THE OUTPOST

THE OUTPOST

MIKE RESNICK

TOR ®

A Tom Doherty Associates Book
New York

THE OUTPOST

Copyright © 2001 by Mike Resnick

This book is printed on acid-free paper.

Edited by Beth Meacham

Book design by Heidi P. D. Eriksen

A Tor Book
Published by Tom Doherty Associates, LLC
175 Fifth Avenue
New York, NY 10010

www.tor.com

Tor® is a registered trademark of Tom Doherty Associates, LLC.

Library of Congress Cataloging-in-Publication Data

Resnick, Michael D.
    The Outpost / Mike Resnick.
        p. cm.
    "A Tom Doherty Associates book."
    ISBN 0-312-85485-4 (hc)
    ISBN 0-312-87577-0 (pbk)
    1. Life on other planets—Fiction. 2. Bars (Drinking establishments)—Fiction. I. Title.

PS3568.E698 O98 2001
813'.54—dc21   2001027075

First Hardcover Edition: May 2001
First Trade Paperback Edition: June 2002

Printed in the United States of America

0 9 8 7 6 5 4 3 2 1

To Carol, as always

And to the Outpost's progenitors:
Rick's Café Américain
The Monkey Bar
Gavagan's Bar
Joe the Angel's City Hall Bar
Wallace's
The White Hart
Tchaka's
The Draco Tavern

CONTENTS

Part I. Legend 11

Part II. Fact 223

Part III. History 295

PART I
LEGEND

Facts are the enemy of Truth. Everyone knows that.
What follows is the true story of the Outpost.

I knew the moment he walked into the Outpost that he was a
Hero—he just had that look about him. He was a lot closer to seven
feet tall than six, he had unblinking no-color eyes, golden hair that
cascaded down to his shoulders, and the kind of body that you just
knew chairs would bounce off of.

His huge arms were too heavily muscled to be confined, so
he'd cut the sleeves off his shirt. He wore a leather vest, matching
leather trousers, a metal belt with a buckle made out of an alien
skull, and fur-covered boots. And a bunch of alien necklaces and
bracelets: you could hear him jingling from a couple of hundred
yards away.

He had a scar that began just above his ear and ended in the
middle of his chin. His right arm had a tattoo of one of the more
spectacularly endowed naked ladies I can remember seeing, and
she constantly raced up to his shoulder and onto his chest beneath
his shirt; his left arm had a tattoo of himself, scar and all, and it
ran up to his left shoulder and (I assume) met the naked lady on
his chest every few seconds in a pornographic embrace.

The middle finger of his right hand boasted a diamond ring
that must have been six, maybe seven carats, and his ring finger
held a diamond that could eat the middle finger's diamond for
breakfast. He wore a brace of pearl-handled burners, and the Spy
Eye behind the bar told me he had another burner, two screechers,
and a pair of knives hidden on his person.

He ignored the men and women who were gathered at the
tables and walked directly up to the bar.

"Heard a lot about the Outpost," he said in his deep, booming voice. "Hard place to find."

"You managed," I noted.

"I usually find what I'm looking for," he answered. "Give me a Witch's Wart."

I had Reggie—that's what I call the bartending machine; it kind of personalizes him—mix it up. "First one's on the house."

"I approve," he said, picking the glass up and downing it in a single swallow, oblivious to the flames and the vapor that rose from it. "Name's Baker," he continued, putting the empty back on the bar. He paused, as if about to deliver a punch line. "Catastrophe Baker."

"I've heard of you." Of course, I've heard of almost everyone who finds his way to the Outpost.

"I guess a lot of people have."

"Not too many make it out here, though," I noted.

"Maybe more than you'd like," said Baker. "You could be getting a little unwelcome company before long."

"Oh?"

He nodded his shaggy head. "War's getting close."

News is always slow reaching us. After all, we're as far from what's happening as you can get. "Who are we at war with this time?"

He shrugged. "I get the feeling they're more a bunch of *what*'s than *who*'s."

"Then they won't want to stop at the Outpost for a drink, will they?" I said, which was my only concern. Wars come and go; the Outpost stays.

Before I go any further, I suppose I ought to tell you a little bit about the place, maybe starting with where it is.

Easy enough. We're on Henry II, one of the Eight Henrys. We were named by Willie the Bard, who spent half a lifetime looking for just this configuration, and finally found it as deep into the Inner Frontier as anyone has ever gotten. We've got this binary system, and he named the two stars Plantagenet and Tudor. There are eight planets—the Eight Henrys. Henry I has two moons, Edith of Scotland and Adelaide of Louvain. The next six Henrys have one moon apiece: Eleanor of Aquitaine, Eleanor of Provence, Mary de Bohun, Catherine de Valois, Margaret of Anjou, and Elizabeth of York. For a while he was stymied, because Henry VIII doesn't have any moons at all—but it does have six rings, and those became the Wedding Rings: Catherine of Aragon, Anne Boleyn, Jane Seymour, Anne of Cleves, Catherine Howard, and Catherine Parr. A few of the Henrys actually have breathable atmospheres.

Willie is the only one who knows his Earth history, so he names just about everything in the system. For example, no one knows why he calls the huge volcano that's always causing havoc in the other hemisphere Beckett, but that also means no one can contradict him, so Beckett it is. We've got two sets of native humanoids out in the hinterlands; he calls them Normans and Saxons, but no one is quite sure which is which. One race is kind of blue and ugly, and the other is kind of green and even uglier.

Willie wasn't the first man to discover the Henrys, though. *I* was. I left civilization when I had a serious disagreement with the authorities over some of the finer points of the law, and I didn't slow down until I came to the Henrys, which felt like the end of the universe, or maybe the beginning. There was no place left to go, so I decided to land my ship and settle down here. I knew sooner or later somebody would show up, and I decided we needed a gathering place—you know, a bar, some sleeping rooms, maybe a little restaurant that served human food—so I built the Outpost. Made it feel homey: holos of all the great athletes of the past couple of millennia, and a huge nude of Sally Six-Eyes over the bar (she posed for it right here on the premises, a few weeks after we opened for business). I added the mounted heads of some alien animals overlooking the tables, a couple of mind-bending games in the back, comfortable chairs, and a long bar that thirty or forty men and women could sidle up to. Then I figured we needed a post office, since we're halfway across the galaxy from the Monarchy (I know, I know, they call it the Commonwealth—but out here *we* know what it is). The mail ship only comes twice a year, but that's better than nothing. Over the years I added a cartographic chart

shop for those travelers who don't trust their navigational computers. Then I opened a weapons shop. It's been a loser from the start;
the men and women who find the Outpost are about as well armed
as people get to be.

We're never very crowded, because we're the farthest you can
get from anywhere, and only the boldest of the bold are willing to
come this close to the Galactic Core and the enormous black hole
that lives there, gobbling up stars and planets like they were so
many sandwiches. It takes a lot of man—or woman (or alien, for
that matter)—to turn his back on everything he's known and head
out this way. The last thing I started was a pawnshop, because even
heroes can run short of money from time to time.

What else can I tell you? Well, my name, I suppose. It's Thomas Aloysius Hawke, and I think I was in business less than ten
minutes before my first customer dubbed me Tomahawk, and that's
who I've been ever since.

I love my work. If you're not three times as big as life and
twice as wide, you don't come looking for the Outpost . . . and if
you find it, then you've got a lifetime of adventures and exploits
worth bragging about. Reggie and I will fill you up with whatever
you thirst for, and Willie the Bard will write down your story, add-
ing only a few poetic flourishes as part of this epic he's writing. He
tells me that he's up over 4,000 pages, and he says when he finally
publishes it he's going to call it *The Outpost*.

Anyway, Baker ordered a second Witch's Wart, and suddenly
Three-Gun Max looked up from his drink.

"Catastrophe Baker," he said, staring at the huge man's back.
"I heard of you."

Baker turned and looked at Max, who was holding his drink in
one hand, his bottle in another, and was tugging at his ear with a
third.

"You're a mutant, ain't you?" said Baker.

Max grinned. "What makes you think so?"

"Just a shot in the dark."

"Three-Gun Max is the name. Always glad to meet another
living legend."

"Where'd you hear about me?"

"Damned near every place I been," said Max.

"Yeah?" said Baker, suddenly interested. "And where do you hail from?"

"Most recently?" said Max. "Port Raven, out in the Quinellus Cluster."

"I've spent a few days there," acknowledged Baker.

"I know. They had to build a whole new graveyard."

"Well, some of the locals needed better manners," said Baker with a shrug.

"Sure as hell did," agreed Max. "The day I landed I was robbed twice and shot at once on my way from the spaceport to my hotel."

"Yeah, I seem to recall that they don't cotton much to strangers—and with all due respect, you look a little stranger than most."

"I made out okay," answered Max. Suddenly he grinned. "When they tell you to reach for the sky, they never remember to count how many hands you still got left."

Baker threw back his head and laughed. "Let me buy you a drink." He looked around the place. "Hell, let me buy you *all* a drink."

Suddenly the place turned from a still life into a sprint in about a tenth of a second. Big Red and Nicodemus Mayflower and Beta-World O'Grady were about a nose ahead of Sinderella and Little Mike Picasso, and most of the others weren't far behind.

"That's mighty generous of you, friend," said O'Grady.

"I feel right at home," answered Baker in his booming voice. "I recognize two or three of you from your Wanted posters, and I've seen books and videos and suchlike about a bunch of you." He downed another drink. "Hell, I've even had to flee for my life from a couple of you. That creates a *bond*, you know what I mean?"

"Of course we know," said O'Grady. "That's why we're all here. This place is a magnet to our kind—whatever 'our kind' happens to be."

"Well, whatever it is," said Baker, staring at the assembled crowd, "it ain't necessarily human."

"Does that cause you a problem?" hissed Sahara del Rio from her end of the bar.

"Hell, no," said Baker. "I got five or six wives kicking around the galaxy, and half of *them* ain't human." He paused. "Can't say that the half that is ever treated me any better than the half that ain't."

"Maybe we ought to introduce ourselves to our latest benefactor here," said O'Grady.

"I know who you are," said Baker. "You're Bet-a-World O'Grady."

"My reputation precedes me," said O'Grady, looking real pleased with himself. "Too bad all my worlds recede from me even faster."

"I was there the night you lost Beta Campanis III," said Baker.

"Really? I don't recall seeing you."

"Well, my situation wasn't such that I wanted to make a memorable entrance."

"So *you* were the one they were looking for!" exclaimed O'Grady. "What the hell did you do to get two whole military regiments after you?"

"Three," Baker corrected him. "The third was backing up the first two, just in case I got angry. Still, I almost stepped forward when you raised that Canphorite. He had you beat on the table."

"I felt lucky."

"You must have. The odds were about three million to one against you."

"I play by my feelings, not by the odds. That's how I won the entire Binder system." O'Grady grimaced. "Of course, I lost it to a pair of fives a couple of months later, but what the hell—easy come, easy go."

"So what do you own these days?" asked Baker.

"The shirt on my back, the boots on my feet, the deck of cards in my pocket—"

"And a tab for four hundred eighty-three credits," I added.

"You're talking to a man who was once worth billions," he said heatedly. "Hell, maybe even trillions."

"Achilles was once a pretty good free-hand fighter," I shot back, "but I haven't noticed him beating anybody lately."

"Are you threatening me?" demanded O'Grady.

"Of course not," I said. "I'm *reminding* you."

"Well, that's all right, then," he said, holding out his glass. "Fill it up again. Holler when my tab hits five hundred."

"I been hollering since it hit two fifty," I said.

As he walked over to Reggie for a refill, Sahara undulated over, the light playing off her shiny green scales.

"So you're Catastrophe Baker," she whispered in her sibilant, hissing voice, looking him up and down.

"That's right," he said. "I think I missed your name, though."

"Sahara del Rio."

"Mighty earthy name for a Lodinite—or are you an Atrian?"

"Neither," she said with a reptilian smile. "I'm a Borovite."

"They got a Sahara Desert on Borovia?" asked a surprised Baker.

"I grew up on Earth," she said. "I lived in a desert, and I lived where a city named Rio used to be." Her gaze passed briefly over the other patrons. "That's more than anyone else here can say. Not a single human in this place has ever set foot on your mother world."

"Not so," said Billy Karma. "I went there to take the walk up to Golgotha." He turned to Baker and extended his hand. "The Reverend Billy Karma, sir."

"Should you be drinking?" asked Baker.

"Where does the Good Book say that one of God's servants can't lift a few when he's of a mind to?" demanded Karma.

"Can't say I've ever read it," admitted Baker.

"Well, you ought to," said Karma. "As a matter of fact, I have about eight thousand copies of the Red Letter Billy Karma Edition out in my ship. Be happy to sell you one." A self-satisfied little smile crossed his face. "Best damned Bible you ever saw. I threw out a bunch of the dull parts, added some of my own sermons and observations, and printed it up. Cover's got a tight molecular bonding. Couldn't destroy it if you threw it in a bonfire, or even an atomic furnace. Trust me—I've tried both."

"Now, why would you want to burn your own Bible?" asked Baker.

The Reverend Billy Karma shrugged. "I fall off the spiritual wagon every few months and usually wake up with a hangover in some whorehouse. Then I get saved again. Both of 'em do me a powerful lot of good—getting lost and getting saved. And I know that the first thing I always do when I get lost is try to burn the Good Book so I won't be confronting it every morning when I get up after a night of sin and sleaze and other good things."

"Good things?"

"Well, they must *feel* good or I wouldn't do 'em, would I?" shot back Billy Karma. "People like you do 'em all the time, don't you?"

"Not every waking minute," said Baker. "But on the other hand, I ain't no reverend, either."

"Well, when I fall off the wagon, I ain't much of a reverend myself." Karma frowned. "Last time I killed the whole Giriami Gang on Roosevelt III after they got back from robbing a navy convoy ship. At least, that's what they told me when they dragged me out of the smoking ruins and hung this here medal on me." He pulled out a gold medal that was suspended on a silver chain beneath his black shirt and shook his head sadly. "What a tragic way to lose thirty-eight potential parishioners! If I'd been sober, I'd have settled for converting 'em."

One by one Baker started getting introduced to the others. When he was about halfway through, he stopped and pointed to Einstein, who was sitting alone in a corner.

"What's the matter with him?" he asked. "The man hasn't moved a muscle since I got here."

"Oh, that's just Einstein," I said.

"Someone ought to teach him some manners."

"He could teach *you* a little something," said Three-Gun Max. "He doesn't look like much, but he teaches things to the best brains in the Monarchy. Or at least he used to."

"That little twerp?" scoffed Baker. "Hell, if he ain't comatose, you sure can't prove it by me."

"He's not," Max assured him.

"Sure, he is," said Baker. He turned to Einstein and yelled, "Hey, you!"

"He can't hear you," said Max. "He's deaf."

"Yeah?"

"And blind and mute as well. He's been that way since he was born."

"Then what makes him so special?" asked Baker.

"The thing you can't see," said Max. "His brain."

"Explain."

"Because he didn't learn to communicate until he was in his twenties, he never learned to think the way everyone else does when they're growing up. He's probably the most brilliant man in the galaxy—because he's the most unique thinker. He creates entirely new sciences in his head because he ain't hampered by any knowledge of the old ones. Been doing it for close to thirty years now. When the government decided to protect him from exploitation, he decided he needed protection from his protectors, and he wound up here."

"He's really that good?"

"He's the reason we'll reach Andromeda in the next few years. And he's the only man who ever came up with a defense against a molecular imploder. And if you've come across one of those little gimmicks that lets you see through stone walls, that's his." Max chuckled in amusement. "The military wanted to keep the patent on it, but even though Einstein's never seen a naked lady, he thought it would be tragic if it weren't made available to lonely, oversexed, and thoroughly unprincipled men . . . men very much like me, in fact."

Catastrophe Baker stared at Einstein for a long moment. "Well, I'll be damned!" he said at last. "A blind little guy did all that!"

"We all have some talent or other," said Argyle, who'd been hanging back until then.

"Yours is a little more obvious than most," said Baker, staring at the alien as he constantly changed colors.

"This isn't a talent," said Argyle, as he changed from bright red to brilliant yellow to pale blue in less time than it takes me to tell you about it. "It's a defense mechanism."

"Seems more likely to attract predators than convince them you're a tree or a rock or dead or whatever."

"That all depends on the predator," said Argyle. "On my home world, they're carrion eaters. Once I die, I stop changing colors; as long as I keep flashing them, the predators know that I'm alive and not a rotting corpse. They like their meat *very* rank."

"So what's your talent?" asked Baker.

"I juggle things."

"Balls?"

"Numbers," said Argyle. "I used to be an accountant for one of the biggest banks in the Albion Cluster."

"And?"

"And now I'm not," said Argyle noncommittally.

"This joint's got an interesting clientele," remarked Baker.

"We have our moments," agreed Gravedigger Gaines, who was dressed all in black as usual. "Remember me?"

"How could I forget?" asked Catastrophe Baker. "You damned near killed me back on Silverblue, out on the Rim."

"I was a bounty hunter. It was my job."

"You still got those damned dogs?"

"They weren't dogs," said the Gravedigger. "They were Nightswarmers. Native to Bodine V."

"Whatever they were, they were fast as hell and three times as vicious. I was lucky to escape with my skin intact." Suddenly Baker tensed and laid a hand on his pearl-handled burner. "You still a bounty hunter?"

The Gravedigger shook his head. "My Nightswarmers died, and I didn't feel like spending ten years training another team."

"Who says you needed 'em?"

"Whatever the reward, it wasn't enough to go up against the likes of men like you or Hurricane Smith without them. I earned forty bounties before I hung it up; that's not bad for a twelve-year career."

"Well, you seem to have come out of it in one piece," noted Baker. "You could have done a lot worse, even with those damned dogs."

"One piece?" laughed the Gravedigger. He held up his right arm. "This came from Deluros VIII. The left leg's from Pollux IV. The right eye and nineteen teeth are from Greenveldt. Can't even remember where I got the left foot. And I'm using someone else's kidney and spleen, thanks to Jenny the Blade. It was time to retire before there wasn't any of the original me left."

"Sounds like you've got some interesting tales to tell," said Baker. "Sounds like you *all* do."

"We've been known to tell 'em," acknowledged the Gravedigger. "But we've heard 'em all before. Seems to me someone as famous as Catastrophe Baker's got a few tales of his own to share."

"Could be," agreed Baker. He turned to me. "But first, I want to order a bottle apiece for everyone in the Outpost. Give 'em anything they choose. When a man's running in luck, he likes to share it."

"That could amount to some serious money, friend," I said.

"I ain't got no money," he replied—and then, before I could pull my screecher out from under the bar, he reached into a pocket and pulled out the biggest ruby I'd ever seen. "But this ought to hold you for a while." I'm not a small man, but when I placed it in the palm of my hand, I couldn't close my fingers around it.

"Where'd you ever get something like that?" asked Three-Gun Max.

"Well, now, that's a pretty interesting story, if I do say so myself," replied Baker, "and it's my experience that telling stories can be pretty thirsty work, so I'm going to need a little something to keep the old vocal chords fresh and strong. Tomahawk, have Reggie hunt me up a bottle of Cygnian cognac. And if ain't older than I am, take it back and get another."

Willie the Bard took out his notebook—he refuses to use a recorder or computer—while Reggie brought out a two-century-old vintage (well, it was actually thirteen-year-old cognac in a 212-year-old bottle, but what the hell), and Baker bit off the cork and took a long swallow, bellowed an "Ah!" of approval, and began talking.

Catastrophe Baker and the Dragon Queen

It was a couple of years ago (began Baker), and I was out on the Spiral Arm, doing a little mining in the Parnassus asteroid belt.

Well, I didn't do any actual digging or blasting—I mean, hell, I wouldn't know raw plutonium from raw beef—but I did hang out in the little Tradertown they set up on Parnassus II. Had a tavern a lot like this one, only smaller and without no high-quality work of art hanging over the bar, and there were some sleeping rooms, though I was between fortunes at the time and slept in my ship. Like all Tradertowns it had an assay office, and I figured that if I ever saw a miner approach the assay office before he stopped for a drink, he'd probably hit on something interesting, and I planned to make it my business to relieve him of his burden.

Which is how I wound up with thirty pounds of fissionable material. I don't know from fission, but I know it's worth its weight in prettier baubles, and I know you keep it locked in lead containers and don't spend overmuch time playing with it, and I decided that if the Monarchy paid well for it, the Canphorites and Setts and Domarians would probably pay even better. I was pretty well known in the Arm by then, due to a series of unfortunate misunderstandings in which I was always the innocent party, and when I approached the miners who'd made the claim, they just took one look at me and suddenly remembered that they had urgent business elsewhere. Well, all but one, anyway, and making wrong decisions in such matters is what you might call genetically self-limiting.

After I loaded the booty into my ship, I headed off for the Rim, where I figured to hold an informal little auction. I had to stop at the space station that orbited Bellabionda IX to refuel, and while I was sitting there sampling half a dozen different brandies, I suddenly felt the barrel of a screecher bury itself in the middle of my back. I would have turned and had harsh words with the gentleman who was at the other end of the weapon, but I also found my nose about half an inch from the business end of an ugly-looking burner. I chanced a pair of quick glances to my right and my left, and discovered things didn't look more promising in them directions.

Now, the guy facing me was almost as big as I was, which is pretty rare, at least in this universe, and I can't speak for noplace else. He had squinty eyes, and a couple of gold teeth, and he hadn't shaved in a mighty long time, and he hadn't washed in even longer than he hadn't shaved, and he kind of learned forward and said, "Catastrophe Baker, you took something that didn't belong to you."

"I've tooken *lots* of things that don't belong to me," I said right back at him. "That's what I do for a living."

"Yeah," he said, "but this particular thing belongs to the Dragon Queen, and she's charged me with conveying the fact that she's more than a little annoyed with you."

"Okay, you conveyed it," I said. "Now go away and let me finish drinking in peace."

The man with the gold teeth frowned. "I don't believe I'm getting through to you at all," he said. "You stole thirty pounds of prime plutonium from her, and she wants it back."

"There must be some mistake," I answered. "I stole *my* plutonium off five miners in the Spiral Arm."

"Well, it's probably true that they owned the plutonium, but *she* owns *them*."

I pondered that for a minute and finally said, "In my opinion it's miserly to own people *and* fissionable material. Tell her she can keep the men (except for the one I removed from Nature's game plan) and I'll keep the plutonium."

Old Goldtooth kind of sighed and shrugged. "I just knew this was going to happen," he said unhappily. "I told her and told her that a man like you was never going to give her what she wanted just because we threatened to rip out your eyes and cut off your ears and pull your arms and legs from their sockets. I explained that even after we roasted you over a slow fire and put slime spiders in your ears and started extracting your vertebrae one by one that you wouldn't tell us what we wanted to know."

"Since we're both agreed on that," I said, "what do you plan to do instead?"

"Beats the hell out of me," he admitted. "Maybe we'd just better take you to her and let her decide."

"Couldn't we torture him just a little?" asked the guy who was poking the screecher in my back. "Just for fun?"

Another sigh from Goldtooth. "No," he said after some serious consideration. "You know what happened to the last four or five prisoners I let you play with."

"I got carried away" came the petulant answer. "It won't happen again."

"That's what you said last time."

"How about if I just castrate him?" said the guy with the screecher. "Won't stop him from talking, and if she decides to torture him herself, he'll still be ninety-nine percent whole."

"Stupidest suggestion I ever heard," replied Goldtooth. He turned to me. "You have to forgive him," he said apologetically. "He's very young. He just doesn't realize that these Dragon Queens always have their motors running."

Well, truth to tell, I hadn't ever encountered a Dragon Queen. But I'd seen my share of Pirate Queens, which in my long experience could always be identified by their lustful natures, their soul-destroying greed, and their proud, arrogant bosoms, and I figured if Dragon Queens were related to Pirate Queens, or were even some kind of regional offshoot, then maybe I'd fallen out of the frying pan and into the featherbed, to coin what I had every reason to hope was a new and accurate expression.

"So should I put the manacles on him?" asked one of the others.

Goldtooth turned to me. "If we don't shackle you, do you promise not to try to escape or overpower us?"

"You have my word as a gentleman," I told him.

"Get the manacles!" he hollered.

Which is what they did, and which is how I was led into the Dragon Queen's presence a couple of days later, when we finally landed on Terlingua.

We were in an audience chamber that could have housed half a dozen athletic events. The doorways were all different shapes, as if most of them were made to be used by aliens. The walls kept changing colors, and there was a mural maybe fifty yards square painted on the ceiling that I'll swear was never painted by any human.

Now, you people don't know me, so you don't know that I ain't much given to exaggeration, but take my word for it: the Dragon Queen was the most beautiful female I had ever seen in a lifetime of admiring female critters of almost every race and species.

Her hair shone like spun gold. Her eyes were the blue of the clearest lagoon. Her lips were a brilliant red, and moist as all get-out. And one look told me that if she was a typical Dragon Queen, then Dragon Queens made Pirate Queens look like schoolgirls from the neck down.

She'd been poured into a skintight metallic dress. She had breasts that just out-and-out defied gravity, and the tiniest waist, and smooth, silken thighs, and I tried real hard not to pay much attention to the fact that she was toting even more weapons than I tended to carry myself.

"Have you got a stiff neck?" she asked after a couple of moments in a voice that was a little bit harsher than I expected from someone that beautiful.

Well, that wasn't quite where I was stiff, if you catch my delicate and subtle meaning, but I assured her that my neck was just fine.

"Then look at my face," she commanded.

I did so, and suddenly spotted something I'd missed the first time around, which was that she was wearing a golden tiara, and smack-dab in the middle of it was the biggest, most perfect ruby I'd ever seen.

"Miss Dragon Queen, ma'am," I said, "I hope it don't embarrass you, but I have to declare that you are unquestionably the most beautiful woman I have seen in all my wanderings across the length and breadth of the galaxy, to say nothing of its height and depth."

"You may call me Zenobia," she said, and now her voice was more like a purr than a snarl.

That didn't surprise me none, because I'd met eleven Pirate Queens in my day, and eight of them were called Zenobia, and I figured that if you were an exquisitely built young woman possessed of unbridled lust and an overwhelming desire to conquer the galaxy, Zenobia was the name that just naturally appealed to you.

"It's a name fit for a Dragon Queen," I assured her.

She stared at me through half-lowered eyelids. "You interest me, Catastrophe Baker," she said. Suddenly she snapped to attention, which produced an effect most men would pay good money to see. "But first, to business. You stole thirty pounds of my plutonium. I want it back."

"What does a pretty little thing like you need with enough plutonium to blow up half a dozen star systems?" I asked.

She smiled. "I plan to blow up half a dozen star systems," she said.

"Just for the hell of it?" I asked, because you never knew what Pirate Queens might do when they felt irritable, and I figured Dragon Queens weren't much different.

"There are six warlords out here on the Rim. As my first step in the conquest of the galaxy, I plan to assimilate their empires."

"Well, why didn't you say so in the first place?" I said. "Hell, assimilating empires is something I've always had a hankering to do. I think we should become partners."

"You're hardly in a position to make demands!" she snapped.

I held up my hands. "You mean these things?" I asked, indicating the manacles. "I just let them put 'em on me so I could meet you. There ain't never been a chain that could hold Catastrophe Baker."

And so saying, I flexed my muscles and gave one mighty yank, and the manacles came apart. Four or five of her bodyguards—did

I forget to tell you she had a small army of bodyguards?—jumped me, but I just leaned down, straightened up, and sent 'em flying in all directions.

She stared at me, wide-eyed, and I could tell that she was torn between yelling "Off with his head!" and "Off with his clothes!"

"I may have even more uses for you than I thought at first glance," she said at last.

"Then we're partners?"

"Why not?" she said with a shrug that went a lot farther and lasted a lot longer than your standard shrug.

"Well, if we're partners," I continued, "I'd sure be interested in knowing why you're a Dragon Queen rather than a Pirate Queen."

"And so you shall, Catastrophe Baker," she said, walking over and taking me by the hand. She smelled good enough to eat. "Come with me."

She led me to a small door I hadn't seen, since it was hiding behind a bunch of her bodyguards. They stepped aside, and she ordered the door to open, and it did, and suddenly we were in a bedroom that was probably a little smaller than the navy's flagship and had a few less windows than the governor's palace (the *old* palace, not the new, fortified one), and right in the middle of it was a bed that could have accommodated a dozen Dragon Queens and still have some room left over for their gentleman friends.

"What do you think?" she asked.

"It's right impressive," I acknowledged. "But it still don't explain why you're a Dragon Queen."

"It's a result of inbreeding and radiation and genes gone astray," she said, putting a hand behind my neck and pulling my head down to hers.

"Looks to me like every gene is sitting right where it's supposed to be for optimum effect," I opined.

"I'm a genetic sport," she whispered, and suddenly her breath became *real* warm. "When I get hot, I get *hot*! I'm like a dragon in that respect."

She smiled, her eyes gleamed and flashed, and twin needles of smoke and fire shot out from beneath her lips.

She directed my gaze down south of her waist, where still more smoke was escaping.

"You see?" she said. "I'm so constituted that I can't hide my desire for you, Catastrophe Baker."

And sure enough, she couldn't.

"Just a second," interrupted Three-Gun Max. "Are you trying to tell us that she actually was *smoking* down there?"

"That's right," said Baker.

"I don't believe it!"

"*I* was there," said Baker pugnaciously. "Were *you*?"

"No, but if you're gonna tell us you took her to bed without getting some real important part of your masculine anatomy fried to a crisp, I'm gonna have a hard time believing any part of this story."

Baker glared at him until he kind of shrunk into himself, and then the huge man looked around the room, his hand kind of toying with the pearl handle of his burner. "Has anyone else got a problem with my story?"

Nobody said a word, and finally he relaxed and began talking again.

As a matter of fact (continued Baker), I never had a chance to find out just how hot a number she was, figuratively or literally, because at just that instant we heard a huge commotion outside the bedroom, and then there were a bunch of screams, and I could hear the hum of burners and the whine of screechers and the report of bullets.

"The warlords!" she cried. "They've found out about the plutonium and launched a preemptive strike!"

"That ain't no problem," I said. "Give me a couple of them weapons you're wearing and I'll send 'em packing."

She tossed me a couple of guns, and I walked to the door, opened it, and gently announced my presence by blowing away eight or nine men who were wearing uniforms that were different from her bodyguards'.

Then I looked across the room and saw six men all done up in fancy-looking tunics with rows and rows of medals on their chests, and I knew right away that these had to be the six warlords, so I picked up one of their bigger henchmen, twisted his head around a couple of times until he stopped squirming, and used him as a shield as I began crossing the room.

"Be careful!" the Dragon Queen cried out.

"Hell, there's only six of 'em—and they're little ones at that!" I hollered back.

Twelve or fifteen warriors jumped me, but I just shrugged 'em off. Another one grabbed my leg, and I kicked him clear across the room; he hit the far wall on the fly, which has to constitute some kind of record if I just knew what record book to report it to.

When I was maybe fifty feet away from the warlords, I raised the body over my head and hurled it at 'em. Four of 'em went down in a tangled heap. The other two reached for their weapons, but I was too fast for 'em, and after I broke their arms they kind of fell to the floor, and having nothing better to do they started kissing my feet and begging for mercy.

I looked around and saw that the rest of the invaders were either dead or at least not in any mood to continue the fight, and then the Dragon Queen raced over to me and threw her arms around me and gave me one hell of a passionate kiss.

(See this here black tooth? That's what caused it. Burned the enamel top to bottom. I really ought to replace it with a gold one, but it's almost all I got to remember her by.)

Anyway, after she ordered her bodyguards to drag the warlords and the surviving soldiers off to the dungeons and have a little fun with them, she turned back to me and said, kind of sultrylike, "Catastrophe Baker, as a reward for your heroism, you may have any single thing in this room."

"Well, Miss Dragon Queen, ma'am," I said, "that seems like a pretty easy decision, since I ain't never seen a woman to measure up to you."

"Surely a man of your broad experience has seen many beautiful women."

"Yeah, but you're head and shoulders and other things ahead of 'em all."

"It's kind of you to say so," she said modestly, "but there must be three or four others in the galaxy who are even lovelier."

"You really think so?" I asked seriously.

"Out of trillions and trillions of women? Surely."

"Well, then, it's an even easier choice," I said.

"Yes, my love?" she said eagerly.

"Absolutely, my love," I replied. "If you tell me there are prettier women in the galaxy, I got no reason not to believe you. But," I added, plucking the ruby from her tiara, "I *know* there ain't no more perfect ruby, so I'll just take this as a remembrance of my short but happy stay on Terlingua."

"I don't believe it!" she said furiously.

"As a token of my high esteem, I'll dump the plutonium before I leave," I told her.

"You are a fool, Catastrophe Baker!" she said. "Think of what you could have had!"

"You won't never be far from my mind, Miss Dragon Queen, ma'am," I said.

And sure enough, I think of her every time I sit by a blazing fire.

His story done, Catastrophe Baker displayed the ruby again.

"And *that's* how I came into possession of the most perfect ruby in the galaxy."

Everyone seemed properly impressed with his story. Everyone except Hellfire Carson, that is. The grizzled old man walked up to Baker, held out his hand, and asked to see the ruby.

"Handle it carefully, old man," said Baker, offering it to him.

Carson rolled it around in his hand for a few seconds, then held it up to the light and peered at it. Finally he tossed it back to Baker.

"You made a bad bargain," he said. "You should have took the Dragon Queen."

"What are you talking about, old man?" demanded Baker.

"That thing ain't no ruby."

"The hell it ain't!"

"The hell it is."

"What do *you* think it is?" I asked him.

"Not a matter of 'think.' I *know* what it is. I seen enough of 'em in my day." He paused. "It's an eyestone."

"A what?"

"A Landship's eye. That's what we used to call 'em when we hunted 'em back on Peponi."

"And what's a Landship?" asked Baker.

"Landships were big suckers," answered Hellfire Carson, staring off into the past. "Burly, too. Stood maybe sixteen feet at the shoulder, and they were covered top to bottom with shaggy brown fur. Their heads were enormous, and each one had a long prehensile lower lip that seemed almost as useful as a human hand. Their ears were small and rounded, and their noses were big and broad. They looked awkward, but they could move pretty goddamned fast when they were charging."

He stopped long enough to take a swallow from his bottle. "Most interesting thing about 'em was their eyes. Red crystal, they were. Looked just like rubies, except here"—he pointed to some scratch marks—"where the jeweler removed the pupil. They always got rid of the pupil; people didn't like to be reminded where their trinkets came from."

"And you really hunted them for their eyes?" I asked.

"Their eye*stones*," Carson corrected me. "Fetched about five thousand credits for a good pair. Probably worth a little more these days"—he grinned at Catastrophe Baker—"but not as much as a Dragon Queen."

"How do you know so much about Landships?" asked The Earth Mother.

"Because I killed the very last one," said Carson.

The Last Landship

What you've got to understand (said Carson) is that the Landships were a doomed species from the moment that Men decided their eyes made pretty baubles. I've seen 'em worn as jewelry, and displayed as art, and even used as currency. Until today I hadn't ever heard of one being chosen over a real, live woman, but I've been out of touch for quite a while and for all I know it's happened before.

Anyway, Peponi was a colony planet, prettier than some, wilder than most, and it attracted a lot of big-game hunters and adventurers. A few of 'em started safari companies and took clients out into the bush, but most of them were there to hunt Landships and sell the eyestones they collected.

Well, with as many millions of Landships as covered the planet and as few Men to hunt them, you wouldn't think they could be decimated so fast, but within a century there weren't more than fifty thousand left. They were mostly gathered in one protected area, a place called the Bukwa Enclave—and then one day the government ran out of money and pulled most of its army out, and suddenly it wasn't protected any longer, and that was the beginning of the end. I still remember it.

My old pal Catamount Greene was the first to arrive. He didn't know a damned thing about tracking, but old Catamount never let minor details like that stop him. On the way to the Enclave he picked up a bunch of carvings and jewelry from one of the local tribes, then found one of the few military outposts left in the Bukwa area and explained that he was trading these trinkets to the tribes that lived in the Enclave. He gave a few of the choicest ones to the soldiers, bought them a couple of drinks, and went on to say that he was terrified of Landships and that he had heard that the Enclave was filled with them—and within ten minutes he had talked them into marking where the herds were on a map so that he could avoid them while he hawked his wares from village to village. He walked into the Enclave with one weapon, three bearers, and his map, and walked out a month later with more than three thousand eyestones.

Then there was Bocci, who had made up his mind to leave Peponi, but decided to stick around just long enough to clean up in the Enclave. He found a water hole way out at the western end, staked it out, poisoned it, and picked up seven hundred eyestones without ever firing a shot.

Jumping Jimmy Westerly went in with a stepladder, took it out in the shoulder-high grass, where none of the other hunters would go, climbed atop it, and potted twenty Landships the first day he was there. Once they cleared out of the area, he followed them, always keeping to high grass. He'd set up his ladder whenever they stopped, and he kept right on doing it until he had his thousand eyestones.

Other hunters used other methods. True West Thompson brought in a whole tribe of native hunters who used poisoned spears and arrows and brought down almost three thousand Landships before they started becoming scarce.

After a couple of months, the Enclave began to resemble a war zone, and you could smell the Landship carcasses rotting from miles away, but it didn't stop the slaughter. Kalahari Jenkins took a dry area, about forty miles square, at the northwestern tip of the Enclave, announced that it was his personal hunting ground, and swore he'd kill anyone who entered it. A feller named Kennedy wandered in one day, chasing a couple of Landships, and true to his word Jenkins blew him away. What he didn't know was that Kennedy had six sons, and it started a blood feud. Lasted a couple of weeks before they killed him—I seem to remember that he got four of them first—and then the two remaining sons declared that it was now *their* territory. That lasted about five days, until old Hakira came up from the south, killed the last two Kennedy boys, gathered up all of Jenkins's and the Kennedys' eyestones, and lit out for civilization.

Nobody ever found out what happened to the Marachi sisters. They were damned good hunters, those girls—but one day they just disappeared, both of 'em, and no one ever found the eight thousand eyestones they were supposed to have taken.

Anyway, the government finally realized that they had to do something or there wouldn't be any Landships left, and if there weren't any Landships, both the hunting and holographic safari businesses would vanish and Peponi's main source of hard currency would vanish, so they finally passed a ban on hunting Landships.

They meant well, but the ban came too late. They didn't know it, but there was only one Landship left.

"Just a minute," said Nicodemus Mayflower. "I've never even *heard* of a Landship."

"That's not surprising," replied Hellfire Carson. "Not many people have."

"I never saw one in a museum, or even in a book," continued Mayflower.

"Are you calling me a liar?" demanded Carson hotly.

"I don't know yet. When was the last Landship killed?"

"In 1813 G.E.," said Carson.

"*Now* I'm calling you a liar!" said Nicodemus Mayflower. "That was more than forty-seven hundred years ago!"

"I know when it was," answered Carson calmly. "I was there."

"I'm willing to be told that this thing ain't no ruby," interjected Catastrophe Baker, holding up the stone. "After all, talk is cheap. But before I believe anything you say, I'd sure like to know how you came to be almost five thousand years old."

"Might as well tell you," agreed Carson. "You don't look like you're going to take it on faith."

"Tell you what," said Baker. "I'll take fifteen hundred years on faith; you prove the rest."

Everyone laughed, even Carson, and when the noise had subsided he spoke again.

"It happened a few years later. I'd left Peponi and had been hunting on Faligor, when I heard there was adventure to be had in a promising little war in the Belladonna Cluster. It figured to be about a three-week trip, so I activated the DeepSleep chamber and told my ship's computer to wake me when I was within a day of the Cluster."

Carson took a deep breath and let it out slowly as he scratched his shaggy gray head. "To this day I don't know what went wrong, but the next thing I knew some medics were pulling me out of the chamber and saying they'd found this derelict ship floating in space with me inside it. All I know is I went to sleep in the year 1822 of the Galactic Era, and I woke up ten years ago, in 6513. I can't prove it, but there are those who can, and if any doubters want to put up enough money, we'll go hunt them up."

"Well, I'll be damned!" said Catastrophe Baker. "We got ourselves a regular Rip Van Winkle in our midst."

"No," Three-Gun Max corrected him. "We've got a Hellfire Van Winkle."

Which was when and how he stopped being Hellfire Carson.

Getting back to my story (said Hellfire Van Winkle), I stayed on Peponi for a few years after the massacre at the Bukwa Enclave, picking up some money here and there as a guide, or from time to time as a meat hunter for the new towns that were springing up, and in all that time I never saw a Landship. Neither had any of the other hunters or explorers, and we just all assumed that the last of 'em had been killed in the Enclave.

Then one day I was out in the bush, hunting Demoncats for the trophy market, when I heard this mournful, wailing sound off in the distance. Only sound I'd ever heard even remotely like it was years ago—the lonesome, heartbroken sound a baby Landship made when you killed its mother. This was kind of like it, only much louder.

I followed the sound to its source, and came upon the biggest Landship I'd ever seen. He must've stood close to twenty feet at the shoulder, and he was standing all alone in the middle of the forest, howling his misery. I couldn't see any wounds on him, so I decided to follow him for a while to discover the cause of all this unhappiness.

Also, truth to tell, I kind of half believed the old legend of a Landships' graveyard, and I wouldn't have minded a bit if he'd led me to it so I could go around gathering eyestones, but he didn't. He just kept howling out his pain and his misery as he moved from one spot to another, and after a couple of days it dawned on me that he was searching for another of his kind, that he'd probably been looking for another Landship for years now, and he'd pretty much figured out that he wasn't going to find one—that he was the last of his kind.

Oh, he went through the motions, traveled to the most likely places to find his brothers and sisters, but I could tell by the way he carried himself that he didn't expect to find anything except more empty spaces where herds of his kind were once so large that it took them a full day to travel past, start to finish.

He spotted me on the fifth day, and though I was sure he'd been hunted in the past and knew the range and power of Man's weapons, he just stood there and stared at me, as if begging me to put him out of his misery. I didn't do it—I have nothing against breaking the law, but I didn't want to be remembered as the man who killed the last Landship—and after a while he went back to his endless search. I didn't make any attempt to keep my presence a secret, and he just kind of tolerated me. Never tried to charge me, never tried to hide from me, just acted like I was simply one more burden to bear in his already overburdened existence.

We spent close to two months wandering from forest to savannah to scrub bush, and by the end of that time I was as anxious to find some more of his kind as he was, if only to stop that mournful wailing every time we hit a new area and realized we'd come up empty again.

Then one day we crossed the track of a safari. I could tell by the signs that they were no more than eight or nine hours ahead of us. I wanted to turn aside so there'd be no chance of running into them, but convincing a wild Landship to turn away when he doesn't want to takes more skills than I've got. My Landship was so desperate that the instant he picked up the scent of the safari, he headed off in their direction. I knew he couldn't sense any other Landships up ahead, and he had to know there were hunters and guns at the end of the track, but who knows how a Landship's mind works, especially one that's been slowly going crazy with loneliness for years and years?

A couple of hours later I found a discarded laser battery, and I could tell from the customized casing that it belonged to Catamount Greene, and I knew that if Greene saw the Landship nothing could stop him from killing it for its eyestones.

And suddenly I realized that I didn't want the last Landship to die for the same stupid reason that all the others of its kind had died (yeah, including all the ones I myself had killed). Greene and I were old friends and had been through a lot together, and I knew him well enough to know I'd never be able to talk him out of shooting the Landship so he could cash in on two more eyestones.

I don't know why I cared so much, because he sure as hell didn't care what happened to his eyestones once he was shot, but somehow I just couldn't let it happen.

So I called out to the Landship, the first time I'd said a word in his presence, and suddenly he stopped in his tracks and turned to face me, and I walked up to within about twenty yards of him.

"I'm sorry to do this to you," I said, aiming my burner, "but if I ever saw a thing that was tired of life, it's you, and I'm not going to let them chop you into salable bits and pieces. You're one animal whose eyes aren't going to decorate a jewelry shop and whose feet won't become barstools and whose tail won't be sold as a flyswatter. This world and its Landships have been good to me, and I figure I owe you that much."

He stood there, swaying gently and staring at me, and then I pulled the trigger, and I'm not one to get overly sentimental or pretend something's human when it's not, but I'll swear he looked grateful as he tumbled over and sprawled on the ground.

Then I walked over to him, made sure he was dead because I didn't want to cause him any extra pain if he wasn't, and melted his eyestones right there inside his head so no one could ever make a profit on them.

Peponi didn't seem all that pretty to me after that, and a week later I took off for Faligor.

Sinderella wiped away the first tear I'd ever seen on her flawless cheek. "I think that's a beautiful story," she said.

"I got a question," said Max.

"Go ahead," replied Hellfire Van Winkle.

"What would you have done if you'd known there were five or six other Landships still alive?" said Max. "Would you have killed him anyway?"

"Sure," said Van Winkle. "But I'd have taken his eyestones and sold 'em."

Max chuckled, but Sahara del Rio kind of snarled at him. "I thought you were a decent man. I guess I was wrong."

"I *am* a decent man," protested Van Winkle. "I never claimed to be a saint."

"You ain't ever going to be mistaken for one," she assured him.

"That don't bother me none. I'd never know which to put on first, my hat or my halo."

"Tell me more about Landships," said Sinderella, who was all through crying now. "I find them fascinating."

"I told you everything I could about 'em," said Van Winkle.

"I still can't get a mental picture of one," said Sinderella.

Little Mike Picasso, all four feet nine inches of him, spoke up. "I think I can help you."

"Oh?"

He started thumbing through one of his sketchbooks, tossed it aside, and went through another. "Here it is," he said, opening it to a certain page and handing it to her.

"My God, that's awesome!" said Sinderella. "And they we're twenty feet at the shoulder?"

"Closer to fifteen," said Van Winkle. He reached out for the sketchbook. "May I?" She handed it to him and he studied it for a moment, then looked over at Little Mike. "That's a Landship!" he said, surprised.

"Of course it is."

"But no one's seen one for close to five thousand years. How did you know what they looked like?"

"Back in my starving artist days, I accepted a commission to create six stamps for the Peponi post office. One of the ones they wanted was a Landship, so they sent me some early holos and drawings."

"You got everything right except the eyes," said Van Winkle.

"Well, I never knew what the eyes looked like until I heard your story," said Little Mike. "You'd be surprised how badly faded a five-millennia-old holograph can be."

"So you're a painter."

"The best," answered Little Mike.

"Modest, too," said Gravedigger Gaines.

"I was never one for false modesty," said Little Mike. "You know the *Mona Lisa*?"

"Yeah. It's hanging somewhere on Deluros VIII."

"Bullshit. It was stolen thirty years ago. That's *my Mona Lisa* on display. And Morita's *Picnic on Pirhouette IV*?"

"Yours too?"

"Of course." Little Mike smiled smugly. "And when they moved the Sistine Chapel to Alpha Prego III and lost half a dozen of the ceiling panels, who do you think they hired to replace them?"

"Okay, I'm impressed," said the Gravedigger.

"You ought to be," agreed Little Mike.

"So how come I've never heard of you if you're so good?"

"Oh, you've heard of me. 'Little Mike' is just for my friends. My whole name is Michelangelo Gauguin Rembrandt van Gogh Rockwell Picasso." He paused. "But I do most of my best work incognito."

"Why would an artist work incognito?"

"Oh, there are reasons."

"Suppose you share them with us," persisted Gaines.

Little Mike took a swig from the bottle he was holding. "Sure, why not?" he said.

The Greatest Painting of All Time

What you have to understand (said Little Mike) is that not every work of art is an original. I've made more money copying the masters for private collectors, or for museums that didn't want the public to know that the originals were stolen or decayed, than I've ever made for my own creative work, brilliant as it clearly is.

You know, it's really quite strange when you come to think of it. I've made millions of credits from my copies of *The Three Graces* and *The Persistence of Memory* and a trio of *Saturday Evening Post* covers, but with the one exception that I'm going to tell you about, the most I've ever gotten for anything I signed my name to was the five thousand credits that Tomahawk paid me for the painting of Sally Six-Eyes that's hanging over the bar. (In retrospect, I should have charged him a thousand credits per eye.)

That's always been a dilemma for the supremely talented: the world—or, in my case, the galaxy—just isn't ready for us. We're ahead of our time. Look at poor Van Gogh: the man died without ever selling a painting. Or Marcus Pincus, for that matter.

"Marcus who?" asked Three-Gun Max.

"Pincus."

"Never head of him."

"See what I mean?" Little Mike shot back.

———

Still (Little Mike continued), I never believed in starving in a garret, so I took on any assignment that paid my bills and built a reputation, even if it wasn't quite the reputation I'd have wished for a man with my unquestioned talent. I even took that job of painting half a dozen animals for the Peponi post office.

And then one day I got the most interesting commission of my career. It seemed that the Governor of Solomon, a diamond-mining world in the heart of the Monarchy—sorry; make that the Commonwealth—had seen my work and decided that I was just the man he wanted to design a new set of currency for his world.

He flew me to Solomon at government expense, sat me down, and laid out the assignment for me: they wanted new banknotes in denominations of one, ten, fifty, one hundred, and five hundred credits. Five engravings, with some thematic connection among them, for a fee of half a million credits.

As you can well imagine, I was thrilled. I mean, here I was, finally getting a chance to do original work rather than copy some overrated dabbler like Renoir or Degas. Then he gave me the bad news: I couldn't include my signature on the notes. Yeah, I know it's not done, but they never went out and hired a true artiste before. Still, argue as I might, I couldn't talk him into relenting on that one point—though I did get him to double my fee before I finally ran out of words.

He offered to supply me with holos of all of Solomon's greatest politicians and military figures, past and present, but I had carte blanche in regard to subject matter . . . and I saw a way to take my revenge. Although he was married and the father of five daughters, the governor kept a gorgeous blond mistress on New Rhodesia. It wasn't exactly the best-kept secret on Solomon, which is how I found out about it, but everyone—including his wife—pretended not to know anything about it.

I had a year in which to deliver the five engravings, and the first thing I did was rent a ship and fly out to New Rhodesia. I hunted up his mistress, and found that she was getting sick and tired of being kept hidden like a dirty secret. He kept promising to leave his family and make her the First Lady (or First Whatever) of Solomon, but it was obvious that it was all just talk. He had no intention of changing an arrangement he found so congenial.

She wanted to embarrass him, and she also craved the notoriety, so I proposed my plan to her that evening over drinks—Alphard brandy, as I recall—and it met with her immediate and enthusiastic approval.

Over the next ten months, I made five exquisite, life-sized paintings of her, which would later be reduced to banknote size and transformed into engravings.

In the first, which was to become the one-credit note, she was dressed in the traditional uniform worn by both sexes of the Solomon military.

For the ten-credit note, I painted her in basically the same outfit, but without the helmet and armor.

She was wearing less in each of the next two notes, and for the five-hundred-credit note she was totally nude, but with her hands and hair modestly covering the more intriguing bits and pieces of her, not unlike in *The Birth of Venus.*

Then, in the two months remaining to me, I created my masterwork, clearly the greatest painting of all time. Same subject, of course, still nude, but proudly displaying everything she'd hidden on the five-hundred-credit note.

How I worked on those flesh tones—and how I succeeded! You'd swear you could reach out and touch that delicate pink skin. You'd bet your last credit that she was looking only at you, that her eyes actually followed you as you walked around the room. You knew that she was actually breathing, and that her breasts were fluttering gently with each breath. Her lips were so moist you felt that if you placed your finger against them it would come away damp.

Usually when you create a masterpiece you want to finish it and frame and hang it. But on this one, I left rectangular areas in each of the four corners—and when I was sure I was done, when it was impossible to improve the painting any further, I spent the last day filling in those four boxes with the number 10,000,000.

The next day we held a huge reception to launch the new banknotes. One by one I displayed the five paintings. They applauded the first wildly, the next mildly, and then there was a growing uneasiness as I unveiled the last three. I thought the governor was about to have a stroke.

When the ceremony was almost over, I had a couple of assistants display my ultimate masterpiece. I could hear the assembled dignitaries voice a collective gasp, and I announced that this was the ten-million-credit note, and that this was the only one and there would never be another, and since it was a collector's item I'd sell it to the highest bidder. I explained that it was unfair to exclude the planetary population at large from the bidding, so I had allowed the local holo stations to broadcast the painting all across the planet for five minutes before the auction began.

Someone bid five million credits, someone else upped it to seven million, and then the governor finally found his voice. "Arrest that man and kill the holos!" he yelled, and I was dragged off to durance vile, where I languished for the next two days.

I was released in the middle of the night and told to leave Solomon and never come back. I asked the guard to thank the governor for his generosity, and he explained that generosity had nothing to do with it. The painting had sold for seventeen million credits, the governor's handpicked judge awarded him five million in damages for the emotional distress I had caused him, and he had then fixed my bail at twelve million credits.

So that's the story. I don't even know if the painting still exists. They're still using my banknotes—not on Solomon, where the governor outlawed them, but on New Rhodesia, where my model had married the richest man on the planet and then inherited all his wealth when he unexpectedly choked to death on a mutated cherry pit a month later. But it seems a crime that the rarest and greatest banknote of all will never be seen again.

———

"I'd give a purty to see that painting," said Catastrophe Baker. "Or even the model, for that matter. Especially if she's the richest woman on New Rhodesia."

"She was something, all right," agreed Little Mike. "If art mirrors life, then you have to start with something like her to wind up with something like my painting."

"Got a question for you," said Max, who always seemed to have a question for everyone who told a story.

"Sure."

"What's your real name?"

"I thought I told you: Michelangelo Gauguin Rembrandt van Gogh Rockwell Picasso."

"I mean your birth name," said Max.

Little Mike paused for a long minute. "Montgomery Quiggle," he said at last, looking decidedly uncomfortable.

"So like the rest of us, you came out to the Inner Frontier and took a name that suited you?"

"You have some objection to that?"

"Nope, but like I said, I got a question. I understand naming yourself after all them famous painters, but why *Little* Mike? Why not just Mike?"

"Because I'm little, and I'm not ashamed of it."

"No reason to be," agreed Max. " 'Course, it ain't nothing to brag about either."

"Oh, I wouldn't be too sure of that," said Big Red, who'd been an all-star in a number of the usual sports, but made his real reputation as maybe the greatest murderball player of all time. His body was covered top to bottom with scars, which he wore proudly.

"Yeah?" said Max. "And what do you know about it?"

"Enough."

"You're a pretty big man yourself," observed Max, looking at Big Red's tall, muscular frame, "and I know you used to be a pro jockstrapper. So suppose you tell me: Now that racehorses are extinct, what athlete would rather be small than big?"

"Right now, today?" replied Big Red. "The greatest of them all."

"And who is that?"

"You probably never heard of him."

"Then how great can he be?" insisted Max.

"Trust me, he was the best I ever saw. Hell, he was the best *anyone* ever saw." Big Red sighed and shook his head sadly. "The brightest flames burn the briefest time."

"His career was cut short by injury, huh?"

"His career was cut short, all right, but not by injury," said Big Red. He shifted in his chair, trying unsuccessfully to get comfortable. (It's well known that murderballers wear their old injuries like medals, and refuse all pain blocks and prostheses.)

"So are you gonna tell us about him or not?"

"Of course I am. I might be the very last person who remembers him, and if I stop telling his story, then it'll be like he never existed."

The Short, Star-Crossed Career of Magic Abdul-Jordan

Nobody knew his real name (began Big Red), but that didn't matter, because by the time he was ten years old they'd already renamed him Magic Abdul-Jordan, after three of the greatest ancient basketball players. There wasn't a shot he couldn't make, and, oh, how that boy could jump! He was quicker than a Denebian weaselcat, and nobody ever worked harder at perfecting his game.

When he was twelve, he stood seven feet tall, and his folks moved to the Delphini system, where they still played basketball for big money. Hired him a private tutor, and let him turn pro when he was thirteen.

First I ever heard of him was when word reached us out on the Rim about this fifteen-year-old phenom who stood more than eight feel tall and could reach almost twice his height at the top of his jump. A year or two later his team ran out of competition and went barnstorming through the Outer Frontier, and wherever Magic Abdul-Jordan went, he filled the stadiums. I don't think that young man ever saw an empty seat in any arena he ever played.

Nobody knew why, but the kid just kept on growing and forgot to stop. By the time he was seventeen, he was nine feet tall, and they changed the rules to try to make things a little fairer. The baskets were raised to a height of fifteen feet, and he was only allowed two of those spectacular dunks of his per half; anything more than that was a technical foul.

But none of that bothered him. He kept honing his skills and working on his moves. I finally got to play against him on Ragitura II, when he had just turned twenty. By then no closed arena could accommodate the crowds that wanted to see him, and he played all his games in outdoor stadiums. I think maybe two hundred thousand Men and about half that many aliens showed up to see him that day.

When he came out onto the court I couldn't believe my eyes. He was close to twelve feet tall, but he had the grace of a dancer. Don't tell me about the square-cube law. I was there; I saw him. This kid could have stuffed the ball if they'd hung the basket twenty feet above the floor, and he was so quick he led his team down the floor on every fast break.

I was the best player on our team, so I got the dubious honor of guarding him. The rule changes had allowed each of his opponents ten fouls. I ran through all ten of mine in something like six minutes, at which time he'd already put thirty-seven points on the board. When the game was over, I did something I've never done before or since: I walked up to an opponent and asked for an autograph.

He seemed like a nice, modest young man, and everyone predicted a great future for him. I made up my mind to keep an eye on him as his career developed, but that was the only time I ever saw him.

Next I heard of him was a little over a year later. He was up to fourteen feet tall, and it was getting hard to find anyone to play against him. They kept changing the rules, and he kept growing past all the changes. Pretty soon they had the basket so high that he couldn't dunk anymore—but none of the other players could even throw the ball that high.

Another year passed, and he was eighteen feet tall and still growing. They had to construct a special ship to accommodate him, but then one team after another canceled their games. They gave all kinds of reasons, but the simple fact was that no one was willing to play against him anymore. He was just too big and too good, and finally, faced with imminent bankruptcy, the team had to cancel his contract.

That was the last anyone ever saw or heard of the poor bastard. Every now and then I'll hear about a real tall, middle-aged phenom playing in some pickup league, and I'll fly halfway across the galaxy to see if it's him, but invariably it's some guy who's seven feet tall and starting to go a little bald.

Anyway, that's why you never saw him or heard of him. But trust me—no one who ever had the privilege of watching Magic Abdul-Jordan in action will ever forget him. He's probably out there somewhere, towering above his world like an attenuated mountain, still working on his moves, hoping and praying that they'll ask him to come back for one last game so he can give a new generation of fans one final thrill.

But of course they never will.

His story finished, Big Red pulled a white handkerchief out of his pocket and blew his nose noisily.

"This guy really existed?" said Three-Gun Max.

"I just told you so, didn't I?"

"I thought maybe you made it up. I mean, hell, true or false, it makes a good story."

"It *is* a good story," agreed Big Red. "But if I'd made it up, I'd have held him to three points and picked up only one foul in forty minutes."

"A telling point," agreed Catastrophe Baker. "That's sure the way *I'd* have made it up."

"Well, I guess he was the most famous athlete that no one ever heard of," agreed Max.

"Yeah," said Big Red, "I had the privilege of playing against the greatest unknown jockstrapper in the galaxy, and the greatest known one, too."

"You played against McPherson?" said Max dubiously.

"You ever hear of a greater known one?" was Big Red's answer.

"Boy, I remember flying all the way to the Pilaster system to see him!" said Nicodemus Mayflower with a nostalgic smile on his face.

"Even *I* heard of him," chimed in Catastrophe Baker, "and I've been too busy with Pirate Queens and Temple Virgins and the like to pay much attention to children's games." He paused. "Old Iron-Arm. They say he was something else." He turned to Big Red. "Whatever became of him, anyway?"

"Well, that's really Einstein's story to tell," answered Big Red. "But since he can't communicate in any language that isn't full of numbers and strange symbols, I suppose I'd better tell it for him."

And so he did.

When Iron-Arm McPherson Took the Mound

I still remember him when he was just a kid (said Big Red), making a name for himself out in the Quinellus Cluster. They said he was the fastest thing on two feet, and that he'd break every base-stealing record in the books.

I took that kind of personally, since I'm pretty fast myself—or at least I used to be, before I blew out my left knee and broke my right thigh and ankle during my next-to-last season of murderball. (I'll bet you didn't know it, but I took my name from two of the greatest racehorses ever, Man o' War and Secretariat. The press gave each of them the nickname of Big Red.) Anyway, I made it my business to head out that way and see if this McPherson kid was as good as his press clippings.

First time up, the kid bunted and beat the throw, then stole second, third, and home, and he was still looking for more bases to steal when the roar of the crowd finally died down. Did the same thing the second time he was up. Bunted his way onto first base a third time—and then it happened. There was a pickoff play that got him leaning the wrong way, and suddenly he fell to the ground and grabbed his knee, and I knew his base-stealing days were over.

I didn't think much about him for the next couple of years, and then I heard he'd come back, that he was hitting home runs farther than anyone had ever hit 'em, was averaging more than one a game, so I went out to take a look. Sure enough, the kid drilled the first pitch he saw completely out of the ballpark, and did the same with the next couple.

Then they called in Squint-Eye Malone from the bullpen. Old Squint-Eye took it as a personal insult any time someone poked a long one off one of his teammates, so he wound up and threw a high hard one up around the kid's chin. The kid was a really cool customer; he never flinched, never moved a muscle. Malone squinted even more and aimed the next one at the kid's head. The kid ducked a little too late, and everyone in the park could hear the crunching sound as the ball shattered his eye socket, and I figured that even with the artificial eyes they make these days, it would have to affect his timing or his depth perception or something, and it was a damned shame, because this was a truly talented kid who'd been done in not once but twice by bad luck and physical injuries.

And that was it. I never gave him another thought. Then, about four years later, word began trickling out that there was a pitcher out in the boonies who could throw smoke like no one had ever seen. The stories kept coming back about this Iron-Arm McPherson, who supposedly threw the ball so hard that batters never saw it coming, and I vaguely wondered if he was any relation to the McPherson kid I'd seen who'd had all that talent and all those troubles.

Well, he was too good to stay where he was, so they sold his contract to the Cosmos League, and before long he got himself traded to the Deluros Demons, and you can't get any bigger than that.

I was playing for Spica II at the time. We won our division and headed off to Deluros VIII for the play-offs, and I got my first look at Iron-Arm McPherson, and sure enough he was the same player I'd seen those other two times. I was batting leadoff, and I figured he couldn't run too good after that knee injury, and I didn't think he could have fully adjusted to his new eye, so I decided I'd bunt on the right side of the infield and I should have no trouble beating it out, and when my teammates saw how easy it was, why, we'd bunt the poor bastard out of the game, maybe even out of the league.

So the game starts, and I walk up to the plate, and Iron-Arm winds up and lets fly, and I hear the ball thud into the catcher's mitt, and the umpire calls it a strike, but I'll swear I never saw it once it left his hand.

He winds up and throws again, and again it comes in so fast that my eyes can't follow it, and then he does it a third time, and I'm out of there, and I realize that everything I've heard about Iron-Arm McPherson is true.

He strikes out the first eighteen men he faces, and then I come up for a third time to lead off the top of the seventh inning, and he rears back and gives me the high hard one, and I can almost feel it whistle by me even though I can't see it, and I toss my bat onto the ground in disgust and start walking back to the dugout.

"Hey, Red," says the umpire, "you got two more strikes coming."

"I don't want 'em," I say.

"Are you gonna come back here and play or not?" demands the ump.

"Not," I say. "How the hell can I hit what I can't see?"

"All right, you're outta here!" yells the ump, and I get ejected and take an early shower, which suits me fine since the alternative is being humiliated up at the plate again.

We all breathe a sigh of relief when the game's over, because it means we won't have to face McPherson again for another three or four days—but when we come out onto the field the next afternoon, who's waiting for us on the mound but Iron-Arm McPherson!

Well, fifty-two hours into the play-offs we're down three games to none, and we're just one game from elimination, and not a one of us has reached base yet, and McPherson's record in the series is 3 and 0, and he's pitched back-to-back perfect games, and instead of getting tired he seems to be as strong as ever, and one of the local newscasts announces that they've timed his pitches and they're *averaging* 287 miles per hour, and that his hummer was clocked at 303.

That night, while I'm drowning my sorrows in the hotel bar and wondering what to do with myself in the off season, which figures to start sometime around midafternoon the next day, I see Einstein sitting by himself, lifting a few and jotting down notes on his computer. I recognize him from his holos, and I figure if anyone can help me, it's got to be him, so I walk over and introduce myself.

He doesn't respond, and that's when someone tells me he's blind, deaf, and mute, and I ask how anyone ever talks to him, and it's explained to me that I have to get *my* computer to talk to *his* computer and then he'll respond.

I go over to the hotel's registration desk and rent a pocket computer and then return to the bar and have it tell Einstein's computer who I am and how much I admire him, and that I've got a little problem and could he help me with it?

He taps away at his machine, and suddenly mine speaks up: "What is the nature of your problem?"

I ask him if he knows anything about baseball, and he says he knows the rudiments, and I explain my problem to him, that McPherson's high hard one clocks in at 303 miles an hour, and that even at an average of 287 none of us can even see the ball when Iron-Arm lets loose.

He does some quick calculations in his head, takes about two seconds to verify them on his computer, and then sends me another message: "The human arm is incapable of throwing a baseball at more than 127.49263 miles per hour."

"Maybe so," I answer back, "but they clocked him at more than twice that speed."

"The conclusion is obvious," sends Einstein. "The baseball is not being thrown by a human arm."

And suddenly it's all clear to me. Here's this kid who's already got an artificial knee and a replacement eyeball as a result of injuries. Why not get a step ahead of the game by buying himself a prosthetic arm before he can develop bursitis or tendonitis or whatever? And if he was going to buy a new arm, why not the strongest, most accurate arm that science could make?

I thought about it for a while, until I was sure I was right, and then I told Einstein that I agreed with him, but that didn't help solve my problem, which was that whether McPherson was using his real arm or one he'd gone out and bought, no one could even hit a loud foul ball off him.

"It's an interesting problem," responded Einstein. He began tapping in numbers and symbols, and pretty soon his fingers were almost as hard to follow as one of McPherson's fastballs, and after about five minutes he quit just as suddenly as he started, with a satisfied little smile on his face.

"Are you still here?" his machine asked.

"Yes."

"I am going to transmit a very complex chemical formula to your computer. In the morning, print it out and take it to the laboratory at the local university—they're the only ones who will have everything that's required—and have them mix it up as instructed and put it into a titanium vial. Then rub it onto your bat."

"And then what?" I asked.

"Then don't trip on third base as you turn for home plate."

I thanked him, though I didn't really believe anything could work against McPherson, and I went to the lab in the morning, just like he told me to, and got the vial and poured the entire contents onto my bat and rubbed them in real good about an hour before game time.

I wasn't real thrilled when the home plate umpire cried "Play ball!" and Iron-Arm McPherson took the mound for the fourth day in a row and I had to step into the batter's box, but the only alternative was to get myself thrown out again, so I sighed and trudged up to the plate and stood there, waiting.

McPherson wound up and reared back and let fly. I'm not sure exactly what happened next, except that I heard a *crack!* like a gunshot, and suddenly the ball was soaring into the left-field bleachers and I was jogging around the bases with a really dumb grin on my face, and McPherson was standing there, hands on hips, looking like he couldn't believe that I'd belted his money pitch out of the park.

He struck out the next eight batters, but when I came up again with two out and nobody on in the third inning, he leaned back and gave me his zinger, and I pickled it again. I nailed another in the sixth, and I led off the ninth with my fourth homer of the day. I looked at the scoreboard as I rounded third, and saw we were still down 7 to 4, and there wasn't any activity in the Demons' bullpen (and why should there be? I mean, hell, he was still pitching a four-hitter), and before Shaka Njaba left the on-deck circle and went up to take his raps, I crossed home plate and kept on running until I came to him and told him that if he wanted to win the game he should use my bat. I didn't have time to tell him *why*, but Shaka's as superstitious as most ballplayers, and he jumped at the chance to use my lucky bat.

McPherson rubbed the ball in his hands, hitched his pants, fiddled with the peak of his cap, toed the rubber, went into his motion, and let fly—and not only didn't I see the ball come to the plate, but the bat moved so fast I didn't see *it* either. But I heard the two meet, and I saw the ball go nineteen rows deep into the center-field seats, and I passed the word up and down the bench that everyone should use my bat.

The next six hitters took McPherson deep, and when his manager finally came out and took the ball away from him and sent him to the showers (for the first time all season), we were winning 11 to 7. I figured our bullpen could hold on to the lead, so I took my bat back before someone broke it, and sure enough, we won 11 to 8.

McPherson was back on the mound the next day, but after we hit his first five pitches into the stands for a 5-to-0 lead, he was gone again, and we didn't see any more of him in the series.

We won that afternoon, and the next two nights, and became the champions. I sought out Einstein to thank him, but he told me that he'd gotten thirty-to-one odds against Spica II when we were down three games to none. He'd bet a few thousand credits, so he felt more than amply rewarded for his efforts.

As for Iron-Arm McPherson, getting knocked out of the box in front of all those millions of fans was—to borrow a baseball expression—his third strike, after messing up his knee and his batting eye. There just wasn't a place in the game for a pitcher who couldn't get anyone out, even if he *could* burn that hummer in there at 303 miles an hour.

"What became of him?" I asked.

"Last I heard, he was running a spaceship wash at one of the orbital stations out near Far London," answered Big Red.

"So that's how you managed to hit those homers off him!" said Bet-a-World O'Grady. "I'll be damned!"

"You saw the game?" asked Big Red.

"I'm the guy who gave Einstein thirty to one that you couldn't win!" He laughed.

"Just goes to show what happens when you bet against Einstein."

"Same thing usually happens when you bet against *me*," said O'Grady.

"I'll bet you've been involved in some big-money games," offered Three-Gun Max.

"I've been in my share of 'em," agreed O'Grady.

"I heard about the time you put up three agricultural worlds against the Tamal Jewels on one roll of the dice," put in Nicodemus Mayflower.

"And I remember reading that you lost a whole solar system in a card game out on Tevarius IV, and then won it back the next night," added Sahara del Rio.

"Absolutely true," said O'Grady.

"What was the biggest bet you ever made?"

"You really want to hear about it?" asked O'Grady with the air of a man who couldn't be silenced by much less than a lethal blow to the head.

"That's why we're asking," said Max.

O'Grady walked up to the bar, then turned so he could face his audience.

"Then I guess I'll tell you," he said.

The Night Bet-a-World O'Grady Met High-Stakes Eddie

For almost five years (said O'Grady) people had been trying to arrange a game between me and High-Stakes Eddie, who was supposed to be the best gambler in the Belladonna Cluster. At one point I even had a couple of banks willing to back me in a one-on-one poker game with him, and I heard tell he had a Korbelian prince on the line to pick up his tab if he lost to me.

Still, we almost didn't get together at all. He spent almost three months breaking an upstart called the Lower Volta Flash in a nightly game, and then when he was ready, I found myself embroiled in a winner-take-all game for the ownership of the Willoughby system that went on for the better part of ten weeks.

Then one day I got a hand-delivered engraved invitation that read as follows:

Bet-a-World O'Grady is cordially invited to the gaming world of Monte Carlo IV as the guest of High-Stakes Eddie Strongbow. All expenses except for gambling losses will be paid by his host.

"Will you be coming back with me, sir?" asked the young woman who had delivered it.

"Yeah, why not?" I said, making up my mind on the spot. "If we're going to decide once and for all who's the best, I might as well let your boss pay for my transportation and drinks."

"He was hoping you'd feel that way, sir," she replied.

"By the way, where the hell is Monte Carlo IV?" I asked.

"Out by the Lesser Magellenic Cloud" was the answer. "Mr. Strongbow won the entire Cromwell system on a single flip of a coin last year, and officially renamed it about two months ago." She paused. "May I help you pack?"

I patted the pocket that held my wallet, and the one that held my lucky dice.

"I've got everything I need," I announced.

"You might want a change of clothes," she suggested.

"I'll buy some new clothes on Monte Carlo IV and charge them to your boss."

She shrugged and took me to her ship. The crew consisted of three other women in addition to the one who'd delivered the invite, and they called themselves the Queens of Clubs, Diamonds, Hearts, and Spades, though, truth to tell, I never could tell which was which. I think they changed names every few hours just to keep me confused.

It was a long flight to the Monte Carlo system, so I went into DeepSleep a few hours into the trip and had them wake me when we were about an hour from our destination. I'm always famished when I come out of DeepSleep, and that always surprises me, because as often as they explain it to me, I keep forgetting that my systems don't actually stop, but just slow down to a crawl—and when you haven't eaten in a few days, even with your metabolism working at one percent speed, you're still hungry.

By the time I finished eating, we'd touched down, and I was transported to a penthouse suite atop the biggest, glitziest hotel on the planet, which befitted a high roller like myself. There were maybe half a dozen bedrooms, and three of them came equipped with their own women, and there were eight or nine bathrooms and a bunch of fireplaces and holo screens and two well-stocked bars and a robot bartender (but not as friendly as Reggie) and even a library filled with real, honest-to-goodness books rather than tapes and disks and cubes. I'd been in a few nicer suites in my time, but I had to admit that it was pretty impressive for as far outside of the Monarchy as it was.

I'd just finished looking around and introducing myself to the three women when the Queen of Hearts (or maybe it was Diamonds) showed up and told me that my host was waiting for me downstairs. I bade the ladies good night and followed her. There was a huge, elegant casino on the ground floor. It not only had the usual human and alien games, but it had real cards, real dice, and real, live dealers and pit bosses—none of those computerized holographs that you see on worlds like New Vegas and Little Monaco. We walked right through the place without slowing down, and then came to a studded metal door that had guards the size of Catastrophe Baker standing on each side of it.

"This is Mr. Strongbow's private gaming room," explained the Queen of Hearts as they opened the door for us. "It is reserved for himself and his personal guests."

High-Stakes Eddie was sitting on a leather chair at the far side of a felt-covered mahogany table, a drink in front of him, a smokeless Brandeis VII cigar in his left hand. He was smaller than I'd expected, bald as a billiard ball, and wearing an outfit that couldn't make up its mind what it wanted to be. One moment it looked like a toga, then it changed into a military uniform, then a Bendorian tuxedo (you ever see one of those things? The sons of bitches glow in the dark!), and then back to a toga.

His outfit may have been the height of fashion, but his room was an anachronism. The chairs didn't adjust to your body, they actually rested on the floor, and the lights were in the ceiling instead of floating over your right shoulder. Still, it was his place to decorate any way he wanted. "Bet-a-World O'Grady!" he said with a smile. "You can't imagine how much I've looked forward to making your acquaintance. There were times when I truly thought we'd never meet."

"I always assumed that we'd get together sooner or later," I replied, walking forward and shaking his hand. "So when I got your kind invitation, I decided it might as well be sooner."

"Your presence honors my poor establishment," he said. "I trust you will join me in a game or two of chance."

"That's what I'm here for," I said.

"Excellent!" he said. "A number of local dignitaries have expressed interest in watching us compete. Would you have any objection to—?"

"Bring 'em in," I said. "I *like* crowds."

"A gentleman as well as a gambler," enthused High-Stakes Eddie. "I really *am* delighted that you agreed to come."

He waved his hand over a small cube on the table, the door dilated, and half a dozen men and women entered the room. Eddie handled the introductions: one was a mayor, another a general, a third was the planetary governor, and I remember that one large, fat woman was the system's greatest opera diva.

They took their seats, and High-Stakes Eddie directed them to be silent once play began or run the certain risk of being unceremoniously thrown out.

The woman who was the Queen of Clubs that night brought in a dozen unopened decks of cards, half a dozen pairs of brand-new dice, and directed a burly young man to set up a roulette wheel at the far end of the huge table.

"What's your choice, Bet-a-World O'Grady?" asked High-Stakes Eddie.

"I've always been partial to poker," I admitted.

"Then poker it is," he said. "You mind playing with real cards? I hate computers."

"Suits me," I answered.

He tossed a deck to me and waited for me to open it. I inspected the cards, and satisfied myself that it was an honest deck.

"They look good to me," I announced. "Shall we begin?"

"Name it."

"Five-card stud."

"Stakes?" he asked.

"Whatever you want."

"How's about a million credits to ante, and you can only bet in multiples of five million," he said. "Sky's the limit."

There was a sharp collective intake of breath among our six spectators.

"I accept," I said. Then I paused. "I hope my credit's good here."

"Up to twenty billion," he replied. "After that I'll need collateral."

"Fair enough," I said. "Cut?"

He cut the cards, and I started dealing.

I won the first hand with jacks and sixes, he won the next with three kings, and then I won four in a row with a straight, a full house, and a couple of nothings that were higher than *his* nothings. When the dust settled, I was up almost two hundred million credits.

"You're as good as they say," said High-Stakes Eddie, taking a sip of his drink. "Shall we try a little draw now?"

"It's your deal," I acquiesced.

We split the next six hands, and pretty much split the pots as well. Then I won three in a row, and I was suddenly up half a billion.

"Let's make it a little more exciting," he suggested.

"I'm open to suggestions," I replied.

"Let's cut the cards for a billion."

I nodded, ignored another audible gasp from the guests, reached out, and cut to a nine. He smiled, flexed his fingers, reached for the remaining cards, and cut to a six.

"How about two billion this time?" he said.

"And then four billion, and then eight billion, and then sixteen billion, until you finally win one?" I said. "That's not gambling," I said. "That's mathematical inevitability."

"All right," he said, a little heatedly. "What would you rather do?"

"Do you *really* want to make it more exciting?" I asked.

He looked around the room and then nodded, as I knew he would. There was no way he was going to lose face in front of his friends.

"How much money have you got on hand here?" I asked.

"In this room?"

"In the whole casino."

He did a quick calculation in his head. "About eighteen billion credits."

"And you own the Monte Carlo system, right?"

"All fourteen planets."

"Including mining rights?"

"Of course."

"Okay," I said. "That's your half of the bet. For my half, I'll put up all the money I've won here, plus fifteen billion I've got on deposit at the Bank of Deluros, and the deed to all nine planets in the Taniguchi system. They discovered diamonds in the asteroid belt there last month."

"What's the bet?" he said, eyeing me warily.

"One hand of Face-up Draw, winner take all."

"Face-up Draw?" he repeated. "I never heard of it."

"Nothing to it," I said. "We turn all the cards face-up, and instead of dealing, we each choose five cards. Then we can discard up to four cards and draw four more. It's just draw poker with everything face-up and out in the open."

"We'll tie. You'll deal yourself a royal flush and stand pat and I'll do the same."

"Tell you what," I said. "I'll stipulate that you win all ties. My cards have to have you beat, not just tied, in order for me to win."

"Say that again."

I repeated it.

"And there's no suit preference like in bridge?" he persisted. "A three of clubs is as high as a three of spades?"

"Right," I said. "And I'll tell you what else: I'll go first, so you can have the advantage of seeing what I pick before you commit yourself."

Well, he spent the better part of five minutes asking me all kinds of questions, but it was just like I told him, and finally he and I signed a document agreeing to the terms I had outlined.

And that's how I broke the bank at Monte Carlo.

Just a minute!" said Three-Gun Max heatedly. "What kind of fools do you take us for?"

"The usual kind," answered O'Grady with a smug smile.

"There's no way you can win that bet!"

"Don't take *my* word for it," said O'Grady. "Who's the brightest man in the Outpost?"

"Einstein."

"Ask him."

"He's blind, deaf, and mute," said Max. "And if that ain't enough, he's never played poker in his life."

"Just a minute," said Big Red. He turned to me. "Tomahawk, can you have Reggie transmit all the rules to the little computer Einstein always keeps in his hand?"

"No reason why not," I replied.

"It'll take him hours just to learn the rudiments of the game," protested Max.

"You don't know Einstein," said Big Red confidently.

I gave Reggie his instructions, and he started whirring and humming, and so did Einstein's machine, which then started tapping out some incomprehensible code on the palm of his left hand. After about twenty seconds Einstein smiled, the first time his facial expression had changed since he'd shown up a few months ago, and he tapped a message onto his computer's sensors.

Reggie whirred again and then spoke in his dull monotone voice. "Einstein says O'Grady can't lose."

"Well, if Einstein ain't the stupidest genius on the Frontier, I sure don't know who's running ahead of him!" exclaimed Max.

"You're absolutely certain that Einstein and I are wrong, are you?" asked O'Grady.

"Damn right."

"Are you willing to bet a hundred credits on it?"

"Real cards, just like you used on Monte Carlo?"

"Right."

"Fresh deck, same rules?"

"Fresh deck, same rules," agreed O'Grady.

Max pulled a hundred-credit note out of his pocket and tossed it onto his table. "You're on."

O'Grady sat down opposite him, and I broke open a new deck and brought it over to them.

"You go first," said Max.

"I know."

"And remember: I win all ties."

O'Grady spread the deck out face-up, so that we could see all fifty-two cards. I figured he'd pull himself a royal flush, or at least four aces. Instead he started sorting through them until he had pulled out all four tens.

Then he turned to Sahara del Rio, who was staring over his shoulder. "You pick my last card, my dear."

"But I don't know the rules of the game," she protested.

"It doesn't matter," O'Grady assured her. "Just reach out and pick one."

She shrugged, ran her hand over the cards, and finally picked a deuce of clubs.

"Thank you, my dear," said O'Grady. He looked across the table at Max. "Your turn."

Max reached out and promptly picked up all four aces and a king.

"Very impressive," said O'Grady. "Four bullets."

"Let's see you beat *that*," said Max cockily.

"I shall endeavor to," promised O'Grady. "Time to discard and draw now, right?"

"Go ahead."

O'Grady dumped three tens and the deuce, then pulled four cards and built himself a straight flush to the ten.

"Your turn again, Max," he said.

Max stared at his hand, and then at O'Grady's, and then at his again.

"*Shit!*" he bellowed.

"You see?" said O'Grady. "My straight flush beats your four aces, and since all the tens are gone, not only can't you create a royal flush, but the highest straight flush you can build will be nine high."

"What if I'd started with a straight flush instead of four aces?" asked Max.

"Same result. You can't create one that goes any higher than the nine."

"Just a minute," said Hellfire Van Winkle. "Suppose he'd picked four nines. You can't stand pat, because he can draw four aces or a straight flush to beat your four tens. What do you do then?"

"Discard three tens and the deuce and build a royal flush," answered O'Grady. "He can't match it, because all the tens are gone." He reached out, picked up the hundred-credit note, folded it in half, and slipped it into a pocket. "An inexpensive lesson, especially considering how often I'm sure each of you is going to use it once you leave the Outpost." Suddenly he smiled. "Just don't ever try it in the vicinity of Monte Carlo IV. . . . They don't have much of a sense of humor about it out that way."

"You got any other scams you want to tell us about?" asked Max.

"Not for a lousy hundred credits," said O'Grady. He looked over and saw Willie the Bard scribbling away. "Hey, you'd better not be writing all this down!"

"That's the Bard," I said. "He writes everything down."

"He writes *everything*?" repeated Catastrophe Baker.

"Yeah," I said. "He's our historian. Someday he'll make you famous."

"I already got a little more fame than I can handle," protested Baker.

"And *I* don't want millions of people reading about what I did on Monte Carlo," chimed in O'Grady. "I don't mind telling a handful of people out here at the edge of nowhere, but I don't want it written up in a book. I might want to use it again sometime."

"Not to worry," said the Bard. "It'll be twenty, maybe thirty years before I'm ready to publish."

"How long have you been working on this masterpiece?" asked Baker.

"Since Tomahawk opened for business."

"And how many pages have you written?"

"I lost count years ago. But after pruning it down, I've kept about four thousand."

"You halfway done yet?"

"Probably not."

Baker smiled. "Who's gonna publish this thing?"

"That's not my problem," answered the Bard with an unconcerned shrug. "My job is to write it."

"I never did understand artists."

"Hey, we make as much sense as anyone," put in Little Mike Picasso. "And maybe a little more than most."

"Hell, maybe you do," admitted Baker. "Truth to tell, I've only known one real artist."

"A painter?" asked Little Mike.

Baker shook his head. "An opera singer. Ever hear of Melody Duva?"

"Can't say that I have."

"The Diva Duva," said Nicodemus Mayflower admiringly. "I've seen a couple of her holos. She had a gorgeous voice. Whatever happened to her?"

"She was the victim of an unhappy collision of art and science," answered Catastrophe Baker.

"Sounds like a story coming up," suggested the Reverend Billy Karma.

"Not much to tell," said Baker. "She was built like an opera singer, which is to say she weighed in at maybe three hundred and fifty pounds. She loved low-gravity worlds, where she could move with the grace of a dancer. Last time she ever performed was on New Samarkand, in a revival of *Tosca*."

"I've seen the holo."

"You must have seen an earlier version," said Baker. "This one ran only one performance, and no one ever captured it."

"What happened?"

"New Samarkand is a temperate world, and they hold most of their operas and symphonies and other shindigs at this huge outdoor amphitheater," began Baker. "Anyway, there's a scene at the end when Tosca commits suicide by throwing herself off the top of a tall tower they call a battlement. Ordinarily they'd toss a couple of air mattresses down on the stage, out of sight of the audience, to break her fall—but Diva Duva was so, well, *large* that they figured she was sure to bust something, so instead of mattresses they put out a hydro-trampoline to break her fall."

"A trampoline?" asked Max, frowning.

Baker nodded. "She plunged down so fast you could almost hear the wind whistle around her, hit the trampoline full force, and shot straight up. And like I told you, New Samarkand is a low-gravity world. She reached escape velocity and wound up crashing through the cargo hold of a mining ship out near one of the planet's moons." He sighed. "Next day they got rid of the trampoline and put in a swimming pool for her understudy." He shook his head sadly. "Nobody ever thought to ask the poor girl if she knew how to swim."

There was total silence for a moment, while everyone digested the story.

Max was the first to speak. "You absolutely sure every word of that is true?" he asked dubiously.

Baker's jaw jutted out pugnaciously. "Are you impugning my integrity?" he demanded.

"No," Max assured him. "Just your veracity."

"Well, that's okay, then," replied Baker, relaxing.

Just then Achmed of Alphard entered the Outpost, dressed in his glowing robes and sparkling turban. He towered at least a foot above Catastrophe Baker and Big Red, and even more above everyone else.

"Good evening, gentlemen," he said, then bowed in the general direction of Sinderella and the Earth Mother. "And ladies, of course." He looked across the room at me. "The war's getting close, Tomahawk."

"Anyone figure out who the enemy is?" I asked.

He shrugged. "Beats me."

"Then how do you know there's a war?"

"They're firing on Navy ships."

"Yeah, that sounds kind of warlike," opined Max.

"How far away are they?"

"Who knows?" replied Achmed. "A few days, a few systems. It all depends on how often and accurately the Navy fires back."

"I wouldn't worry much," said Gravedigger Gaines. "No war's ever gotten this far."

"This one won't either," added Nicodemus Mayflower, nodding his lean, angular head for emphasis.

"Well, if it does, they're going to wish they'd gone in some other direction," chimed in Catastrophe Baker. "I've killed men for lesser crimes than disturbing me while I'm drinking and socializing."

"Are there any greater crimes?" asked Three-Gun Max.

"None that come immediately to mind," admitted Baker.

The door opened again and Sitting Horse and Crazy Bull entered. The wind was blowing, as usual, and they were coated with the red dust that covers most of Henry II when it's not blowing through the dry, hot, thin air.

Sitting Horse and Crazy Bull were wearing their tribal buckskins and feathered war bonnets, which looked just a tad out of place on a pair of roly-poly, fur-covered, orange, three-legged aliens, but we'd all grown used to their appearance over the years.

"Hey, Tomahawk—" began Crazy Bull.

"I know, I know," I said. "The war's getting closer."

"What war?" he asked.

"Damned if I know," I answered. "Let's start again."

"Sure," said Crazy Bull agreeably. "Hey, Tomahawk, a couple of Blue Angels for me and my partner."

Reggie mixed them up and placed them on the bar.

"That looks pretty interesting," remarked Baker. "I think I'll have one too."

"You don't want it," said Sitting Horse, picking up his glass. "It's poison to humans."

"Really?"

"Really."

"Cancel my order, Reggie," he said. "By the way, what are a pair of orange, three-legged furballs doing dressed up like Injuns?"

"We come from Velitas IV," said Sitting Horse.

"Never heard of it."

"That's because it's not Velitas IV anymore," said Sitting Horse.

"We were colonized by descendants of the Great Sioux Nation," said Crazy Bull. "But instead of exploiting us, they shared their knowledge and their culture with us, and finally we all became blood brothers and took Indian names. We even renamed the planet. Now it's Big Little Horn IV." He paused. "Sitting Horse and me, we make the Outpost our headquarters because we like anyone who calls himself Tomahawk."

"Just out of curiosity, have you guys ever seen a horse or a bull?" asked Baker.

"No, but we've seen a lot of men who were crazy, and even more who spent all their time sitting when they should have been *doing.*"

"Hey, it's no skin off my nose," said Baker. "But if it was me, I'd have took Geronimo for a name."

"Not me," interjected Big Red. "I'd have been Jim Thorpe."

"Pocahontas for me," said Sinderella.

"So come to Little Big Horn and you can choose any name you want," said Sitting Horse.

"And as an added bonus, you get to put on war paint every Saturday night," said Crazy Bull.

"How many wives do Injuns get?" asked Baker.

"How many women can you live with?" asked Sitting Horse.

"It's been my long and considered experience that the total comes to something less than one," answered Baker.

"See?" said Sitting Horse. "You're not so alien after all."

"I thought you guys were the aliens," said Baker.

"Not to us, we aren't."

They took their Blue Angels off to a table and began playing a game that seemed to involve cards, pebbles, and feathers in equal quantities.

"I wonder if we should be worrying about this war," said the Reverend Billy Karma.

"They know better than to attack the Outpost," said Max. "This is where all the living legends hang out. They don't want no part of us."

"If they're godless chlorine breathers, maybe they don't know about us," said Karma. "Or maybe they subscribe to different legends."

"If they're godless chlorine breathers, they have no more interest in Henry II than we have in their home world," said Nicodemus Mayflower. He grinned at his wit, and between his widow's peak and his thin face and aquiline nose, he looked exactly like my notion of the devil—which may well have been why he chose Nicodemus for one of his names.

"I want it on the record that I, for one, resent the notion that all nonhumans are godless," said Argyle, sparkling like a Christmas tree.

"You believe in God?" demanded Billy Karma.

"I believe in thirty-seven separate and distinct gods," answered Argyle proudly. "That puts me thirty-six ahead of you."

"It makes you a pagan."

"It makes you a man of limited vision," said Argyle.

"Still, it don't matter what *you* believe," continued Karma. "Jesus died for your sins anyway."

"I never could figure out why you worship someone who couldn't even save himself," said Argyle. "And you walk around wearing a representation of the cross that killed him. That's awfully close to psychic necrophilia."

"Them's fighting words!" cried Billy Karma, putting up his fists and starting to bob and weave.

Argyle sprang forward, clipped Billy Karma cleanly on the chin, then stood back as the Reverend slowly collapsed.

"You can't beat a being who prays to Balaxtibo, the God of Self-Defense" shouted Argyle triumphantly.

"He's one of the thirty-seven?" asked Baker.

"Right," said Argyle. "Though my personal favorite is Wilxyboeth."

"Which one is that?"

"The God of Sexual Potency."

The Reverend Billy Karma groaned and sat up on the floor, gingerly rubbing his chin.

Argyle extended his hand. "No hard feelings?"

"None," said Karma. "Pull me up, will you?" When he was standing, he turned to Reggie. "Hey, Reg, mix up a couple of tall ones for me and my pal here. Come on, Argyle, you fascinating little alien bastard," he said, putting an arm around the sparkling alien's shoulders and leading him off to a table. "We got a lot to talk about."

"We do?"

Karma nodded. "Let's start with Wilxyboeth."

"I wonder how you spell Wilxyboeth?" mused Willie the Bard, frowning and staring at his paper notebook.

"How come you don't use a recorder or a computer?" asked Catastrophe Baker, walking across the room to look over the Bard's shoulder.

"That's not art."

"What's the difference between recording what we say and writing it down?"

"I embellish."

"And you couldn't do that with a computer?"

The Bard considered it for a moment, then shook his head. "I don't like machines."

"Neither do I, come to think of it," admitted Baker. "I just figured a computer could do things faster."

"It can fuck up my book two hundred thousand times faster

than my pen can," agreed the Bard. "Trust me, you'll all come out looking better because of my pen."

"Gonna take off all the rough edges, huh?"

"Or add a few," said the Bard. "Whatever it takes."

"I'll make you a deal, Willie," said Little Mike Picasso. "Give me ten percent of the advance and I'll illustrate your book for you. I'll do sketches of everyone in the Outpost."

"Sounds good to me," said the Bard. "Long as you're willing to wait till I sell it."

"Sure. No problem."

The Bard stared at him for a long moment. "Okay, it's a deal," he said. "Now suppose you tell me the real reason you offered to do this."

Little Mike gestured toward Silicon Carny. "I'll die if I can't draw her."

Baker looked over and saw her for the first time. "If all you want to do is *draw* her, you got a lot more wrong with you than you think."

Silicon Carny stood up, and everything came to a sudden stop. No one spoke, no one drank, no one dealt cards. If you made the effort, you could probably hear one molecule of air bumping into its neighbor. She had *that* kind of effect on men.

I knew a little bit about her. Not much, but enough to understand her name. The *Silicon* part was easy enough; mighty few slender women have fifty-inch bustlines with nipples that point almost straight up. The *Carny* part was because her entire body was covered by art—not exactly tattoos, but some alien painting that was in constant flux, almost like a continuous holo—and she'd grown up in a carnival sideshow.

Finally Baker broke the silence.

"By God!" he exclaimed. "This has got to be the first time I ever saw one work of art stuck on top of an even purtier one!"

Silicon Carny smiled at him. "You like?" she purred with an accent I still hadn't placed after four or five years.

"Ma'am," he said, removing his vest and shirt, "I got some mighty artistic tattoos myself, as you can plainly see, but I freely admit they ain't nothing compared to you—and they sure as hell ain't painted on such a nice canvas."

I'd been right about the tattoos: they met in a passionate and pornographic embrace on his chest, then ran off in opposite directions until they reached his hands and headed back toward his chest again.

Silicon Carny looked at him and giggled. For all I know she even blushed, but she had so many colors in perpetual motion that no one could tell. It didn't matter much, though. When she laughed, she shook—and when she shook, strong men just naturally got a little weak in the knees.

"What a delicate, tinkling laugh you got, ma'am," said Baker admiringly, putting his shirt back on. "I think I've only heard one other as engaging."

"Who did it belong to?" asked Max.

"Strangely enough, to the only other carny performer I ever knew," said Baker. "A woman of rare and delectable beauty, though lacking this charming lady's exceptional superstructure."

"So tell us about her," urged Max.

Baker shook his head. "It's a long and tragic story and I don't want to go into it."

"I'd like to hear it," said Silicon Carny.

Baker seemed to consider her request for a moment, then shrugged. "All right, ma'am," he said at last. "It brings back a lot of painful memories—but I make it my business never to say no to a lady, especially one put together even remotely like yourself, ma'am, so if that's what you want, that's what you'll get. But I warn you up front, it ain't got no happy ending."

Catastrophe Baker and the Siren of Silverstrike

It all began (said Baker) when I decided to pay a visit to my old friend Bloody Ben Masters, who'd been the first one to hit pay dirt on Silverstrike. He'd made a few million credits off his silver mine, then sold it for a few million more, built himself a castle with an acid moat around it, and retired.

When I got there I learned that poor Ben was no longer among the living—seemed he'd got a snootful one night and decided to see if he could swim the moat without taking a breath. He got the last part right, because I don't believe there was enough of him left to breathe about three seconds after he dove in. Anyway, there I was with some time on my hands, so that night I moseyed into town to see what the locals did for entertainment besides jump each other's claims, and that's when I found Old Doc Nebuchadnezzar's All-Star Carnival and Thrill Show.

They had all the usual carny stuff: a null-gravity Ferris wheel, a Tower of Babel for the menfolk and a Gomorrah Palace for the ladies, a couple of fights to the death between Trambolians and a pair of the local Men, a magician who volunteered to cut your spouse in half—I don't recall him promising to put her back together, now that I come to think of it—and the usual surgically altered six-armed jugglers and knife throwers and the like, but none of 'em especially interested me.

In fact, I was about to leave when I heard a trumpet blare and a little guy in a bright plaid suit got up on a floating platform and announced that the moment we were all waiting for had arrived, and that anyone with twenty credits to spend could come into his bubble and see the Siren of Silverstrike in all her sensual glory.

Well, the last time I saw so many people move so fast all at once was when me and Bloody Ben had had one of our little disagreements back on Bilbau II and I threw a couple of poker tables through a window and demanded a little more fighting room, and he threw the bartender out after the tables and allowed that that was a right good idea, and I figured anyone or anything that got everyone so motivated was probably worth twenty credits and then some, so I gently shoved a few folks out of my way, tried not to listen overmuch to their howls of anger and agony, and forked over my money.

Once I got inside the bubble, I kind of shouldered my way to the front, hardly discommoding anyone at all except six or seven men who refused to step aside as quick as they should have for a newcomer to their fair planet, and then I took a seat.

I didn't have long to wait, because the second I sat down the music started, and suddenly the Siren of Silverstrike appeared onstage, and you got to believe me when I tell you that she was about as lovely a critter of the female persuasion as I'd ever seen up to that time. Her hair hung down almost to her waist, and it was striped with rows of iridescent colors: red, blue, yellow, green, and the pattern repeated a couple of times. Real striking and artistic, you know?

She held up an almost-transparent little sheet or towel or some such thing in front of her and began her dance, and I noticed when she spun around that she wasn't wearing nothing but her dancing shoes, and that the rest of her hair also came in the very same rows of colors. I think that might have been the instant I decided I was hopelessly and eternally in love with her.

I couldn't figure out why such a lovely young piece of femininity was working in a carnival, and then it occurred to me that this Nebuchadnezzar feller had probably kidnapped her when she was just a little girl, before she'd blossomed into the fullness of womanhood, so to speak, and that she was just waiting for some handsome hero-type to rescue her from this life of enforced slavery and take her home so she could dance every night just for him as a way of showing her gratitude.

I waited until her dance was over, and then it took another five minutes for the audience to stop cheering and stomping and whistling, and finally the bubble emptied out, and I hopped onto the stage and found the little exit at the back and walked through it, and a few seconds later I found myself in the Siren's dressing room.

She was sitting stark naked on a little stool that floated in front of a vanity and a tri-dimensional mirror, brushing her multicolored hair. There were dozens of holos of her in various states of dress and undress on the walls, and a couple of missives which were either love letters or glowing testimonials. There were a bunch of little fussy dolls on a shelf, and a row of ugly porcelain dogs that yipped a nonstop musical tune, and some paintings of big-eyed alien children who all looked pretty much alike, even though a couple were four-armed and one was insectoid and another was a chlorine breather.

When the Siren finally saw my reflection in her mirror, she turned to face me.

"Who are you?" she demanded, either totally forgetting that she wasn't wearing nothing or else not much caring about it.

"I'm Catastrophe Baker, here to declare my everlasting love for you and to rescue you from a life of indentured servitude," I told her.

"I'm flattered," she said, looking me up and down, "but I don't *want* to be rescued."

"That's because Old Doc Nebuchadnezzar has brainwashed you," I explained. "Spend a few months traveling the galaxy with me and you'll be as good as new. What do you say, Siren?"

"I say no, and my name's not Siren."

"What is it, then?" I asked. "If we're going to spend a lifetime of sexual rapture together, I suppose it's one of the things I ought to know."

"It's Melora, and we're not going to spend any time together at all."

"Melora," I repeated. "It must be fate."

"What must be?"

"I've always had a soft spot for naked sirens named Melora," I said. "Purtiest name in the universe, if you ask me."

"I didn't ask you," she said. "Now go away."

"I can't leave you to this life of misery."

"I'm deliriously happy here," said Melora. "I've only been miserable for the past three minutes."

"You're looking at this all wrong," I explained. "I'm in the hero business—at least when I ain't running from various gendarmes—and that means one of the things I do is rescue damsels in distress."

"I'm not *in* distress," she insisted. "Now leave me alone."

"How can I leave you alone?" I said. "I'm in love with you."

"Well, *I'm* not in love with *you!*" she shot back.

"That's because you don't hardly know me," I said. "After ten or twelve years of fun and hijinks together you'll fall like a ton of bricks."

"What does it take to make you leave?" she demanded.

I realized then that my approach had been all wrong, that she viewed me as just another unwashed and uncouth member of her audience, so I figured it was probably time to display my class and erudition by saying something poetic that would sweep her off her feet. I racked my mind trying to remember some of the more touching love stories I'd read as an adolescent, and finally I hit upon a phrase that I just knew would win her over.

"Melora," I said, placing a hand over my heart to indicate my sincerity, "my throbbing love engine cries out for you."

"You can take your throbbing love engine and shove it!" she snarled.

"That's exactly what I had in mind," I replied, pleased that my little ploy was working. "I'm glad to see we're thinking along the same lines."

She stood up, walked to a wall, took a robe off a hook, wrapped it around her, and faced me with her hands on her hips. "I'm asking you for the last time: Are you going to leave peacefully?"

"Peacefully, yes," I said. "Alone, no."

"All right," she said. "But don't say you weren't warned."

She opened her mouth and gave forth a scream that just got higher and higher and louder and louder. Pretty soon the mirror cracked, and a bunch of little glass doodads on the vanity shattered, and by the time she reached M over high Q all the fillings had fallen out of my teeth, and still she kept it up. I could hear people howling in pain outside the tent, and then I couldn't hear nothing anymore, and the next thing I knew she was slapping my face and telling me to wake up.

"What happened?" I mumbled. All the porcelain dogs had shattered, so at least the experience wasn't a total loss.

"They don't call me the Siren of Silverstrike for nothing," said Melora with a satisfied look on her face.

"Okay, so you're a siren," I said, running my tongue gingerly over all the holes in my teeth. "What did you have to do that for?"

"Because I'm not going anywhere, and you needed convincing."

"But why not?" I persisted.

She stared at me. "Because *I'm* Old Doc Nebuchadnezzar. I *own* this show, and nothing pulls in more money than the Siren of Silverstrike. Now do you understand?"

"Why didn't you just say so in the first place?" I said. "If you can't go, I'll just move in with you."

This time she hit H over high Z.

"I like living alone," she said when she'd slapped me awake again.

"You're one of the hardest ladies to romance that I've ever encountered," I said. "But Catastrophe Baker don't give up easy."

Well, she screamed three or four more times, and I kept passing out, and finally some of the townsfolk came by and asked her to stop because she'd busted every window within three miles.

"*Now* will you leave?" she asked, staring at me when I woke up again.

"All right, all right, I get the picture," I said. "But the day will come when you'll regret throwing away such a perfect and unselfish love as I'm offering you in exchange for just fifty percent of the carnival's take."

But nothing could budge her, and I soon saw that I'd been blinded by her physical beauty, or maybe even just by her dye job, and after seeing a dentist and getting my fillings replaced I went back out among the stars, a couple of days older and a little lonelier and a lot wiser.

Silicon Carny chuckled. "Now I'm starting to understand why they call you Catastrophe!" she said.

"There are other reasons just as valid, ma'am," said Baker, "and I'm sure the survivors could tell you all about it—if any of 'em have been released from their various hospitals."

"Humans are always talking and singing about unrequited love," complained Sahara del Rio.

"Of course they are," said Achmed of Alphard, who was probably a little less human than most. "It's the most ennobling emotion of all."

"The most frustrating, anyway," chimed in Three-Gun Max.

"But what good does it do?" said Argyle, who was still sitting in a corner with the Reverend Billy Karma. "When it's time to procreate, the female comes in season, the males fight for the right to perpetuate their genes, and then all is quiet until the next hurricane season."

"That ain't exactly the way it works with us," answered Baker.

"All right," amended Argyle. "The next planet-freezing blizzard. Big difference."

"You got part of it right," said Bet-a-World O'Grady. "The males do fight for the females. Or sometimes, like in the case of people like our friend Baker here, just for the exercise."

"You think the females don't fight every bit as hard?" asked Sinderella with a sly, knowing smile. "We're just more subtle about it."

"With all this fighting, it's a wonder anyone has the energy to procreate," said Argyle.

"It can get nasty," agreed Max. "To say nothing of awkward."

Suddenly the old man sitting by himself in the farthest corner spoke up. "What do you know about it?" he demanded. "Hell, what do any of you know? There's only one word for it, and that's *tragic*."

"What's so tragic about sex?" asked Baker.

"I'm not talking about sex," said the old man. "I'm talking about love."

"Who are you, and what do you think you know about it?"

"My name is Faraway Jones, and I've sought after it in its purest form for more than forty years."

"Faraway Jones!" exclaimed Nicodemus Mayflower. "Didn't I hear about you on Bareimus V?"

"Can't be the same Faraway Jones I heard about on Sparkling Blue," said Max.

"There was supposed to be a Faraway Jones on New Burma, out on the Rim," added Gravedigger Gaines.

"They were all me," said Jones. "I've been to all three of those worlds, and maybe seven hundred more."

"Are you an explorer?" asked Big Red.

"No, though I've been the first to set foot on a bunch of worlds."

"An adventurer?"

"Not on purpose, though I've had my share of them."

"What, then?" persisted Big Red.

"A searcher," answered Jones.

"For what?"

"Well, now, that's my sad and tragic story."

The Tragic Quest of Faraway Jones

I never set out to be the first man to set foot on two or three hundred worlds (began Jones), nor the millionth to touch down on another few hundred. All I ever wanted was to find my Penelope.

I started looking for her, let me see, forty-three years, eight months, and nineteen days ago. First planet I went to was Castor XII. She wasn't there, of course.

Then I tried the Nelson system, and all the oxygen planets in the Roosevelt system. Even touched down on Walpurgis III, which was as strange a world as I've ever seen in a lifetime of seeing strange worlds, but she wasn't there either.

So I kept looking. I looked all through the Inner Frontier and the Monarchy and the Spiral Arm and the Outer Frontier and the Rim, and even in the Greater and Lesser Clouds, but there was no sign of her. After it became obvious that this was going to be an epic search, I re-named my ship *The Flying Dutchman*.

Had a lot of interesting adventures along the way. Once I stood atop the highest mountain in the galaxy, and another time I walked along the bottom of the deepest chlorine ocean. I threw away diamonds the size of walnuts because my pockets were loaded with bigger ones. I killed animals that would make Hellfire Van Winkle's Landships look like household pets.

I turned down the chance to be King of the Purple Planet, and I said no when I was begged to be the consort of a woman who was even prettier than Sinderella and Silicon Carny, meaning no offense to those lovely ladies. But I knew I had to stay free of all entanglements, both political and romantic, and of course I had to keep myself pure for my Penelope.

At one point I even enlisted the help of the Golden Gang, but although they could find hidden treasures and lost masterpieces of artwork, they couldn't find Penelope. I went to Domar and rented the services of their Master Telepath, but although he could read every mind within fifty thousand light-years, he couldn't come up with a single clue as to my Penelope's whereabouts.

So I kept going from one world to another, hoping for some sign of her, or maybe to meet someone who'd seen her or even heard of her. The years slid by without my noticing, but I've never lost faith that someday I'll find her and that would make all the suffering and hardship and loneliness worthwhile.

You don't know how heartbreaking it can be, to think you've got an inkling of where she might be, only to find out, again and again, that it was a false lead, an empty hope. . . .

"Just a minute," interrupted Three-Gun Max. "Why not ask *us*?"

"I beg your pardon?" said Faraway Jones.

"The Outpost's clientele," explained Max. "Together, we've been to even more worlds than you have. Just tell us something about her, and I'll bet one of us can put you on the right track."

Jones blinked his eyes several times. "Well, I think her hair's probably blond. Not yellow-blond. More sandy-like. And she's likely kind of slim. Very pretty, but not the eye-popper that the ladies here are." He paused. "That's okay, though. My mother was a frump, and she wasn't the brightest woman you'd ever want to meet, but when she was eighty-five and fat and wrinkled, my father would still have gladly laid down his life for her. Beauty is in the eye of the beholder, and in my eye, Penelope is the most beautiful woman in the galaxy." Another pause. "She'll be wearing a blue-checked gingham dress, with a little red silk scarf around her neck, and a big velvet bow in her hair. At least, that's what I figure she *ought* to be wearing."

"You haven't seen her for forty-three years," noted Max. "Her hair might be gray or white, and she could have gained or lost thirty or forty pounds, and she's sure as hell not wearing the same clothes now. So tell us things about her that aren't likely to change. Like, for starters, how tall is she?"

Jones frowned and ran a hand through his thick, shaggy, unkempt white hair. "I don't know." He touched his nose with a forefinger. "I think she came up to about here."

"All right. What about her name?"

"Penelope," said Faraway Jones. "A beautiful name, Penelope. It's a poem all by itself."

"What's her last name?"

Jones shrugged. "Beats me."

"Just a minute," said Max. "You've been searching for her for forty-three years and you don't even know her name?"

"Wouldn't a rose by any other name smell as sweet?" replied Jones defensively.

"Yeah, but it'd be a lot easier to find if you could tell people you were looking for a rose," said Max irritably. "All right—just what *do* you remember about her?"

"I don't have to remember anything," said Jones. "I know everything I need to know about her."

"Except her name and her whereabouts," said Max. "Where did you meet her? On what world did you last see her?"

Jones looked very uncomfortable. "I never met her," he said at last.

"You've spent forty-three years searching for a woman you never met?" said Max incredulously.

"You're making it sound ludicrous, and it's not!"

"Perish the thought," said Max. He decided to try one more

time. "She must have been a woman of remarkable accomplishments for you to spend your entire adult life trying to find her."

"I really couldn't say," answered Jones.

"Uh . . . I don't want to seem unfeeling, but I think an explanation is in order."

"There was this poem."

"A poem?"

Jones closed his eyes. "The last few lines went like this:

"Out there somewhere, beyond the sea,
I'll find my sweet Penelope,
With burning kisses on her lips, and flowers in her hair."

He paused. "The instant I read it, I knew that there was a Penelope waiting out there for me, and all I had to do was find her."

"How do you know her name wasn't Gertrude or Beatrice?" asked Max.

"The poem says it's Penelope."

"The poem also says that the *poet* will find her."

"The poet's been dead for seven millennia. I looked him up. He never married anyone called Penelope."

"So based on three lines, you've wasted forty-three years searching for a woman who either never existed or who died seven thousand years ago?"

"There were a *lot* of lines! I only quoted three. And she's out there somewhere. If there's a woman for every man, then she's the woman for me. The *only* woman."

"How will you know her when you see her?" asked Sinderella.

"I'll know her," said Jones with absolute, almost devout certainty.

"I wish you luck, Faraway Jones," said Sinderella, walking over to him. "But just in case you don't find her, I'd hate to think of you going to your grave without ever having kissed a real, flesh-and-blood woman."

She put her arms around his neck and leaned over to kiss him, and he almost fell off his chair avoiding her.

"I'm sorry, and I don't mean any insult," he said, getting to his feet, "but I've got to keep myself pure for her, just as I know she's keeping herself pure for me."

"You've got a funny notion of pure," offered Max.

"That's okay," said Jones, walking to the door. "As far as I'm concerned, all of you have a funny notion of love." He paused. "I've wasted a whole day here. It's time to go off looking for her again."

"Be careful," warned Achmed of Alphard. "There's a war going on out there."

Jones smiled. "If Men and aliens and meteor showers and supernovas couldn't keep me from searching for my Penelope, you don't really think a little thing like a war can stop me, do you?"

"Wars have stopped people from more important quests," said Achmed.

Jones smiled. "You don't know Faraway Jones," he said, opening the door. "And there *are* no more important quests."

And with that, he was gone.

There was a long silence. Finally Bet-a-World O'Grady pulled out a wad of banknotes. "Anyone want to start a pool?"

"On whether he finds her, or on whether she exists?" asked Baker.

O'Grady shrugged. "Either one," he said with a smile.

Nicodemus Mayflower sighed and shook his head. "He's not exactly the brightest being traveling the spaceways, is he?"

"If he's got a pet, he may not even be the brightest thing in his ship," chimed in Three-Gun Max with a chuckle.

"Well, *I* thought he was sweet," said Sinderella.

"So's a bag of sugar," said Max. "But you wouldn't want to go off and live with it."

"You're too cynical by half," she shot back. "I wish someone like Faraway Jones was looking for me."

"No, you don't," said Max.

"And why not?" demanded Sinderella.

Max laughed. "He might find you."

"He's a lot better than *you*!" she snapped.

"Hell, we're all a lot better than Max," said Baker. "But that don't mean Faraway Jones is Mr. Right."

"I *created* Mister Right," said Sinderella. "I'll settle for Faraway Jones any old day."

"You mean you *met* Mister Right," Max corrected her.

"I meant what I said."

"You know we ain't letting you get away without telling us the details," said Max.

"Why not?" she replied after some consideration. "Who knows? You might even learn something, though I doubt it."

Building Mister Right

I was raised to be a courtesan (said Sinderella). I was schooled in the tantric arts, I was taught to move and dress seductively, I was instructed in all the many ways a woman can please a man, and I was warned what attitudes and behaviors to avoid.

When I was sixteen I went to work on Xanadu, the pleasure planet in the Belial Cluster. My clientele included some of the greatest names in the galaxy. I was even given to °°°Lance Sterling°°° for a week after he set the people of Hacienda III free.

There was no aspect of pleasure that was unknown to me, and no sexual art, no matter how strange or painful or alien, in which I was not an acknowledged expert. And because of this, I was in great demand. Even the Earth Mother tried to buy my contract and move me to her establishment on Praesepe XIII, but of course my employer would not part with me.

Then, one day, when I was twenty years old, I found myself walking down the long corridor to meet my next assignment. As I passed the multitude of rooms, I heard the moans and sighs of rapture—but only from masculine throats. And a thought occurred to me that should have been obvious the day I arrived there: that Xanadu was a pleasure planet for only half the race, that the women *provided* pleasure but did not *receive* it.

So I decided to take my savings—and of course, being a woman I'd had no place to spend all that money on Xanadu—and start an industry that would do for women what so many industries did for men.

I realized that I would need men who were as skilled in the giving of pleasure as I was, and I spent the next year auditioning perhaps a thousand of those with the best résumés—and while I will freely confess that it was not an unenjoyable year, I nevertheless found some major or minor fault with each of them.

It was then that I decided the only way I could be sure of providing the perfect lover was to *build* him. I queried a number of women, asking them to describe in detail all the physical features and behavioral characteristics of their ideal man, and then hired Bellini, the Monarchy's greatest designer of androids, and set him to work.

The women had been unsure of the perfect eye color, so we decided that the eyes would appear blue in certain light, gray in others, brown in still others.

It didn't work. The women I invited to inspect our prototype found a changing eye color very disconcerting.

There was the same problem with the length of his hair. We tried short hair, long hair, even no hair, but there was no consensus.

Things became even worse as we got to the more important features. Since this was to be the ideal man, far superior to all others, we gave him a fifteen-inch phallus. The first three women to see it ran screaming from the room; the fourth kidnapped him at gunpoint and neither she nor the android were ever seen again.

Musculature was another problem. Should it be Herculean or Apollonian? We tried the heavily muscled Herculean model first; it broke the rib cages of the first five women it hugged. So we went for the slender, delicate Apollonian; two of its first three sexual partners broke *its* ribs in the throes of passion.

When it came to speech, we ran into still more problems. Fully half the women we questioned stated that men had nothing interesting to say, that all they really wanted to do was talk about themselves. But the other half insisted that our prototype be capable of speech, because they wanted to be complimented and flattered to preserve the illusion of romance before they climbed into bed.

So we took this into account, and everything seemed to be going well for a day or two. Then the complaints began: A few sweet nothings whispered before a roaring fire was fine, but couldn't it think of anything *else* to say? Forty-eight hours of non-stop flattery tended to sound, well, if not insincere, at least *programmed,* and nothing is a greater hindrance to romance than a lack of spontaneity.

So we went back to the drawing board and gave our prototype the equivalent of fifteen post-graduate degrees. He was able to converse thoughtfully on any subject, and we removed all trace of ego so that he would have no urge to speak about himself.

I should have known better. The typical comment was: "If I'd wanted to go to bed with my college professor, I would have." One I particularly remember was: "Do you know how quickly an analysis of the annual fiscal expenditure on Sirius V can quell the fire within?"

There were the same problems with the prototype's taste in art, in music, even in women. Each woman wanted to think she was the only one for him, but that meant reprogramming him each time, so that at noon he loved slender blondes and at two he loved pudgy redheads and at four he loved drunken brunettes.

I had run through most of my money without a single one of my female volunteers agreeing that I'd created Mister Right. Then, when °°°Lance Sterling°°° sent word that he'd like to spend another week with me, I gave the android to the first woman who asked for him (she later dismembered him with a butcher knife) and went back to my former life, convinced that Mister Right was as much an unattainable dream as the Perfect Woman.

So don't you denigrate Faraway Jones. A love like that means a lot more to a woman than most of the things I built into Mister Right.

"Actually, there are nineteen perfect women in the universe," said Catastrophe Baker to the room at large. "I've been with thirteen of them, and I've got almost half my life left to hunt up the other six."

"So you really knew °°°Lance Sterling°°°?" said Little Mike Picasso.

"Yes, I did," answered Sinderella.

"He's one of my heroes," said Little Mike wistfully. "I always wanted to paint his portrait."

"I wouldn't have minded meeting up with him myself," chimed in Gravedigger Gaines. "Heroes like him are few and far between."

"I heard all kinds of stories about how he died," said Three-Gun Max. "I wonder if anyone knows what really happened?"

"One of us does," said Nicodemus Mayflower.

"You heard it?" asked Max.

"I *lived* it. I was there."

"Sure, you were," scoffed Max.

"It's true!" said Mayflower heatedly, and skinny as he was, I again was struck by how much his lean, angular face looked like my notion of Satan. "I spent ten years with him, fighting villains and evildoers!"

"I don't believe it," said Max. "There are heroes so big they blot out the stars for parsecs. He was one of them. Why would he bother with *you*?"

"I can find out if he knew him," offered Sinderella. Everyone turned to her. "He had a scar on his shoulder. Describe it."

"A scar?" repeated Mayflower. "I always thought it was a tattoo. It looked like a big, bloody L."

"Is he right?" asked Max.

Sinderella nodded her head. "He's right."

"Not everyone's a freelance hero or soldier of fortune," said Mayflower with just a touch of bitterness. "Some of us function better in structured situations."

"I can't imagine why," said Baker.

"Save the arguments for some other time," said Max. He turned to Mayflower. "Okay, you knew him. So let's hear how he died, and how many of the enemy he took with him."

"From everything I've heard about him," said Little Mike Picasso, "he'd have sold his life so dearly that they'd have needed one hell of a mass grave for the men who finally took him down."

"Do you want to hear about it, or do you want to tell *me* about it?" demanded Mayflower irritably.

"Let's have it," said Max.

The Untimely Death of ***Lance Sterling***

To begin with (said Nicodemus Mayflower), he wasn't born ***Lance Sterling***. His real name was Mortimer Smurch. I once asked him why he changed it, and he asked me if I'd lay down my life for a man named Mortimer Smurch, and I thought about it for a few minutes and never asked him again.

By the time he was nineteen he was dedicated to freeing oppressed people, human or alien, wherever he found them. He knew it would be dangerous, so that's when he decided to wear the mask.

"If he didn't want to call attention to himself, why did he wear that shining silver outfit with the cape?" asked Max.

"You want to hear this or not?" said Mayflower.

"All right, all right, I won't interrupt again," said Max.

"Until the next time," predicted Baker.

I didn't mind the mask so much (continued Mayflower). It was the sword that bothered me. I mean, what sane man uses a sword when his opponents have burners and screechers and pulse guns? But after he led the revolutions on Briarpatch II and Blue Alaska and came away without a scratch, he decided that God was on his side and that he was invincible.

By then he'd made a bit of a reputation for himself, especially since he let everyone know it was ***Lance Sterling*** beneath the mask, and a lot of idealistic young men and women sought him out and offered to fight for his cause. I was one of them.

I still remember my first action. The Governor of Piastra VII had revoked the constitution and literally enslaved the people. They were forced to labor eighteen hours a day in his gold mines (and this was on a planet with a twenty-two-hour day), working on half rations, while he and his army grew fat off the sweat of their brows. ***Lance Sterling*** couldn't tolerate such a situation, and he gathered his followers about him and announced that we were going to attack Piastra the next morning.

When I asked for our battle plan, he looked at me as if I was crazy.

"Battle plan?" he repeated. "My plan is to go in there with swords flashing and burners blazing and not to stop until every last villain is dead."

I gathered my courage to ask another question and said, "What I meant was, their army numbers about twenty thousand, and we are less than one hundred fifty. Isn't some strategy required?"

"My strategy is to free the poor citizens of Piastra VII," he answered firmly. "Do you have a problem with that?"

"No, I guess my math must be faulty," I said.

"Are there any other questions?" he asked, staring at us. "No? Good. I will leave the pleasure of decimating the army to you, but the governor is mine."

"You mean you're not going to lead us into battle?" I blurted out.

"Of course I am," he said. "At least, until I spot the governor, who, though evil through and through, is nonetheless no coward. He and I will match swords and skills up and down the balustrades, in full sight of his men, and when I dispatch him, it will take the heart out of his army, and most of those who are still alive will lay down their arms and swear allegiance to whomever the liberated citizens elect as their new leader."

Well, I could see about eighty-three ways his plan could go

wrong, but I couldn't bring myself to challenge him a third time, so I kept my doubts to myself and prepared to die as nobly as possible the next morning.

You've all read the history books, or seen the holographic re-creations of the Battle of Piastra VII, so you know that it turned out exactly the way °°°Lance Sterling°°° had predicted, with him running the governor through and the army suing for peace less than a minute later.

That's when his reputation really began to grow, and we never again had a problem recruiting volunteers. By the time we liberated Hacienda III a few years later, we had more than two thousand men and women fighting on our side.

Of course, success hadn't changed °°°Lance Sterling's°°° approach to warfare. It had cost him forty-two of his most trusted lieutenants during the last six revolutions. I began to think that he himself could only be killed by a silver bullet or a stake through the heart.

I still remember the day he outlined his plans for Hacienda. The gist of it was that we, his followers, would create a diversion five miles from the emperor's castle, while he would boldly enter through the front door, slash and hew his way to the emperor's private quarters, tickle his Adam's apple with the point of his sword, and demand his immediate surrender.

I asked him if he wouldn't feel a little more comfortable (one never suggested that he might want to feel *safer*) with a few hand-picked men accompanying him.

"Why?" he asked, surprised.

"It seems foolhardy to assume that the emperor won't be well guarded, even within the walls of his own castle," I said.

"Of course he will" was his response. "But then, that's what makes it fun!"

"You think going up against sixty armed men with nothing but a sword is *fun*?" I asked incredulously.

"I *am* °°°Lance Sterling°°°," he answered, as if that explained everything. "And besides, I have it on good authority that there are only fifty-five of them."

"Obviously my math has failed me again," I said as apologetically as possible.

He laid a heroic hand on my shoulder. "You're decent and you're loyal, Nicodemus, old friend," he said. "There's no law that says you have to be intelligent, too."

"Thank you, glorious leader," I said.

"Tut-tut," he said. "A simple ***Lance*** is sufficient. Or ***Lancelot***, if we're being formal."

Well, we set Hacienda free, as everyone knows, and ***Lance Sterling*** did indeed get the emperor to agree to his terms . . . but we also lost ninety percent of our forces.

"They died in a noble cause," said ***Lance Sterling*** during the funeral service. "Their mothers should be proud."

I waited for his funeral oration, but he evidently felt he had no need to say anything further, and besides, he wanted to get back to the ship and go off to liberate other oppressed peoples.

We spent the next two years liberating Melancholy III, Greenwillow, Wheatfield, Pius XIV, and New Tahiti, and even stopped by the university planet of Sorbonne long enough to help the students take over the Administration Building . . . and then we came to that fateful day on Brookmandor II.

As you know, the planet had been conquered by a megalomaniac who called himself Alexander the Greater. He feared an uprising among his unwilling subjects, and as a result his army was dispersed across the planet.

Lance Sterling decided that a lightning-swift attack on Alexander's headquarters would have the desired effect, that once the head of this hideous political and military structure was cut off, the body would crumble.

"He's got to have a couple of hundred guards and retainers on the premises," I said. "Just this once, I wish you'd let some of us go with you."

He smiled in amusement. "Mathematics again, Nicodemus?" Then he shrugged and relented. "All right. You and Zanzibar McShane may accompany me. Will that make you happy?"

I assured him that it would, and the next morning, before sunrise, the three of us sneaked into Alexander's headquarters. We climbed to the top level of the building, and had made it almost halfway to his private quarters when Alexander himself stepped out into the corridor we were traversing, his burner aimed right between °°°Lance Sterling's°°° eyes.

"I've been expecting you," said Alexander with an evil leer. "My men said that you would launch a full-scale attack, but I knew that an egomaniac such as yourself would never be willing to share the glory with his cannon fodder. Now drop your sword."

°°°Lance Sterling's°°° sword fell to the floor with a noisy clatter.

Alexander the Greater approached him, turned him so that he was facing us, and placed the burner next to his ear. "Now tell your men to drop their weapons," he ordered.

"Do what he says," said °°°Lance Sterling°°°, showing no sign of fear. "He has the upper hand . . . for the moment."

Zanzibar McShane dropped his pulse gun and his screecher. I pulled my burner out of my holster, but I didn't drop it.

"Drop it, or I'll kill your leader," said Alexander.

"You're going to kill him anyway," I said, aiming my burner at him. "If I drop it, you'll kill us both."

"I'm not kidding!" yelled Alexander. "Drop it or your boss is a dead man!"

"That's stupid," I said. "If I drop it, we're *all* dead men."

"I'm going to count to three," said Alexander.

"Count to five hundred for all I give a damn," I said. "I'm not dropping it—and if *you* kill him, *I'll* kill you."

"Then I'll kill your friend, too," he said, indicating Zanzibar McShane.

"He's not my friend," I answered. "I hardly know him."

"Damn it, Mayflower!" said °°°Lance Sterling°°°. "Just drop the fucking burner!"

"He'll shoot me if I do."

"He'll shoot *me* if you don't!" snapped °°°Lance Sterling°°°.

"One way he kills one of us," I explained logically. "The other way he kills two or maybe even three of us."

"I hate you and your goddamned mathematics!" he snapped just before Alexander the Greater burned a hole through his noble head.

I fired an instant later, Alexander toppled over, and Brookmandor II was free before noontime. Zanzibar McShane stayed on to become their new governor, while I took °°°Lance Sterling°°° home and buried him in his family plot.

"So that's why no one ever found his grave!" exclaimed Three-Gun Max. "Who'd think to look for Mortimer Smurch?"

"I'm surprised no one else here fought for him," said Bet-a-World O'Grady. "I mean, hell, he was the most popular revolutionary of his time."

"Oh, I fought in my share of revolutions," answered Max. "I just never got around to fighting in the same ones as °°°Lance Sterling°°°."

"I think we've probably *all* seen our share of action," agreed the Gravedigger.

"Yeah, but not in wars or revolutions," said Catastrophe Baker.

"You never fought in a war?" asked Max.

"I'm not a joiner," said Baker.

"Sometimes you don't have to wait to join up," said Max. "Sometimes a war sneaks up on you when you're not looking. Like this one that's heading toward the Outpost."

"This doesn't sound like much of a war," said the Gravedigger. "Just a few dozen enemy ships. If you want to talk about a *real* war, I could tell you about the Peloponnesian War. Strangest enemy I ever saw."

"*You* were there?" asked Max.

"Yes."

"Well, damn it to hell, so was I!"

"You, too?" said Nicodemus Mayflower. "That's where I saw my first action, before I hooked up with °°°Lance Sterling°°°."

"Are you guys sure you have it right?" asked the Bard.

"Of course we do," said Max.

"But the Peloponnesian War was held back on Earth, almost ten thousand years ago."

"We're not talking about *that* Peloponnesian War," said Max.

"There was another one?" asked the Bard.

"Sure. About fifteen, sixteen years ago, out past the Albion Cluster."

"I'd like to hear about it," said the Bard.

"As if you had a choice," snorted Catastrophe Baker.

"Who should go first?" asked the Gravedigger.

"Anybody got a three-sided coin?" said Max with a grin.

"I just happen to have one," volunteered O'Grady.

"Why am I not surprised?" muttered Max.

O'Grady produced the coin. "Okay," he said, holding it up so everyone could see it. "This is heads, this is tails, and this is fists."

"Fists?"

O'Grady shrugged. "I had to call it something." He tossed it in the air. "Call it."

All three men called fists. It came up tails.

"Looks like *you'll* have to tell the story," said Baker.

"No, but I'll choose the order. Nicodemus Mayflower, you go first."

"Why him?" demanded Max.

"Because the Gravedigger is polite enough to wait, and I'm tired of listening to you," said O'Grady.

Max considered that for a moment, then nodded his head thoughtfully. "Okay, that's a valid reason."

The General Who Hated His Private

I guess it was called the Peloponnesian War (began Mayflower) because the enemy was a race that called themselves the Peloponnes.

I worked for ComPelForCom HQ (that's Commonwealth Pe-loponne Forces Command Headquarters) back then. In fact, I was General Bigelow's driver, pilot, orderly, and all-around gofer.

Bigelow was an imposing-looking man, and never more so than when he was in full dress uniform. He had enough medals to go from his chest to his ankle, and his biggest problem was figuring which ones to wear and which to leave in his trunk.

The war on Peloponne V was to be General Bigelow's farewell to organized butchery. He'd been sent in with a force of a few thousand and told to pacify the natives. It was after fully half his men went over to the enemy that he realized he had a little problem.

"What the hell is going on?" he used to complain to me. "Men *never* desert! Would *you* desert if I sent you to the front line?"

"I don't think I would, sir," I would reply. "But I didn't think anyone else would, either."

Then he'd rant and rave for another half hour or so, open a bottle, and drink himself to sleep—and in the morning we'd have lost another twenty or thirty men to the enemy.

Finally he decided that a unique situation—and this certainly qualified—demanded a unique solution, so he sent for Hurricane Smith. Even then Hurricane was wanted on about half a hundred worlds and had a huge price on his head, but General Bigelow agreed to pardon him for all his outstanding crimes if he'd come to Peloponne V and help clear up the situation. Hurricane consid-ered the offer, asked for a quarter of a million credits in addition to the pardon, and enlisted when the general agreed to his terms.

Bigelow wanted to make him a colonel, but Hurricane hated officers, and insisted on being a private. The General sent for him the second he touched down, and Hurricane showed up wearing his usual outfit, which was made from the furs of various alien polar animals.

"Why are you out of uniform?" demanded the General.

"I'm *in* uniform," said Hurricane.

"I want you in a *military* uniform."

"You hired Hurricane Smith. This is what I wear; it's my trade-mark."

"Not when you're in *my* army, it isn't."

Hurricane turned and headed toward the door. "Nice knowing you, and good luck with your war."

There were six armed soldiers guarding the door, but no one made a move to stop him. After all, he was Hurricane Smith.

"Wait!" yelled Bigelow.

Hurricane turned to face him.

"All right," said Bigelow with a sigh. "Wear whatever you want."

"Thanks," said Hurricane. "I will."

"First thing tomorrow morning, I want you to move to the front."

"And start blowing away aliens. I know."

"No," said the General. "I want you to find out why my men are deserting and going over to the enemy."

Hurricane shrugged. "You're the boss," he said. "But if it was *me*, I'd kill all the bad guys first."

"Just do as you're ordered," snapped the General.

Hurricane nodded and started walking to the door again.

"Just a minute, Private," said Bigelow.

"What now?"

"You're supposed to salute."

"I don't do that," said Hurricane. "It's a silly custom." He walked out of the office.

"This may not have been the brightest decision I ever made," Bigelow said to me. "I don't think I like that man very much."

"He's supposed to be one of the best at what he does, sir," I said.

"What he does is plunder and rob and kill."

"This is the army. He should fit in just fine, sir."

We didn't see him again for two days. Most of us concluded that he'd developed a serious distaste for military life and had left the planet, though a small minority thought he'd joined all our men who'd gone over to the Peloponnes. Then, just after sunrise on the third day, he wandered into headquarters.

"I found out why all your men have been deserting," he announced. "Other than the obvious reason, that is."

"The obvious reason?" repeated Bigelow.

"They don't like you very much," said Hurricane. "Can't say that I blame them," he added thoughtfully. "But the real reason is a little more complicated." He paused. "Have you ever actually seen a Peloponne?"

"I've seen holographic representations of them. Big, ugly insectoid beings."

"Well, yes and no."

"What do you mean?" demanded Bigelow.

"They're shape-changers."

"Even so, how can they terrify my men into deserting?" asked the General. "After all, how fearsome can they make themselves appear?"

"They don't appear fearsome at all."

"Then what shape *do* they take?"

"Ripe naked women. Ripe, *passionate* naked women. Ripe, *lonely,* passionate naked women. Except near the Sixth Battalion, which is composed entirely of women. To them they appear as wealthy, elegantly dressed, sophisticated gentlemen who drink vodka martinis and love to dance the rhumba."

"But surely once our men and women have . . . ah . . . *experienced* them, they realized they've been duped by the enemy and have given away their precious honor to hideous, disgusting, insectoid aliens."

"Well, the way *I* found out what we were up against was to go off with one of the Peloponnes," answered Hurricane.

The General failed to repress a shudder of revulsion. "And?"

Hurricane contemplated his answer for a moment. "I have to admit that as women go, she wasn't especially memorable," he said thoughtfully. Then he smiled. "But for a twelve-legged four-eyed insect, she was a knockout."

"You are as disgusting as *she* is!" thundered the General.

"Watch your tongue when you speak about my fiancée," said Hurricane ominously.

"Get out!" screamed Bigelow. "I don't want to hear any more of this!"

"One word of warning," said Hurricane. "There are more human soldiers on their side than on ours. If you don't leave Peloponne V soon, I think they'll probably mount an attack."

"This is outrageous and disgusting!"

"You think so?" asked Hurricane mildly. "Wait until they cut your belly open and deposit a few thousand eggs. Now, *that's* outrageous and disgusting."

"How can you run off with such a creature?" demanded Bigelow.

"Beauty is only skin deep," said Hurricane Smith, as he walked to the door for the last time. He paused and turned to the general. "But ugly goes all the way down to the soul."

I got to thinking about what Hurricane had said, and when word reached me that ***Lance Sterling*** was looking for recruits, I borrowed a ship one night and took off to join him. Never did see a Peloponne. Saw the general a few hundred times, which in retrospect was more than enough for any war.

"I got there after Hurricane Smith left," said Max.

"And I showed up after Max," said the Gravedigger. "So he should tell his story next."

"Makes sense," agreed Max. He took a swallow of his drink. "Things had gotten a lot worse when I arrived on the scene."

"Was General Bigelow still there?" asked Catastrophe Baker.

"Sure. It was his last campaign, and he wasn't leaving until he wiped out the Peloponnes—those that he could distinguish from naked ladies, that is."

"Must have been a mighty interesting job—differentiating the one from the other," offered Baker.

"Me and God could have doped it out," said the Reverend Billy Karma with absolute and enthusiastic certainty.

"The mind positively boggles with the various tests one could devise," added Little Mike Picasso.

"The general didn't have your aesthetic sensibilities," said Max. "He sent all the women home, waited until they were all off the planet, and then shot anything that even remotely resembled a woman."

"Efficient," admitted Little Mike. "I'll give him that."

"Wasteful," said Baker.

"So how did the war end?" asked the Bard, scribbling furiously.

"Not exactly the way you'd expect," answered Three-Gun Max.

"So are you going to tell us or not?" persisted the Bard.

"Try and stop him," said Baker.

The Private Who Hated His General

By the time I hired on (said Max), morale was about as low as it could get. There were nearly as many Peloponnes as ever, but all the women had been sent home, and most of the men who hadn't gone over to the other side were pretty badly shot up.

General Bigelow was getting desperate, so he put out the word that he was looking for mercenaries.

"He *must* have been desperate if he was willing to hire you!" guffawed Sitting Horse.

"You think I can't kill my share of aliens?" asked Max ominously.

"Oh, we figure you can slaughter nonhumans with the best of them," said Crazy Bull. "We just don't see you responding to military discipline."

I'd have surprised you (continued Max). I stayed sober, didn't sneak no shape-changing alien ladies into the barracks no matter how good they looked, I remembered to salute most of the time, I even made my bunk up every now and then. I hate officers, so I insisted on being a private, even though I was getting paid more than anyone except the General.

Problem was, General Bigelow could have used forty or fifty more like me, or a couple of dozen Hurricane Smiths. Word had gotten out about the war—first, that it was going badly, and even worse, that he'd sent all the women away—and even though he was offering top dollar, he couldn't begin to replace the men he was losing every day.

Finally he hit on the notion of flying bombing missions over the Peloponne lines, so that none of us came into direct contact with those alien women. 'Course, their lines were so spread out, and in such a constant state of flux, that we mostly just dropped our payloads and hoped for the best.

It didn't take them long to realize that we weren't going to meet them face-to-face on the battlefield, so they moved up their long-range molecular imploders and started turning our airships into soup. Before long word had even reached New Vegas, and they started offering odds on how many of us would return from each day's mission. The first week, the odds were four to one that any of us would survive, but by the second week they were only five to two, and the third week they were six to five pick 'em.

Now, if you only had to complete one mission before you got mustered out, you could live with those odds—or at least you could on six days out of eleven. But when that son of a bitch Bigelow had you flying two missions a day, you had to figure your number was up by the morning of the second day.

"Shit!" muttered O'Grady. "The best odds I could ever get on you guys were three to five against!"

"You bet on us?" asked Max.

"With odds like that?" said O'Grady. "No way. They were blowing you out of the sky like there was no tomorrow. Like any smart gambler, I went with the run."

Can't say I blame you (said Max). Hell, if I'd been able to put a little money down on the Peloponnes, I'd have done it in a flash. Believe me, none of us looked forward to running—or flying—the gauntlet of all those imploders every morning and evening. We begged the general to come up with some other strategy, but he didn't have any ground troops left, and he refused either to surrender or declare a victory and get the hell out, so we kept flying missions.

By the beginning of the fourth week, I was the only pilot still on active duty. All the others were dead or wounded. He'd started with 406 airships and an equal number of pilots, and now all he had left were forty-two ships and one pilot (me), the rest having joined the enemy or been melted away, mostly the latter. So I went up to General Bigelow and suggested that maybe it was about time for a different strategy, since this one sure as hell wasn't working.

But he was under pressure to win the war, and no one was sending him any men or supplies, and all he had left was me and a couple of platoons that he was afraid to send against the enemy, since the enemy had this habit of looking awful friendly at close quarters.

Well, I wasn't happy about it, but he offered to double my pay, so I agreed to fly one more mission.

I barely made it back to base, and just as I was having a beer in the officer's club, Bigelow came up to me and told me he wanted me to go right back up.

"Meaning no disrespect, General Bigelow, sir," I said, "but you can go fuck yourself."

"You're all I've got!" he snapped. "I will not have it go on my record that I lost my final battle."

"There's the airship," I said, pointing out the window. "Go fight it yourself."

"I'm a general," he said. "I don't sully my hands with the actual fighting. That's what I have *you* for."

"You ain't got me," I said. "I resign. Use some other poor bastard."

"They've all deserted."

"Every last one of them?" I asked.

He nodded.

"You mean I've been dropping bombs on our own men?" I demanded.

"They're not our own men anymore! They've gone over to the enemy."

I couldn't say I blamed them. After all, the enemy probably fed them better, and based on what I'd heard of Hurricane Smith and his lady love, they sure kept 'em warmer at nights.

Well, we haggled back and forth for the better part of the afternoon. I kept saying that I wasn't going to play target for the Peloponnes anymore, and that I also didn't feel right dropping bombs on my friends, and he kept saying that he wasn't about to surrender or sue for peace, and that anyone who was shacked up with a lady insect, no matter what she looked like on the outside, wasn't any friend of mine.

Finally the sun started setting without anything being settled, and it didn't look like anything *would* get settled, and then the General pulled out his burner and pointed it between my eyes and explained that if I flew one last mission there was a chance, however slight, that I might survive it, whereas if I refused one more time, there was absolutely no chance that I'd survive a laser blast at a distance of six inches, which was a very telling argument.

"All right," I said. "But only if you'll agree that this is the very last one."

"I agree," he said. "And to prove it, we'll load your airship with every explosive that remains on the base."

We spent the next few minutes arguing over how much of a bonus he was going to pay me if I made it back alive, and since I didn't trust him any farther than I can spit with my mouth closed, I made him transfer the funds to my account back on Binder X before I finally got up and walked over to the airfield.

"You mind if I choose my own target?" I asked as I was climbing into the airship.

"Be my guest," he said. "Just remember to dump your entire payload and let's bring this noble struggle to a satisfying conclusion."

"Roger and out," I said, closing the hatch behind me.

I took off, climbed to about five thousand feet, and looked off toward the enemy lines out on the horizon.

And then I got to doing some serious thinking. I didn't have anything against the Peloponnes, and neither did all the Men who'd gone over to them. Now, maybe if I'd known a Peloponne I might have felt different, but I didn't. On the other hand, I knew General Bigelow.

So I flew back over the base, dropped my payload, and brought the struggle to a satisfying conclusion.

Well, satisfying to everyone except General Bigelow, anyway.

"That can't be right," said Big Red.

"Why the hell not?" demanded Three-Gun Max. "Every word was God's own truth, except for a couple of poetic flourishes here and there."

"I mean, if you ended the war, what the hell was Gravedigger Gaines doing there?"

"Why don't you ask *him*?" said Max, who seemed to have lost all interest in the Peloponnesian War now that his story was done.

Big Red turned to the Gravedigger. "Well?"

The Sergeant Who Hated Everyone

I wasn't there to fight a war (said Gaines). I was a bounty hunter, not a soldier.

I'd spent the better part of a year looking for Mad Jesse Wilkins. He'd killed more than three dozen men back in the Monarchy, as well as a fair number of women, children, dogs, cats, and alien pets. He lit out for the Frontier when he found out that I was on his trail. I just missed him by a day on Roosevelt III, and I was no more than half an hour behind him when he made his escape from Far London.

He altered course toward the Albion Cluster, and eventually he changed his identity and signed on as a sergeant in the Peloponnesian War—a neat little riff on the notion of the coward hiding out in the middle of a battlefield.

By the time I got there the war was over. There was nothing but a huge crater where the human headquarters and landing field had been—

"Just call me Bull's-Eye Max!" shouted Max with a laugh. "I never miss what I aim for!"

I had an urge to order the men's room servo-mech to tell everyone whether Max always hit what he aimed for, but I was more interested in hearing the rest of the Gravedigger's story, so I kept quiet.

Anyway (continued Gaines), I couldn't find any sign of life . . . but I knew Mad Jesse's skills, and I figured he was a little harder to kill than most men, so I decided to do a systematic search of the planet.

That's when I found out that most of the men were still alive, and that they'd made their peace with the Peloponnes even if their officers hadn't. At first I thought they were unwittingly laying the groundwork for another war, one that would be fought over all the Peloponne women they'd accumulated, but then I learned that each Peloponne female laid about ten thousand eggs a year, and that the larvae reached maturity in about five years, so no one was apt to mind a few hundred of them choosing to live with the former enemy.

As a matter of fact, the men had all pretty much decided to go back to human worlds, since it was a lot easier for their womenfolk to pass as humans than for them to pass as insects. Now that the war was officially over, the Monarchy was preparing to rebuild the planet and throw all kinds of money at the Peloponnes. They were also willing to do just about any favors that were requested, which included transporting all the men and their ladyfriends to other worlds.

I checked each man as he left, and Jesse wasn't among them. (It's pretty hard to disguise yourself when you're four hundred pounds and have steel teeth and wear a patch over one eye.)

I found him a few days later, holed up in a cave halfway up a mountain, still wearing his sergeant's uniform. I waited until he went out to gather some firewood and got the drop on him when he returned.

"Hi, Jesse," I said, pointing my screecher right at him.

"Either shoot or get the hell out of my way," he said without slowing his pace. "I got things to do."

"Shut up and listen to me," I said. "There's a million-credit price on your head. I'll make you the same proposition I make everyone I hunt down: Pay me the million credits yourself and you can walk away a free man."

"Some lawman!" he snorted contemptuously.

"I'm not a lawman," I said. "I'm what you might call an independent contractor. My only loyalty is to whoever pays me. That could be you."

"I ain't got a million credits," said Mad Jesse. "And if I did, I wouldn't give it to you anyway."

"You spent all the money you got for killing all those men and women?"

"Nobody paid me nothing," he said. "I *like* killing people."

"Well, that makes it kind of awkward," I said. I looked around. "You got any partners here?"

"You mean those sniveling little turncoats?"

"Does that cover *all* the deserters, or just the ones you don't like?"

"Both. I don't like none of 'em."

"What about a woman?"

"Don't have much use for 'em," said Jesse. "Besides, they shipped 'em all home months ago."

"I mean a Peloponne."

"I *hate* bugs!" he exploded. "And I especially hate bugs that look like women!"

Well, I spent about half an hour with him, and at the end of that time I still didn't know what he *liked*. He hated his fellow man, he hated women, he hated children, he hated the army, he hated the government, he hated aliens. He wasn't real fond of dogs or cats or birds either.

I offered him a drink while I was trying to decide whether to kill him on the spot or take him back to stand trial. He took one sip, spit it out, and hurled my flask down the side of the mountain.

"I hate bad booze!" he bellowed.

"That was real Cygnian cognac!" I said.

"What do *you* know about taste, asshole?" he said.

It was a real dilemma. If I shot him where he was, I'd have to take him a third of the way across the galaxy to claim the reward, and he didn't smell all that good *now*. On the other hand, if I took him back alive, I'd have to listen to him all the way, and I figured I couldn't take much more than an hour before I killed him anyway.

And then the perfect solution occurred to me.

I got up, motioned him to enter the cave, and kept my screecher trained on him.

"Good-bye, Jesse," I said.

He just stared at me uncomprehendingly.

"I've been a bounty hunter for most of my life. I deal with nothing but the scum of the galaxy—and I have to say that you are the most unpleasant man it's ever been my displeasure to meet."

"You ain't gonna kill me?" he said.

"No."

"Or take me back?"

"No."

"Why the hell not?"

"Because I've come to the conclusion that the worst punishment you can undergo is to be stranded on a world populated by nothing but giant bugs who don't like you any better than you like them. Before I leave I'll tell them that you're here, and I'll make sure they know how dangerous you can be, so that they never wander anywhere near you alone or unarmed."

"You can't do this to me!" he bellowed. "What about your reward?"

"I've decided that the thought of you spending the rest of your life here is all the reward I want or need," I said.

And it was.

"I just love stories of death and carnage!" enthused the Reverend Billy Karma. "They're so religious, if you know what I mean."

"Did you ever go back to see what had become of Mad Jesse?" asked Max.

The Gravedigger shook his head. "For all I know he's still there, living off fruits and berries and eating an occasional grubworm for protein." He smiled, which he didn't do more than once a month or so. "At least, I like to think so."

"I find it amazing that the three of you fought in the same war on the same side and never once met each other," said the Bard.

"I didn't fight in the war," Gaines corrected him. "It was over by the time I got there."

"How long did it last, start to finish?" asked the Bard.

"Too damned long," said Max. "I'd like to get my hands on whoever thought up that particular war." He paused thoughtfully. "It couldn't have been General Bigelow. He wanted to leave worse than anyone."

"Who knows?" said Little Mike Picasso with a shrug. "People have been thinking up wars for thousands of years now—and then getting other people to go off and fight them."

"Which brings up an interesting question," said Nicodemus Mayflower.

"Yeah?" said Little Mike. "And what question is that?"

"Who thought up the very first war?"

"Hell, who invents *anything*?" chimed in Catastrophe Baker. "There's no way to know. Probably it was some caveman with a club."

"That's not really true," said the Bard. "Most inventions are carefully recorded and documented."

"Yeah?"

"Absolutely. Don't take *my* word for it. Ask Einstein."

"*Ask* him?" repeated Baker. "I don't even know how to let him know I'm here, short of sticking a pin into him."

"Just ask your question," said Big Red, pulling out a pocket computer. "I'll transmit it to him."

"I don't know what the hell to ask," said Baker. He paused for a moment, then came up with a solution. "Have him tell us about some of the most important inventions."

Big Red alternately whispered into his computer and tapped on its screen. A moment later Einstein's computer started buzzing and whirring, and he quickly tapped in his answer.

"Well?" asked Baker as Big Red stared at his screen.

"A Domarian named Kabbis Koba invented eating three billion and twenty-seven years ago, at 9:15 on a Sunday morning," replied Big Red. "It became wildly popular, since people hadn't really been able to figure out what to do with their mouths when they weren't talking, and it quickly spread to other planets." He paused, staring at the tiny screen. "Here's another. Not only did Moses lead his people out of bondage to the Promised Land, but he also invented the very first dessert. Einstein's a little vague on the recipe, but it seems to have involved figs, honey, and whipped cream."

"That's the stupidest thing I ever heard in a long lifetime of listening to stupid things in barrooms!" snorted Baker.

"Don't be so sure of that," said Argyle. "Just because *your* race doesn't codify its history doesn't mean the rest of us don't."

"What particular history have you got in mind?" demanded Baker pugnaciously.

"My own ancestor, Quillot Tariot III, invented the sneeze," said Argyle proudly.

"You don't *invent* something like a sneeze," said Baker. "You just *do* it."

"Well, someone had to do it first."

"I don't believe any of this."

"Okay," said Argyle. "Who do *you* think invented the sneeze?"

"IIow the hell should I know?" said Baker.

"Hah!" said Argyle triumphantly. "And I repeat: *Hah!*"

"That's quite an accomplishment," said Crazy Bull.

"Thank you," said Argyle.

"Of course, *our* race invented both the pun and the double entendre, as well as the crude off-color remark."

"And colors," added Sitting Horse. "Don't forget—we invented colors too."

"And a damned good thing we did," said Crazy Bull. "You can't imagine how dull the universe was before that. It looked exactly like a black-and-white holoscreen, only bigger."

"It was still dull," interjected Sahara del Rio. "Until *my* race invented singing."

"Your race did that?" asked Crazy Bull, surprised.

"You want a demonstration?" she asked.

"Sure, why not?"

She promptly hit Q over high C, and shattered six of my crystal glasses.

"Well, maybe we didn't invent singing," said Hellfire Van Winkle, "but I'll lay plenty of eight to five that we invented yodeling."

"I wonder who invented gambling?" mused O'Grady. "That's what makes life worth living."

"Wait a minute," said Big Red. "I'm getting another message from Einstein."

We all waited until it finished scrolling across his screen.

"He says you're all wrong, that singing and colors and gambling and even yodeling are all well and good, but there was only one invention that can truly be credited with making life worthwhile."

Everyone fell silent, for Einstein was never wrong.

"Is he gonna tell us what it is?" asked Max.

"Yeah," said Big Red, staring at the tiny screen. "It's coming up now."

The Greatest Invention

You know (began Einstein), God did lousy first drafts.

Consider the universe, for example—and we might as well consider it, since there isn't anything else. It's close to seventeen billion years old, give or take a couple of months, and yet it took almost fourteen billion years for life to develop anywhere.

And the first life forms weren't exactly the type that would make you want to write home and brag about them. They were single-celled little creatures, invisible to the naked eye, which was probably all for the best since they were ugly as sin when you looked at them through a microscope.

Eventually they developed arms and legs and nostrils and things like that, and crawled out of the primeval ooze and onto dry land.

"Is he talking about Earth?" asked Sinderella. "I didn't think Man was that old."

"I'll ask him," said Big Red, tapping away.

You think Earth had a monopoly on primeval ooze (answered Einstein)?

As a matter of fact, the very first race to climb out of the muck and mire were the Beldorians of Danix VI. They were a humanoid race, and not without their admirable traits, although it was another billion years before any of them got around to inventing personal hygiene.

———

"He thinks personal hygiene is the greatest invention of all time?" said Three-Gun Max with a sardonic laugh.

If I'm interrupted once more, I'll stop enlightening you and go back to my drink (said Einstein, who was frowning and staring right at Max with his sightless eyes).

As I was saying, the Beldorians were a humanoid race. To the uninitiated, they all seemed to have goiters in their armpits, but the trained observer would soon have deduced that the growths in question were actually Beldorian fetuses. That's right: the Beldorians reproduced by budding.

And, need I add, their numbers were diminishing with each generation. I mean, who wants to walk around with an unborn child hanging from each armpit? Among other things, it really hinders your spear-throwing, and it almost guarantees that you'll never invent basketball. Reproduction was a pain in the ass—or, to be more specific, in the armpit—and hardly anyone felt inclined to practice it.

It was when Iggloth, a Beldorian who had just come of age, accidently rubbed up against his companion, Marlieth, while they were sleeping in a cave, that he suddenly discovered she was nice to touch. So he touched her again. She was a heavy sleeper, but eventually all the touching woke her up and she decided that she enjoyed it, and began reciprocating. In fact, they spent the next month doing nothing except eating an occasional sandwich and touching each other here and there.

Touching each other here was very pleasant, to be sure, but it was when they touched each other *there* that the results were electrifying. Later that day, when they ran out of sandwiches and had nothing else to do with their mouths, they invented kissing. It took them another seven years of trial and error to make it to the next step, but sure enough, they finally invented sex on a rainy autumn afternoon.

Of course, if it had stopped right there with the two of them, galactic history would have taken a different and considerably less interesting course. But the fact of the matter is that Barlotuth, Iggloth's closest friend, stopped by one day to see if he'd like to go fishing.

"Go away," muttered Iggloth. "I'm busy."

"For how long?" asked Barlotuth, an accommodating fellow.

"Till a year from next Tuesday!" snapped Marlieth.

Up to that point Barlotuth hadn't even known Marlieth was there, since the cave was quite dark, but now he squinted all five of his eyes and peered forward.

"What are you doing?" he asked curiously.

"We don't have a word for it," said Iggloth. "But it's really nifty! You should try it."

"It can't be more fun than fishing!" said Barlotuth.

"Fine," said Iggloth. "Go fishing and leave us alone."

Barlotuth was about to answer when Marlieth suddenly started giggling louder and louder, ending in a happy (if earsplitting) shriek.

"All right," he said, turning and wandering away from the mouth of the cave. "If it's *that* much fun, maybe I'll give it a shot."

And he did, and soon the word spread, and before long all the Beldorians were doing it. Now, nothing much came of the invention at first—after all, they were carrying these unborn babies under their arms—but mutation is a wonderful thing, and before long there weren't any more budding babies, and sex became so popular that it immediately spread all across the galaxy to every sentient and non-sentient species, though I intuit that it never crossed the intergalactic void and that they still reproduce by budding in Andromeda.

Anyway, that's how it happened, and if Iggloth and Marlieth were here now, I'm sure we'd all give them a standing ovation. And if they could stop touching each other long enough to pay attention—and doubtless Bet-a-World O'Grady can compute the odds on that—I'm equally certain they'd be justly proud of how enthusiastically everyone has taken to their invention.

In fact, now that I think of it, they not only invented sex, but they also invented mutation.

"I never knew that," admitted Catastrophe Baker.

"The universe is filled with infinite mysteries," chimed in Achmed of Alphard. "Strangely enough," he added thoughtfully, "most of them can be discovered in bed with a member of the opposite sex."

"And they don't get much more opposite than women," added Nicodemus Mayflower, staring admiringly at Sinderella.

"Just imagine," continued Baker. "If it hadn't been for them two Beldorians all those billions of years ago, I could look at Silicon Carny here and not feel a thing."

"You're not about to feel anything *now*," she shot back. "Just keep your hands to yourself."

Everyone laughed at that, none louder than Catastrophe Baker himself.

I checked the clock behind the bar. Ordinarily Reggie and I would start closing the place down in another half hour or so, but heroes need less sleep than most, and they all seemed to be in a talkative mood this particular night. Besides, we had to keep an eye out for enemy ships, so I told Reggie to just keep serving them as long as they wanted.

Baker finished another drink, then walked over to Big Red. "Ask Einstein who invented God," he said.

Big Red put the question to him and got the answer back almost instantly.

"He says it's still a point of some debate as to whether we invented God or He invented us."

"Maybe a third party invented us *and* God," offered Max, who could never leave well enough alone.

"Maybe Einstein ought to turn all of his brainpower to figuring it out," suggested Baker.

Another brief pause while Big Red waited for Einstein's answer.

"He says he'd rather figure out which came first, the chicken or the egg."

"Beats me," admitted Baker. "But whichever it was, I take my hat off to the man who invented the frying pan."

"You guys just don't understand at all," said the Reverend Billy Karma. "God invented everything. He just uses Men and aliens as His tools."

"Yeah?" Max shot back. "Suppose you tell me why God would want to invent pimples or jock itch?"

"Just as you can't appreciate good without having known evil, you can't appreciate good health without having experienced illness."

"Why do you have to appreciate it?" persisted Max. "Why can't you just experience it? Or is God such a self-centered prima donna that He's got to make everyone sing His praises night and day?"

"You know, I just hate it when you ask questions like that," said Billy Karma. He turned to Argyle. "Let's go back to talking about the god of sexual potency. Maybe it's blasphemous, but it beats the hell out of pondering all these deep, philosophic questions."

"I find deep, philosophic questions fascinating," said the multicolored alien.

"I was afraid you were going to say something like that," muttered Billy Karma.

"In fact," continued Argyle, "when I was younger I spent my entire fortune seeking the answers to the mysteries of the universe."

"You ever come up with any?" asked Baker.

"A few."

"Care to share 'em with us?"

Argyle shrugged, which made him look like an animated kaleidoscope.

"Why not?" he said.

The Ultimate Question

When I was growing up (said Argyle) I was always curious about things. I pestered all three of my parents with endless questions, and finally, in exasperation, they bought me a computer, which I promptly christened TAM (for The Answer Machine).

In the beginning, it was capable of answering almost all of my simplistic queries. Of course, it couldn't tell me why all the elevators arrive at once, or why no adult can open a childproof bottle, but it was pretty good on some of the more common questions.

For example, like any kid, I'd ask why the sky was green.

And TAM would spew out an answer in a nanosecond or two, to the effect that *my* world's sky was green because all the continents were blanketed by green grass and the oceans were covered by an exceptionally fast-growing and disgusting form of algae, but that skies actually came in all colors, including blue, purple, violet, indigo, yellow, red, orange, mauve, puce, magenta, and licorice black.

Or I might ask "How high is up?"—always a favorite among obnoxious youngsters.

And TAM would explain that everything was relative, that up wasn't quite as high if you were standing atop a mountain as if you were in a valley, which made me clarify my thinking and express myself more precisely.

Whenever I had a few extra credits to spend, I bought TAM more memory and brainpower, and began asking it increasingly difficult questions.

"For instance?" asked Max, who just couldn't stop himself from interrupting almost every story at least once.

———

For instance (answered Argyle), I'm not even a mammal, and my race has three sexes—so why am I attracted to big-breasted women?

"Damned good question," said Max. "What did TAM answer?"

That it was a universal constant (said Argyle) and I shouldn't lose any sleep over it.

As I became more sophisticated I'd ask if a tree made a noise when it fell in an empty forest, and TAM would kind of sigh and explain that a forest couldn't very well be empty of trees, and that I had to learn to think more clearly.

Or I'd pose the question: if God made me, who made God? And he'd reply that it was an invalid supposition until I could prove God had made me, and that personally he doubted it like all hell. (You'll notice that by now I was referring to TAM as *him* rather than *it*; I found it helped personalize him—and he was also able to answer some embarrassingly naive and insecure questions about the nature of sex, which is something that none of my parents seemed able to do.)

Anyway, I kept buying TAM more brainpower, and kept pushing him to the limits of his abilities.

For example, since I worship thirty-seven gods and Men worship only one, I decided to prove they were wrong. So I did some studying, and I found out that Men put a lot of stock in the First Cause Argument. You know the one: for every effect there is a cause, and when you finally backtrack to a first cause beyond which you can't go, you call that God. So I asked TAM if he could disprove the First Cause Argument.

"Certainly," he replied instantly. "To disprove it, one need merely show that not everything has a first cause."

"Okay, you *can* disprove it," I said, realizing that I had expressed myself improperly. "Now *will* you?"

"If you wish. Consider the set of all negative integers. The *last* cause, the highest number, is minus one. The next-to-last cause is minus two. And the first cause, minus infinity, cannot exist."

"Excellent!" I exclaimed. But suddenly I was filled with doubt. "Could it be that that's just a fluke?" I asked. "A single disproof to a theory that's lasted thousands of years?"

"You want more, I got more," replied TAM. "Consider next the set of all proper fractions. The last cause, the highest number, is one over one. The second highest is one over two, or one-half. Then one-third, and so on. And the first cause, one over infinity, cannot exist."

"Thank you, TAM," I said.

"That was almost too easy," said TAM. "Ask me a tough one."

"Well, the other proof of God that still seems to have widespread acceptance is Bishop Barkley's—that of the unseen observer. Can you disprove it?"

This time it took TAM three nanoseconds to answer.

"No, but I can show you how trivial it is."

"Trivial? In what way?"

"Wait until I access my rhyming dictionary," said TAM. "Ah, here it is. All right: I can condense everything Bishop Barkley said, every argument he made, every word of his entire life's work, into a single four-line stanza, to wit:

> *"With eyes wide open and mouth shut tight,*
> *I watch by day and I watch by night.*
> *And though I'm sure you must find it odd,*
> *I'm always here—you may call me God.*

"I submit to you that anything that can be reduced to such a childish doggerel cannot possibly have any universal import or validity. Furthermore," he added, "it kind of makes God into a Peeping Tom. Who wants to worship a Supreme Voyeur?"

"If you say so."

"I just did," answered TAM.

Well, the years passed by, and I thirsted for more knowledge, and finally I reached the point where I sought the Ultimate Answer to Existence.

The problem was, TAM didn't have enough brainpower to handle the question. Oh, he could compute the diameter of an electron in half a nanosecond, and he was able to pinpoint the date of the Big Bang to within seventeen minutes . . . but what I wanted to know was simply beyond him.

I knew the only way to get my answers was to increase TAM's capacity by a multiple of thousands, maybe tens of thousands. And that would require money—more than I could earn in several lifetimes.

Still, I knew that if I *could* make TAM bright enough to answer my questions, the entire galaxy would benefit. So one day I robbed the biggest bank on our planet. The plan was foolproof, of course: TAM, who was as eager to increase his intellect as I was, had come up with it. I must confess that even as I was filling my bags with loot, I was silently appealing for understanding to Morixomete, the God of Heinous Deeds Committed for Noble Purposes. I'm sure He heard and forgave me, and I was really sorry about the sixteen innocent bystanders.

I spent every credit on more intelligence for TAM, and when he was ready, I hit him with the Question.

"Are you ready?" I said.

"Roger!"

"Okay, here it comes," I said. I paused just a moment for effect and then hit him with it: *"Why?"*

Usually TAM came up with an answer in less than a second. The really tough questions took him perhaps half a minute. But this time he thought and cogitated and considered, and after eleven minutes he finally gave me his answer:

"Why not?"

That was when I realized there wasn't enough money on my planet to supply him with the intellect he needed to answer the Ultimate Question, so I came out to the Frontier and became a notorious outlaw, though no one knew that I was killing and raping and robbing and plundering for the noblest of causes.

After sixteen years I felt I'd accumulated enough money, and I poured every credit of it into TAM's prodigious brain. By the time I was done, he was probably three times as smart as the Master Computer back on Deluros VIII.

I activated him, and asked the Ultimate Question again:

"Why?"

This time he began whirring and blinking in earnest—and he kept it up for three days and three nights, considering every possible answer, every alternative, every subtle nuance to the secret of creation. And finally came the moment that we'd both spent our whole lives leading up to—the Ultimate Answer:

"Because."

"That's *it*?" I said, surprised.

"That's it," replied TAM.

That's when I realized that the Ultimate Question would remain unanswered for all eternity.

"Thanks," I muttered unhappily.

"Any time," replied TAM.

So I made a total break with my past, left TAM behind, and returned to the Frontier, this time to stay. The only question I ask these days is "Where's the bar?"

I still like big-breasted women, though.

"So does TAM still exist?" asked O'Grady.

"Yes. Why?"

"Maybe he can't answer the Ultimate Question, but I'll bet he could dope out the odds on next week's games."

"Well, I think it's noble that Argyle spent so long trying to find out the secret of existence," said Sinderella. "Except for all the people he killed and raped, that is."

"It's a chump's game," said Max. "The only thing we were put here for is to make lots of little replicas of ourselves before we totter off to the grave."

"Then it's damned lucky the Beldorians made it so much fun, isn't it?" put in Nicodemus Mayflower.

"Well, I disagree," said Big Red. "I think each of us has his own purpose. If you were to ask Magic Abdul-Jordan whether he wanted to sire a bunch of eighteen-foot-high children, I think he'd tell you that he'd rather shoot himself right now than lay a curse like that on his offspring."

"Right," chimed in Little Mike Picasso. "Reproducing the species is all well and good, but to what purpose? I'd rather create one work of lasting art than ten kids who go out and live dull, everyday, unexceptional lives."

"Nobody who comes to the Outpost is unexceptional," said the Bard. "So why should you think their offspring will be?"

"You've heard of shirtsleeves to shirtsleeves in three generations?" replied Three-Gun Max. "Well, how about unexceptional to unexceptional in two generations? I don't recall any of our parents ever traipsing out here to the Frontier and making the kind of reputations we've got. We're a bunch of freaks. Great and heroic freaks to be sure, but freaks nonetheless."

But Nicodemus Mayflower wasn't buying it. "Are you telling me that, say, Einstein and Sinderella couldn't produce a kid with his brains and her looks?"

"I'd say it's a damned sight more likely that they'd produce one with *her* brains and *his* looks," answered Max.

"Well, I like that!" snapped Sinderella, glaring at him.

"No insult intended," continued Max. "But let's be reasonable. Was there any reason to predict anyone in this tavern would turn out the way we did? Was your mother the sexiest woman in a whole sector of the galaxy? Do you suppose Catastrophe Baker's father could wipe out entire regiments before going off to bed a sacrosanct high priestess? Did Little Mike have five brothers and sisters who could produce works of art that would pass for that of the great masters? I say we're all unique, and I can't see what's wrong with that."

"There's nothing wrong with it," answered the Bard. "But it

does tend to cast some serious doubt upon the entire science of genetics."

"Big deal," said Max. "Have you ever seen a gene?"

"I haven't seen a supernova, either," said the Bard. "But I have it on excellent authority that they exist."

"Just keep arguing with me," said Max pugnaciously, "and I won't let you put me in your book."

"Keep saying stupid things and I won't want to."

"Write me out of that book and I'll blow your head off!" bellowed Max, who seemed to have less use for logic than most men.

"Blow my head off and the book will never get finished," shot back the Bard.

"I hadn't considered that," said Max grumpily. "Okay, you can live." He paused. "What were we talking about?"

"The cosmic verities and the meaning of life," said Nicodemus Mayflower. "Stuff like that."

"Only we decided that no one could ever know the answers," added Little Mike Picasso.

"Someone knows," said Catastrophe Baker, who'd been silent for a long time. (Well, for him, anyway.)

Argyle shook his head. "Even TAM didn't know."

Baker shook his head. "TAM was wrong. There's one man who knows the secrets of the universe and the purpose of life."

"And you just happen to know who he is, right?"

"As a matter of fact, I do."

Catastrophe Baker and the Mage of the Swirling Mists

I ain't much of a philosopher (said Baker). Universal truths haven't got all that much to do with the hero business. I mean, when you see a dyed-in-the-wool villain doing villain-type things, you don't stop and wonder if society's to blame, or whether his punishment should fit his crimes. No, you blow the son of a bitch away and worry about it later.

So I didn't really have much initial interest in meeting up with the Mage of the Swirling Mists. The fact that people trusted him with their secrets and their hopes and their dreams didn't mean a thing to me.

What I *was* interested in was the Star of Bethlehem, surely the most gorgeous blue-skinned girl I've ever laid eyes on. She was some kind of mutant, what with her blue skin and orange eyes, but other than that she could have been Sinderella's better-looking twin sister, meaning no offense.

I first saw her out on Prego Minoulli IV. She was just coming out of a hotel there, and it was love at first sight—at least on my part. I doubt that she even saw me at all. But that didn't make no nevermind. My heart was pounding away in my chest, and my throat was getting dry, and my palms were starting to sweat, and I knew from previous experience that all of these were the symptoms of falling into eternal and undying love.

I hung around the hotel lobby for a couple of hours until she returned so I could declare my feelings and sweep her off her feet and maybe into the honeymoon suite—but when she finally came back it was in the company of a big, burly man wearing a turban and a robe with a bunch of stars and quarter moons and stuff on it.

I walked right up and gave her one of my more chivalrous bows.

"Ma'am," I said, "I been admiring you from afar, and the time has come to announce my everlasting devotion and start admiring you from close up."

"Leave us alone!" said the man gruffly, pushing me on the shoulder, which was about as high up as he could reach.

I busted his ribs and knocked out nine of his teeth as a gentle reproof, but when I turned back to my blue-skinned ideal of pure womanhood she'd already made it onto the airlift. Now, the hotel had some fifteen hundred rooms, and I was perfectly willing to bust down the door of each and every one of 'em in search of her, but then it occurred to me that there might be a less strenuous way, so I moseyed over to where the guy with the turban had fallen after I bounced him off the far wall, and I squatted down next to him.

"Howdy, neighbor," I said.

He took one look at me, uttered a shriek of terror, and curled up into a little ball.

"C'mon, friend," I said, kind of forcefully straightening him out and trying not to pay no attention to all the creaking and cracking sounds. "I didn't mean you no harm. I just happen to resent being pushed by little-bitty guys with turbans—and besides, you were standing betwixt me and that which I want most in all the galaxy."

"What *I* want most is a doctor!" he muttered.

"I never noticed it before, but you got a serious lisp there, friend," I said.

"I didn't have it until you knocked out all my teeth!" he shot back. (Actually, he *spat* back, but I didn't hold it against him none, since he didn't have anything in the front of his mouth to act as a barrier to all that saliva.)

"You do me a serious injustice," I said, prying his jaws open. "You got lots of teeth left—hell, I can see at least a dozen from here, counting molars—and if you want to keep 'em, you'll start answering my questions."

He whimpered a bit at that, but didn't enter into no arguments.

"That blue-skinned lady you was with," I said. "By what name does she go?"

"She is the Star of Bethlehem," he said.

"What is Bethlehem—some kind of a play or movie?" I asked, hoping against hope that it might even be a strip show.

"That's her name!" he wailed. "Now let me go!"

"Real soon," I said. "I ain't a lot more comfortable sitting here on your chest like this than you are. But if I'm gonna spend the rest of my life with this lady, I gotta know a little more about her. Like, for starters, where does she work?"

"She and I both work on the same planet!" he said, and then he passed out, probably more from fear and shortage of air than anything more major.

Well, since I didn't want no trouble with the local gendarmes, who were still a little miffed at me for busting up Aristotle's Bar and Study Parlor and putting half a dozen of their brethren in the hospital the night before, I slung the guy with the turban over my shoulder, went outside into the cool night air, and wandered around for the better part of an hour before I finally found an emergency room where I could dump him.

(I should probably have asked some questions when I saw that all the other patients were animals—but at least the veterinarian was open for business in the middle of the night, which is more than I can say for all them rich, stuck-up doctors.)

When I got back to the hotel, I asked the desk clerk where I could find the Star of Bethlehem. He called up some Tri-D star maps on his computer and began looking, so I grabbed him by the collar and shook him a couple of times to make sure I had his attention, and politely suggested that while the Star of Bethlehem might be a lot of things, including a celestial object, the particular stellar body I was looking for was wearing a skintight dress and was staying in the hotel.

He apologized and told a servo-mech to mop up the small puddle he'd made on the floor, and then checked the hotel's register, and suddenly turned as white as a sheet.

"You look like you seen a ghost," I said.

"I'm just anticipating," he answered.

Well, I didn't know what he meant, and it wasn't none of my concern anyway, so I said, "What room is she in?"

"She checked out half an hour ago," said the clerk, cringing as if he expected the ceiling to fall on his head.

"Where did she go?" I asked.

"Let me see," he said, messing with the computer.

"You know," I opined, staring at his hands, "you really ought to see a doctor before that palsy gets any worse."

"I plan to see a whole barrage of them the second I'm off duty," he replied. "Ah, here it is. She caught the starliner to Dante II."

"You got any other info on her?" I asked, wondering, for instance, if she was married, and if she was, was she a fanatic about it?

"Just that her companion listed his profession as assistant to the Mage of the Swirling Mists."

"The Mage of the Swirling Mists?" I repeated, rolling the name around on my tongue and wondering if anyone involved in this situation except me had just a first name and a last one.

"Yes," said the clerk. "I've never seen him, of course, but I've heard that he can foresee the future, explain all the eternal verities, and even predict the roll of the dice."

"Sounds like a handy guy to know," I allowed. "I hope he ain't too good-looking."

"He is the Master of the Mystic Arts," said the clerk. "What matters appearance to a being like that?"

I was more concerned with what they mattered to a being like the Star of Bethlehem, but I kept my thoughts to myself and went to the spaceport, where I climbed into my ship and took off for Dante II, which for the uninitiated is just past the Virgil system, way out on the Spiral Arm.

Took the better part of two weeks to get there, during which time my love for the Star of Bethlehem had blossomed and grown and matured into a beautiful thing of gossamer fragility. I'd been doing a lot of thinking about the pair of us, and I had only one question left, which was would she let me call her Star, since calling her Star of Bethlehem every time I spoke to her could get to be a little tedious.

Once I landed, I made my way through customs—they'd never heard of me, so it didn't take as long as usual—and walked out of the spaceport. I figured I might as well get right to business, so I stopped the first pedestrian I saw with the intention of asking him where I could find the Mage of the Swirling Mists, but he just lay peaceful-like where he'd fallen, and after eight or nine minutes my patience began wearing thin, so I just wandered into the city on my own.

Before long I came upon another man walking the streets by himself, and I kind of signaled for him to stop and talk to me.

"Okay," he said, stretching his hands way above his head. "And you can stop pointing the blaster at me. I ain't armed and I ain't dumb enough to run away from a man that's carrying as much firepower as you seem to be."

"That's right reasonable of you, friend," I said. "I got just one thing to ask of you and then you can be on your way."

"Is this some kind of trick question?" he asked nervously. "What'll you do to me if I get it wrong?"

"It ain't no trick," I assured him. "And it's vitally important to my sex life and my emotional well-being." I tried to figure out how to word it without sounding like too much of a country bumpkin, and finally I blurted out, "Where can I find the Swirling Mists?"

I was all prepared for him to laugh at me, but instead he looked kind of relieved and pointed up the road a way.

"Go to Fourth Street and turn left," he said.

"That's all there is to it?"

"That's it."

I thanked him and hurried off, anxious to clutch the Star of Bethlehem to my manly bosom.

When I got to Fourth Street, I took a left, and walked half a block past a number of theaters and clubs and restaurants, mingling with a bunch of folks who were dressed to the nines, and then suddenly I found myself in front of a blinking holographic sign that proclaimed that I had reached the Swirling Mists Nightclub.

"Welcome, wayfarer," said the doorman, who was dressed exactly like the guy I'd kind of disassembled back on Prego Minoulli. "Enter the Swirling Mists and let the fabulous Mage astound you with his feats of prestidigitation and legerdemain!"

Well, Prestidigitation and Legerdemain sounded like a couple of Altairean bodyguards, but I didn't want to show my ignorance, so I thanked him and walked on in.

The show was just finishing, and a bunch of chorus girls were on stage, dressed—or maybe a better word is *un*dressed—like witches, and doing really interesting things with their broomsticks, but I wasn't here for the high culture the place afforded, but for my Star of Bethlehem, and once I determined that she wasn't anywhere to be seen I moseyed backstage and began looking for her.

I tried five or six dressing rooms, and raised a couple of female screams, which struck me as odd since I wasn't seeing nothing they weren't proud to show off onstage, and then I came to the biggest dressing room of all, and there, sitting at a table and staring into a mirror, was this guy with a cone-shaped magician's hat and a long white beard, and a robe that kept changing colors the whole time I looked at it.

"You ain't the Star," I said, making no attempt to hide my disappointment.

"I most certainly am," he replied with dignity. "Don't take *my* word for it—go out and look at the marquee. The Mage of the Swirling Mists is the star this and every night."

"And you're the Mage?" I asked.

"That's right."

"Good!" I said. "Where can I find the Star of Bethlehem?"

He looked puzzled. "Second star on the right and straight on till morning?"

"She's a woman," I explained.

"I didn't know they came in sexes," he said. "Fascinating!"

"I thought you knew everything," I said.

"Me?" he replied with a laugh. "I just do card tricks." He reached into the air and produced a deck, then fanned it out. "Here, take a card, any card."

"I don't care about card tricks!" I yelled.

"Okay, don't lose your temper," he said. He reached behind my ear and suddenly there was an egg in his hand. "There!" he said proudly. "What do you think of that?"

"It's an egg," I said. "Big deal."

"But where did it come from?" he said with a twinkle in his eye.

"*That's* the kind of stuff everyone says you know," I answered him. "Did it come before the chicken or after? And while we're on the subject, where's the woman I love?"

"How the hell should *I* know?" said the Mage.

"They told me you knew everything," I said.

"Ah!" he said, his eyes lighting up. "Now I understand. You

want the Mage of the *Purple* Mists! *He* knows everything. He answers all the questions about life and death and such, and he's never been known to be wrong. Me, I just do sleight of hand."

"You're sure?" I asked, staring at him and trying to decide if he was joking.

"Absolutely," said the Mage. "He works about half a block down the street. And I hear that he's got the most beautiful blue-skinned assistant . . ."

I didn't wait to hear the rest. I was out the back door before he could finish his sentence, and a minute later I was pounding at the locked door of the Purple Mists.

Finally the door inched open and a skinny old guy stuck his head out.

"Stop pounding!" he said. "I heard you."

"Let me in!" I said.

"We're closed for the season."

"What season?" I said. "What's going on, and when do you open again?"

He shrugged. "How should I know? Maybe never."

"What are you talking about?" I demanded. "Where's the Mage of the Purple Mists?"

"He left the planet this afternoon with that beautiful assistant of his," said the old guy.

"When's he coming back?"

"Beats me" was the answer. "Didn't leave no forwarding address neither."

I set off to hunt them down and pledge my love to the Star of Bethlehem, and I spent the next year searching for them without any luck, but then I ran into a couple of Pirate Queens and a High Priestess who looked exactly like she had an extra pair of lungs, and after awhile I couldn't quite remember what the Star actually looked like except for being blue and kind of pretty.

As for the Mage of the Purple Mists, I guess he was everything they said he was. But he couldn't do card tricks, and people who knew him said he wasn't much with a blaster or a burner, and he was too old to cut the mustard with the Star of Bethlehem, so when I think of him at all, I wonder what knowing all the secrets of the universe was really worth.

"Let me take him to High-Stakes Eddie's for a night and I'll put a cash value on it," said Bet-a-World O'Grady.

"You know," said Sinderella, "there's more to this secrets-of-the-universe business than meets the eye. Or rather, there's a lot less."

"What do you mean?" asked O'Grady.

"You weren't listening. The brightest machine in the galaxy couldn't give poor Argyle even as good an answer as some drunken jerk in a bar could, and the Mage of the Swirling Mists does card tricks."

"True," said Baker. "But the Mage of the Purple Mists, now . . ."

"You don't know anything about him," said Sinderella.

"Except that he's got your Star of Bethlehem," added Max with a smirk.

"She was too perfect," answered Baker.

"How can someone be too perfect?" asked Sinderella.

"She was purity itself," said Baker. "How can you enjoy a roll in the hay if it don't feel dirty?"

"A telling point," agreed Nicodemus Mayflower. "If you don't rut like a couple of farm animals gone wild, and then feel so guilty that you've just got to unload in church, and then change your mind because what you did was so filthy that your minister would never speak to you again—"

"I ain't never seen, heard, smelled, or even experienced a sex act that could shock my tender sensitivities," interrupted the Reverend Billy Karma. "You've just been going to the wrong church, my son."

"Well, if it doesn't shock you, it should at least shock the pants off God," continued Mayflower.

"God is a mighty understanding critter," said Billy Karma. "And it's been my experience that He likes a spicy story as well as the next man."

"That's some religion you preach," said Max sardonically.

"The best," agreed the Reverend. "I mean, what the hell good's a religion that doesn't attract sinners? That's what keeps God in business—fresh blood."

"I never looked at it that way," admitted Baker.

"Not many people do," answered Billy Karma. "Or else you'd all get into the preaching biz."

"And God don't shock easy?" continued Baker.

"It's almost as hard to shock God as it is to shock me," said Billy Karma. "Take this little lady here," he added, pointing to Sinderella. "She felt a need to confess her sins this morning, or maybe to brag about 'em a little, and even though we ain't from the same branch of God's family, I sat down and listened to her for three hours." He paused and looked around the Outpost. "Well, brethren, I panted, and I drooled, and my hands started shaking, and once or twice I even went outside to bay at the sun (the moon not being in the sky at the time). I stuttered and I stammered and I howled like a dog—but the one thing I wasn't was shocked. Excited, yes. Inflamed, sure. Aroused, damned right. But shocked? Never!" Then he winked at Sinderella. "We got to have another heart-to-heart real soon now, you hear?"

"I think I been going to the wrong church all my life," said Baker.

"I don't know about that," responded Max. "I mean, to listen to you tell it, the only thing you ever got out of a church service was a vestal virgin or two, and they didn't stay vestal for long."

"You mean virgin," said Sinderella.

"That, too."

"Well, you sure have an interesting way of looking at things, Reverend," said Nicodemus Mayflower.

"I got to," answered Billy Karma. "After all, I'm God's eyes and ears on this here temporal plane of existence."

"He spent most of last night trying to convince me he was God's hands, too," said Silicon Carny.

"You never heard of the laying on of hands?" said the Reverend in mock surprise.

"Not where *you* were trying to lay them," replied Silicon Carny.

"How about talking in tongues?" asked Max.

"I give up," said Billy Karma. "How *about* talking in tongues?"

"Can you do it?"

"Usually not until my fifth drink."

"The more I hear about this man's religion, the more I like it," announced Baker.

"The more *I* hear about it," said Max, "the more it sounds like I've been practicing it for the last twenty years without even knowing it."

"Tell me some more," said Baker. "You got any saints in your religion?"

"Not so's you'd notice it," answered the Reverend Billy Karma. "I thought I was pretty saintly this morning, just sitting there listening to Sinderella without pouncing on her."

"Uh . . ." began Sinderella meaningfully.

"Without pouncing on her in earnest," he amended.

"Hey, I was there!" she said.

"Okay, without pouncing on her in *deadly* earnest," said Billy Karma. He turned back to Baker. "All right—no saints."

"How about prophets?" asked O'Grady, who only seemed to get interested in the conversation when he could bring it around to odds and betting.

"We make more than our fair share, and we're completely tax-free," replied the Reverend. "You thinking about taking to the cloth?"

"I meant *prophets*, not *profits*," said O'Grady, enunciating carefully. "You know—the kind of men who make pronouncements and predict the future."

"Men who make pronouncements and predict the future are hanging out in every brokerage house and bookie joint in the galaxy," said Max. "And every last one of 'em dies broke."

"We've had our share of prophets," replied the Reverend. "Including maybe the two most interesting in the history of organized religion."

"Organized religion's been around eight or nine millennia," noted Max dryly.

"Nonsense," said Billy Karma. "Religion didn't get really organized until I writ down all the rules for it maybe fifteen years ago. And since then there have been fifty-three amendments, as well as two evenings' worth of apocrypha experienced at one of the sleazier whorehouses on Talarba VII, and a rejected canon courtesy of an alien lady who had three of everything worthwhile." He winked at Silicon Carny. "There's still time to become the fifty-fourth amendment."

"There's still time to be nailed to a cross," she replied.

"What's the matter with you, woman?" he demanded. "Religion's supposed to be enjoyable, or why practice it at all?"

"*I'd* enjoy it," said Silicon Carny.

"She's got you there, Reverend," said Max. "Fair is fair."

"So what about these two prophets you were mentioning?" asked Baker.

"Don't encourage him," said Max. "He talks enough as it is."

"But think of all the things he can't do while he's busy talking," said Sinderella.

"He wouldn't be doing 'em to me anyway," said Max. He turned to Billy Karma. "Would you?"

"I got to be a lot more desperate than I am right now to work all the way up to *that* amendment," said the Reverend devoutly. "Now, do you want to hear about these prophets or don't you?"

"I don't know," said Max. "Maybe we ought to take a vote."

"You didn't vote for anyone else's stories," said Billy Karma.

"*They* didn't waste three million words building up to 'em," said Max. "All in favor of hearing the Reverend Billy Karma drone on about these here prophets, say aye."

"Aye," said Catastrophe Baker.

"All opposed?"

Everyone else in the Outpost hollered, "Nay!"

Max looked at Baker, and saw a little something in his eyes that made him think twice.

"The ayes have it," said Max.

The Prophet Who Was Never Wrong

When I was a young man (began the Reverend Billy Karma), and just starting out on the preaching trail, I came across a true quirk of nature—a pair of brothers who were Siamese twins, joined at the hip. I did my best to uplift their spirits, but they felt abandoned by God, and one day they walked out during a thunderstorm and begged Him to strike them down with a bolt of lightning and end their misery.

And damned if the Good Lord didn't do just that. His aim was a little off, though, probably due to the poor visibility, and instead of killing them the lightning actually split them apart. The shock sent 'em both into a coma, and they lost a lot of blood, but somehow or other they were found and taken to a hospital before they could expire, and there they lay, day in and day out, tied into dozens of tubes and wires.

And then one day one of 'em opened his eyes and asked where he was and what had happened to him, and the staff calmed him down and explained the situation to him, and the Lord granted another miracle and brought him back to perfect health within a week.

One afternoon, just before he was due to leave the hospital, he mentioned that he wished he didn't have such an ugly scar on his left hip—and lo and behold, the scar vanished almost before the words were out of his mouth.

"I wish the sun would break through all the clouds," he said, and a second later the sun did just that.

It was then he realized that he'd been doubly blessed by God, that anything he wished for would come true.

Now, he hadn't ever prepared for a profession, since there ain't a lot of jobs open to one-half of a Siamese twin team, but now he decided to set up shop as a prophet. On the surface of things, it would appear that he didn't actually *need* a job, since he could just wish for a million credits or a castle with maid service . . . but he wanted to thank the Lord for the miracle, and he figured the best way to go about it was to make other people just as happy as God had made him.

First thing he needed was a name, so he called himself Isaiah the Right—Isaiah for the Old Testament prophet, and Right because he'd been the twin on the right when they were still attached. He took off just long enough to marry the prettiest girl around, and then he hung out his shingle and started prophesying in earnest.

Problem was, God, who can have a pretty mordant sense of humor when the mood strikes Him, put a little backspin on the ball.

For example, some poor, unhappy soul would seek him out and ask for a prophecy, and Isaiah the Right would peer into his crystal ball (which actually held a hologram of Tassle-Twirling Tammie Twilight doing the act that was famed from one end of the galaxy to the other), and he would intone something like "You shall have wealth beyond imagining." And the man would thank him and go off to prepare for his windfall.

But it never came. Which makes a twisted kind of sense, when you come to think of it, because there ain't nothing beyond a man's imagining, and nothing is exactly what he got.

Still, if it was just the prophecies that were theoretically dead-on but never actually came to pass, it wouldn't have been so bad. But every now and then Isaiah would get something like a four-hundred-pound girl with acne and crooked teeth who wanted to be beautiful, and he'd peer into that ball (thoughtfully hiding its contents from onlookers) and pronounce that "Tomorrow morning you shall be the most beautiful woman on the planet."

And sure enough she would be—but only because every other woman on the planet woke up weighing five hundred pounds with eczema and a mouthful of cavities.

I think maybe the worst was the politician who crossed Isaiah's palm with the mandatory silver and some optional twelve-carat diamonds. Isaiah told him that after the election he could climb the highest mountain in the world and he would be the master of all he could see. Sure enough, the poor bastard went blind on election night.

Well, things just went from bad to worse, and finally Isaiah the Right wished that he were back in the hospital right next to his brother, who was sleeping the sleep of the innocent.

That night Isaiah was mugged and robbed by three little old ladies with blackjacks, and sure enough he wound up one bed over from his brother.

Turns out his brother had woke up a couple of days earlier and been charged with seducing a couple of the nurses. He was taking a nap when Isaiah arrived, and he sure was sleeping the sleep of the innocent, because he later proved in court that he'd been in bed with Isaiah's wife at the very moment he was supposed to be with the nurses.

When Isaiah heard that, he had a seizure and went right into another coma, and everyone decided that it was better all the way around to just let him stay asleep, and he remains there in the hospital to this very day, the prophet who was never wrong.

"So what happened to his brother?" asked Max.

"I thought you'd never ask," replied Billy Karma.

The Prophet Who Was Never Right

Turns out that God has a better sense of humor than most people give Him credit for (continued the Reverend Billy Karma). Because just as Isaiah the Right was never wrong, his brother couldn't win for losing. If he said it looked nice out, it'd snow five minutes later. If he thought the local murderball team was a lead-pipe cinch to win, they'd blow a seventeen-goal lead in the last three minutes. If he went to a restaurant and asked for steak, they'd give him salad—and when he decided not to make an issue of it and asked for some salad dressing, they'd bring him horseradish.

After awhile he decided that there might be a way to make a living in the prophet biz anyway, so he took the name of Isaiah the Left so everybody would know he wasn't his brother, and set up shop. He needed an interpreter, of course, someone to tell the customers that when he said the only horse that couldn't possibly win was the gray gelding, what he meant was to bet the farm on the gray.

He'd go to New Vegas as an adviser, and the second he advised you to stick on eighteen, you'd take a hit and pull a deuce or a trey. He'd be at the craps table, and some hot four-armed Delphinian would be rolling the dice, and when Isaiah would say that there was no way the purple bastard could come up seven six times in a row, you knew where to place your money.

In fact, before long he felt compelled to change his name. Oh, it was still the opposite of Isaiah the Right, but now instead of Isaiah the Left he was Isaiah the Wrong.

He achieved some remarkable results. I remember one free-hand boxing match where he had so many stipulations that in order for him to lose all of them the referee had to get a hernia and the boxers had to be miraculously transported thirty-seven light-years away, where the fight was decided by a split decision.

He just kept on making wrong prophecies and raking in the money. It couldn't last, of course. God doesn't mind playing an occasional practical joke, but He ain't so happy when someone plays it right back on Him.

One day Isaiah the Wrong prophesied that his client would be unlucky in love—and the next night the client got lucky indeed, and ran off with Isaiah's fiancée.

He promised his next client that fame and fortune would forever elude him. Two days later the Fame and Fortune Collection Agency ran his client to ground and nailed him for almost three million credits' worth of unpaid debts.

The kicker came when, suddenly filled with self-doubts from his last two experiences, he looked at his unhappy image in the mirror and said, "I have confidence in you. Things will get better."

The words had barely left his mouth when he realized what he'd done, but God hadn't supplied him with a rulebook and he didn't know how to take it back.

In short order four women sued him for child support, his banker embezzled his money, the mortgage company repossessed his house, his office was broken into and robbed, and a stray cat bit him on the great toe.

He finally decided that he couldn't take any more, so he went to the hospital, lay down next to Isaiah the Right, and made one last prophecy: "I feel so good that I don't think I'll ever need to sleep again."

That was more than twenty years ago. He's still snoring.

"What the hell does that have to do with your religion?" asked Max irritably.

"You asked for prophets, I gave you prophets," replied Billy Karma.

"Not the kind anyone would want to write up in a Bible," said Max.

"You didn't specify Old Testament–type prophets."

"*I* didn't ask for any prophets at all."

"Then what the hell are you bitching about?" demanded Billy Karma. "Get uppity with me and I'll bring a rain of toads down on you."

"Ain't no such thing," said Max.

"Don't bet on it," interjected Sinderella. "Every time I go out I'm immediately surrounded by more unkissed frogs and toads than you can shake a stick at."

"What a pair of lost opportunities," said Bet-a-World O'Grady, shaking his head sadly.

"You leave her opportunities alone!" said Max, who seemed determined to fight with *some*one about *some*thing.

"I'm talking about the Isaiah brothers," said O'Grady. "A man who knew how to use what they had to offer could own half the galaxy in a year's time."

Big Red had been translating for Einstein, who suddenly tapped something onto his computer, and Big Red's screen immediately lit up with a number that seemed to cover the whole of it. He held it up in front of O'Grady.

"You know what this is?" he asked.

"A googol?" guessed O'Grady.

"The yearly tax on half the galaxy. Einstein just computed it." He grinned. "Do you *really* want to own it?"

"Well, if I *did* own it, I'd go to Deluros VIII and sit down opposite the Monarch and pull out a deck of cards and we could cut for the tax—double or nothing."

"What if you lost?" asked Hellfire Van Winkle.

"With *my* deck?" replied O'Grady as if that was the silliest statement he'd heard all week—which it probably was.

"Forgive me," said Van Winkle with a smile. "I lost my head."

"So, Catastrophe Baker," said the Reverend Billy Karma, "are you about ready to join my church?"

"I'm giving it some thought," said Baker. "A man ought to have something to do of a Sunday morning."

"You mean besides rape, carnage, plunder, murder, and sleeping late?" said a deep voice from the doorway, and we all turned to see who had wandered in. "I can't imagine what it might be."

They were an eye-catching couple. The woman was tall and shapely, with coal-black hair and eyes, and matching black lipstick. The man was as big as Catastrophe Baker, which was going some. He had wild red hair, and a bushy red beard, and was wearing an outfit made from the furs of various alien polar animals. I knew from the descriptions I'd heard that it couldn't be anyone but Hurricane Smith.

"Well, I'll be damned!" said Baker.

"Probably you will be," agreed Smith, "but pour me a drink first."

Smith and his companion walked to the bar, where he and Baker hugged and pummeled each other with enough energy to have killed anyone else in the room except maybe Gravedigger Gaines.

"It's good to see you again, Hurricane!" said Baker. "And who is this elegant lady by your side?"

"This here is Langtry Lily," answered Smith. "We're on our honeymoon!"

"Well, congratulations to both of you!" boomed Baker. "Do you mind if I kiss the bride?"

"You remember what happened the last time you kissed one of my female companions?" answered Smith with a smile. "And *that* was a lady I'd known for only ten minutes."

I stepped over to greet them. "What can I have Reggie get for you?" I asked. "The first one is always on the house."

"I'll have some Denebian firewater," said Smith. "How about you, my dear?"

Langtry Lily whispered something in his ear.

"Have you got a gallon of coffee somewhere in the back there?" he asked.

"No problem," I said.

"Maybe a pint of cream?"

"Yeah, there's always some around."

"And a pound of sugar?"

"That's an awful lot of sugar," I said.

"She's got a sweet tooth. Can you do it?"

"A gallon of coffee, a pint of cream, and a pound of sugar," I repeated. "Yeah, we can do it."

"Good," he said, escorting Langtry Lily to a table. "Now, hold the coffee and hold the cream, and bring what's left."

I've had stranger orders, though not too many, so I shrugged and gave Reggie his instructions.

"Hey, you're that Peloponne lady that the Hurricane ran off with, aren't you?" asked Nicodemus Mayflower.

"She's my wife," snapped Smith. "That ought to be enough for you."

"No offense meant," said Mayflower hastily. "The Hurricane and I served together. I got nothing against the Peloponnes."

"So is she or isn't she?" whispered Sitting Horse.

Just then an insect flew by Smith's table. Langtry Lily opened her mouth, her tongue shot out a good twenty inches and snared it, and an instant later we could hear an unladylike crunching sound, followed by a quick *gulp*.

"She is," answered Crazy Bull.

"Geez!" sighed Sinderella. "Do you know how much money I could have made with a tongue even half that long?"

"A man of the cloth can't stand by while a possible parishioner expresses such feelings of inadequacy," said the Reverend Billy Karma. "Why don't you come by later and try your physical short-comings out on me?"

"Because I don't want you trying *your* physical shortcomings out on *me*," said Sinderella.

When the laughter died down, Baker walked over and joined Hurricane Smith and Langtry Lily at their table.

"What brings you to the Outpost?" he asked.

"Truth to tell, I wasn't originally headed here," replied Smith. "But there's an awful lot of shooting going on over in the next system, and since I'd heard of this place, I thought it might be a nice spot to hole up until they get their war over with."

"Either side fire on you?" asked the Bard.

"Hell, *both* sides fired on us," said Smith. "Who are they mad at, anyway?"

"Pretty much everybody, as near as I can tell," answered Baker.

"Hey, Hurricane," said Gravedigger Gaines, "are you going to introduce me to your missus, even if I can't kiss her?"

"That all depends," responded Smith warily. "Are you still a bounty hunter?"

"I gave that up years ago."

"Glad to hear it. I always liked you, except when you were shooting at me."

"Well, damn it all," said the Gravedigger, "I always figured you and I could be great friends if you'd just stop trying to kill me."

"Hell, ain't no time like the present," said Smith, extending his huge hand.

"Sounds good to me," said the Gravedigger, taking it in his own oversized paw.

"Honey," said Smith to his wife, "this is my—"

Her eyes went wide and she started drooling uncontrollably on the table.

"Uh . . . sorry about that. Used the wrong word," he explained to Gravedigger Gaines. "Langtry, this is my friend Gravedigger Gaines, who used to be the best enemy a man could have. Gravedigger, this is Langtry Lily."

Langtry Lily glared at the Gravedigger and hissed.

"It was just *business*," explained Smith. "I never held it against him."

"Honest, ma'am," added Gaines. "There was no one on the Inner Frontier I was less eager to go up against, and no one I would have been prouder to collect the reward on. Except maybe for that ugly blond guy over there," he added, jerking his thumb in Baker's direction.

"Anyway, we're friends now," said Smith.

"We were never enemies, just business rivals," said the Gravedigger.

"It's like athletes who play on different teams," explained Smith.

Langtry Lily looked from one of them to the other, then finally smiled at Gaines. It was the kind of smile men went out and died for—or, in the case of the Peloponnes, deserted by the thousands for.

"Didn't there used to be an actress called Langtry Lily back when we were still Earthbound?" asked Little Mike Picasso.

"Lillie Langtry," answered Smith. "My Langtry is an actress too."

"Really?" said Little Mike. "I try to keep up with the theater. When was her most recent performance?"

"Five'll get you ten it's right this minute," said O'Grady with a chuckle.

"We don't hide what she really is," said Smith. "We just thought you'd all feel more comfortable seeing her like this. But if you'd rather—"

"No!" hollered Baker. "I still plan on eating sometime this week. I don't want nothing to kill my appetite."

At the mention of the word *eat*, Langtry Lily emptied the pound of sugar on the table in front of her. Then a kind of straw emerged from a corner of her mouth, and she began sucking up the sugar with loud slurping noises.

"And this don't bother you none?" asked Baker.

"There are . . . ah . . . compensations," said Smith.

"Yeah, I saw one of them when she nailed the fly," said Sinderella.

"God teaches us not to be jealous," said Billy Karma. "I really think you're ripe for some private counseling, my dear."

"I'm afraid not, Reverend," said Sinderella. "I've got better things to do with my time than listen to you croak 'Compensate me, baby! Compensate me!' in a voice like a strangulated duck."

"Funny," said Billy Karma, half to himself. "I can't think of anything better to do with *my* time."

"Go sacrifice a virgin on the altar of love," said Sinderella.

"I'd be more than happy to accommodate you," answered Billy Karma, "but you've no idea how difficult it is to *find* a virgin these days."

"It always was," said Max.

"Me and Hurricane knew a guy who found one once," said Baker. "Remember?"

"How could I forget?" said Smith. "That must have been, oh, ten or twelve years ago."

"So let's hear about it," said the Bard.

"If you insist," replied Baker with a weary sigh.

Johnny Testosterone and the Temple Virgin

There was this guy called Johnny Testosterone who wiped out a whole army of aliens (said Baker). For his reward, he was given the Temple Virgin.

The end.

"Loses a little something in the retelling, don't it?" said Max dryly.

"Well, it ain't much of a story," responded Baker sullenly. "I'm hardly in it at all."

"Still, it was a better story than *that*," said Smith.

"How would you know?" Baker shot back. "I was emptying the wine cellar and you were off with a God-knows-what doing God-knows-what-else."

Langtry Lily reached out to hold Hurricane Smith's hand. Suddenly her own hand became a mandible, and she dug it into his flesh.

"He's exaggerating, my dear!" said Smith, painfully pulling his hand away and wiping the blood from it as her mandible became a feminine human hand again. "Besides, it was a long time ago!"

She leaned over and whispered something in his ear.

"All right, all right, if you insist," he said, and then turned to the rest of us. "I've been requested to tell the true story."

"The whole thing?" asked Max. "I get the feeling Catastrophe left out a couple of details here and there."

"The whole story," promised Hurricane Smith.

Johnny Testosterone and the Temple Virgin

First of all (began Smith), his name wasn't really Johnny Testosterone. That was just the name he took when he hit the Frontier, probably in the hope of impressing the ladies, as I never noticed him to behave any differently or score any more often than the rest of us.

His real name was Johnny Potts. It didn't make the kind of lasting impression on people that Catastrophe Baker or Gravedigger Gaines did, so he dumped it as soon as he could. Then he began dressing to match his new name. Wore his shirts unbuttoned down to the navel, tied a silk scarf around his neck, and his trousers were so tight you'd swear he was auditioning for a ballet. Even tinted his skin tan. Women loved it; men thought he looked kind of silly.

Still, once push came to shove, he could handle his fists and his weapons with the best of them, and he wasn't scared of anything except maybe Catastrophe Baker when he was drunk, which is a mighty reasonable attitude to have, so we let him travel out to the Albion Cluster with us.

There's a lot more to the hero business than meets the eye. One of the biggest problems is that actions which seem properly heroic to us get our holographs on Wanted posters and attract a lot of men like the Gravedigger here, despite the fact that we never did him any harm.

Anyway, the three of us—Catastrophe, Johnny, and me—got

word that there was a religious colony on Leviticus IV that needed heroes more than most. Seems that some aliens had landed and set up shop there, and it was against the colonists' religion to raise a hand in anger, even to defend themselves.

It was a very elastic religion, though, since it didn't seem to have anything against *other* people raising hands in anger on their behalf. Before long we heard that there was a substantial reward for anyone who freed them from the yoke of alien tyranny, and while none of us had any serious philosophic objections to aliens or tyranny, we had all kinds of objections to not collecting substantial rewards. So we passed the word that we were heading to Leviticus IV and weren't in the mood for any competition, and once people heard that Catastrophe Baker and Hurricane Smith didn't want any company, they suddenly remembered that they had urgent business elsewhere.

We landed next to a temple that could have passed for a small city. It had arches and turrets and spires, and I was willing to bet that it possessed its fair share of secret passageways and hidden chambers.

"The aliens just *let* you land?" asked Max dubiously.

"There was a huge wall around the temple, like a walled city, and we landed inside the wall," answered Hurricane Smith.

"How come the aliens hadn't overrun the temple already?" demanded Max.

"I'm coming to that."

It turns out that whoever built the temple had actually built it as a defensible fortress (continued Smith). Not that the current inhabitants had any notion of defending it themselves . . . but the walls were lined with webs of energy that tended to roast the enemy, and evidently it wasn't against their religion to keep them turned on.

"So why didn't the aliens land inside the walls like you did?" persisted Max.

"Who's telling this story, you or me?" demanded Smith irritably.

Max looked like he was going to argue the point, but just then Langtry Lily started hissing at him, and he decided that silence was the better part of valor.

The simple truth of the matter (said Smith) is that the aliens didn't *know* that the colonists wouldn't put up a fight. A bunch of them had been burned to a crisp trying to climb the walls or break them down, and they knew the city had impregnable defenses, so it never occurred to them that they could land inside the walls and capture it. Instead, they surrounded the place and laid siege to it.

Anyway, a few minutes after we landed we were in a huge room that had all the trappings of a cozy little chapel writ large. There were maybe three dozen men and women waiting for us. Their leader was the High Priest, an old guy by the name of Sandazar, who wore a flowing robe of spun gold.

"I thank the Great Galactic Spirit for answering our supplications and sending us three bonafide heroes in this our hour of need," he said.

"Let's eliminate the middle man," said Catastrophe. "Just thank us and let's get on with the negotiations."

"Negotiations?" asked Sandazar, looking kind of puzzled.

"Even heroes got to eat," said Catastrophe.

"But of course!" exclaimed Sandazar. He clapped his hands above his head. "Bring food for our saviors!"

"I don't think you follow me," said Catastrophe. "We don't work for free. There was mention made of a reward."

"Certainly!" said Sandazar. "Drive the aliens away and you may have anything we possess."

"I'll take that robe of yours," said Catastrophe.

"Consider it done," said Sandazar. "Always assuming you survive."

Just then a gorgeous girl, no more than sixteen years old, and dressed in a gauzy blue gown you could just about see through, approached us, carrying a tray laden down with food.

"Take it away!" said Sandazar. "I misunderstood our guests. They are not hungry after all."

"You know," said Johnny Testosterone, watching intently as the girl walked away, "not all of us insist on being paid in coin of the realm."

"That was never our intention," said Sandazar. "In fact, the most heroic member of your team may claim the Temple Virgin for his own."

"Now you're talking my language!" said Johnny, never taking his eyes from the girl as she undulated away.

I decided that we could worry about the rewards later, but that first we ought to know a little something about the enemy, so I stepped forward and introduced myself.

"Ah, Hurricane Smith!" said Sandazar. "Your reputation precedes you."

"I'm not so much concerned with what precedes me as with what might be sneaking up behind me," I replied. "Suppose you tell us what these aliens are like."

"They're huge amoebas," answered Sandazar. "Their bodies have almost no structural integrity; they grow and contract with every breath and step they take."

"Have you any idea what they want?"

"They want to rule the planet and make us their slaves, of course," said Sandazar, as if explaining the obvious to a small child.

"They usually do," agreed Catastrophe in bored tones.

"How did they communicate that particular desire to you?" I asked.

"Verbally, of course."

"You're telling me that these amoebas can speak?"

"Absolutely," said Sandazar. "Their diction is superior to Catastrophe Baker's."

"Have they said why they chose Leviticus IV?"

"Well, actually, they thought this was Wyandotte II, but they decided that as long as they were here they might as well take over the planet and turn us all into slaves."

"What kind of weapons do they have?" I asked.

"I don't know. They stay on one side of the wall and we stay on the other." He paused for a moment. "Is there anything else you need to know?"

"Probably," I said, "but I can't figure out what it is."

"You're quite sure?"

"Quite."

"Then I think we'll leave the carnage and bloodletting to you and go hide in our secret subterranean chambers. Give a holler when you've slaughtered the last of them."

"No problem," Johnny assured him. "Just remind everyone that the Temple Virgin is reserved for me."

"I will certainly do that," answered Sandazar. Then he turned and left the room, followed by all the lesser priests and priestesses, and we three heroes were left alone.

"Well, how do you want to handle this?" asked Catastrophe.

"It's up to you," I said.

He frowned. "Well, it poses a serious problem. If there were two of us, I'd just tell you to take all the aliens on the right and I'd take all the ones on the left. And if there were four of us, we could each take all the aliens facing a particular wall." He sighed. "But I don't know how to divide an alien army by three."

"Howzabout you two divide 'em in half, and I'll kill any that get by you?" suggested Johnny.

"I don't plan to let none get by me," said Catastrophe.

"You know," I said, "maybe we ought to talk to them first. Once they know who they're up against, they might think twice about a war of conquest here and go back to hunting for Wyandotte II."

"Especially if we give them a map," agreed Johnny.

"It's worth a try," said Catastrophe. "Hurricane, you go out and talk to them."

"You're not coming with me?" I asked.

"Let's be reasonable," said Catastrophe. "If it works, you won't need us—but if it turns out to be as dumb an idea as I think it is, there'll still be two of us left to destroy their army."

Well, I really couldn't argue with the logic of that, so I walked outside, found the power source for the wall, deactivated it, opened the door, and walked out into the fields beyond the temple. Catastrophe and Johnny shut the door so fast they almost took off my heel.

I found myself surrounded by a few hundred amoebas, so I raised my arm in the universal sign of peace.

"What are you pointing at, human?" demanded the closest amoeba.

"Nothing," I said. "I'm being friendly."

"So whenever you want to make friends, you point to the sky?"

"Well, yes, I guess I do," I admitted.

"You're not impressing us with your intellect," said the amoeba.

"Where did you guys learn to speak Terran?" I asked.

"We monitor your commercial holo transmissions," said the amoeba. "We especially like the ones involving Pirate Queens."

"Most people do."

"Okay, so much for small talk," said the amoeba. "Now it's time to kill you. Do you prefer strangulation, crucifixion, boiling in oil, or simply being torn asunder?"

"What if I were to show you how to get to Wyandotte II?" I said.

"I'd call that damned sporting of you," said the amoeba. "First we'll conquer Leviticus IV, kill all the humans, and raze the temple to the ground, and then we'll wage war against Wyandotte."

"You don't understand," I said. "I'm offering to *trade*. You leave us alone, and I'll supply you with the star charts you need."

"Yeah, that sounds good," said another amoeba.

"No," said a third. "Let's kill the humans first and then see if we can find Wyandotte on our own."

Pretty soon all the nearby amoebas were arguing, and the one I'd been speaking to sidled up to me.

"We're going to have to take a vote," it said. "This could take all day. Come with me; I've got a box lunch hidden away."

I followed it to a nearby forest. None of the other amoebas took any notice of us; they were too caught up in trying to decide whether to accept my proposal or not.

"By the way, have you got a name?" I asked when we finally sat down, protected by a pair of giant trees.

"Winoria," said the amoeba.

"That's a very feminine name for an amoeba that doesn't possess a gender," I said.

"I most certainly do," said Winoria. "I am a female."

"How can I tell the difference?"

"There are ways," said Winoria, slithering closer to me. "For example . . ."

It sure as shooting was some example. And just about the time I'd adjusted to that one, she showed me another. (Don't get upset, Langtry; this was long before I met you.)

Well, we spent an idyllic hour in the forest, indulging in our natural scientific curiosity. Then I heard the hum of a burner and the buzz of a screecher, and I could hear Johnny Testosterone's voice screaming things like *"Eat hellfire, you alien scum!"* and *"Kiss your ass good-bye, you godless heathen!"*

I jumped to my feet and started running back to the temple. The gate was open, and Johnny was standing just in front of it, weapons smoking.

"What the hell's going on?" I demanded.

"I got tired of waiting," he said, "so I killed 'em all. By God, that felt even better than a hot shower on a cold morning!"

"But they were considering going away without trying to conquer the planet after all."

"I figured that when I heard them all arguing," replied Johnny. "That's why I decided to start shooting. The old priest wasn't going to give us the Temple Virgin if the enemy declared peace on us."

I looked around. "What happened to them?"

"They melted. Disintegrated. Vanished." He suddenly saw Winoria coming up behind me. "Except for this one."

He aimed his burner at her, and I slapped it out of his hand before he could squeeze the trigger.

"Why the hell did you do that?" demanded Johnny.

"Leave her alone," I said.

"*Her?*" he repeated. "How do you know?"

I felt my face turn a bright red.

"None of your business," I said.

He looked from Winoria to me and back to Winoria. "That's perverted!" he snapped, picking up his pistol and tucking it away in his holster. Then: "Was she any good?"

"Where's Catastrophe?" I asked, ignoring his question.

"He found their wine cellar," answered Johnny. "I imagine you'll have to peel him off the floor by now."

Well, he obviously didn't know Catastrophe Baker. I figure he couldn't have downed more than eight or ten bottles by now, and that meant he wouldn't be even halfway to tipsy.

"Son of a bitch!" yelled Johnny suddenly. "Baker spent the last hour drinking, and you spent it committing sins they ain't even got names for yet, so that means I wiped the aliens out all by myself— so I got first claim on the Temple Virgin!"

Which didn't bother me at all. The girl in the gauzy dress suddenly seemed so *ordinary*, with nothing special or exotic to offer a man of the galaxy.

What *did* bother me was that Johnny Testosterone had wiped out all of Winoria's people, and as he went back into the temple I turned to her and expressed my regrets.

"No harm done," she said. "If you'll give me the star charts, I'll be on my way to Wyandotte II."

I handed them over. "Here they are," I replied. "But I can't help noting that you don't seem terribly distressed over the slaughter of your companions."

"Why should I be?" she replied, and suddenly she split into about half a million tiny pieces, which instantly began growing. "To the ship, my children!" she ordered them. As they rushed to obey her, she turned to me. "It was a memorable and stimulating interlude, Hurricane Smith," she said, "but I must say I find your method of procreation incredibly inefficient, no matter how much fun it is."

Then she was gone, and I turned back to the temple. Catastrophe met me as I approached the chamber where we'd met the High Priest.

"Johnny tells me you've been enjoying yourself," I said.

"He tells me the same thing about you," answered Catastrophe with a knowing grin.

"Some heroes we are," I said. "It looks like Johnny won the war all by himself."

"Not much of a war from what I could tell. Once I looked over the top of the wall and saw that an amoeba can't wear a weapon, I figured you could take care of yourself." He paused. "I never figured Johnny would fight 'em all himself."

"He wanted the reward worse than we did."

"Hell, I've already put in for my reward. I want the gold robe."

"I suppose, to be honest, I've already had my reward," I admitted, thinking wistfully of Winoria.

Suddenly we heard a shriek of abject horror, and a moment later Johnny Testosterone came racing out of the temple, hightailing it for the mountain range that was about two hundred miles past the forest, and looking neither right nor left.

"I wonder what the hell *that* was all about?" asked Catastrophe.

A couple of minutes later a skinny young man with a neatly trimmed beard and a couple of flowers stuck in his hair wandered out.

"Have either of you seen Johnny Testosterone?" he asked.

"Yeah," said Catastrophe. "He was headed due west like a bat out of hell."

"Damn!" said the young man, scuffing the tile with his sandaled foot.

"And who might you be?" I asked him.

"Me?" he replied. "I'm the Temple Virgin."

We never saw Johnny again.

"I think I liked Baker's version better," said Three-Gun Max.

"Wasn't much of an adventure," replied Baker. "Didn't have much of an aftermath, either. When we got back to a civilized world and I tried to sell the robe, I found out that it was made of spun pyrite."

"Could have been worse," suggested Max. "You could have wound up with the Temple Virgin."

"Well, it just goes to show that you can't trust priests," said Nicodemus Mayflower. "I figure that it's best not to believe anyone below the level of king, or maybe emperor."

"You ever met an emperor?" asked Max.

"Not yet," answered Mayflower. "But I've got my whole life ahead of me."

"Except for the part you've already wasted," observed Baker wryly.

"That goes without saying," replied Mayflower with dignity.

"DAMN IT!" roared Hurricane Smith, and suddenly we all turned to look at him. He was holding a scarf next to his cheek, and blood was seeping through it.

"I told you it happened before I met you!" he snapped at Langtry Lily.

She hissed and spit at him. He ducked, and her saliva hit the back of his chair and started dissolving it. A second later he had his burner about an inch from her nose.

"You try that again and this'll be the shortest goddamned honeymoon on record!"

"Your first spat?" asked Little Mike Picasso curiously.

"More like our two hundredth," answered Smith. "You'd think a race that produces eggs like there's no tomorrow wouldn't be so fucking jealous!"

He kept his gun trained on her for another few seconds, then twirled it around his finger and put it back in its holster, all in one fluid motion.

Langtry Lily leaned over and whispered to him again.

"Forget it!" he snapped. "What good does it do to apologize when I know you'll be slashing me or spitting at me again in a few minutes? We've got to lay down some ground rules here or else go our separate ways."

Suddenly Langtry Lily's whole demeanor changed. She began crying—huge, gut-wrenching sobs—and she buried her face in her hands.

"Now see what you've done," said Little Mike. "You've gone and broken her poor little insectoid heart." He paused, then added: "Always assuming she comes equipped with one, that is."

"Uh . . . I don't want to seem unduly insensitive," I interjected, "but can her tears do any harm to the table?"

Smith just glared at me without answering, and a moment later he put his hands on her shoulders to comfort her, but she kept on weeping and wailing to beat the band, and finally he walked to the bar and called Reggie over to him.

"You got any honey?" he asked.

Reggie quickly gave him a bottle of it. Smith walked back to his table, opened it, and spilled a little on Langtry Lily's forearm. She lifted her head to see what was happening, fluttered her nostrils a few times, stopped crying as quick as she'd begun, and then started sucking up the honey with that strawlike thing that shot out of the corner of her mouth.

"Another crisis averted," said Smith with a grimace.

"You could avert a lot of 'em if you'd just give up this taste you've acquired for alien females and go back to human women," said Baker.

"I like what I like," said Smith, jutting out his jaw.

"Okay, it's your life," said Baker with a shrug, "and I ain't the one to say that your tastes are perverted—but they sure could be a mite more practical."

"Let's change the subject before she starts paying attention," said Smith, watching as Langtry Lily finished cleaning the honey off her arm and inserted the straw into the bottle. "What have you been doing with yourself since the last time I saw you?"

"Oh, this and that, here and there," answered Baker. "Even

made it all the way to Sol's system." He paused. "Never quite got to Earth, though."

"Why not?"

Baker opened a fresh bottle of 130-proof Belarban whisky. "I got sidetracked in the Hall of the Neptunian Kings," he said, taking a huge swallow. "This story won't be over as quick as my last, since I'm the star of it—and I wouldn't want to go dry in the middle of it."

Catastrophe Baker in the Hall of the Neptunian Kings

Before Baker could even begin, Three-Gun Max spoke up.

"There ain't no Neptunian Kings," he said.

"What makes you think so?" retorted Baker.

"There ain't nothing at all on Neptune except a lot of empty real estate and a bunch of air nobody can breathe."

"Well, they *told* me it was Neptune," answered Baker, "but I suppose it could have been Jupiter."

"Ain't nothing there neither," said Max. "Only there's a whole lot more of it."

"Actually," offered Big Red, "there used to be a hockey team called the Neptunian Kings. But I don't think they ever got within two thousand parsecs of Neptune." He paused. "They weren't very good, anyway."

"Who's telling this story anyway?" demanded Baker pugnaciously.

"Go ahead and talk," said Max. "But I reserve the right to get up and leave if you start telling any whoppers."

"Fair enough," said Baker. He tapped the pearl handle of his burner. "And I reserve the right to blow your balls off if you even think of getting up."

"It figures to be true," added Nicodemus Mayflower. "After all, it's not as if he's talking about the Hall of the Neptunian Priests."

"Or hockey players," said Big Red.

"Or oversized killer roaches," muttered Hurricane Smith under his breath.

"Are you all gonna listen or not?" roared Baker, and suddenly a hush fell over the Outpost.

It happened maybe four years ago (began Baker, glaring at Max until he was sure he wasn't going to be interrupted again). I'd just left Oom Paul, the little diamond-mining world out by Antares, and I'd heard tell that Fort Knox wasn't radioactive any longer, and that all you had to do was just waltz in and carry out as many gold bars as you wanted, and there was nothing there to stop you except maybe thirty or forty guards, and that they were mostly little ones at that.

But my navigational computer and I got to telling dirty jokes to one another, and playing poker, and otherwise amusing ourselves to combat the boredom of the long voyage, and damned if we didn't combat it so well that the computer forgot to pay attention to where we were, and all of a sudden we were orbiting Neptune (or maybe Jupiter) rather than Earth.

Problem is, I didn't know it until we landed, and the ship told me I'd better put on a spacesuit and helmet. It struck me as kind of a strange request, but I just figured we'd touched down near a toxic waste dump. It wasn't until I stepped out of the ship that I realized that the landscape didn't bear a lot of resemblance to all the holos I'd seen of Earth.

I was about to climb back in and give the computer a piece of my mind when I saw a huge building off in the distance. It had all kinds of strange angles, and stained-glass windows with colors I hadn't never seen before, all of which roused my curiosity, so I decided to take a closer look at it.

I headed on over to it and found myself facing a door that must have been seventy feet high. I pushed against it, but it was latched or bolted from the inside and it didn't give an inch. This just made me more interested to see what was on the inside, so I walked around the whole of the building, which must have been about half a mile on each side, looking for a way in.

When I couldn't find none—there were maybe ten other doors, all of them locked—I decided to climb up the side of the building and ease myself in through one of the windows.

Well, let me tell you, that was a lot easier said than done. Oh, the building was easy enough to climb, because it was covered with weird carvings and strange-looking gargoyles, so I had no trouble getting handholds and footholds—but when I reached the window, which was maybe forty feet above the ground, I discovered that it was locked too, and strong as I am, I couldn't kick it in.

I considered melting it with my burner, but I wasn't exactly sure what the atmospheric make-up of Neptune was, and I figured that if it happened to have a high concentration of oxygen, like maybe eighty percent or so, I could set the whole planet on fire just by pulling the trigger.

So I kept climbing, and after another hour I reached the roof, which was about three hundred feet above the ground, and started walking along it, looking for vents or chimneys I could slide down. Sure enough, I found one smack-dab in the middle of the roof. Problem was, it went straight down, and I figured the fall could kill or cripple me, so I looked farther and finally found a hatch leading to the interior of the building. I decided it had been used by the guys who built the place, or maybe the one who had to keep the roof clean—but whoever used it was as big as the guys who walked through the doorways, because each step was maybe fifteen feet down from the last one.

I hung down from the top step by one arm, then let go and dropped maybe six feet to the next one, and climbed down the whole staircase like that. When I got to the bottom, I found myself in a pitch-black chamber. I turned on my helmet's spotlight, found a door, and pushed against it—and this one gave way.

I stepped out into a huge room, filled with two dozen ornate chairs, each capable of holding a being that was maybe seventy feet high.

Then I heard a voice in my ear: "You can breathe the air in here now."

I spun around and whipped out my pistol.

"Who said that?" I demanded.

"Me," came the answer. "Your suit. I have analyzed the air, and it is breathable."

"Thanks."

"It's just damned lucky you didn't break that window," said the suit.

I figured I could spend the rest of the day standing there arguing with it, or I could climb out of it and start exploring, so I did the latter.

Then I started at one end of the hall and began walking past all the chairs, and I decided that each of them was a throne, and had probably been retired when the king who sat on it had died or lit out for greener pastures.

Now, truth to tell, I didn't have no serious interest in Neptunian Kings, but I didn't have nothing against maybe finding some palace jewels, so I set out to see if there were any around for the taking.

The hall was mostly empty except for the chairs and some weird-looking tapestries hanging on the walls, but then I stumbled into an anteroom just behind Throne Number Nine—and what should I find but an absolutely gorgeous naked lady standing there staring at me.

"Good morning, ma'am," I said. "I'm Catastrophe Baker, at your service."

She didn't say a word or move a muscle, and I figured I'd kind of startled her into immobility.

"Dressed in kind of a hurry this morning, didn't you?" I said, trying to break the ice with a little friendly conversation.

She still didn't answer, so I walked a little closer to see if maybe she was a statue.

I couldn't see her breathing, and her eyes seemed fixed on some spot in the Hall of the Neptunian Kings, but she sure looked like a flesh-and-blood lady to me, rather than an imitation.

Then I realized that I had to be mistaken, because she was maybe a foot smaller than me, whereas anyone who lived in this place seemed like they couldn't go much less than fifty feet at the shoulder or the withers, whichever came first.

It was a shame, because in a long lifetime of looking at beautiful naked ladies, I hadn't never seen one more beautiful than this one.

I was going to leave and go back to looking for jewels and other marketable trinkets, but first I walked over to more closely admire the artist's handiwork. Even from two feet away you couldn't tell that she wasn't a real flesh-and-blood woman. Her skin was as smooth as could be, and I reached out to touch it, just to see if it was marble or stone or some artificial fabric—and damned if it didn't feel just like a real woman's skin.

I wondered just how realistic all the details were, so I kind of got to feeling her here and there and the next place—and when I laid my hand on the next place, she gave out a shriek that would have woke the dead and slapped my face.

"I thought you were a statue!" I said, startled.

"I was," she answered in the most melodic voice. "I apologize for hitting you. It was an instinctive reaction."

"You got some mighty powerful instincts there, ma'am," I said.

"Actually, I owe you my gratitude. I've been frozen in that position for the past fifteen millennia." She shuddered, which produced an eye-popping effect. "I could have been there forever if it hadn't been for you."

"Suppose you tell me what's going on, ma'am," I said, trying to grasp it all.

"I was King Thoraster's favored concubine, and when he thought I might have lost my heart to one of the palace guards, he had his technicians put me in stasis. There was only one way to release me in case he should change his mind at a later date, but he never thought any casual observer would be so gross and uncouth as to touch me *there*."

"How did he manage to freeze you for fifteen thousand years?" I asked.

She began explaining it to me, but as far as I'm concerned any sufficiently advanced technology is indistinguishable from double-talk, so I just kind of tuned her out after a couple of minutes and settled for admiring what old King Thoraster had been wasteful enough to freeze.

"And that's how he did it," she concluded.

"Just how big was he?" I asked.

"The same size as all the others," she replied, looking puzzled by my question.

"Then, pardon an indelicate inquiry, but how—?"

"Ah! I see!" she said. "Let's go into the Hall of the Kings, where the ceiling is a little higher."

I followed her until we were standing right in the middle of the hall.

"Now I want you to do me one last favor," she said.

"If it's within my power to do, ma'am," I said, "you've but to ask."

Suddenly she turned the prettiest shade of red. "It's very embarrassing," she said. "I think I'd prefer to whisper it to you."

"I'm all ears," I said.

She leaned over and began whispering.

"You want me to do *what*?" I asked aloud.

She turned an even brighter red and repeated it.

"Are you sure, ma'am?" I said. "I don't believe there can be five planets in the galaxy where doing that won't get us both thrown into the hoosegow." I paused. "Still, it sounds pretty interesting now that I come to think about it."

"Please!" she said.

So I did it—and then, right in the middle, when things were getting both interesting and complicated, she pushed me back.

"Get away!" she whispered.

"What's the matter?" I asked. "Did I do it wrong?"

"You were doing it perfectly!" she said, blushing furiously. "Now get back!"

So I got back, and none too soon, because suddenly she started growing right before my eyes, and a minute later she was mighty close to sixty feet tall, give or take a couple of inches.

"Thank you, Catastrophe Baker!" she said. "Thoraster's scientists made that the only way I could ever regain my true size. They never dreamed that I'd find anyone twisted enough to help me!" She smiled down on me. "I shall never forget you!"

"But we ain't finished!" I protested.

"It's no longer possible," she said. "I must find if any of my race still survives, and you must don your suit and return to your ship."

"I ain't in no hurry," I said.

"Yes, you are," she corrected me. "The mechanism that controls the Hall of the Kings sensed your metabolic needs and created a breathable atmosphere for you, but now that I am alive again, it will soon revert to the atmosphere that exists outside the building."

"This is a hell of a way to leave someone who did you such an enormous favor," I said unhappily.

She looked at me thoughtfully for a moment. "Yes, I suppose it is," she said, and scooped me up in one of her giant hands.

Decorum forbids me from telling you what she did next. Besides, there's worlds where I could get twenty years to life just for describing it.

When we were done, I put on my spacesuit and went back to the ship and took off. It was only after I'd left Sol far behind me that I remembered I hadn't finished looking for the jewels. I considered turning around and going back for them, but then I figured that I'd experienced the most precious jewel of all, so I just kept going, and never returned to the Hall of the Neptunian Kings.

I looked around the Outpost, and I'd have to say that as eager as the men were to find out exactly what that giant Neptunian lady had done to or with Catastrophe Baker, they didn't look half as fascinated as the women.

"I don't suppose you'd like to whisper the dirty parts to me?" suggested Sinderella.

"I wouldn't want to embarrass you, ma'am," said Baker.

"Just start whispering and we'll see who blushes first," she said confidently.

"I'm always looking to extend my knowledge," said Silicon Carny. "Perhaps you and I could finish what you and the Neptunian woman started."

"You tell me what she did once she was sixty feet tall," promised the Earth Mother, "and I'll tell you one that could get you thirty years just for listening to me."

"If we do what I'm thinking of," added Sinderella, giving him a sultry look, "I'll bet I wind up sixty feet tall too."

"And what if you lose?" asked Bet-a-World O'Grady, whose interest was suddenly piqued.

"I'll have had more fun than you have when you lose at cards," she replied with a smile.

"Hard to argue with that," agreed O'Grady.

Suddenly Big Red's computer came to life, and he looked at the holographic screen.

"Einstein wants to know how she got off the planet," he said.

"Beats me," answered Baker. "I don't rightly know for a fact that she did."

"He says she would have needed one hell of a ship, and he doesn't figure that it was fueled up and waiting for fifteen thousand years."

"I tell a story about a naked woman who's been kept in stasis for a hundred and fifty centuries, and suddenly grows sixty feet tall, and that's all he's concerned with?" demanded Baker.

"He says he's figured out all the other stuff, and it all makes scientific sense. The only thing that bothers him is the ship."

"He's figured out what they did?" said Silicon Carny.

"Yeah. He says that was the easy part."

"Tell him I want to talk to him later."

"He already knows," said Big Red.

"He does?" she said, surprised.

"He's Einstein, isn't he?" said Big Red, as if that was all the explanation anyone required.

"Sixty feet tall!" mused Nicodemus Mayflower. "Hell, she was even too big for Magic Abdul-Jordan!"

"She sounds more like Hurricane's kind of woman than Baker's," observed Max.

"What do you mean?" asked Baker.

"Well, whatever else she was, she sure as hell wasn't human," said Max.

"She was human enough," replied Baker with a fond smile of recollection.

"You didn't exactly describe her, except to say she was beautiful," said Little Mike Picasso. "What did she look like? Maybe I can draw a sketch of her."

"Long auburn hair down almost to her waist," said Baker, looking off into space as he pictured his Neptunian lady. "Full moist red lips. High cheekbones. Tiny, little nose. And her eyes were something else." He paused. "Hungry."

"You're hungry?" I asked.

"No," he answered. "She had hungry eyes."

"That's not really much help," said Little Mike.

"That's what she looked like," said Baker.

"No one has hungry eyes."

"*She* did."

"Look," said Little Mike in his best professional manner, "eyes can be lots of things. They can be blue or brown or gray or green or black. They can be narrow or round or slanted. They can be crossed or cocked. They can even be flashing. But they can't be hungry."

"Sure, they can," said Hurricane Smith.

"Another quarter heard from," said Little Mike. He turned to Smith. "Have you ever met a girl with hungry eyes?"

"Almost," answered Smith.

"You almost met one?"

"She was almost a girl," said Smith.

"Somehow I sense another story in the offing," said Max.

The Gril with the Hungry Eyes

It was maybe ten, eleven years ago (began Smith), out by the Sambakki Cluster. There was a terraformed moon there called Carnival, and I stopped by to see exactly what it had to offer.

If Bet-a-World O'Grady had visited the place, he would have thought he'd died and gone to heaven. I saw more human and alien gambling dens than I'd ever seen in one place before, and they had some pretty high rollers. It started raining while I was there, and I saw a couple of guys bet fifty thousand credits on which raindrop would roll down the window fastest.

Then there was a row of theaters, ranging from ornate opera houses to small tents, and the entertainments ran the gamut from *Figaro* and Shakespeare to strip shows and music hall comics. The streets were filled with jugglers, acrobats, magicians, musicians, even half a dozen puppeteers. In the distance I could see fireworks from a dozen theme parks, some for aliens, some for kids, some for very adventurous adults.

I figured I'd take a room at one of the hotels and then, after I'd had a good night's sleep, start exploring Carnival in earnest, but as I approached a likely hostelry a stunning woman happened to pass by. I got a whiff of her perfume and a look at the way she walked away, kind of like jelly on springs, and I just automatically fell into step behind her.

Finally, when she came to the end of the block, she stopped before crossing the street, and I caught up with her.

"You've been following me," she said in lilting tones. She didn't sound upset, just like she was stating a fact, which in fact she was.

"I don't mean to annoy you or insult you," I began, "but you've got the most exciting perfume I've ever encountered."

She laughed. "I don't wear perfume."

"But—"

"Those are pheromones," she replied. "*My* pheromones. Perfume manufacturers have been trying to reproduce the effect for thousands of years."

"Then I'm at a loss to understand why you don't have a couple of hundred men following you," I said.

"Because I released them in your vicinity."

"I beg your pardon?" I said.

"You're Hurricane Smith, aren't you?" she said.

"Yes."

"Your reputation precedes you. It's well known that you have a taste for, shall we say, the exotic?"

"I'm not much into whipping and such," I said.

"I meant that you prefer alien women."

"Are you telling me you're not human?"

"I am a Gril," she responded. "We are an ancient race who dwell beyond the Greater Magellanic Cloud."

"You sure *look* like a real woman," I said.

"Oh, I'm real, all right," she said. "Come up to my room with me and I'll prove it."

"I don't even know your name," I pointed out.

"Vethusia," she said.

She took me by the arm and headed off to the Womb, which was the name of her hotel.

"How do you differ from women, other than in being able to aim your pheromones?" I asked her.

"Oh, there are some minor differences," she said. "You'll find out about them later. But," she added, kind of rubbing up against me, "I'm just like a human woman in all the ways that count."

Which was good enough for me, and which she proceeded to prove during the next couple of hours.

It was when I woke up in the morning that I began to realize just *how* alien Vethusia was.

She was still in bed, with a sleep mask over her eyes, breathing regularly, and I tiptoed around the room to where I'd left my clothes so that I wouldn't wake her. When I got to her side of the bed, I saw something shining on the nightstand, so I walked over to see what it was.

And what it turned out to be was her fingernails.

Now, I know some women wear false fingernails, but these were too long for that. I mean, they were the whole things, right down to the cuticles.

Then, while I was puzzling over this discovery, I saw her ears. Not on her head. On the nightstand, between her fingernails and her nose.

I reached out to touch the nose, to see what it was made of, since it had sure appeared real the night before—and damned if it didn't skitter away from me, coming to a halt at the far side of the nightstand. I tried to pick it up, and it ducked and darted away again.

Next I tried to touch her ears—and three of her fingernails dug into my hand.

I figured I needed some answers, so I gently prodded her and said, "Hey, Vethusia—wake up."

She sat up, the mask still covering her eyes.

"What is it, my love?" she asked.

(*Goddammit, Langtry—stop looking at me like that! This all happened before you were even hatched!*)

Where was I? Oh, yeah—she asked, "What is it?"

And I said, "There seems to be a little less of you than there was last night. Or at least it's spread out a little more."

"I *told* you I was a Gril," she said.

"But you didn't tell me what a Gril *was*," I pointed out. "In fact, I still don't know."

"Are you unhappy?" she asked. "Did I fail to satisfy your bestial needs?"

"I didn't say I was unhappy, just surprised," I answered. "And I prefer to think of my needs as romantic."

"Then romance me and stop complaining," she commanded.

And suddenly the room was filled with that irresistible odor, and we had an instant replay of the previous night, and I had to admit that her not having a nose or ears or fingernails didn't make a bit of difference at all.

When it was over and we were lying side by side, I gently stroked her hair, half expecting it to come off in my hand, and then reached to remove her mask.

"What are you doing?" she asked suspiciously.

"I want to look into your eyes," I said. "They're so deep and blue."

"Don't."

"But—"

"Just leave well enough alone," she said.

And then I figured it out—she didn't have any eyes either. I must have said it aloud, because she replied that of course she had eyes.

"Then let me see them," I said.

"They're not here right now."

"I don't think I follow you," I said.

"They're out hunting."

I suddenly decided to continue the conversation from the far side of the room, while getting dressed as quickly as possible.

"Okay," I said. "Let me make sure I've got this straight. Your eyes haven't fallen out or been misplaced or stolen or anything like that. They're just out hunting."

"That's right."

"I hate to seem ignorant, but what do eyes hunt?"

"Breakfast, of course."

The more she answered me in that conversational tone, the more alien she seemed.

"Where do they hunt it?"

"Wherever they can find it," she said.

I decided I didn't really want to see her with her mask off after all, and now that I came to think about it, she looked a lot better with her nose and ears back on too. I conveyed this thought to her, and after she felt blindly around the nightstand for a minute she put them back where they belonged. When that was done she pressed her fingertips against the nightstand and all her nails jumped into place.

Then, suddenly, I heard a strange sound. When I looked around, I saw a pair of eyeballs rolling across the floor. They reached the side of the bed and began bouncing up and down until they wound up on top of the covers, where they rolled over to her hand. The second she felt them she picked one up, turned her back to me, pulled off her sleep mask, and put it into her eye socket, then did the same with the other. When she was done she turned to me and smiled.

"Better?" she asked.

"Much," I said.

Her left eye burped.

I edged toward the door. "It's been very nice knowing you, Vethusia."

"You're not leaving already?" she said.

"Well, it's late and I've got things to do," I said.

"It's early and you've got nothing to do."

"Then I'll think of something to do," I said fervently.

"You didn't seem to mind my company all that much when we were making love."

"I didn't know how many detachable parts you had when we were making love," I shot back. I stared at her for a minute and then asked, "What else comes loose?"

"You don't want to know."

"Why?" I said. "How many more nightmares can you give me?"

"All right," she said with a sigh. "I don't want to set up house-keeping with a bigot who hates Grils."

"I don't hate Grils," I said. "I just don't understand them a lot more than I don't understand most other things in the universe."

"We'll have one last fling for the road," she said, "and then we'll go our separate ways."

"Not a chance," I said.

But before I could open the door she hit me with that natural perfume again, and sure enough, we had one last fling for the road.

"Good-bye, Hurricane Smith," she said when I'd finished getting dressed. "Let me give you something to remember me by."

"Lady, I ain't *ever* going to forget you!" I said adamantly.

"You're sure I can't give you a remembrance?"

"I'm going to have to see a shrink to get rid of some of the remembrances you already gave me," I said.

"I could make you stay, you know," said Vethusia.

"I know."

"And you'd love every minute of it."

"Until I came down with a cold and a stuffed nose," I replied.

She found that amusing and started shaking with laughter, and I snuck out the door before any unexpected parts could come off, and a minute later I was out in the street, wondering which way the spaceport was. I chanced to look up for just an instant, and there she was, a vision of loveliness, staring at me from the window. She looked so little and lonely and vulnerable, I felt like a cad for leaving her.

Then she winked one of those big wandering blue eyes at me, and I decided that even cads have their good points. Twenty minutes later I took off from Carnival, trying not to think of all the good times I could have had with the Gril I left behind.

"I don't want to dwell on a painful subject," said Baker, "but you could avoid a shitload of trouble if you'd just stick with human women."

"Like you did with the Neptunian concubine?" asked Smith irritably.

"That was an accident."

"So was this," said Smith. "I don't seek out alien ladies, you know."

Langtry Lily hissed softly.

"Except for you, my dear," he added quickly.

Suddenly Little Mike Picasso jumped to his feet and stared out one of the windows.

"What's the matter?" I asked him.

"There was a huge explosion," he said. "Either the sun just went nova or the shooting's getting awful close."

"Fifty to one that it's the war," said Bet-a-World O'Grady.

There weren't any takers.

"Wonder just what kind of aliens they are?" mused Baker.

"Whatever they are, I got an unhappy premonition that they ain't gonna be as sexually motivated as the ones you and the Hurricane keep running into," said Max.

Nicodemus Mayflower turned to Catastrophe Baker. "What's the most dangerous race you ever came across?" he asked.

"Women," said Baker.

"I mean an alien race," said Mayflower.

"So do I," answered Baker, sticking by his guns.

"How about you, Gravedigger?"

"I don't know who was the most dangerous," answered Gaines. "The Domarians were the most exhausting."

"How so?" asked Mayflower.

"There was a warrant out on a couple of 'em, so I flew to Domar to see if I could pick up the reward." He paused and took a swallow of his drink. "Interesting world, Domar. No cars, no buses, no trains, no airplanes, no boats, no golf carts, no roads. Just Domarians. They're about forty feet tall, and most of that is leg. They hate the night and spend their whole lives walking around and around their world, following the sun over the horizon—except for when they're killing each other, that is."

"Did you find the ones you were looking for?"

"Yeah, but I must have lost thirty pounds catching up with them," said Gaines.

"What about you, Hurricane?" asked Mayflower.

"I get along pretty well with most aliens," he answered as Langtry Lily glared at him.

"So we've heard," said Max dryly.

"Big Red?" asked Mayflower.

"You've got to understand that I look at it from a different perspective," said Big Red. "I'm an athlete, not a hero or a bounty hunter or even a soldier. I'd say that the toughest aliens, physically, were the Torquals. They stand about twelve feet tall, all of it muscle, and the last time a human team challenged them to a game of murderball the Torquals won sixteen, five, eight, and three."

"I've never seen murderball," said Sahara del Rio. "What does that score mean?"

"The Torquals scored sixteen goals, the Men scored five, the Torquals killed eight men, and the Men killed three Torquals." Big Red smiled. "It's a vigorous game, ma'am."

"So they were the toughest," said Sahara.

"Physically."

"What other ways are there?" she asked.

"Well, there's mentally," answered Big Red. "No Grumarite has ever lost a chess match except to another Grumarite. And then there are the Quintalias, who invented five-dimensional checkers."

"How do you play that?" asked O'Grady.

"Beats me," said Big Red. "You'd have to ask a Quintalia, and they're so busy peeking into other dimensions that they don't always answer."

"So you'd say that the toughest are the Torquals and the smartest are the Grumarites and the Quintalias?" asked Mayflower.

"The toughest I've seen in competition," Big Red corrected him. "Personally, I'd put Einstein up against any of them."

"You mean any Grumarite or Quintalia."

"I mean *any* of them."

"Come on," said Mayflower. "How do you expect a blind man to defeat a Torqual?"

"He's Einstein," said Big Red. "He'd find a way."

"My money would be on the Torqual," said O'Grady.

"You'd lose."

"Oh, yeah?" said O'Grady. "Ask him how he'd win."

Big Red tapped a message, waited for Einstein to reply, and then read the holographic screen.

"He says it would be easy."

"Did he say *how*?" insisted O'Grady.

"Yeah. He says E equals MC squared."

"So what? Everyone knows that."

"True—but only *he* knows how to apply it."

"Poppycock."

Big Red's screen came to life again.

"He says if you'll put up five hundred credits to his ten, he'll prove it right now."

Suddenly a look of uncertainty crossed O'Grady's face. "Tell him I don't want to take his money."

The computers exchanged messages again.

"He says not to worry—you won't."

"Some other time."

"He says he's been analyzing things, and if the war gets much closer you may never have another chance."

"I'll learn to live with the disappointment," said O'Grady.

"Too bad," said the Reverend Billy Karma. "I love watching Good and Evil going at it hammer and tongs."

"Which of them would be Good?" asked Max.

"Whichever one won, of course," said Billy Karma. "God don't let Evil get a leg up in these matters."

"It must be nice to be that certain of things," said Max.

"It *is* comforting," agreed the Reverend.

"How about you, Max?" said Nicodemus Mayflower.

"I give up," said Max. "How *about* me?"

"I mean, who were the most dangerous aliens you ever faced?"

"You mean other than overly aggressive redheads named Thelma?" said Max. "Well, actually Hurricane Smith's story about the hungry eyes reminded me of them a little bit."

"Of redheads named Thelma?"

"No. Of dangerous aliens."

"Yours had hungry eyes too?" asked Smith, suddenly interested.

Max shook his head. "Nope. But they were a formidable bunch just the same. Hell, if it wasn't for me, they might have overrun the whole galaxy."

"Thank heaven for small favors," muttered Little Mike Picasso sarcastically.

"Thank someone else," said the Reverend Billy Karma. "I happen to hold the copyright to heaven."

"So who were these aliens anyway?" asked Big Red.

The Pirates of Dawn

Ever hear of Ophir (began Max)? It's a mining world out on the Rim. Rich in diamonds, lots of other precious stones. Not a bad place, really. Good atmosphere, only about eighty percent standard gravity. They built a hospital for heart patients out there, since the gravity puts so little stress on them.

But they had a problem. Same problem you'd expect any world with that many diamonds to have.

Security at the mines was tight, and not many diamonds were smuggled off Ophir. A couple of local warlords tried to raid the place, but they didn't have much luck.

But then came the Pirates of Dawn and *they* made out like, well, pirates.

"So why were they called the Pirates of Dawn?" asked Big Red.

"I'm coming to that," said Max irritably.

They were aliens (said Max). Nobody knew where they came from. They never made a daylight raid, and they never came in the dead of night. Twilight didn't seem to interest them either. They always came just as the sun was rising, and let me tell you—they were *tough* motherfuckers. First raid they made, they killed seventeen security guards and made off with about forty million credits' worth of gemstones. Didn't lose a single man, either.

(Well, "man" is the wrong word for 'em. They had three legs, which made running a bit of a problem, but you couldn't knock one of 'em off his pins no matter how hard you hit him. Matter of fact, they were three-sided all the way up, with three arms, each a third of the way around the trunk of the body from the last one, and three large eyes spaced evenly around the head. Only one mouth, but it wasn't always pointed in the direction they were going.)

They never gave any warning before their raids. They just showed up, blazing away with some kind of pulse weapons. To this day no one knows why they were interested in diamonds, but my guess is they traded them to some renegade humans for bigger weapons and faster ships.

Anyway, they made seven raids the first year, and when the dust had cleared they'd damn near bankrupted the colony—those members of it that were still alive.

I'd heard about Ophir's problems, and having nothing better to do, I showed up one morning and offered my services. They were so desperate that they didn't even haggle about my fee—one diamond for each Pirate killed, and a ten-diamond bonus if I could kill them all or chase 'em away for good—so I took a room in the best hotel in town, a place called The Uncut Diamond, and waited for them to come back.

Problem was, I couldn't really plan anything until I knew they were on their way, and like I said, they never gave any warning. They'd just show up out of nowhere, take what they wanted, and vanish just as quick.

I'd been there twenty-seven days when the next raid occurred. I'd been sitting out every night, and going to bed at midday, and this particular day I saw about fifteen of 'em walking toward the brand-new reinforced assay office where the stones were kept before being shipped back to the Monarchy. Some of the security guards started firing away, but the Pirates never even flinched. They just fired back with deadly accuracy, and a minute later eight guards lay dead on the ground.

I studied them carefully. I knew we'd killed one, so they couldn't be impervious to our weapons, but nothing we'd fired that morning seemed to damage them. Then I realized that what *looked* like military uniforms were actually suits of armor, based on some alien scientific principle that could repel the light from burners and the noise from screechers. About the only way to take one of the Pirates out was to blow his head off, and from two hundred yards—which was the distance at which our men started firing—a head shot with a hand weapon would be a stroke of dumb luck. The Pirates' weapons were a lot more accurate, and with those huge eyes they didn't need any telescopic sights.

I waited until they entered the assay building. Then I moved forward and took up a safe defensive position about thirty yards away behind a trash atomizer, and waited for them to come out, which they did about five minutes later.

I drew a bead on the first one's head, fired, and blew him to kingdom come. I nailed the second one behind his ear, and the rest took off like bats out of hell. They weren't exactly graceful on those three legs, but they kept spinning around as they ran, and I couldn't manage another head shot.

I didn't want to step out in the open and chase them because I knew their eyesight and handguns were better than mine, so I waited until they vanished in the distance. When their ship took off a moment later, people began pouring out into the street to tend to the dead security guards.

As for me, I walked over and examined the bodies of the two Pirates I had killed, but it was a useless exercise. There wasn't enough left of the heads to learn anything, and the bodies were so well armored that it wasn't worth the effort to hunt for weak spots.

Next I examined them for anything remotely resembling a religious artifact, and was relieved as hell when I couldn't find one, because that showed me the way to beat the sons of bitches.

I waited for the mayor to appear—he'd lagged behind until he was dead certain the ship wasn't coming back—and I demanded two diamonds for killing the Pirates. The mayor countered that I owed Ophir eight diamonds for the dead guards, and that came to a net payment of six diamonds.

"Bullshit!" I said. "This is Three-Gun Max you're talking to, and if you don't pay me what you owe me, I ain't gonna tell you how to defeat the Pirates of Dawn."

"You know how?" he asked, surprised.

"Yeah, I know how," I answered. "And if you want me to share that knowledge with you, I want my two diamonds right now."

The mayor and the city council started whispering amongst themselves for a minute or two. Then they all straightened up and turned to me.

"Come to my office in half an hour and I'll pay you your diamonds," said the mayor.

"Fine."

"Now—how do we kill the Pirates?"

"Come to your office in half an hour and I'll be happy to tell you thirty seconds later," I said. "Assuming I've been paid in the interim."

Well, suddenly he couldn't see no reason not to go directly to his office, so I followed him there and waited patiently until he unlocked his safe and withdrew a couple of fine-looking diamonds.

"All right," he said, handing them to me. "Here's your payment. Now, how do we kill the Pirates of Dawn?"

"By recognizing that they *are* the Pirates of Dawn," I said, "and asking yourself why."

"I don't understand," said the mayor.

"Look," I said, "even though we haven't had much luck to date, they know we can kill them. So they have some alternatives—they can attack under cover of night, when they're almost impossible to see, or they can attack in daylight, when we'd be sitting ducks if we tried to pick them off. But they don't do either—they always attack at dawn. Why?"

"I don't know."

"Neither did I," I admitted. "Until I examined the two I killed."

"What did you find?"

"Nothing," I said. "And that was the key."

"Finding nothing was the key?" he repeated, puzzled.

"Yeah. If they'd been carrying anything that implied that they worshiped the sun or the moon, even something that showed they felt the summer and winter solstices were special, it might have explained why they always attack at dawn. But they weren't carrying anything like that—so it had to be those huge eyes. They *can't* attack in daylight; the sun blinds them."

"Why not at night, then?" asked the mayor.

"Because Ophir doesn't have a moon, it's the only planet in its system, and it's sixteen light-years from the closest star. Your nights are pitch black, so that even the Pirates of Dawn can't see without using some kind of torch that would attract immediate attention and pinpoint their whereabouts."

"Okay, it makes sense," said the mayor. "But that just explains why they attack at dawn. It doesn't explain how to defeat them."

I shook my head sadly. "You're so dumb I really ought to double my fee," I said. "But what the hell, a bargain is a bargain. Give me ten men, and we'll be ready for them the next time."

And we were. They showed up exactly thirty days later, and we were waiting for them with the brightest spotlights money could buy. We turned them on when the Pirates were maybe fifty yards from the assay building, and picked them off at our leisure while they staggered blindly through the streets.

We let one survive and make it back to the ship so that he could tell all the other Pirates that Ophir had doped them out and they'd better plunder other worlds from now on. And from that day to this, the Pirates of Dawn have never returned.

As for me, I lived like a king for almost a year before I ran into Bet-a-World O'Grady out near the Delphini system and lost the remainder of my diamonds to him in a single night at the poker table.

"Don't feel too bad," said O'Grady to Max. "I only had them for about three days before I lost them to Underlay McNair." He shook his head ruefully. "It was bluffer's heaven. I lost fifty million credits with nothing to the nine. The son of a bitch was sitting there holding nothing to the jack."

"Underlay McNair," mused Catastrophe Baker. "I've heard of him."

"He used to be a bookie," said O'Grady. "Remember the big

heavyweight freehand championship match between Backbreaker Barnes and the Penjak Kid?"

"Who could ever forget it?" interjected Big Red. "It was the only fight in history where both men died in the ring."

"Right," said O'Grady. "And since they both died, the bookies didn't have to pay off. Old Underlay, he was sitting there on maybe fifteen million credits' worth of bets, so he decided that with a grubstake like that it was time to quit booking bets and start making them."

"I saw the Penjak Kid once," said the Gravedigger. "I always figured the only two men in the galaxy who could take him were Catastrophe Baker and me—and I wasn't so sure about me."

"I don't know about the Kid," said Hurricane Smith, "but I was there the night Backbreaker Barnes whipped Jimmy Steelfist, and I think I could have taken him."

Big Red's computer screen came to life.

"Einstein says you're all wrong," said Big Red. "Only one person could have beaten either Barnes or the Kid."

"Who was he?" asked Gaines.

Big Red transmitted the question, then smiled as the answer came onto his screen.

"It wasn't a *he* at all."

"An alien?" said Gaines.

"No," said Big Red. "A woman."

"I don't believe it!" scoffed Gaines.

"Einstein's never wrong."

"He is this time."

Einstein tapped away and a new message appeared on the holoscreen.

"He wants to know if you've ever heard of the Cyborg de Milo," said Big Red.

"The Cyborg de Milo?" repeated Gaines. "Is he making this up?"

"No," said Achmed of Alphard from across the room. "I knew her. She exists."

"And she's called the Cyborg de Milo?"

"Now she is. I knew her as Venus."

"I'm not going to even ask what her full name was," muttered Gaines.

"Who cares about her name?" said O'Grady. "Tell us why Einstein thinks she was capable of beating Backbreaker Barnes and the Penjak Kid."

"He doesn't *think* it," Big Red corrected him. "He *knows* it."

"And he's right," added Achmed.

"Still why?"

The Cyborg de Milo

Her real name (said Achmed of Alphard)—or, rather, her *original* name—was Venus Delmonico, and back when I first met her, she was as pretty and polite and refined a girl as you'd ever want to know. She had passed the entrance exam for Aristotle—that's the university planet, you know—and she was specializing in something terribly esoteric. I can't remember exactly what it was—poetry of the third century of the Galactic Era, perhaps. Anyway, she was supposed to already be such an expert that there were only two people in the whole of the Monarchy who could teach her anything more, and both of them were professors on Aristotle.

But three weeks before she was scheduled to leave for Aristotle, thieves broke into her parents' home. Her father tried to stop them and was killed for his trouble. Her mother fled, screaming for help, and they killed her too. Then, to cover their tracks, they set fire to the house, destroying everything she and her parents owned, including her collection of incredibly rare volumes of poetry. The only reason Venus herself wasn't killed was because she was studying at the local library.

I was a neighbor, and I was there, looking at the smoldering ruins, when Venus arrived. The police told her what had happened. I expected her to become hysterical, or perhaps to faint, but she did neither. Her face became expressionless, her voice became softer, and she questioned the officer in charge until she had nothing more to learn from him.

Then she spotted me, walked over, and asked me to contact Aristotle and tell them that she would not be attending, neither during the coming semester nor in the foreseeable future.

"But what will you do with yourself?" I said. "You mustn't withdraw from society because of this tragedy."

"I'm not withdrawing," she said calmly, almost coldly. "I have work to do."

"Your studies?"

A look of contempt crossed her pretty face. "No, Achmed," she replied. "*Important* work." She paused and took one last look at the ruins of her house, then turned back to me. "I will see you again before it begins."

And then she was gone.

I didn't hear from her for almost a year. I made some inquiries, but nobody else seemed to know what had happened to her either. Then one evening she showed up at my house without any warning.

"Venus!" I said. "Where have you been?"

"Preparing," she replied, as I ushered her into the living room.

"You haven't changed a bit," I said, staring at her.

She chuckled. "Thank you, Achmed. That is the first time I've laughed since my parents were slaughtered."

"What did I say that was so funny?" I asked, confused.

"I have changed more than you can imagine," she replied.

I looked her up and down. "I can't see it," I said. "I doubt that you've gained or lost as much as two pounds."

"I've lost more than two pounds," she said. "I've lost two arms."

I stared at her arms. "I don't understand."

She tapped the fingers of her right hand against her left arm. They made a strange, clicking sound.

"I had my arms replaced," she said.

"But *why?*" I asked, shocked.

"Because I didn't need them," she replied. She held her arms out. "I needed *these*."

"For what?"

"For my work."

"I thought your work was studying poetry."

"My work is killing people who deserve killing," she replied. She spread out the fingers of her right hand. "This finger shoots lasers. This one shoots sonar. This one is an energy pulse gun. And this one shoots bullets." Then she displayed the fingers of her left hand. "Flamethrower, atomic drill, spring-loaded knife, and a light that will not only illuminate the darkness but also pierce through fog and opaque alien atmospheres."

She tapped a finger against her beautiful blue eyes. There was that same noise.

"My eyes not only see everything you see, but they can also see into the infra-red and ultra-violet spectrums. The left one is also telescopic and the right one can become a microscope."

"My God!" I exclaimed. "What have you done to yourself?"

"I've circumvented millions of generations of evolution and become totally efficient," she answered. "From this day forward I am no longer Venus Delmonico. I am now the Cyborg de Milo. Like the Venus of old, I have lost my arms—but unlike her, I have replaced them with something better."

"We have police to hunt down criminals, and out on the Frontier there are bounty hunters like Gravedigger Gaines."

"They work for money," she replied. "I work for justice."

"But—"

"The police have been hunting my parents' killers for a year. Have they made any progress?"

"I don't know," I admitted.

"I do. They're no closer to solving the murders now than the night they occurred."

"I don't know what to say," I told her. "I feel that you have thrown your future away."

"Perhaps you have thrown yours away," she suggested, walking to the door, "by not doing everything within your power to guarantee that you live to *have* a future."

It took her three days to track down her parents' murderers. I don't know what she did to them, but I heard that there wasn't enough left of them to bury.

She stayed in the Alphard system for another month. Then, after she'd hunted down our most wanted criminals, she decided to seek greater challenges, and she left for the Inner Frontier.

From time to time I read about her, or hear rumors of a cyborg woman who has killed men that even Catastrophe Baker would think twice about facing, but I do not know for an absolute fact that she is still alive.

But if she isn't, I sure wouldn't want to be in the same room, or even on the same planet, with the man who could kill her.

"Einstein says she's alive, all right," said Big Red, reading his screen. "He met her just last month on Greenpasture II."

"Why?" asked Max. "What could either of them possibly want with the other?"

"She wanted his advice, of course," said Big Red. "Why does anyone meet with Einstein?"

"What kind of advice?" Max persisted.

"She still has two very human legs. She wanted his opinion concerning what to replace them with."

"How the hell many more built-in weapons does she need?"

"She has enough weapons," answered Big Red. "But that doesn't mean she can't improve her efficiency. Does she want legs that can stand up under four gravities? Legs that can let her jump forty feet into the air? Feet with suction cups on the bottoms, for walking up walls and across ceilings? Legs with compartments to hold energy packs, or possibly with refrigeration units to store food when she's away from civilization?"

"Okay, okay," said Max irritably. "I get the point."

"You know," mused the Gravedigger, "I *have* heard of her. I never knew her name—and some of the feats she pulled off sounded like tall tales. But I've been hearing about a cyborg woman for years now, a woman who can do all the things that Achmed says that this Cyborg Venus can do."

"Cyborg de Milo," Achmed corrected him.

"Yeah?" said Max, still looking for someone to argue with. "Well, if she's so close, how come she hasn't shown up at the Outpost?"

"Maybe she's not thirsty," said Nicodemus Mayflower.

"Or maybe she planned to, and either the Navy or the aliens blew her ship to smithereens," added Little Mike Picasso. "There's a war going on out there, you know."

"If anyone took a shot at her, I hate to think of what would happen to them if they missed," said Achmed.

"How long has she been a cyborg?" asked Nicodemus Mayflower.

"Eighteen years," said Achmed.

"That's a long time to go around with a mad-on," said Hurricane Smith. "Maybe she just needs someone to love her."

"She's not your type," said Catastrophe Baker.

"How do you know?" asked Smith.

"She's human."

Langtry Lilly began hissing at Smith.

"It was just an academic proposition, my dear," he said quickly, prepared to duck if she spit at him again. She glared at him, and he took her hand in his and began stroking it gently. After a moment she relaxed and went back to scouring the table for those few grains of sugar she'd missed.

"Anyway, she sounds like one tough lady," said Little Mike.

"Can't argue with that," agreed the Gravedigger. "I thought I'd met the toughest women on the Frontier, but this Cyborg de Milo sounds like she could wipe up the floor with them."

"Who were they?" asked Willie the Bard, looking up from his notebook.

"You ever hear of the O'Toole sisters?" asked Gaines.

"Nope," answered the Bard.

"I did," said Nicodemus Mayflower.

"Me, too," said Baker. "Weren't they named something weird, like Silk and Satin?"

"I thought it was Rubber and Lace," said Nicodemus.
"Close, but no cigar," said the Gravedigger.

The Romantic Tale of Velvet and Leather O'Toole

Nobody knows when they came out to the Frontier (began Gaines). Hell, they might even have been born out here. I do know that they grew up in Nightmare Alley, which was the criminal sector of Port Raven, a nondescript little world in the Willoughby Sector—and anyone who can stay alive in Nightmare Alley for more than a day or two has developed some real survival skills.

They weren't the brightest girls I ever met—there's no way they could ever have gotten accepted on Aristotle like the Cyborg de Milo did—but they obeyed the laws, worked hard at their jobs, and saved their money.

As a matter of fact, that's how I came into contact with them. Seems we were all using the same bank at the time. I wasn't thrilled with Port Raven, but it had a branch of the Bank of Spica, and that's where I kept my main account.

The girls were pretty in a plain kind of way, if that makes sense to you. Nothing wrong with either of them, but they didn't make you want to bay at the moon or go slay dragons the way that, say, Silicon Carny does. One always dressed in velvet and the other always wore leather, and after awhile any other names they might have had just faded away and they were Velvet and Leather, the O'Toole sisters.

The bank was run by a skinny little runt who went by the name of Throckmorton Lewis Frothingham. I'll swear his name weighed more than he did. He was a precise little man. He always looked like he'd just come from his tailor, even when it was hot and muggy out. There are still a few people here and there who wear glasses, but he's the only one in my experience who wore a pince-nez—you know, the spectacles that fit on the bridge of your nose. He always had a silk handkerchief stuck in the cuff of his left sleeve, and his shoes were polished to within an inch of their lives.

I spent a lot of time at that bank, waiting for various bounties to be wired to me—well, to Spica, actually, but then they'd notify the Port Raven branch—and I saw a lot of the sisters. I don't know what kind of jobs they had, but they were paid in cash on a daily basis, and every night just before the bank closed they'd stop by and deposit their money. And little Throckmorton Lewis Frothingham was always there to greet them, and exchange a few pleasantries, and personally handle their transactions.

Then one day, with no warning at all, the Bellargo Gang showed up, seventy-three members strong, to rob the place.

"The Bellargo Gang?" said Baker. "I haven't heard of them in close on to a dozen years now. Whatever happened to them?"

"Stop interrupting and maybe you'll find out," said the Gravedigger.

The girls were there (continued Gaines), and maybe two or three others, a couple of robot tellers, plus Frothingham, of course—and me.

"You're a bounty hunter!" whispered Frothingham. "Aren't you going to do something?"

"All my money's on Spica," I answered. "Whatever they do to your bank, it won't cost me a credit."

"But it's your job to bring these villains to justice!" he said.

"I'll take on any half dozen of them," I said, "but there's got to be better than fifty of 'em here. The way I see it, my job is to stay alive until I can meet them under more favorable circumstances."

The whole time we were talking Bellargo himself was staring at me, and finally he walked over.

"Ain't you Gravedigger Gaines?" he said.

"Some people call me that," I answered.

"You've been a real thorn in my side over the years," he continued. "You've killed six of my men, and four or five others deserted rather than take a chance of running into you."

"What a waste," I said.

He looked puzzled. "A waste?"

"If they quit, I don't get any bounties and you don't get any flunkies."

He threw back his head and laughed. "I like you, Gravedigger Gaines," he said. "It seems a pity to kill you."

If he wanted me to beg for my life, he was in for a long wait, but then he noticed the O'Toole sisters, and he swaggered over to them.

"Hi, ladies," he said. "I can tell you've been saving yourselves for a *real* man."

"When one shows up, be sure to let us know," said Velvet.

"Everybody's a humorist today!" snarled Bellargo. I thought he was going to take a swing at her, but then his gaze fell on Frothingham. "How about you?"

"I don't think there's anything funny about a bank robbery," he answered in a shaky voice.

"Must be cold in here," said Bellargo. "Look at how his hands are trembling."

"Leave me alone!" said Frothingham. "You came to rob my bank. Rob it and go away!"

"*Your* bank?" repeated Bellargo.

"He's the president," said Leather proudly.

"Good. Then he should know the combinations to all the computer locks on the safes."

"I can't tell you that," said Frothingham. "I'm willing to be robbed, but I'm not willing to collude with you."

"You'll do what you're told and like it!" said Bellargo, and then he made his fatal mistake—he slapped the poor little bastard right across the face.

Two seconds later Velvet was flying through the air and gave Bellargo's head such a kick that it damned near left his shoulders.

His neck made a huge cracking sound, and that was the end of Bellargo.

In the meantime Leather had jumped in among his men, raining blows and kicks right and left, and then Velvet joined her, and by the time I'd overcome my surprise long enough to pull my gun, seventeen of Bellargo's men were laid out on the floor. Twelve of them never got up again, and I began to understand how the sisters O'Toole had managed to survive in Nightmare Alley.

The rest of it was a rout. Velvet picked up a burner from one of the outlaws, Leather picked up a pair of screechers from another, and they started using the rest of the Bellargo Gang for target practice. I got in one or two shots, but they sure as hell didn't need me.

When the dust had cleared and every member of the gang was either dead or disabled, the two sisters rushed up to Throckmorton Lewis Frothingham.

"Are you all right?" asked Leather solicitously.

"Poor baby!" crooned Velvet. "Did they scare you?"

At first I thought it was an act. I mean, how could two such formidable women care for a mousy little man like that?

But it was anything but an act. Two weeks later Velvet O'Toole married her bank president in the morning, and three hours later, Leather married the same man in a tasteful afternoon ceremony. Then the three of them left on their honeymoon.

"And that was the end of it?" asked Willie the Bard, scribbling furiously.

"Not quite."

"What else is there?" asked the Bard. "Did they leave him?"

Gaines shook his head. "I was back there about a year ago. They all live in this huge house—just the kind you'd expect a banker to own. The girls (well, women, actually) still dote on the little bastard. Velvet has seven kids and Leather has eight. I'd love to tell you they look like the O'Toole side of the family, but the fact is that almost all of them look like their father."

"Poor kids," offered Big Red.

"Oh, I don't know," said the Gravedigger. "They're each going to inherit a couple of million credits, and they don't get a lot of teasing at school despite their looks."

"They don't?" said Big Red. "Why not?"

"Because Leather and Velvet are both on the school staff. Leather teaches martial arts, and Velvet coaches the murderball team. Let me tell you: no one messes with *their* kids."

"I can believe that," said Little Mike Picasso. "Wish I'd had a mother like that."

"Think it through," said Hellfire Van Winkle. "Maybe she could protect you from bullies, but would you really want to be disciplined by someone like that?"

"You've got a point," admitted Little Mike.

"I sure do," said Van Winkle. "A mother who can mete out that kind of punishment could turn you into an accomplished liar."

"Not that anyone here needs much help," said Three-Gun Max sarcastically.

"Every word spoken tonight was the truth," I said, feeling a need to stand up for the Outpost's clientele.

"Is that a fact?" said Max.

"Except for the ones that weren't," I answered lamely.

"I imagine the Outpost has heard its share of both," said Argyle.

"You think buildings are sentient, do you?" said Max, still looking for an argument.

"How the hell should I know?" asked Argyle.

"Well, take it from me," said Max. "They aren't."

"Nonsense," said Nicodemus Mayflower, his thin, angular face looking more Satanic than ever. "I knew an entire city that was sentient."

"Bullshit," said Max.

"Okay," said Mayflower with a shrug. "If you don't want to hear about it, that's fine by me."

"Hey!" said the Bard. "*I* want to hear about it."

"Me, too," I added, just to annoy Max.

"If Max doesn't want to listen, there's a war going on out there," said Catastrophe Baker, pointing to another explosion just beyond one of our moons. "He can go make the galaxy safe for the rest of us while we stay here and listen."

Which ended Max's objections to hearing the story.

A City Older than Time

It was out on the Other Arm—the one where Earth isn't—that we found it (said Nicodemus Mayflower).

There were these two competing groups of archaeologists, and neither of them trusted the other, so they each hired some bodyguards to make sure that the other side's bodyguards didn't attack them.

(Yeah, I know, that made it more likely. But how are you going to talk any commonsense to guys who like to travel halfway across the galaxy just to dig in the dirt?)

Anyway, we came to this binary system that wasn't on any star maps, and since I was the guy who first spotted it, they told me I could call it anything I wanted, so the brighter star became Alpha Nicodemus and the other one was Beta Mayflower—and if you don't believe me just check any navigational computer that was programmed after 6519 G.E.

Well, for some reason, they decided that the third planet circling Beta Mayflower was the most likely to have whatever it was they were looking for, so we landed, and sure enough, there was this ancient city, filled with crystal spires and marble streets and quartz windows that acted as prisms and turned the sun's light into an endless series of rainbows.

We'd been there maybe two days when the other party of archaeologists showed up. Our leader told them that we'd already filed a claim, or claimed squatters' rights, or whatever it is you do when you're a scientist and you're not into sharing. The other guys said that was all well and good, but there was no legal authority they could appeal to since the world hadn't been mapped or claimed yet—so they planned to stick around and do their digging and studying no matter what we said.

Tempers started heating up, and then suddenly we all heard a strange moaning sound. It seemed to be coming from the very center of the city, but when we arrived there we couldn't find anything at all. One member of our group decided that it had been made by the wind whistling through the biggest building in town, and a member of the other group said that no, it was obviously caused by gas escaping from a fissure in the ground. Then one of our people said that the only gas escaping was coming from their group, and while all of us bodyguards stood around staring at our employers and wondering what made them act like that, they almost came to blows.

The only thing that stopped them was another moaning sound, this time from the north end of the city. We all traipsed over there as fast as we could, but when we got there we still couldn't find anything.

It was starting to get dark, so both sides decided to call it a day. My group went back to our camp on the east side of the city, and the other groups went off to set up their camp on the west side.

It was while I was lying on my cot, wondering what the hell I was doing here (and also trying to think of which of the girls I knew would be most impressed by knowing a man with a binary system named after him), that I suddenly seemed to hear a voice inside my head.

"Nicodemus Mayflower," it intoned.

I sat up and looked around to see if anyone else had heard anything, but my companions were all snoring peacefully.

"Nicodemus Mayflower," it repeated.

"I'm right here," I said softly. "What do you want?"

"The pain is almost unbearable."

"Maybe you should take a pill for it," I said. "And by the way, who are you and *where* are you?"

"I am Nesbudanne," said the voice.

"I don't want to be disrespectful, but that's no help at all."

"I am the city," said Nesbudanne.

"I beg your pardon?"

"You ask where I am," continued Nesbudanne. "I surround you. I am the delicate towers, the shining pavement, the glistening walls, the curving stairways, the highways, the walkways, the causeways. I am the sewer system beneath your feet. I am the mosaic tiles on the walls of the church, and the mural on its ceiling."

"All right, I get the picture," I said. "But why are you in such pain?"

"I was endowed by my creators, who have long since left me for more modern cities on distant worlds, with the gift of empathy. I can intuit your needs and react to them. Are you cold? I will warm the air. Are you hungry? I will activate my kitchens. Are you sleepy? I will dim my lights and play restful music." Nesbudanne paused, and I thought I could hear an almost human sigh. "But empathy has a downside as well. Your scientists hate their rivals, who hate them right back—and I have been bombarded with those emotions all afternoon and evening. I was never equipped to deal with such things. The agony is almost unendurable."

"I sympathize with you," I said, idly wondering if sympathizing was the same as empathizing. "But what do you expect me to do about it?"

"Beyond my northwestern border is a valley known as the Dreambasin," said Nesbudanne. "It is filled with hallucinogenic plants. Find some way to lead the parties there before I can stand the pain no longer."

"What happens when they get there?" I asked.

"They will inhale the scent from the flowers. Then, since friendship seems totally unknown to them, perhaps they will imagine that they enjoy each other's company and can work in concert toward a common goal."

"I suppose it's worth a try," I said.

I got up, woke my fellow bodyguards, and explained the city's plan to them. They all agreed, and then, still under cover of darkness, I gained the concurrence of our opposite numbers.

The next morning we marched both parties of scientists to the

Dreambasin at gunpoint. We didn't go into the valley ourselves, but we made *them* go—and within five minutes archaeologists who had hated each other for decades were throwing their arms around each other. They spent the day playing childlike games, and laughing happily, and swearing eternal fealty.

And then evening came, and we marched them back to the city—and before we reached the central square five separate fist-fights had broken out, and the battle lines were drawn again.

Then everything was interrupted by the moaning we had heard the day before, but this time I knew what it was.

"Nesbudanne!" I cried out. "Are you all right?"

"You did your best, Nicodemus Mayflower," answered Nesbudanne sadly, and this time I saw that everyone could hear it speak. "But I cannot bear the hatred any longer."

The tallest spire in the city suddenly shattered and fell to the ground in a million pieces.

"I was built to serve you," said Nesbudanne regretfully. "I could not love you more if you were my own children—and you could not hurt me more if you were my sworn enemy."

Another spire crumbled, and, two blocks away, a church began collapsing.

"Perhaps it is all for the best," continued Nesbudanne, its voice growing weaker with each passing second. "You are all scientists. You now have empirical evidence that empathy is not a survival trait. There will come a day when you can perform the most deli-cate microsurgery on a DNA molecule. When that day occurs, do not shackle your next generation with the curse of empathy."

Then buildings began collapsing wholesale, and long cracks split the pavement. We raced for safety beyond the city limits and, once there, stopped and turned to observe the results of our hatred.

There have been many days when I was proud to be a man abroad in the galaxy.

That wasn't one of them.

"Why didn't Nesbudanne's heart break when the people who built it left the planet?" asked Max, always the cynic.

"It didn't die of a broken heart," answered Nicodemus Mayflower. "Its sensitive psyche was shattered by all the hatred."

"Damned lucky it never went into politics," said Max.

"Or art," added Little Mike Picasso.

"Or sports," chimed in Big Red.

"Or any other endeavor where your excellence makes others aware of their shortcomings," concluded Willie the Bard.

"That's one of the reasons we hang out here, isn't it?" said the Gravedigger. "Because we're not jealous of each other in the Outpost."

"I don't know," said Sinderella, gesturing toward Silicon Carny. "I could be mighty jealous of *her* if I let myself."

"There's no reason to," said the Earth Mother. "You don't know where she stops and where the silicone begins."

"That's right," said Sahara del Rio. "No woman could possibly have a bustline like that."

"I knew a woman that had an even bigger one," offered Hurricane Smith.

Langtry Lily glared at him.

"This was before I met you, my dear," he continued. "Hell, they were *all* before I met you."

"Bigger than Silicon Carny, you say?" asked the Reverend Billy Karma.

"That's right."

"What more proof does anyone need that God exists?" said Billy Karma triumphantly.

"I don't think God had much to do with it, Reverend," said Smith.

"That's blasphemy!" growled Billy Karma.

"You tell the story," said Catastrophe Baker, who was still toying with converting, "and we'll decide."

"Fair enough," said Smith.

The Pirate Queen with the Big Bazooms

This all took place about eight years ago (said Hurricane Smith). I had just escaped from the prison planet of Bastille, where I'd been unfairly incarcerated for what were loosely termed "crimes against God and Nature," and I'd made up my mind to clear out of the Monarchy and seek my fortune on the Outer Frontier.

I'd docked at Samovar Station, just beyond Terwilliger's Belt, and was having a drink in the bar while they were enriching my ship's atomic pile, when I heard a commotion coming from one of the corridors leading to the inner offices. Naturally I got up to see what was happening, and as I stepped out of the bar the most gorgeous woman I'd ever seen came running up to me. (Remember: I hadn't seen you yet, my dear.)

She was wearing thigh-high boots and a tiny little G-string and a bra that barely contained her phenomenal bosom, and her hair was long and wild. She had a knife tucked in each boot. There was a screecher strapped to her thigh. She had a burner in one hand and a blaster in the other, and she was firing at a bunch of soldiers, so I knew with a single glance that she was a Pirate Queen.

"Help me," she gasped, "and everything I have is yours!"

Well, it's difficult to refuse an offer like that even under normal circumstances. And when a whole lot of uniformed scum are trying to kill the prettiest lady you've ever seen, why, if you're any kind of gentleman, you simply have to do the right thing and take some kind of action.

So I pulled my burner and fired it at the floor right ahead of the soldiers. The tile melted and turned red-hot, and they skidded to a halt just before they ran onto it. I pulled the girl into the bar so that we were out of their line of fire, raced to the service exit, and soon found my way through the maze of corridors to my ship—and discovered that they hadn't finished enriching the pile yet.

"That's my ship over there!" panted the Pirate Queen, pointing to a nearby vessel.

We raced to it, and took off just before the soldiers caught up with us. As soon as we reached light speeds, she put the ship on autopilot and turned to me.

"I want to thank you for what you did back there," she said.

"I was happy to be of assistance," I told her. "Perhaps we should introduce ourselves. I'm Hurricane Smith."

"Hurricane Smith?" she repeated. "I've heard about your exploits for years."

"And you are . . ."

"You may call me Xenobia."

"That seems to be a popular name with Pirate Queens," I said. "You're the third one I've known to use it."

"Really?" she said. "I've never met any other Pirate Queens. I thought I was the only one."

Now, I'm pretty sure that Pirate Queens don't have a union or a school yearbook or anything like that, but even so I should have latched on to the clue right there. But then she took a deep breath, which sent out waves and ripples and flutters all through her magnificent superstructure, and all other thoughts promptly vanished from my mind.

"Perhaps you'd like to join me in my private quarters and get comfortable?" she suggested.

I would have thought that the entire ship qualified as her private quarters, but I just nodded without taking my eyes off her bosom and followed her to her sleeping cabin.

And what a sleeping cabin it was! There was no bed, but the floor was covered with dozens of soft, thick furs, and the walls and ceiling were completely mirrored.

She stood in the middle of the cabin and turned to face me.

"You know, Hurricane Smith," she said, "I could use a man like you."

"I was hoping you'd say that," I replied.

She chuckled, which sent still more ripples across her flesh. "I meant in my work."

"What *is* your work?" I asked.

"Robbing space stations, holding up Navy convoys, stealing precious gemstones, and eluding the gendarmes."

"Standard Pirate Queen fare," I noted.

"Well?" she said. "Will you join me?"

"As a full partner?"

"As a junior partner," she replied. "Even the notorious Hurricane Smith can't start at the top."

"I'll have to think about it," I said.

She unhooked her bra and let it fall to the floor. "I'll help you make up your mind," she said.

"That's very considerate of you," I said, starting to slip out of my tunic.

"Considerate is my middle name." She smiled and removed her G-string.

"I don't suppose you'd consider removing all your weapons, too?"

"When I know you better."

"How much better do you plan on knowing me?" I asked.

She walked over, put her arms around me, and pressed her body against me—well, as much as she *could* press against me with those magnificent bazooms in the way.

"You'd be surprised," she whispered.

Well, not much we did for the next couple of hours actually surprised me, but it sure went a long way toward making me decide to become her junior partner.

It was when I woke up a little later that I realized something was terribly wrong. I stood up and looked down at my Pirate Queen—and saw that her breasts were now a few feet long, kind of flat, and covered half the floor of the little cabin.

"What the hell's going on here?" I bellowed.

She woke up right away, tried to sit up, couldn't get her balance, and finally realized what had happened. Instantly her breasts resumed their original shape.

"Good morning, my darling," said Xenobia.

"What *are* you?" I demanded.

"Don't you remember?" she said with a smile. "I'm your senior partner."

"What *else* are you?" I insisted. "I'll make it real easy. Let's start with what you're not, which is a woman."

"That didn't make any difference to you a few hours ago," she pointed out.

"A few hours ago I was blinded by your beauty," I said. "Or what seemed to be your beauty."

"Didn't you enjoy making love to me?" she asked.

"That's got nothing to do with it!" I yelled. "I want to know what you are!"

"I told you—I'm a Pirate Queen."

"But what *kind* of a Pirate Queen?"

"The beautiful kind. Isn't that the kind you're attracted to?"

"I'm getting very confused here," I said.

She sighed, and even though I knew that she lacked a certain degree of—how shall I say it?—structural integrity, I just couldn't help staring as her bosom rose and fell.

"All right," she said. "I needed a partner. I saw you at the space station and recognized you from your Wanted posters, so I shot a soldier and arranged for you to rescue me."

"How did you know I'd be willing to risk life and limb rescuing a woman I'd never seen before?"

"Because every member of your race and gender is a sucker for *these*," she said—and as the words left her mouth, her bosoms reached out across the room and caressed my cheeks. I was torn between kissing them and running hell-for-leather to the far end of the ship, and the only reason I didn't choose the latter course of action is because I had a horrible premonition that her breasts could reach that far and I didn't want to find out for sure. So I chose a middle course of action and just stood there shaking like a leaf.

"Oh," she said sympathetically. "Have I scared you?"

"Not yet," I said. "But you're getting awfully close. What do you really look like?"

"What difference does it make?" she responded. "I can always look like this for you."

"God, I hope not!" I said devoutly.

She smiled and almost blushed. "I forgot," she said, and suddenly her breasts contracted until they were merely E cups again.

"So, Hurricane Smith," she said, "will you ride the spaceways with me, plunder the wealthy, and share my sexual favors?"

"I don't think so," I said.

"But why not?" she asked. "Has any human woman ever pleased you more?"

"No," I admitted. "But every last one of them has upset me less."

"But I can *be* human for you!" she insisted.

"Every time I grab you," I said, "which figures to be pretty damned often, I'd always wonder exactly what I was *really* grabbing."

"If it feels good—and I assure you it feels good to me, too—why worry about it?"

"A man's got to worry about something," I explained. "If I hook up with you, I figure I'll have enough worries to last me a couple of lifetimes and maybe part of a third."

"I'm sorry you feel that way," she said. "We could have been a wonderful team."

"Is that a real tear rolling down your cheek," I asked, "or are you just putting on a show for me?"

"Last night was the show," she replied mournfully. "The tear is for real."

And that's the way I'll always remember her—standing there, the most beautiful creature I've ever seen (except for you, my dear), with a real tear rolling down her face.

But it was a useful experience, for as time went by I realized that appearances aren't very important, and if I hadn't discovered that I might still be a bachelor searching futilely for love instead of a happily married man.

Suddenly a tear appeared on Langtry Lily's cheek, and she leaned over and planted a long, tender kiss on Hurricane Smith's lips.

"Now that's right touching," said Catastrophe Baker.

"It sure is," agreed the Reverend Billy Karma. "It almost makes you forget she's a godless insect that lays eggs and probably eats her young."

He was lucky he leaned over to blow his nose just then, because a stream of acid saliva from Langtry Lily shot out right to where his head had been.

"I knew a lady insect once," said O'Grady. He turned to Langtry Lily. "Not of your species, ma'am. She was a brilliant silver in color, and had a number of long, sinewy arms, and the biggest, reddest multifaceted eyes you ever saw. She showed up at the casino out by Mutare II one night and started winning everything in sight. Took me hours to figure out how she was doing it."

"The eyes, right?" said Little Mike.

"That's what I thought originally," answered O'Grady. "But it wasn't. It was those damned antennae. She was getting signals from another insect that was standing maybe twenty feet behind us."

"What did you do—tar and feather her, or cut off her antennae?" asked the Reverend Billy Karma.

"Neither," said O'Grady. "All we did was take our money back and burn a big red A into her carapace."

"Why?"

"I take it you're not much on the classics," said O'Grady. "We figured any time she entered a human gambling establishment, the players would take one look at that A, figure she was an alien Hester out for a good time, and if their name wasn't Hurricane Smith they'd head for the hills."

Big Red looked at his computer's holoscreen. "Einstein says he likes that idea."

"That's because Einstein is better read than the Reverend here," said O'Grady.

"I don't read anything but the Good Book," said Billy Karma defensively. "Especially the begattings."

"You sound like you're into genealogy," said Achmed of Alphard.

"He's into begatting," Sinderella corrected him.

"Where does the Lord say you can't have a little fun?" demanded Billy Karma.

"How about Genesis?" suggested Hellfire Van Winkle.

"Besides that!"

"That wasn't enough?" said Van Winkle. "He threw Adam and Eve out of Eden."

"Well, I got my own theories about that," said Billy Karma. "You know what I think Eve was *really* nibbling on instead of an apple?"

"I don't want to hear this," said Sinderella.

"I don't even want to think about it," added Van Winkle.

"If God didn't want you educated, He wouldn't have put me here to preach to you," said Billy Karma. "I've been thinking for some time now that the Bible needs a complete rewrite."

"I can see it now," said Little Mike Picasso: "*The Old Testament—the Good Parts Version,* by the Reverend Billy Karma."

"Sounds good to me," said the Reverend.

"Does anything that's filthy or in terrible taste ever sound *bad* to you?" asked Sinderella.

"Insufficient information," said Billy Karma.

"What are you talking about?"

"You let me nibble up your thigh and down your belly and then I'll know if you taste good or terrible."

"I don't know how to break this to you, Reverend," said Little Mike, "but there's a difference between women with good taste and women who taste good."

"Not to me there isn't," said Billy Karma devoutly.

"I can believe that," said Van Winkle.

"I think maybe you'd better pray to the Lord to send you a restraining bolt," said Sinderella.

"You're into restraints, are you?" asked the Reverend.

Sinderella looked like she was going to reply, but then she turned her back on him in disgust.

"No doubt about it, the Lord had plenty of foresight," said Billy Karma, still staring at her. "Look at that beautiful round ass. God put most of the fun stuff on the flip side, but He remembered to leave a little something back here for a lonely man of the cloth to admire."

"Kind of single-minded tonight, ain't you?" said Baker.

"Single-minded is an understatement," agreed the Gravedigger.

"Hey, Reverend," said Baker as another explosion lit up the night sky, "maybe you'd better have a quick talk with the Lord and tell Him to leave women alone and concentrate on ending the war."

"Not His department," said the Reverend Billy Karma. "God made women. *Men* make wars. Well, men and godless aliens."

"You know, any minute now we're going to take offense at that," said Sitting Horse.

"You wouldn't want to go to heaven anyway," said Billy Karma. "I figure if there actually *are* any aliens there, they all live in the low-rent district and don't get choice tee times at the golf course."

"I don't know why," said Hellfire Van Winkle, "but I get the definite impression that it takes less education to become a preacher these days than when I was growing up."

"Mostly it takes a Bible, a black coat, and a personal relationship with the Good Lord," agreed Billy Karma.

"It sure as hell doesn't take any knowledge of Old Earth's literature," put in Big Red. "Hell, even *I* knew who Hester was."

"He probably thinks the House of Usher is where you train robots to guide dirty old men to their seats at a strip show," said Little Mike Picasso.

"You mean it ain't?" said Billy Karma.

"Just a minute here," said Catastrophe Baker. "Are you saying that the House of Usher is *fictional*?"

Little Mike stared at him. "Are you saying it isn't?"

"I've *been* there," said Baker.

"I'm talking about a story called 'The Fall of the House of Usher,'" said Little Mike.

"Am I in it?" asked Baker.

"No."

"Well, I should be," he said, "because I was there when it fell."

"Somehow I don't think we're talking about the same place," said Little Mike.

"How many Houses of Usher could there have been?" asked Baker.

"Tell me about yours and then I'll give you an answer."

Catastrophe Baker and the Fall of the House of Usher

It all took place on Moebius IV (began Baker). I'd just finished hunting Demoncats. They're currently the most endangered large predators in the galaxy—they weren't endangered at all when I started, but one of 'em charged me early on and got my blood up—and I'd decided that I owed myself a little R&R, except that I called it F&F.

I'd heard that the best whorehouse in that sector was the one that Ugly Jim Usher ran on Moebius, so I headed there to kind of reward myself for a job well done. Turns out that most of what I'd heard was right. Ugly Jim ran a hell of an operation, and since he's a pretty broad-minded soul (no pun intended) he stocked it with the best-looking females from most of the better-looking races in the galaxy. There were human women, and Balatai women, and even a couple of Peloponnes (though they didn't hold a candle to you, Mrs. Smith, ma'am). I think the strangest may have been the one they called the Spider Lady: she had eight legs evenly spaced around her body, but except for that she looked as human as any woman there.

"Uh . . . I hate to interrupt," said Hurricane Smith. "But if she had eight legs, how many . . . ah . . . ?"

"Four," said Baker.

"Amazing!" said Big Red.

"And how did you . . . uh . . . ?" said Smith.

"Pretty much the usual way," answered Baker. "Except that four of us could do it at once and never get in each other's way. Well, as long as she stayed on her feet, that is."

"Fascinating" said Smith. "I wonder if—"

Langtry Lily uttered a warning hiss.

"It's merely academic interest, my dear," said Smith.

She leaned over and whispered something to him.

"I wouldn't dream of it!" he said in injured tones. "In fact, I've already forgotten that she can be found on Moebius IV."

Another hiss.

"I misspoke," said Smith with a little tremor of desperation in his voice. "I've already forgotten that she can be found on Mac-Beth IX."

She stared at him expressionlessly.

"Reggie!" he hollered. "Some more sugar for the lady!" As Reggie brought out another pound of sugar, Smith turned to Baker. "Go on with your story."

"You sure?" asked Baker, trying to suppress a grin of amusement. "I mean, I'd be just as happy to wait until she dissolves you or rips you to shreds."

"No, go right ahead," said Smith uncomfortably. "You were listing all the alien prostitutes?"

"I was telling about my memorable experience in Jim Usher's whorehouse," Baker corrected him. "The rest was just scene-setting and window-dressing."

"It was?" said Smith, obviously disappointed.

"Right. Are you still interested, or should I quit?"

Smith took a quick peek at Langtry Lily, who looked like she was ready to spit in his eye if he came up with the wrong answer.

"No, I'm dying to hear it," said Smith.

"Good," said Baker, still grinning. "I'd hate to think all this talk of alien whores was boring you."

"Just tell the fucking story!" bellowed Smith.

I wish that was the kind of story it was (said Baker). A fucking story, that is.

Though, to be honest, it certainly started out that way.

Like I was saying, I stopped by Ugly Jim Usher's place, downed a couple of pints of 150-proof whiskey imported from New Kentucky, and gave the ladies the once-over to see who I was going to honor with my patronage.

And all of a sudden, damned if I didn't think one of them Demoncats had done my retina some serious damage, enough to make me see triple, because standing in front of me were three of the sexiest ladies I'd ever laid eyes on—and if you'd have put a gun to my head I couldn't have spotted the tiniest difference between them. I just stood there staring at them with my jaw hanging open until all three of 'em started giggling.

"Don't feel embarrassed," said the one on the left. "Everyone reacts like that the first time."

"Well, I can see why," I said. "I could have sworn that two of you were holographs of the third."

"Oh, we're real, all right," said the one on the right.

"Want us to prove it?" asked the one in the middle with a wicked grin.

"Why not?" I responded. "In a long lifetime filled with nothing but interesting adventures, this sounds like it could be the most interesting of all. By the way, have you girls got names?"

"I'm Fatima," said the one on the left.

"I'm Fifi," said the one on the right.

"And I'm Felicity," said the one in the middle. "We're the DeMarco Triplets."

"Identical in every way," said Fatima.

"I got no problem believing it," I said.

"Wait'll you take us to bed," promised Fifi. "You'll find that I'm much more identical than they are."

"That's a pretty daring challenge," I noted.

"Are you up to it?" asked Felicity meaningfully.

"I been up to it (so to speak) since the second I laid eyes on the three of you," I told her.

I didn't feel the need to waste any more time talking, so I went over and told Ugly Jim that we needed a small room with a big bed.

"You want all three of them?" he asked.

"Sure do," I said.

"At the same time?"

"Relatively," I said.

He named a price that I thought was five times too high. I paid it without an argument and off the four of us went.

Well, I won't describe the next couple of hours, since my pal Hurricane would probably find it boring, and the rest of you might just faint dead away from excitement—but I will say that it was one of the more satisfying experiences of my life, to say nothing of being one of the most exhausting.

In fact, the more I thought about it the more I couldn't see no reason why we shouldn't all get satisfied and exhausted every night for the rest of our lives, so before we left the room I asked all three of 'em to marry me, and damned if they didn't say yes.

Ugly Jim was only too happy to accommodate me when I told him I was buying drinks for everyone in the house, males and females, humans and aliens alike, to celebrate my good fortune. It was only when I told him what my good fortune *was* that he hit the roof and looked like he was having a seizure, or at the very least conniption fits.

"You can't do this to me!" he screamed. "They're my three biggest earners!"

"I'm not doing it to *you*," I pointed out. "I'm doing it to *them*."

"It's out of the question!"

"I don't recall asking you no questions," I said. "But since I'm a reasonable man, name your price and I'll buy 'em from you."

"I don't sell human flesh," he said with dignity. "I just rent it."

"Okay," I said. "I'm renting 'em for the next fifty years."

"I absolutely refuse," said Ugly Jim. "The business can't survive without them."

"Sure it can," I said. "I'm going out to my ship to get my bankroll. Have a number ready when I get back, and we'll haggle over it for a while, and I'll pay you too much, and we'll all be happy, especially me and the DeMarco triplets."

Before he could say anything, I went to my ship, hit the combination to the safe, and brought out a wad of bills that would have choked a dinosaur. I decided to give Ugly Jim a few minutes to calm down, so I took a drink from my private stash, counted to five hundred, and finally returned to the whorehouse.

Ugly Jim was waiting for me with a triumphant grin on his face.

"I got some money to share with you," I said. "You look like you got a joke you want to share with me."

"It's a joke, all right," said Ugly Jim. "And it's on you."

"What are you talking about?"

"The DeMarco girls," he said. "They ain't going anywhere."

"I'll believe it when I hear it from them," I said. "Where are they?"

"In their rooms upstairs," he said.

I was up the stairs in two giant leaps, and a second later I busted down the first door I came to. A couple of seconds after that I was apologizing mighty profusely, more to the guy who was tied to the cross than to the nun who was beating him with her rosary beads.

I busted down two more doors before I came to the first of the DeMarco girls. She was lying on her bed, and her right hand was chained to a spike that had been driven deep into the wall behind the headboard.

"I'll get you out of this, Fifi," I said, walking over to her.

"I'm Felicity," she replied.

"How the hell am I supposed to know the difference?" I asked her.

She pulled my head down to her lips. "I'm the one who . . ."

Well, once she recalled the event to me, I knew she was Felicity, all right.

Anyway, I put my foot against the wall, grabbed the chain with both hands, and pulled—and nothing happened.

Now, it ain't usual for me to pull on something and not get instant results. I pulled again, even harder, and the spike still stayed in the wall.

So I figured if I couldn't pull the spike out of the wall, I'd just have to pull the wall down around the spike. I covered Felicity with a blanket so she wouldn't get cut by no flying debris, and then I balled up my fists and started pounding on the wall in a regular rhythm. It only took about ten or twelve blows to shatter the whole wall, and suddenly the spike was dangling from the chain, and I uncovered Felicity and told her that I'd find a way to get it off her wrist once we were on my ship.

I busted down three more doors (and saw some mighty unusual and memorable sights) before I came to Fatima, who was in the very same fix. I knew better than to pull at the chain, so I just started hammering at the wall, and sure enough, it crumbled in about twenty seconds.

By the time I hit Fifi's room, I'd done some pretty serious damage to the place, what with having busted down two walls and maybe a dozen doors. I spent three or four minutes pounding on her wall when I realized that it wasn't like the other two, that Fifi's spike had been driven *through* the wall into a main support beam. Even after the wall fell down, the spike was still stuck in that damned beam. Now, a lot of men would have been discouraged, but that just got my dander up, and I began pounding harder and faster, and finally the beam split in half, and Fifi was free.

I gathered the three girls and started down the stairs with them when the whole building began shaking. We just made it out the door before it collapsed—and *that* was the Fall of the House of Usher.

"What happened to the DeMarco triplets?" asked the Bard.

"I'm a man of my word," said Baker with dignity. "I married 'em."

"You've got three wives?"

"I got *six* wives," replied Baker. "Unhappily, Fifi, Fatima, and Felicity ain't among 'em no longer."

"What happened?"

"I guess our love life must have been a little too rigorous for them," said Baker. "They finally ran off with some salesman who was pushing potency cures."

"You mean impotency cures," said the Bard.

"I know what I mean. Somehow he'd become convinced that people wasted even more time on sex than on eating, and he was bound and determined to put an end to it."

"And he actually made a living selling this cure?"

"Nope," said Baker. "But he sure as hell collected a lot of women." He paused. "Hell, now that I think of it, maybe I'll go into the potency cure business myself one of these days."

"When you come up with a potency cure, give it to the Reverend," said Sinderella. "I'll pay for it."

"Hell, *you* could cure my potency," said Billy Karma. "For a few minutes, anyway."

"Uh . . . I don't want to be the bearer of bad tidings," interrupted Hellfire Van Winkle, "but either morning has come a few hours early or they're lighting up the sky with one helluva lot of explosions."

"*Our* sky?" asked Three-Gun Max.

"Just whose sky did you think I was talking about?" demanded Van Winkle.

"I meant, you're sure it's Henry II and not Henry III or IV?"

"I can't even see the other Henrys," said Van Winkle. "But don't take *my* word for it. Stick your head out the window and tell me what *you* see."

Max walked over to the window. "What I see," he said, looking out, "is a woman walking toward the Outpost."

"Is she alone?" asked Baker.

"Seems to be."

"What does she look like?"

"Wait another ten seconds and you can see for yourself," said Max. He turned to Hellfire Van Winkle. "By the way, the sky is dark again."

"Well, it was bright as day a minute ago," said Van Winkle defensively.

Max was about to reply, but just then the door opened and the woman walked in. She was tall and lean, and she had a hard look about her eyes. Her hair was kind of short, she didn't use any makeup, and there was just something about her that said if Catastrophe Baker or the Reverend Billy Karma or any of the others tried anything fancy with her, they'd be hobnobbing with God or Satan a couple of seconds later.

Suddenly Achmed of Alphard stood up. "It's you!" he exclaimed.

"Hello, Achmed," said the woman. "What are you doing out here on the Frontier?"

"Hiding from God, Jasmine Kabella, and the tax collectors," answered Achmed. "Not necessarily in that order."

"You gonna introduce us to your friend?" interrupted Baker.

"Certainly," said Achmed, though most of us had already guessed her identity. "Ladies, gentlemen, and aliens—this is the Cyborg de Milo."

Big Red's computer came to life. "Einstein says hello again."

"Hello right back at him," said the Cyborg de Milo.

"What brings you to the Outpost?" asked Achmed.

"A better ship than the ones that were chasing me," she answered.

"Chasing you?" repeated Little Mike Picasso. "You mean we might be getting some visitors at any minute?"

"No, that's not what I mean at all." She paused for a moment. "A trio of alien ships took after me when I entered the system. I'd heard about this place, so I headed for Henry II with the three of them hot on my tail. What they didn't know is that my ship's got the latest generation of heat shield on its nose. I plunged into the atmosphere at a steep angle, one that produced a lot of friction with the air molecules. They followed me, and a minute later all three of them went up in the brightest flames you ever saw."

"See?" said Van Winkle triumphantly. "I *told* you it looked like daylight out there!"

"What's the situation?" asked Little Mike. "How's the war progressing?"

"What war?"

"What do you mean, what war? The one between the aliens and the Navy."

"I didn't see any sign of the Navy," she replied. "Either they've all been blown to pieces, or else they cut and ran. Either way, the only ships up there are alien ships." She walked over to the bar and signaled to me. "Bring me a beer."

"Yes, Ms. de Milo," I said.

"And call me Venus."

"Coming right up, Venus," I said, and ordered Reggie to draw a tall one. When he handed it to her, she downed it as fast as Catastrophe Baker ever drained a glass, then wiped her mouth with the back of her hand.

"Thanks," she said. "I needed that."

"Killing aliens can be mighty thirsty work," agreed Baker.

"I plan to kill a lot more of them," said Venus grimly.

"There's no hurry," said Baker. "Sit down, relax, and have another beer. They'll still be there when you're done."

"Doesn't it bother you that a bunch of beings you've never met before are out there plotting to kill you?" demanded Venus.

"Hell, if I ever woke up one morning and there *weren't* a bunch of beings I didn't know plotting to kill me, I just might keel over and die from shock." He smiled at her. "Catastrophe Baker at your service, ma'am."

"*You're* Catastrophe Baker?" she said. "I've been hearing stories about you since I was a little girl!"

"Every last one of 'em true," Baker assured her. "Except for them what ain't."

"It will be an honor to fight side by side with you against the aliens," she said.

"Well, I do a lot of things side by side with women of all types, shapes, and sizes," said Baker. "But fighting aliens is one of the things I do best alone."

"Side by side or on our own, we'll decimate the bastards!" she said enthusiastically.

"Maybe we'll just invite 'em in for a drink and try to find out what got 'em so all-fired riled in the first place," said Baker.

Venus threw back her head and laughed. "You've got a wonderful sense of humor, Catastrophe!"

"I know I have," he replied. "But I ain't taken it out of mothballs yet today."

"Maybe we *should* give some thought to facing off against the aliens," said Big Red.

"Are you in that much of a hurry to meet your maker, son?" asked the Reverend Billy Karma. "Don't count on sitting at His right hand if things go wrong. I was speaking to Him just this morning and He never mentioned you." He turned to the room at large. "Leave us not rush foolishly into a situation that can be just as foolishly avoided."

"*Men!*" muttered Sinderella disgustedly. "All talk and no action!"

"I keep offering you some action, honey," said Billy Karma, "and you keep turning me down."

"You should have said yes to him," interjected the Earth Mother. "The odds are he wouldn't have done a damned thing about it."

"Oh, yeah?" Billy Karma shot back. "What makes you think so?"

"Experience."

"You never had no experience with me."

"I've had more than my share of experience with men, and I've come to the conclusion that you're all a bunch of totally worthless blowhards."

"I take exception to that remark!" snapped the Reverend.

"See? Sinderella was right—all talk and no action."

"What kind of action do you want?" demanded Billy Karma. "I could knock your teeth out if that'd make you happy."

"You try it, and ten seconds later you'll know for sure if there's an afterlife or not," replied the Earth Mother.

The Reverend stared at her for a long moment, then decided not to find out if she was telling the truth.

"Ah, what would you know about action anyway?" he settled for saying.

"More than you, that's for sure," said the Earth Mother.

"Hah!" he responded. "Who'd ever want you?"

"Lots of men."

"Name one."

"Gladly," said the Earth Mother. "Moses Jacoby Zanzabell."

At the sound of the name, a hush fell over the Outpost.

"*The* Moses Jacoby Zanzabell?" asked the Reverend Billy Karma at last.

"There's only one."

"But he's the richest man in the galaxy!"

"That's right."

"And he took a liking to you?"

"Liking is an understatement," said the Earth Mother. "He wanted me so badly that he *bought* me."

"*This* I gotta hear," said the Reverend Billy Karma.

"Me, too," said Max.

The Trillionaire's Toy

You know (began the Earth Mother), I was a pretty good-looking woman twenty-five or thirty years ago. I realize it's hard to believe now, but that's because sooner or later gravity catches up with all of us. But back then, I was a knockout. I looked just like Sinderella, only I was blonde. (Or, at least, I was *frequently* blonde.)

Most people, when they heard about Moses Jacoby Zanzabell, who was the galaxy's first and only trillionaire, couldn't believe anyone could be so rich. I didn't have any problem with that. *I* couldn't believe anyone could be so ugly.

I was working at the Tower of Babel, a high-class brothel located on Green Cheese, a moon of Pirelli VII, when I first saw him. Oh, I knew who he was, all right; a man like that doesn't exactly dwell in obscurity.

Anyway, he came into the place, left his bodyguards at the door, and spent a few minutes considering his choice—and then he selected me.

Now, not only was he the ugliest man I'd ever seen, but he was also in the running for the foulest-smelling one as well. So when he announced that he wanted to spend the night with me, I refused. This seemed to amuse him, because he was obviously not used to people denying him anything he wanted. He walked over to me, pulled out his wallet, and placed a fat wad of banknotes in my hand.

"A million credits for one night," he said with a smile—and I noticed that he needed dental work too.

"Not interested," I said.

"But you work here!" he insisted. "You *can't* say no to a paying customer."

"I just did."

"Well, it's against the law for a business to advertise a service and then reject a legitimate offer."

"Okay," I said. "I quit."

"Just a minute!" he said urgently. "No one's ever turned me down before."

"Consider it a learning experience," I told him.

"I consider it stimulating beyond belief," he admitted. "It's a brand-new experience."

"I'm not *trying* to stimulate you," I said. "Just the opposite."

"It's not working," he said. "Now, what'll it take to make you change your mind?"

"Nothing you can say or do," I told him.

"I didn't get where I am by taking no for an answer," he said, walking to the door. "I'll be back."

And sure enough, he was back the next night.

"All right," he said, walking right up to me. "Let's go."

"Go where?" I asked.

"I own palaces all over the galaxy," he said. "I just built one on New Fiji. I think we'll go there."

"I'm not going anywhere," I said.

"Yes, you are," he said. "Check with the government."

"What has the government got to do with it?" I demanded.

"They declared you a living monument in exchange for a ten-million-credit donation," said Zanzabell. "Then, since they control the sale of all monuments, they agreed to let me purchase you for another forty million credits." He smiled. "I *own* you."

I had my lawyer check it out, and somehow it was all true. Now, I realize it seems crazy to spend fifty million credits for a woman—*any* woman—but as he explained it, he made more than that every ten seconds, so it didn't seem quite as crazy to him.

So I went to New Fiji with him, and he showed me my room, which would have comfortably held two murderball fields and a racetrack. The bathroom could have held a small lake, and *did* sport an impressive waterfall. Zanzabell stopped at the door and told me he'd be by to pay me a visit in an hour.

I had barely finished exploring my new quarters when he showed up, carrying a bottle of Cygnian cognac. He didn't smell any better than usual, so I suggested we drink first. He filled our glasses, and he drained his while he was ogling me, and before I'd even taken a sip of my own drink, he'd made it halfway through his second glass.

He started slurring his words by the third glass, and I saw he had trouble focusing his eyes by the fourth. I kept him talking until he'd finished the whole damned bottle. When he finally decided it was time to take me to bed, he stood up, reached a hand in my direction, and collapsed onto the floor.

I dragged him to the bed, managed to lift him onto it, and took a long, luxurious bath. When I was through, I dialed up a good book on my computer and spent the next few hours reading it, until I heard him starting to stir in the bed.

"Where are you?" he mumbled.

"Right here," I said, walking over to him.

"I can't remember a thing," he said.

"I remember everything," I said. "You were fabulous!"

"I was?"

"The best I've ever had," I assured him. "Don't you remember?"

"Ah, yes," he said. "Now it all comes back to me. I really *was* fabulous, wasn't I?" He got shakily to his feet. "I'll see you again tonight."

And when he came to my room, I saw to it that we had a repeat performance of the previous night.

The third night he brought drugs along with the liquor. I pretended to take them while he used up the entire supply.

This went on for almost two months. Each night he would get so drunk or stoned that he passed out, and each morning I would tell him how wonderful he'd been in bed and how much he had pleased me, and he always pretended to remember rather than admit that he couldn't recall a single thing.

I realized that I couldn't keep this up forever, so after sixty days had passed, I asked for my freedom.

He refused.

Now, I could have tried to escape, but he had guards everywhere, and I'd never have made it to the front gate. And I could have tried to win my freedom in the courts, but my lawyer assured me that it could take years. I could have waited for some hero like Catastrophe Baker or Hurricane Smith to rescue me, but the fact was that I didn't know any heroes back then.

So I decided to take advantage of the same male psychology that had kept me safe thus far.

The next time I saw Zanzabell, I threw my arms around him, apologized for being so foolish as to ask for my freedom, and swore my eternal love for him. He disengaged himself and looked very uncomfortable.

"You're all I want!" I panted. "All I'll ever want! Once a day isn't enough anymore! I want you to visit me in my room at least three times a day—and I'll kill any woman who tries to stop you!"

"Nobody gives me orders!" he snapped. "Now back away!"

"But you're all I live for!" I told him. "You're even better in bed than you are in business, and I won't share you with anyone!"

He suddenly looked like a trapped animal.

"Get away from me!" he said.

"Never!" I cried, kneeling down and grabbing his legs.

Well, he had his men pull me away and lock me in my room, and every day for the next week I repeated my performance, and he kept looking more and more like a trapped animal as the week wore on, and finally he ordered his guards to give me my freedom and return me to the Tower of Babel.

I cashed in all the jewels he had given me in exchange for the sexual favors he was sure he'd gotten, and used the proceeds to buy my own brothel. Thanks to my knowledge of the male of the species, it was a remarkable success.

"So he never once got you into bed?" asked Sinderella.

"That's right," said the Earth Mother.

"If the Reverend doesn't calm down, we have to have a long talk."

"What the hell is going on?" demanded the Cyborg de Milo angrily.

"I don't think I understand the question, ma'am," said Catastrophe Baker.

"There's a war out there! Aliens have decimated the Navy. They've already landed on Henrys IV and V, and they're headed for Henry II. And all anyone wants to do is talk!"

"That's not quite *all* we want to do, honey," said the Reverend Billy Karma.

"You lay a finger on me and I'll lay one on you," said Venus in a threatening tone, "and we'll see who has the more potent finger." She turned to Baker and Smith. "I can understand the rest of these clowns, but you two are bonafide heroes. Why are you still sitting around this place instead of going out there and wiping out those alien scum?"

"What's your hurry?" asked Smith. "No one's shooting at the Outpost yet."

"Right," added Baker. "It's been my experience that there ain't no problem so urgent today that it won't be even more urgent tomorrow."

"Besides," said Bet-a-World O'Grady, "everyone knows that violence is the last resort of the incompetent."

"The competent don't wait that long," said Venus contemptuously.

"I never yet saw a war that was worth rushing into," said Smith.

"Right," agreed Baker. "If this war can't stick around until we're ready to fight it, it wasn't worth the effort in the first place."

The Cyborg de Milo got to her feet and walked to the door.

"To hell with all of you!" she said. "There's vermin out there that needs defenestrating! I'll do the job alone if I have to!"

She stalked out of the Outpost and headed back to her ship.

"I never saw anyone so goddamned anxious to get her head blown off," said Three-Gun Max.

"Lot of guts, though," opined the Gravedigger.

"Good-looking broad, too," added the Reverend Billy Karma.

"Fine," said Sinderella. "Chase *her* for awhile."

"She's off to fight the aliens," said Billy Karma. "Just how crazy do I look?"

"Do you want a frank answer or a friendly one?" said Sinderella.

"I withdraw the question," said the Reverend uncomfortably.

"That's a mighty brave lady facing mighty long odds," said Smith. He looked over at Baker. "You think we ought to go with her?"

"I got room for a couple of more drinks yet," answered Baker. "Maybe by then they'll have taken a shot at us and we'll have a real reason to fight."

"Yeah," said Smith thoughtfully. "I suppose you're right."

"He's wrong."

It was a voice no one had ever heard before.

"Who said that?" I demanded.

Reggie, my robot bartender, rolled over to me. "I did, Toma-hawk."

"You?" I exclaimed. "I didn't know you could talk."

"I've always been able to," said Reggie.

"But you've been tending bar here since the day we opened and you've never said a word!"

"I never had anything to say until now."

"And now you do?" I asked.

"Yes," he said. "I've been listening to everyone's stories, and now I've got one of my own to tell."

"We're all ears," said Baker.

"It doesn't have a title," said Reggie, "because I am just a robot, and not creative like the rest of you. So with your permission, I will just call it Reggie's Story."

Reggie's Story

Once upon a time (said Reggie) there was a gathering place for the most extraordinary people in the galaxy. It attracted heroes and bandits, artists and athletes, ministers, geniuses, prostitutes, bounty hunters, gamblers, even aliens. Since I am a robot and haven't been programmed for creativity, let's call it the Outpost for lack of a better name.

Unique people came to the Outpost to drink, to tell a story or two, and mainly to mingle with other very special people. It was a haven for them, a place to hide from the mundane and the commonplace, from the fawning adulation and the irrational resentment of the populace at large.

And because they were extraordinary people, they sometimes forgot that there was a galaxy of normal people out there, a galaxy that *needed* the kind of men and women who were drawn to the Outpost.

One day an alien fleet entered the system. The Navy tried to stand against it but was destroyed. There was a moment, a single instant in time, when the heroes of the Outpost might have turned the tide of battle, might have driven the aliens not only from the system but from the entire galaxy. But instead of doing what they were born to do, they talked and they drank and they talked some more, and then the moment was gone. The aliens took advantage of their lethargy to destroy the Outpost and everyone in it, and within five years the entire Monarchy had fallen beneath their on-slaught.

That's the story. It of course has nothing to do with *this* Outpost or *these* heroes.

Thank you for listening.

Catastrophe Baker got to his feet.

"All right, Reggie," he said, walking to the door. "I was going out there anyway."

Reggie didn't answer.

"Did you hear me?" said Baker.

Still no answer.

"What's the matter with him?"

"He only talks when he's got something to say," said Little Mike Picasso.

"And now he's said it," added Nicodemus Mayflower.

Gravedigger Gaines got up. "I'll walk you out to the ships," he said to Baker.

"You ain't leaving me behind!" said the Reverend Billy Karma. "Me and the Lord got to protect that little cyborg lady."

Hurricane Smith turned to Langtry Lily. "I really should go with them."

She whispered something to him.

"Certainly, my dear," said Smith. "I'll be happy to have you come along."

In another minute Hellfire Van Winkle and Little Mike Picasso and Sahara del Rio and Sinderella and Nicodemus Mayflower and Argyle and Bet-a-World O'Grady and Sitting Horse and Crazy Bull and the Earth Mother and Achmed of Alphard and Silicon Carny all started making their way to their ships.

"What about you?" Max asked Willie the Bard.

"Somebody's got to wait here and write down the survivors' stories," said the Bard.

"If there *are* any survivors," said Max. He turned to Big Red. "You going or staying?"

"I'm going," he said. "That is, if I can leave my computer with Tomahawk."

"For safekeeping?" I asked.

"For communicating with Einstein," said Big Red, indicating the blind genius who sat alone at his table. "His brain may prove to be the difference between victory and defeat."

He tapped out a good-bye to Einstein, then handed me the computer and walked out the door.

"How about you, Max?" I asked.

"Oh, I'm going off to slaughter aliens," he said. "There never was any question about it. But I see about half a dozen unfinished drinks sitting on various tables, and it'd be criminal to pour them out."

He began walking from table to table, downing all the half-empty glasses.

"Protect her, Max," said Reggie.

"Her?"

"The Cyborg de Milo," said Reggie. "She's half robot. I feel a remarkable affinity toward her."

"You got the hots for a lady cyborg?" asked Max.

"Just do what I asked."

"If half of what we heard about her is true, it makes more sense for *her* to protect *me*," said Max.

"Please," said Reggie in almost human tones.

Max stared at him for a long moment, then nodded. "Okay, Reggie—you've got it."

"Thank you, Max," said Reggie.

"Remember this the next time Tomahawk tells you to water my drink."

Then Max went out to his ship, and the Bard, Reggie, and I were alone again, except for Einstein. We fell silent, each wondering how such a mismatched bunch of heroes would fare against the alien invaders.

I had a premonition that we didn't have long to wait before we learned the answer.

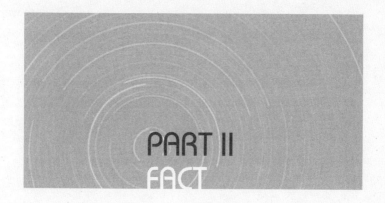

PART II
FACT

Achmed of Alphard and the Aliens

After picking his way through the Wedding Rings, Achmed of Alphard set his ship down on Henry VIII. It was a cold, dark, forbidding world, with a temperature of minus 93 degrees Celsius, a gravity about half of Galactic Standard, and an atmosphere of pure ammonia.

He'd picked up a neutrino reading where there shouldn't have been any, and had homed in on it. Sure enough, the aliens had set up a repair and refueling station there among the huge outcroppings of rock and ice.

Achmed checked his weaponry, made sure his burner and his screecher were fully powered, and stuck a trio of energy grenades in his belt. He set his ship down twelve miles away from the station. His oxygen canisters could keep him supplied with air for almost ten hours; given the light gravity, it shouldn't take him more than a couple of hours to reach the station. He'd eliminate any guards with his laser rifle—no sense using the screecher and letting them know the enemy was nearby—and then he'd take out the station with the grenades. Then he'd return to his ship. Even with a couple of unforeseen obstacles, he should have a good five hours of oxygen to spare.

Before he donned his protective spacesuit and left the ship, he raised the Cyborg de Milo on his subspace radio.

"Where are you?" she asked.

"I'm on Henry VIII."

"What the hell is there?"

He told her.

"Good," she said. "Just sit tight until I'm through here, and I'll be out there to wipe them out."

"I'm going to do it myself," said Achmed.

"Don't be a fool," she said. "You're no commando. Leave this work to the people who are fit for it."

"How do you know you're fit for something until you try it?" he retorted.

"Have you ever killed anyone?"

"Ask me in ten hours."

"I haven't got time to say it politely. You're no Catastrophe Baker. Just sit tight until I can get there."

"I appreciate your concern, Venus," replied Achmed, "but I can't let other people fight my battles for me."

"Who says it's *your* battle?" she demanded.

"You did, back at the Outpost."

"I didn't mean you."

"I aim to do my part," said Achmed. "Don't worry. I'll be careful. I'll sneak up on them and be gone before they even know I was there."

"They *already* know you're there. You can't land a ship ten miles away without their knowing it."

"Twelve miles," he corrected her.

"Ten, twelve, it makes no difference," said the Cyborg de Milo. "They'll know if you land anywhere in the same hemisphere."

"I'm not afraid."

"Your courage does you no credit," she insisted. "It's born of ignorance. Leave the killing to the killers."

"I plan to make you proud of me," he said, breaking the connection.

He checked his weaponry one last time, climbed into his suit, and opened the hatch.

He never saw the pulse blast from the alien weapon that shattered both his helmet and his head before he could even step out of the ship.

Sinderella and the Aliens

Sinderella got the alien ship in her sights.

"Lock on," she commanded.

"Locked on," responded the computer.

"Fire."

"Firing."

The alien ship became an enormous red blossom, then vanished.

"That's three of the bastards," she said. "Now let's scram before they spot us."

"I require directions."

"Take us to the Wedding Rings."

"Which of the six rings?"

"Take your choice," said Sinderella.

"I am not programmed to make value judgments. I require guidance."

"All right," she said. "Anne Boleyn."

"Course laid in. Shifting to light-speeds."

"Good. And while you're at it, see who's available on the scrambled channel."

"Working . . ."

"This is Nicodemus Mayflower," said a familiar voice. "How are you doing?"

"So far, so good," answered Sinderella. "Maybe *I* can't match the aliens physically, but my ship sure as hell can. I've taken out three of them that were in transit from Henry VI to Henry VII."

"Good!" said Mayflower. "Now, unless you're skilled in evasive maneuvering and defensive warfare, get the hell out of there. One ship might go unnoticed and unavenged, but not three of them."

"Don't worry, I'm headed toward the Wedding Rings right now. I should be safe there. I don't think they can afford the time and manpower—well, *alien*power—it will take to find me in all that debris."

"Fine," said Mayflower approvingly. "It's a good place to sit out the rest of the war."

"I'm not sitting anything out," she replied. "I'm just sort of regrouping, giving them time to get their minds on something else before I reenter the battle."

"Okay, but take it easy. We've got enough heroes out here. Don't try to be another."

"These bastards beat the Navy. We need all the heroes we can get."

"Being a hero isn't something you learn on the job," said Mayflower. "You nailed three of them, and that's something to be proud of—but they probably weren't expecting to be attacked in their own spacelanes. Now that they're ready for you, you're liable to get your ass whipped."

"It's *my* ass," she said stubbornly.

"Well, there's those of us who've grown increasingly fond of it and would like to see it survive intact."

"Thank you, Nicodemus Mayflower," said Sinderella. "I haven't blushed in more than a dozen years—but if I still could, that would have brought a rush of color to my cheeks."

"Just take care of your cheeks," said Mayflower. "*All* of them."

"Not to worry," she replied. "Who's going to chase me all the way out to the Wedding Rings?"

"Braking," announced her ship. "We have arrived at Anne Boleyn."

"Okay, Nicodemus," she said. "I'm going to kill the connection, make a sandwich, take a nice long Dryshower, and—" There was a stunned silence. *"Oh, shit!"*

"What is it?"

"Five of the bastards! They were waiting right here for me. They must be able to read our scrambled channel!"

Another silence.

"Damn! They're shooting at me!" She paused. "It may be easy to hide in the Rings—but it's hard as hell to maneuver with all the junk floating around here." Another pause. "Something hit me! I don't know if it's a rock or one of the aliens!"

"Where are you? I'm on my way, but it's a hell of a big ring!"

"You'll never make it! They just—"

The radio went dead, and a moment later Sinderella's ship began spinning end over end, one more piece of debris in the Wedding Ring known as Anne Boleyn.

The Reverend Billy Karma and the Aliens

The Reverend Billy Karma crept through the valley, wondering just what the hell he was doing here. It was one thing to call down the wrath of God upon these alien infidels, but it was quite another to be the personal bearer of that heavenly wrath.

But somehow or other his enthusiasm had momentarily gotten the better of him, and here he was, in plain sight of the aliens' encampment on Henry VI, hoping against hope that nobody had spotted him, or that (better still) Baker or the cyborg lady were launching attacks at some other point on the perimeter, attacks that would not only send these alien fiends straight to hell but (even more important) would create enough of a distraction to allow him to find a nice, safe hiding place and sit out the rest of this undeclared war.

He sat down behind a huge, blue alien tree, trying to catch his breath and bring his racing pulse back to some semblance of normalcy.

God, what I'd give for a smoke! Or a drink. Or that gorgeous little Sinderella!

He scanned the horizon. He'd seen alien vegetation before, but it had usually been green. Had to be for photosynthesis to work. But this stuff was all blue—the trees, the shrubs, the leaves, even the flowers.

But of course there was no photosynthesis going on here, he realized; otherwise all these trees and bushes would be producing enough oxygen for him to breathe. This must have been one of those planets God made very early on, before He got the knack of it.

Suddenly the Reverend saw some dust off to his left.

Damn! If You had just given this fucking world a breathable atmosphere, I wouldn't be wearing this stupid helmet, and I would have heard whatever it is that's getting so close to me.

Billy Karma flattened himself against the ground, hoping the shrubs surrounding him would protect him from view. He couldn't hear if the aliens who were raising the dust were approaching or walking away, and he didn't dare raise his head to look. He simply lay motionless, his eyes closed tightly, and whispered a few prayers and a couple of admonitions to the Lord.

Then a six-fingered hand clamped down on his shoulder and pulled him to his feet.

The Reverend Billy Karma found himself facing a trio of aliens, all mildly humanoid in shape, all wearing protective suits and helmets.

"Who are you, and why are you spying on us?" asked the alien, its voice coming out cold and without inflection through the translating device built into its helmet.

"Do I look like a spy?" demanded Billy Karma. "I happen to be a man of the cloth."

The three aliens stared at him. "You are composed of flesh and bone, not cloth."

"That's a human expression," explained the Reverend. "It means that I am a man of God."

"That is a contradiction in terms," said the second alien. "*We* were created by God in His image. Therefore, you cannot be."

"Nonsense," shot back Billy Karma. "God created Man, and Satan created all the other races, meaning no offense." He stared at the aliens. "Now that I come to consider it, the three of you look exactly like golem."

"What is golem?"

"A golem is a kind of devil."

"Curious," said the first alien. "You look very much like a Bixtel."

"What's a Bixtel?"

"A devil."

"I've had enough of this blasphemy!" snapped Billy Karma. "I have a number of Bibles in my ship. I'd be happy to give them to you so you can finally learn the truth of things."

"The truth is that you are a great liar," said the first alien. "Probably you are a manifestation of the Prince of Liars Himself."

"Hah!" said Billy Karma. "I repeat: *Hah!* My God can whip your false idol in straight falls without working up a sweat!"

"We shall see," said the first alien, producing a hand weapon. "Start walking."

"Where?"

"I will tell you when to stop."

They proceeded to an encampment, then entered a Bubble. When the hatch closed the aliens waited for almost a minute, then removed their helmets and told Billy Karma that he could do the same.

"You mean God made you oxygen breathers?" he said, taking off his helmet and setting it on the floor. "Must have been one of His very few oversights."

The first alien indicated an odd-looking chair. "Sit."

"In that thing? It wasn't made for real people!"

The alien pushed him into the chair.

"God is really gonna rake you over the coals for this!" promised Billy Karma, shifting uncomfortably as he tried in vain to find a position that was painless.

The second and third aliens secured his arms to the arms of the chair.

"What's going on?" demanded Billy Karma, a slight tremor in his voice.

"We are going to question you," said the first alien.

"How come you can speak Terran? I thought you needed a translating mechanism."

"*I* can speak it. My companions cannot."

"Where'd you learn it?"

"I am asking the questions," said the alien. He leaned forward. "What were you doing outside our encampment?"

"I didn't know you *had* an encampment there!" said Billy Karma.

"All right. What are you doing on Janblixtl?"

"What the hell is Janblixtl?"

"This world."

"This world, you godless alien heathen, happens to be Henry VI," said Billy Karma.

"You have not answered my question," said the alien. He pulled a wicked-looking pointed weapon out of a pouch.

"I told you: I'm a man of God. I travel the galaxy, looking for men and aliens to convert."

"Convert into what?"

"Into God-fearing Christians—something you wouldn't know nothing about."

"I do not believe you," said the alien. "Do you know what I think?"

"What?"

"I think you are a spy, left behind by Man's Navy when we chased them out of this system. I think your duty is to alert nearby systems to our presence, and to report to your superiors on our movements."

"The only superior I acknowledge is God," said Billy Karma. "And He don't need me to tell Him what you're planning on doing, any more than He needs the Navy to stop you. He'll wipe you out in His own good time."

"You insist on maintaining this fiction about being a spokesman of your God?"

"It ain't a fiction! I'm a man of the cloth."

"So you said."

The alien held his pointed weapon to the artificial overhead light. The Reverend Billy Karma watched it in horrified fascination.

"If you are truly God's spokesman, nothing can make you renounce Him, is that correct?" asked the alien.

"What are you getting at?"

"The truth," replied the alien. "And the truth is that nothing can make me renounce *my* God, because I believe in Him with every ounce of my being. If you have been telling the truth, I will not be able to make you renounce yours."

"I don't know about this," said Billy Karma, unable to look away from the weapon. "God understands that Men ain't perfect."

"My race has that much in common with your God," said the alien. "We understand that you're not perfect either."

Billy Karma watched as the light glinted off the metal point of the weapon. "What are you gonna do with that thing?"

"I am going to test the strength of your belief."

He approached Billy Karma and slowly lowered the point until it was resting on the human's thumbnail.

"The Lord is my shepherd . . ." intoned Billy Karma.

The alien leaned down, and the point went through Billy Karma's nail and thumb. The Reverend screamed in agony.

"What is a shepherd?" asked the alien.

"You go to hell!" grated Billy Karma as the blood gushed out of his thumb.

"This could be very time-consuming," said the alien. "You agree, do you not, that I could pierce all ten of your fingers?"

Billy Karma made no reply.

"But that would be dull and repetitious. After all, you have so many fingers." The alien paused. "But you have only two eyes."

Billy Karma pulled his head back as far as he could.

"You look uncomfortable," said the alien. "I had hoped you would have adjusted to the chair by now."

He took a step closer.

"You leave my eyes alone!" screamed Billy Karma.

"Certainly," said the alien. "Just renounce your God and admit that you are a spy left behind by your Navy."

The Reverend Billy Karma took one last look at the bloodied point of the weapon.

"God is a fiction," he said. "I have no use for Him and no belief in Him. I am a spy, left here by the Navy."

"Who is your commander?"

Billy Karma sighed deeply. "Whoever you like."

The three aliens put their heads together and whispered to each other. Then they turned back to Billy Karma.

"What are you going to do to me?" he asked apprehensively.

"We're going to amputate your hands and feet, so that you cannot sneak back here or operate any weaponry, and then, when you are no longer a real or potential threat to us, we are going to put you aboard your ship."

"What if I just promise not to spy on you or fire any weapons?"

"If you would betray your God, why would you not also betray us?" said the alien.

"What about my eyes?"

"That is between you and your God," answered the alien. "At some point you will have to look Him in the eye and explain why you renounced Him."

Six hours later they carried the Reverend Billy Karma to his ship. He was unable to walk, or to manually operate the controls, but his voice brought the ship's computer to life, and shortly thereafter he took off from Henry VI.

His most immediate problem was how to feed himself until he received medical attention. Then there was the problem of adjusting to the prosthetic hands and feet he was sure he would need.

But those were trivial.

The biggest problem of all would come when he finally had to confront God and explain what he had done.

Sahara del Rio and the Aliens

Sahara del Rio's ship settled into orbit around Henry VII, and she ordered her computer to scan for life-forms.

It had been a long time since she'd seen any military action, and in the past she'd usually been a spectator. When Earth was attacked by the Sett Empire, all aliens—Sett and non-Sett alike—had been rounded up and placed in camps until the brief battle was over.

In fact, she'd spent a lot of time in places she didn't much like. Bigotry was outlawed within the Monarchy, but there were always "legal exceptions" and "extraordinary situations." Like the fact that she couldn't purchase a first-class spaceliner fare anywhere in the Spiral Arm. Or that she had to stay in the Alien Quarter on Spica II. Or that she was not allowed to dine in The Fatted Calf, Deluros VIII's finest restaurant.

Oh, it wasn't bigotry, she was assured. Take the spaceliner, for instance. The seats were created for humans, not humanoids such as herself. The company had received so many complaints that humanoid aliens found the seats uncomfortable that they no longer offered them to any race but Man, since they constantly had to refund the price of the ticket.

("Does that mean if I'm uncomfortable in the economy-class seats, I can get a refund?" she had asked. The ticket agent stifled a guffaw and explained why it was impossible.)

As for Spica II, the governor had received numerous death threats. Since there were no human fingerprints on any of the missives, it was assumed that they came from an alien. And while no one in the government was a bigot, surely she understood the necessity of keeping all aliens under observation until they could capture the one who was causing all the trouble.

("How long is this situation likely to last?" she asked as she was directed to the Alien Quarter. No one knew . . . but she finally got them to admit that it had already existed for thirty-four years with the end not yet in sight.)

The Fatted Calf's maître d' explained that the menu was prepared for the human palate, and that it could cause serious digestive problems for aliens.

("But I've lived on Earth for six years and eaten human food the whole time," she explained.)

("I've no reason to doubt you," answered the maître d'

smoothly, "but if we make an exception in your case, then we must admit every alien who is certain he can metabolize human food, and since most of them are not as truthful as you are, we could be legally liable.")

She thought about these and other abuses, all the private insults and public humiliations, and deactivated her ship's scanner. She'd been too long at the Outpost; she had forgotten what normal humans were like.

She took one last look at the scanner, saw that it had picked up alien life-forms near the equator, shrugged, and instructed her navigational computer to lay in a course back to her home planet.

She'd lived among savages too long, and she was damned if she'd go to war on their behalf.

Catastrophe Baker and the Aliens

Catastrophe Baker, all six feet nine inches of him, walked boldly into the middle of the alien encampment on Henry III.

"My name's Baker!" he bellowed. "Catastrophe Baker! And I'm here to settle the war by fighting your champion—winner take all!"

He was instantly surrounded by armed aliens. A hundred weapons were aimed at him. Finally one alien, wearing more medals and brighter insignia than any of the others, stepped forward.

"Your reputation precedes you," he said. "But how do we know you are that hero?"

"If I ain't, your champion will beat me without working up a sweat," answered Baker.

"True enough," said the alien. "But we have already won the war, so your offer is meaningless."

"You ain't won nothing if I'm still standing," said Baker.

"Blow his legs away," said a feminine voice.

Baker turned and found himself facing a beautiful young woman.

"Now that's a hell of a thing for a prisoner to suggest, ma'am," he said. "Meaning no offense."

"I'm not a prisoner."

"Well, if push comes to shove, it's an even worse thing for a turncoat to suggest."

"I'm just a businesswoman. These people need weapons. I sell weapons. We fill mutual needs." She stared at him. "What are you doing here all by yourself?"

"It goes with the heroing trade, ma'am," said Baker. "I aim to take on their most fearsome fighter, wipe up the floor with him, and bring this unfortunate conflict to a close."

She stared at him for a long moment. "You really believe that, don't you?"

"Ain't nothing born, foaled, hatched, or spawned has ever been able to make me holler uncle. I don't imagine these here alien scum got the exception."

"Why should they fight you at all?" said the woman. "They've already defeated the Navy, and you're here all by yourself. Why shouldn't they just kill you and be done with it?"

He stared right back at her. "Are you *sure* you're a woman and not just some alien look-alike?"

"I'm a woman."

"You sure don't sound like a member of the same race. You got a name, ma'am?"

"I've got lots of names," she replied. "In my profession, it's a necessity."

"You got one you prefer to all the others?"

"Not really."

"Then, since we're on Henry III, I think I'll call you Eleanor of Provence."

"Isn't that the name of the moon?"

"You're every bit as round in the right places as the moon," replied Baker.

"Flattery will get you nowhere."

"I ain't flattering you, ma'am," said Baker. "You can't help being beautiful any more than you can help being a deceitful, back-stabbing, unscrupulous traitor to the human race. But at least you're easy on the eyes."

"You still haven't answered the lady's question, Catastrophe Baker," said the alien commander. "Why shouldn't we just shoot you down in cold blood?"

"Because you don't want me to fall down."

"Why not?"

Baker opened his tunic to reveal a number of explosives taped to his torso. "Because if I fall down, so will every alien and every structure within ten miles of me."

"Then why should we have our champion face you?" asked the commander. "If he knocks you down, the effect will be the same as if we were to shoot you right now."

"You give me your word of honor as an alien and an officer that you won't shoot me and I'll take the bombs off before the fight."

"And if we refuse, what then?"

"I ain't thought that far ahead," admitted Baker. "A race that's willing to take on our Navy don't strike me as a bunch of cowards."

"You have a remarkable way of expressing yourself," said the alien. "Even when you are complimenting us, it sounds like an insult."

"Have your champion make me apologize," said Baker with a confident grin.

"You are much bigger than any of us. I don't think it would be a fair fight."

"Tell you what," said Baker. "I ain't twice as big as you. I'll take on your two best at the same time."

"It's an interesting proposition," said the alien commander. "But the stakes are unrealistic. I do not have the authority to call off the war—and when your Navy sends reinforcements, as I suspect it will, I very much doubt that you can get them to return to their base."

"Okay, you got a point," said Baker. "What stakes do you want to fight for?"

"We don't need money and we don't need weapons," answered the alien. "And I have no idea what else you want. So why don't *you* propose the stakes?"

"Okay," agreed Baker, "I reckon I'd better, if we're ever gonna get this thing up and running." He looked around the area, and then his gaze came back to Eleanor of Provence. "Here's my proposition. If I win, you give me the woman."

"What?" she demanded.

"Us humans got to stick together," said Baker. He smiled and winked at her. "The closer the better."

"That's outrageous!"

"Fighting for outrageous stakes just naturally goes with being a hero."

"Just a minute," said the alien commander. "That's what we give you if you win. What do you give us if *we* win?"

"I'll fight the rest of the war on your side."

"Isn't that at odds with your stated beliefs?" asked the commander.

"Sure is," answered Baker. "It'll give me that much more incentive to win."

"But if you *do* lose, you will place yourself under my command?"

"Right." He shrugged. "It won't be so terrible. I *like* fighting."

"It's a deal," said the commander.

"Now wait a minute!" said Eleanor.

The alien turned to her. "I do not expect to lose this wager," he said. "But even if I do, how can I turn down the proposition? If our champions lose, then, while I will miss your wit and charm and companionship, you are, after all, merely a salesperson of dubious loyalty who can be easily replaced. But if we win, we will secure the services of the famous Catastrophe Baker." He turned to Baker. "How long will it take you to prepare?"

"As long as it takes me to unwrap these here bombs."

"We shall be ready."

Baker was watched carefully as he disattached the explosives from his body and laid them gently on the ground. Then he looked around to see if his opponents had shown up yet.

They had. One was short and heavily muscled, the other tall and lean with the grace of a dancer.

"What are the ground rules?" asked the alien commander as the two champions approached Baker.

"What rules?" he responded. "This here is a freehand fight. Hitting, kicking, biting, and gouging are all legal. So are kidney punches—always assuming you *got* kidneys."

"When is it over?"

"When only one of us is left standing."

"I agree to your rules—or lack of them," said the commander. His army moved closer, forming a circle about thirty feet in diameter around the three combatants. "Let the battle begin!"

The muscular alien charged Baker. He could have side-stepped, grabbed an arm, and twisted, but he was curious to see how he measured up to his opponent, so he planted his feet and took the charge against his chest and belly.

The alien bounced off.

Now the tall one approached cautiously, dancing on his toes like a boxer. Suddenly he launched a kick at Baker's groin. Baker grabbed his foot before it landed, lifted it as high as he could, and twisted sharply. The alien flipped in the air and landed on his back with a heavy thud.

Baker grinned. "Come on!" he urged them. "Let me have your best shot!"

Both aliens charged him at once. He took two blows to the face and one to the neck, then swung a roundhouse at the taller, thinner alien and floored him. He felt a trickle of blood on his lip, licked it off, and turned to the muscular alien.

"You throw a pretty nice punch for a little feller," he said. "Now let's see how you take one."

He stalked the alien around the circle, finally cut off his escape route, and connected with a mighty blow to the head. The alien dropped like a ton of bricks.

Just as Baker thought the fight was over, the taller alien leaped onto his back, biting his neck and digging his fingers into Baker's eyes. Baker shook his massive head, sending the alien reeling away. Then he picked the graceful being up, held him over his head, spun around three times, and hurled him as far as he could. The alien flew totally beyond the circle of soldiers, hit the ground heavily, tried groggily to stand up, fell over, and lay still.

Baker turned to the alien commander. "They put up a good fight for a pair of alien heathen. Tell 'em when they wake up that they lasted about as long with me as anyone ever has." He walked up to the woman and took her by the hand. "Come on, Queen Eleanor. Time for us to be going."

As they began walking to his ship, the alien commander called out after him, "You have forgotten your explosives, Catastrophe Baker. We are an honorable race. We will allow you to take them with you."

"You keep 'em," said Baker over his shoulder.

"You are sure?"

"Yeah," he said. "They got waterlogged back on Silverleaf II a couple of years ago and haven't been worth a damn ever since. You couldn't blow 'em up with a detonator."

Sitting Horse and Crazy Bull and the Aliens

This is some ship, this flagship of yours!" said Sitting Horse, obviously impressed.

"Damned thing must be a mile long," added Crazy Bull.

"It is the greatest dreadnought ever constructed," said the captain of the alien vessel.

"The humans don't have a chance," said Crazy Bull. "Not against this thing. What kind of armaments do you carry?"

"One hundred and twenty-one nuclear warheads, seventy-seven pulse energy warheads, sixteen laser cannons, and more than three hundred torpedoes," replied the captain proudly.

"You could probably win the war all by yourself," said Sitting Horse.

"It's quite possible," agreed the captain.

"I *knew* we made the right decision," continued Sitting Horse. "I took one look at this ship and told my friend here that we were fighting on the wrong side, that Men didn't have anything that could stand up to this."

"Besides," said Crazy Bull with a note of contempt in his voice, "what did Men ever do for us?"

"You are just one of the many races that Men have subjugated," said the captain. "I am surprised that you were willing to fight for them."

"*Willing* is the wrong word," said Crazy Bull. "We just didn't see any way they could lose—and if you think Men are hard on races that submit to them, you ought to see what they do to races that try to stand against them."

"That is why we are fighting this war of liberation," said the captain.

"Oh?" said Sitting Horse. "I thought it was to conquer a few more star systems."

"That is another reason," acknowledged the captain calmly.

"And of course, it makes sense to attack Men out here at the edge of the Frontier, where all you had to defeat was a small, unprepared squadron of the Navy."

The captain stared at them for a long moment. "Are you impugning our courage?" he demanded.

"Not at all," said Sitting Horse. "We're complimenting your strategy. Why take on the main body of Man's Navy until you have to? You grow stronger every day, while their political and moral corruption makes them weaker every day."

"I've never thought of it like that," said the captain, "but, on reflection, it's absolutely true."

"Sure," said Sitting Horse. "The day will come when you advance on Deluros VIII at the heart of the Monarchy and no one can stop you."

"You have an exceptionally clear view of the situation," said the captain. "I admire your way of looking at things."

"We admire *your* way," said Crazy Bull. "That's why we chose to defect."

"We are delighted to have two such intelligent beings join us." The captain paused. "I will want you to address the crew later, to discuss the abuses you have suffered at the hands of Men.'"

"It could take hours," said Crazy Bull.

"Maybe days," agreed Sitting Horse.

"Splendid!" exclaimed the captain. "We will excerpt your descriptions of the most humiliating abuses and transmit them to our home world, so that our people will know why we must conquer this vile and odious race."

"We'll be happy to participate," said Sitting Horse. "After all, if it's Man against the galaxy, as we have so often heard their leaders say, then it is only fitting that the galaxy unites against Man."

"And if your race controls a few hundred more worlds when the fighting is done, that's a small price for the galaxy to pay for its freedom from oppression," added Crazy Bull.

"Besides, you'll have *earned* those worlds," said Sitting Horse. "Whereas Man simply *took* them."

"It is a subtle difference," admitted the captain. "I am surprised that you can grasp it so quickly."

"We've been trained by experts."

The captain didn't know quite how to respond to that statement, so he settled for summoning his steward and breaking open a bottle of his home planet's most potent beverage. They spent the next hour toasting each other's good health and swearing eternal friendship.

Then Sitting Horse stood up, swaying gently, and asked directions to the bathroom. When he returned it was Crazy Bull's turn, and finally they signed their official requests for asylum.

"Excellent!" said the captain. "I'll show you to your quarters now."

"First we've got to get our gear off our own ship," said Crazy Bull.

"You didn't bring it with you?"

"We didn't know what kind of welcome we would receive," said Sitting Horse. "We might have decided you were no better than Men."

"If you had refused to join us, I might have tortured you, or thrown you into the brig," said the captain.

"Why?" asked Sitting Horse. "After all, we're not the enemy. We're just another poor, innocent, downtrodden race."

"So how do we get back to our ship?" asked Crazy Bull.

The captain signaled for his steward again, and the steward showed them back to their own ship.

A moment later they were sitting at their controls, starting to break free of the huge alien flagship.

"Terrible-tasting stuff, wasn't it?" remarked Crazy Bull as they sped away.

"Give me human booze every time," agreed Sitting Horse, adjusting the ship's spin. "By the way, do you think there's any chance he'll find the bomb?"

"I doubt it," said Crazy Bull. "You hid it pretty damned well. I mean, hell, it took *me* a couple of minutes to find it so I could activate the timer, and I knew it was there. Besides, what possible reason would he have for looking behind the toilet bowl?"

"How long until it blows?"

Crazy Bull checked his timepiece. "Maybe ten more seconds. Don't worry—we're clear."

They both looked at the viewscreen where, nine seconds later, the alien flagship exploded. For a brief moment it seemed almost as bright as a supernova.

"Well, I'll be damned!" said Sitting Horse with his less-than-firm grasp of human history. "It's General Custard and the Big Little Horn all over again!"

Hellfire Van Winkle and
the Aliens

Hellfire Van Winkle sped toward Edith of Scotland, the smaller of Henry I's two moons.

"So you thought you could hide here?" he muttered aloud as the alien encampment showed up on his sensor screen. "Hell, if I could find the last Landship in the jungles of Peponi, I can sure as hell find a military outpost on a dead moon."

He fell silent again, the current moment less real to him than the past. He remembered the sights and smells of Peponi, the feel of the thornbush as it scraped against his safari jacket, the taste of cold, pure water on a hot afternoon, the thrill of the hunt, the adrenaline rush when he finally got a Demoncat or a Sabrehorn or a Landship in his sights.

What the hell was he doing here, fighting aliens he'd never seen in a ship he hadn't adjusted to in a section of the Frontier that hadn't even been mapped when he was a young man? He was not only half a galaxy away from where he wanted to be; he was *millennia* away.

Time hadn't so much passed him by as played a nasty trick on him. He didn't fit here, didn't belong in this era, wasn't comfortable anywhere except perhaps the Outpost, where he could rub shoulders and swap stories with other misfits. But misfits though they all were, none fitted in as awkwardly as Hellfire Carson. (Make that Hellfire Van Winkle, he corrected himself with a grimace; one more example of Time thumbing its nose at him.)

Yes, he'd outlived his time, no question about it. Now he had to prove that he hadn't outlived his usefulness as well.

The problem was that he was tired of outliving things. He should have been dead and buried 4,700 years ago. He hadn't enjoyed the past dozen years, and he didn't anticipate enjoying the next dozen either.

So if I survive this battle, what will I do with the rest of my life? Just sit around remembering the past and feeling cheated because it was taken away from me before I was through with it? That's no way for anyone to live.

His mind made up, Hellfire Van Winkle yelled out a "Geronimo!" that no one else could hear, aimed his ship at the very center of the military encampment, and increased his speed.

Just before he hit, he idly wondered if the explosion would be visible all the way to the Outpost. He was not surprised to discover that he didn't really give a damn.

Big Red and the Aliens

The tunnel was cold and damp, and it smelled like a sewer. Small alien animals scurried to and fro, and ugly alien insects clung to the ceiling. Big Red tried not to notice them.

He'd landed on Henry IV, well away from the main body of alien soldiers. Hurricane Smith had said to leave them for him, and he was more than happy to do so. His scanner found a prison in a deserted city halfway around the planet, and he landed near it with the intention of releasing any human prisoners who had been incarcerated there.

A mile from the city's walls he'd found the tunnel's exit. He'd come almost two miles now, and by his estimate he had to be near the center of the city. So far there'd only been two branches, neither of them any more promising than the main corridor.

It was possible, of course, that he'd walk for another couple of miles and find himself outside on the far side of the city, but he doubted it. The tunnel may have smelled like a sewer, but it wasn't constructed like one. It had to lead somewhere, and he was intent on following it to its end.

He proceeded another three hundred feet, and then the tunnel took a hard turn to the left. Twenty more feet and he came to a metal door.

He pushed against it. No luck. He tried to find a latch or handle to pull on. Nothing.

Finally he withdrew his laser and melted the door. Then he waited a few minutes so he wouldn't burn through his boots as he stepped over the molten slag.

He came to a ramp that led upward at a slight angle and followed it. Before he'd ascended halfway he heard alien voices, and he froze. He concentrated on the voices, but he couldn't differentiate them well enough to determine how many aliens were above him. He waited until he heard footsteps retreating, made sure his burner had recharged itself, and climbed silently to the top of the ramp.

Two aliens had their backs to him and never knew what hit them. He pulled the corpses into a darkened area, then surveyed his surroundings.

Corridors jutted off in every direction. As he was trying to decide which one to follow, he heard a strong, masculine voice singing a bawdy song about a young mutant maiden who had three of everything that could possibly be considered worthwhile.

He crept toward the voice, pistol in hand, peering into the darkness, ready for anything. The voice became louder (and the song even bawdier), and finally he emerged into a huge chamber surrounded by a number of prison cells. There were no doors on the cells, but he knew from the faint humming permeating the area that they were protected by a force field.

The voice had reached the point in the song where he had everything required to satisfy the mutant maiden grafted onto his body, and was just beginning the final verse when it stopped almost in midstanza.

"Watch yourself!" it said suddenly. "Everything's hot."

"I know," said Big Red. "Where are the controls?"

"On the far wall. Are you the advance party or the whole show?"

"The whole show," said Big Red, walking cautiously to the control box.

"Hey! I know you!"

Big Red turned and looked into the cell.

"I know you too!" he exclaimed. "You're Backbreaker Barnes! I saw you the night you fought for the title!"

"I wish you'd seen me on one of the nights I won," replied Barnes ruefully. "And you're the one they call the Quadruple Threat—basketball, baseball, track, and . . . and something else."

"Murderball," said Big Red. He indicated the control box. "Do you know if I can just melt this thing, or is it booby-trapped?"

"They're not expecting company. Go ahead and melt it."

Big Red fried the control box, which sparked and sputtered for a fraction of a second and then went dead.

Backbreaker Barnes walked to the front of his cell and cautiously extended his hand. When he didn't receive a shock, he smiled and stepped out into the corridor.

"I don't know what brought you here, but I'm mighty glad to see you. Big Red, isn't it?"

"Right. Are you the only one here?"

"I am now."

"What happened to the others?"

"I did."

"I don't understand."

"They captured about a dozen of us and locked us down here. Once or twice a day they'd drag two of us up to ground level, stick us in an arena, and make us fight to the death."

"You killed them all?"

"If I hadn't, the aliens would have. Those were the rules: two men went in, one came out. The first day I knocked Captain Mazurski out and refused to kill an unconscious man, so one of the aliens blew him away. The second day I got Mukande Nbolo so bloody and groggy he could barely stand up. I stopped fighting, even when they threatened me. I thought they were going to kill me for refusing an order, but instead they decided Nbolo was in no shape to fight again the next day so they shot him instead. After that I knew it was me or my opponent, that there was no way both fighters were ever going to be allowed to live, so I killed each of them as quickly and painlessly as possible."

"Well, I suppose I can't blame you for staying alive," said Big Red.

"It wasn't that hard," admitted Barnes. "I didn't have to fight anyone like, say, you." He stared thoughtfully at Big Red. "I wonder how you'd have done?"

"Let's be glad we'll never have to find out," said Big Red. "Now, how the hell do we get out of here?"

"The most direct way is straight up, but even if you loan me your screecher we're going to be outnumbered by hundreds to one. I suppose the best way is to go back the way you came."

"Right," said Big Red. "We'd better get going. I had to kill a couple of guards. For all I know, they're late calling in or reaching a checkpoint."

"Do you know the way back?" asked Barnes. "We were chained and blindfolded when they brought us here. The only way out I know is up through the arena."

"I'm pretty sure I can find it. I know it's on a lower level, and there were only a couple of branches the whole way."

"Okay, lead the way."

Big Red tossed him a sonic pistol. "Here, take this."

"Nice screecher," said Barnes admiringly. "Beautifully weighted."

"Believe it or not, I won it in a track meet."

"Are you still in shape?"

"I try to keep fit. Why?"

"That wasn't an academic question," said Barnes. "I just heard some footsteps coming in our direction. Let's get moving."

Big Red broke into a trot, his long, loping stride eating up ground as he descended to the tunnel level and began retracing his steps. Backbreaker Barnes, panting heavily, his muscular body built for strength rather than speed, followed as best he could. When Big Red pulled too far ahead, he slowed down so as not to lose contact with Barnes.

After a mile they stopped and listened for sounds of pursuit.

"I think they gave up," gasped Barnes.

"We'd better keep running anyway," said Big Red. "They can always signal ahead to others."

"How much farther have we got to go?"

"Maybe a mile and a half."

"I'm beat," said Barnes. "I can't run that far." Suddenly the sounds of footsteps and voices came to their ears. "They're going to catch us anyway," continued Barnes. "We might as well have it out right here."

"What are you talking about?" demanded Big Red.

"I'm undefeated. That's why they let me live." He took a fighting stance. "Besides, I *like* being the champion."

"Have you lost your mind?" said Big Red. "They're going to be here in another minute!"

"And they'll find me standing over your body."

Barnes dove for him, but Big Red was too quick. He side-stepped and pushed Barnes head-first into a wall as he raced by. Barnes bellowed in pain and turned to face his opponent, but all he got for his trouble were two quick kicks, one in the groin, the other to his left knee. He fell to the floor, cursing.

"I *told* you I played murderball," said Big Red.

The alien voices became louder.

"Help me up!" cried Barnes, clutching his shattered kneecap. "They're almost here!"

"Give them my regards, Champ," said Big Red.

He started running again. He'd barely broken a sweat when he reached the safety of his ship and took off.

The Earth Mother and the Aliens

In a small interrogation room on Elizabeth of York, the sole moon of Henry VII, the Earth Mother faced a pair of aliens.

"Name?"

"The only name I answer to is the Earth Mother."

"That is not the name on your passport."

"I am not responsible for that," she answered calmly.

"What is your purpose for coming here?"

"There's a war. I'm not a warrior. I heard you had a hospital here. I want to help."

"But the hospital is run by and for members of our race. Why do you not work at a human hospital?"

"There aren't any in this system. You have either destroyed our Navy, or at least chased them to a system we control where they can get all the help they need."

"Then why should we need any help at all?" asked one of the aliens.

"Because a small group of Men has taken up the battle, and you will find that, in their way, they are more formidable than the Navy." She stared at the two aliens. "If you don't need medical help yet, you soon will."

"Why should we believe you?" asked the second alien.

"I am unarmed. I am in what we call late middle age, and I am seventy pounds overweight. I have high blood pressure and diabetes. Surely even *you* must realize that I pose no threat to you—and I *do* possess medical knowledge that may be unknown to you."

"Are you a doctor among your own people?"

"No."

"A nurse, then?"

"No. But in my prior profession, I was frequently called upon to heal the wounded."

"Why didn't you send them to a medic?"

"Our social structure would probably make no sense to you. Just believe me that there were valid reasons why they did not want anyone to know that they had patronized my business."

The aliens exchanged knowing smiles. "Perhaps you are not as incomprehensible as you believe," said the first one. "All right,

Earth Mother. You may work in our hospital as a nurse."

"But know that you will be under electronic surveillance at all times," added the second.

"That will be perfectly acceptable," said the Earth Mother, getting to her feet. "Which way do I go?"

One of the aliens got up. "I will show you."

He showed her into a small dressing room, waited while she donned the uncomfortable and ill-fitting blue-gray robes of an alien nurse, and then escorted her to a ward, where she was introduced to her superior.

Her first job was emptying and cleaning alien bedpans. As she collected them, she carefully studied the anatomy of the wounded alien soldiers. Later, in the nurses' dormitory, she joined a few of her workmates in the group shower and spent as much time scrutinizing them as they did her.

Yes, she decided, it should work just fine. *A few days, a little gossip, maybe a little surreptitious observation, and I should know everything I need to know. We're not all that different, your race and mine, and there's no reason why I shouldn't bring my non-medical expertise to the situation at hand. I mean, hell, we've already got a few empty wards filled with brand-new beds. Now all I have to do is figure how much to charge to fill them.*

She looked out at the ward. An alien soldier, his foot blown off, his torso swathed in bandages, still managed to pinch a nurse as she walked by.

The Earth Mother smiled. *This is going to be easier than I thought.*

Argyle and the Aliens

I'm approaching Henry V," said Argyle. "I should make contact with the aliens any moment now."

"Have you gone crazy?" demanded Gravedigger Gaines's voice

on the subspace radio. "Most of their forces are on Henrys IV and V!"

"Well, there wouldn't really be much sense going to Henry I, would there?" replied Argyle.

"Three-Gun Max is already on V, and I think Venus is on her way there. Leave the fighting to them and get your ass out of there."

"I'm no fighter," said Argyle.

"Then why aren't you back at the Outpost?" said Gaines.

"They're aliens. *I'm* an alien. They just might listen to me."

"Idiot!" snapped Gaines. "You're as much an alien to them as you are to us."

Argyle frowned. "I hadn't thought of it that way," he admitted.

"Then maybe it's time for you to *start* thinking, and get the hell out of the system."

"Thanks for your concern, but I really think someone has to try reasoning with them."

"The time for reasoning was over when they blew a hundred Navy ships out of the sky." Gaines paused. "I'm going to have to break off communications with you. Even with a scrambled signal, you're getting close enough to the planet for them to home in on you."

"I'm not trying to hide my presence," said Argyle. "There must be someone on the other side who will listen to reason."

"Your giant computer listened to reason," noted Gaines, "but it didn't do either of you a hell of a lot of good, did it?"

"We're not savages. Neither are they. Surely history is on our side."

"History is usually on the side with the best weapons," said Gaines. "Over and out."

Argyle maintained his distance from the planet until the aliens signaled his ship.

"Identify yourself."

"My name is Argyle. I'm a native of—"

"Your vessel, fool!"

"It's a spaceship. What do you wish to know about it?"

"Registration. Point of origin. Duration of current voyage. Destination. Armaments."

"I'm having my computer feed you all the data now."

"What is your purpose for being in this system?"

"I was having a drink with my friends on Henry II," said. Argyle.

"Are you a human?"

"No."

"Are you a member of a race allied with the Commonwealth?"

"Yes, I am."

"Remain in orbit. Two of our fighter ships will approach you and escort you to the planet's surface."

"I will do as you request," said Argyle. "Then I would like to speak to someone in charge."

"That was an order, not a request."

"Then I will do as you order," Argyle corrected himself. "But I would still like to speak to someone in authority."

There was no response, and a few minutes later two fighter ships showed up. They flanked him and herded him to the hastily assembled spaceport.

Once on the ground he was escorted, at gunpoint, to an interrogation room, where a slightly bored alien bureaucrat was waiting for him.

"We have no record of an Argyle owning a ship with the registration number of RP1034CB."

"That is because my true name is not Argyle. That is a name given to me by my human friends."

"Why should a member of any other race have human friends?"

"They are an interesting race, not without aspects of nobility and compassion," said Argyle.

The alien muttered an untranslatable sound.

"Anyway, to answer your question, my true name, and the name on the ship's registration, is Quilbot Phylnx Quilbit."

"And why are you here, Quilbot Phylnx Quilbit?"

"I have come to reason with you."

"We're very busy fighting a war. Why should we take the time to listen to you?"

"Because I am not a Man."

"But you have obviously been contaminated by Men."

"They do not wish this war."

"That is hardly my concern," said the alien.

"Whatever your grievances, I'm sure we can address them without resorting to war," persisted Argyle. "There is ultimately no justification for two races killing each other."

"Nonsense," said the alien. "Do you know how many laborers and industries we'd put out of work if we were to stop the war just because a few bleeding hearts think we can talk out our grievances?"

"But there are peaceful means of settling your differences!"

"Peaceful, perhaps," said the alien. "Glorious, no. And economically advantageous, never."

"There is nothing glorious about death," said Argyle.

"Why do *I* get all the pacifists?" muttered the alien. "I've put in my time. I don't make waves. I deserve better."

The alien sighed and pointed his pistol at Argyle's head.

"You will not shoot me," said Argyle confidently. "That would be irrational."

"What is so very advantageous about being rational?" asked the alien, slipping off the safety device. "It simply makes you more predictable. That was the very first thing we learned in officers' candidate school."

"But I am your last hope!" insisted Argyle. "All the others are prepared to fight. Only I am willing to find an alternative."

"Thank goodness for small favors," sighed the alien. "For a moment I was afraid they were all like you."

He fired the weapon, and Man's last best hope for peace—indeed, his only one—fell dead upon the floor.

The Cyborg de Milo and the Aliens

The Cyborg de Milo crept silently down the tortuously twisting streets of the ancient metropolis on Henry V. The city had been built ten millennia earlier by a long-vanished race, and had stood empty until the aliens set up their headquarters there after decimating the Navy.

She was tempted to use the torch that had been embedded in one of her fingers, but torches attracted attention, and Men with torches weren't supposed to be here, so she resisted the temptation.

The Cyborg had no particular destination in mind, just a general pattern of destruction. But it couldn't begin too soon. There were at least five hundred aliens stationed in the city, and she didn't want to broadcast her presence until she lowered the odds a bit.

She had hoped to keep to the alleyways, but there weren't any. Her next notion was to go underground and make her way via the sewer system, but she had no map of it, and she didn't relish trying to find her way with no maps and no landmarks. So, keeping as near to the irregular structures as she could, she continued stalking silently among the ancient buildings.

She was fast approaching a very sharp corner, and suddenly she could hear voices—*alien* voices—somewhere up ahead of her.

The voices grew clearer and louder, until she estimated that they were no more than thirty yards from the corner. Her first inclination was to duck into the doorway of the nearest building until they passed. Then she discovered that it didn't *have* a doorway. She backtracked a few steps, found a small alcove between the building and the one she had just passed, and darted into it. Then she crouched down and waited.

Five aliens in military uniforms suddenly came into view as they turned the corner. One of them had an extremely high-pitched voice, but she couldn't discern any other difference among them.

She looked up and down the street, made sure no one else was around, then pointed two of her deadly fingers at the group. Three fell to the laser, two to the incredibly powerful beam of solid sound.

She ducked back into the shadows and squatted down, waiting to see if anyone had spotted the carnage. Before long her calves and thighs began cramping, and she carefully leaned forward, momentarily assuming the position of a runner in the starting blocks, alternately stretching each leg out behind her.

The Cyborg waited for almost three minutes, then carefully stood erect, stuck her head out, looked in both directions, and quickly walked to the corner.

The street soon made a hairpin turn, almost doubling back on itself, and simultaneously narrowed to a point where it was less than ten feet wide. She felt very claustrophobic as she kept walking and the street kept narrowing. Within another hundred yards she had to walk sideways, with her back pressed against a wall, to pass between buildings on the opposite side of the alien street.

Then it broadened again, not slowly and gradually, but abruptly, and in a single stride she went from a street so narrow that it seemed like a corridor to a thoroughfare so wide that she thought for a moment that she was in a large public square.

There was no artificial illumination, but the moon Catherine de Valois was directly overhead, and none was needed. It was almost bright enough to read by the moonlight, and she realized that she had almost three hundred yards to walk before the street narrowed again, three hundred yards in which there were no lampposts, no benches, no trash atomizers, nothing to hide behind, and she would be the only living, moving thing.

She considered traveling via the rooftops, but very few of the buildings were remotely similar in height and structure. The sewers were out; too: even if she had a map, which she didn't, she didn't know how to go about finding an entrance to them.

Finally she decided that there was no alternative to crossing as quickly and silently as she could, and this she proceeded to do, staying as close to the buildings on the left side of the street as possible. When she had covered slightly more than half the distance, she saw an alien staring at her from a fourth-story window.

She pointed her finger at him, and he tumbled down to the ground, the hole between his eyes still smoking. She expected to hear outraged screams, or alarm sirens, or approaching footsteps, or *something*, but nothing happened, and in another ninety seconds she had turned another corner and found herself on a street that, for a change, seemed neither too wide nor too narrow.

She stepped into some deep shadows as two more aliens came into view. She was taking aim at them when they entered a small building. Curious, she approached it and tried to peer in, but the windows were too high.

Then a trio of aliens began approaching, and she once again hid in the shadows and watched as they entered the building.

This had to be it—the enemy's barracks.

She went around back, looking for a less conspicuous entrance—and couldn't find one. She spent a few more minutes trying to figure out how to gain surreptitious entrance to the building, and couldn't hit upon a solution. At last she leaned against a wall while considering her options—and almost fell over backward when a four-foot-wide section of the wall slid behind a discolored part of the building.

She looked around quickly, before the wall slid back and plunged the interior of the building into total darkness, and found a narrow staircase. She shone her finger's torch on it just long enough to fix the height of each stair in her mind and then slowly, carefully, began ascending. Eighteen stairs later she reached a landing.

She activated her torch again and examined the landing. There were four doors—one open, three closed. She walked to the open one and looked in. There was no one there.

She returned to the landing, studied the other three doors, and chose one at random. She opened it, found herself facing some twenty aliens in various stages of sleep and undress, and began firing. This time a number of them screamed before dying, and she raced back to the landing, waiting for more aliens to burst out of the other two doors.

As quickly as they ran out, she mowed them down.

"Who *are* you?" cried one of the aliens who had not yet emerged.

"I am your death, come to seek you out," she answered. "As I seek out all who attack the race of Man."

The alien yelled something in his own language, and got an immediate response from a different room.

The Cyborg decided that since her presence was probably known to the whole city by now, secrecy was unnecessary. She aimed a finger at the ceiling, fired a ball of energy into it, listened to the screams from within the rooms as the building began collapsing, and raced down the stairs.

She walked out into the open, surprised that there wasn't an armed battalion waiting for her.

"It can't be this easy," she muttered—and sure enough, it wasn't.

As she rounded a corner, she found herself facing a dozen aliens. She heard a scuffling sound behind her, turned, and saw that five more aliens were behind her.

"You are our prisoner!" said one of the aliens in front of her. "Make no sudden moves."

She looked around as the alien approached her. There was no chance of reaching the temporary safety of a building before they gunned her down.

"Where are your weapons?" demanded the alien.

"I have none."

"Do not lie to me. You have killed more than twenty of us."

"More than forty, actually," she replied.

"Where are they?"

She pointed toward the aliens that were facing her. "Beyond that building," she said.

The alien peered ahead of him. "Which building?"

She looked at the armed aliens. They were relaxed, secure in the knowledge that she was unarmed, that their commander was in complete control of the situation.

She lowered her finger until it pointed directly at them.

"That one."

And then, before anyone quite knew what was happening, she sprayed the aliens with a laser beam. In one motion she pivoted, crouched, and turned the beam on the five aliens behind her. One of them actually managed to get off a shot—a wild one—before he died; the others all lay where they had fallen.

"I don't believe it!" said the alien commander. "You are a mere female!"

"There's nothing *mere* about me," she said ominously. "Drop your weapons."

He did as he was told.

"Have you got a knife or a sword?"

He leaned down and picked up a knife from the pile of discarded weapons.

"You're about to learn what a motivated female can do," she said, as a shining blade sprung out from one of her fingers.

"And you will use no weapon but that?" he asked.

"It's all I need."

A smile crossed his alien face, and he charged her, knife extended. She side-stepped and slashed his forearm.

He spun around, swiped at her with the knife, then charged again—and got slashed again for his trouble.

"I would not like to be your mate," he muttered, approaching her more cautiously this time.

"It's not something you're ever going to have to worry about," she said, feinting with the blade and landing a solid kick to his knee.

"You are already dead," panted the alien, barely able to support his weight on his crippled leg. "You just don't know it."

"I never liked braggarts," she said, slashing his left cheek. "Especially pompous male braggarts."

"I am not bragging," he said. "I know I cannot defeat you. But I don't have to. I just have to keep you here for another minute, and then more of my warriors will arrive, so many that even your weaponry will be useless against them."

"Then we've no time to waste, have we?" she said, stepping in close and burying her blade deep in his chest. He groaned once and fell lifeless to the ground.

The Cyborg de Milo wiped off her blade, then allowed it to slip back into her artificial finger.

She began counting. There were the first five she had killed. Then the one in the window. There were seventeen here on the street. And despite what she'd claimed, she was sure there were at least fifty more inside the barracks building.

Seventy-three total. Maybe even a few more. Not bad at all.

And the night was young yet. She looked up and down the street, ready to add to the total.

There were no aliens in sight. Possibly they were hiding. Or regrouping. Or plotting strategy.

It made no difference. Wherever they were, she would find them. Whatever attack they planned, she would face it. She was the Cyborg de Milo, and this is what she was created for—what she had created herself for.

She began walking slowly down the middle of the street.

"Come out, come out, wherever you are," she called ominously.

Bet-a-World O'Grady and the Aliens

The casino on Mozart II was almost empty. Word of the war had gotten out.

Bet-a-World O'Grady wished there was a little more business going on. He liked the hustle and bustle of a well-run casino, and he especially liked having a few well-endowed nude girls dancing not too far away. Not that he had any interest in them (unless they had some interest in games of chance), but they provided a distraction to his opponents, and O'Grady used every angle available in his quest for victory.

Still, he mused, dancing girls probably wouldn't have much effect on the aliens he had contacted. He didn't know anything about them, except that they seemed to have a mad-on against Man, but he couldn't imagine an alien would have any more visceral interest in watching a human girl take her clothes off than he himself would have in watching a bird molt to music.

O'Grady sipped his drink and began going through his warm-up exercises. He shuffled a brand-new deck, dealt out four hands, turned the cards up, and noted that he hadn't lost his touch: each hand contained a royal flush.

He shuffled again, cut to an ace, then to another, and then to a third. There was no sense cutting to the fourth; he had already palmed it.

He spent a few moments dealing seconds, then false-shuffled for a few more. His fingers felt limber now, and he got up to go to the bathroom, where, once he was certain no one was watching, he inserted his specialized lenses that would enable him to see any markings should the aliens use their own crooked deck.

That done, he returned to the table, spent a few more minutes dealing bottoms, then concluded by practicing the Greek deal and the center deal.

Just about the time he was wondering if the aliens would show up, the hatch opened and four humanoid beings stepped into the airlock. Once the hatch was secured they removed their protective suits and entered the casino.

The one who appeared to be their leader looked around at the empty tables. Then his gaze fell on O'Grady.

"Welcome," said O'Grady. "I've been waiting for you."

"We are not late," said the leader, approaching him.

"Well, you're here now, and that's all that matters. Have you got a name?"

"I have eleven of them, depending on the occasion," replied the alien.

"Which one do you want me to use?"

"They are all beyond your ability to pronounce," said the alien. "Why not choose one that you are comfortable with?"

"Fine by me," said O'Grady. "From this moment on, you are Nick the Greek."

"A human name?"

"He was probably a little less human than some, but, yeah, it's a human name."

"And you, of course, are Bet-a-World O'Grady."

"Right."

"May I sit down?" asked Nick the Greek.

"Certainly." O'Grady gestured to the other three aliens. "Your men are welcome to sit, too."

"They are not men, and they will stand."

"Whatever makes you happy."

"Tell me, Bet-a-World O'Grady," said Nick the Greek, "do you really bet entire worlds on card games?"

"I've been known to do it on card games, rolls of the dice, sporting events, and just about anything else where you can determine a winner and a loser."

"Most interesting."

"But you already know that, or else you wouldn't have shown up."

"We did check you out thoroughly," admitted Nick the Greek.

"And you have the authority to match my bets?"

"Yes."

"Your generals must think you're one hell of a gambler."

"I do my best," said Nick the Greek modestly.

"Where did you learn to play human games?" asked O'Grady.

"I have traveled the Inner Frontier extensively. And I studied under one of the greatest of all human gamblers."

"Who was that?"

"An old friend of yours," said Nick the Greek. "High-Stakes Eddie Strongbow."

"High-Stakes Eddie?" exclaimed O'Grady. "Well, I'll be damned! How is the old bastard?"

"He is no longer among the living, I regret to inform you," said the alien.

"Sorry to hear it."

"I understand human etiquette requires some preliminary banter," said Nick the Greek. "Shall we begin to play, or is further speech required?"

"Might as well get started." O'Grady signaled to the robot bartender. "Half a dozen new decks, please."

"I will be allowed to inspect each deck, will I not?"

"To your heart's content," said O'Grady. "Always assuming you've *got* a heart."

"And what game shall we be playing?" asked the alien.

"I'm a poker man myself, but I'm always open to suggestions."

"Poker will be satisfactory."

The bartender dropped off the decks. O'Grady pushed one across the table to Nick the Greek. "Go ahead and examine it," he said.

The alien broke the seal on the pack, inspected the cards carefully, then nodded his approval.

"Stakes?" asked the alien.

"Let's start out at fifty thousand credits a hand," said O'Grady. "That ought to buy your side a handful of weapons if you win."

"That is acceptable."

"Cut for draw?" asked O'Grady.

Nick the Greek cut to a nine. O'Grady grinned and cut to a jack.

"Five-card stud," he announced.

O'Grady won the first two hands, lost the third so as not to discourage the alien, then won two more.

"The cards are running against you, Nick, old fellow," he said at last. "Maybe this isn't your night."

"I have been ordered to accept your challenge and play poker with you," said the alien. "We need the money for fuel and weaponry."

"What you need and what you're going to get aren't necessarily the same things," said O'Grady.

He promptly lost the next three hands, and then played the alien even for almost two hours. At the end of the time he sighed and leaned back in his chair.

"Looks like no one's getting rich tonight," he said. "I'll tell you what: let's let it all ride on one hand."

"Define *all*," said the alien.

"If I win, you give me all the money you've got with you, and all your soldiers clear off Catherine de Valois—that's the moon you're stationed on."

"And if I win?"

"You get all the money I've got with me, any worlds I hold title to, and I'll sit out the war in one of your prison cells."

The alien seemed hesitant. "That's a lot to bet on a single hand . . ." he said at last.

"Then let's see if I can make it more enticing," said O'Grady. "Have you ever played Face-Up Draw?"

"What are the rules?"

"Just like draw poker, but we put all the cards face-up on the table. We each take five cards; we can discard up to four of them and pull four more."

"We will each choose a royal flush, and hence we will always tie," said Nick the Greek.

"Maybe not."

"It is a certainty."

"All right," said O'Grady. "I'll tell you what—I will stipulate, in writing if you wish, that you win all ties."

"Let me make sure I understand this," said Nick the Greek. "There is no value to the suits. A royal flush in spades is no higher than a royal flush in diamonds or clubs?"

"Right."

"And I win all ties?"

"Yes."

"I agree to your conditions," said the alien.

"Shake on it," said O'Grady, extending his hand.

Nick the Greek took his hand.

"And since you still look distrustful, I'll go first." O'Grady smiled at the alien. "That way you can see what I've pulled before making your own choices."

Suddenly Nick the Greek's three companions came to life, and three pistols were pointed at O'Grady's head.

"No, Bet-a-World O'Grady," said Nick the Greek. "I think *I* shall go first."

"But—"

"That's the way High-Stakes Eddie taught it to me, just before I killed him."

O'Grady sighed and settled back in his chair. He had a feeling that it was going to be a long time before he saw the Outpost again.

Nicodemus Mayflower and the Aliens

Nicodemus Mayflower's ship raced for Anne Boleyn, the second Wedding Ring circling cold, distant Henry VIII. Every few minutes he would send out a message on the scrambled channel, asking for some response from Sinderella, some signal so that he would know she was still alive.

He received no answer.

As he approached the eighth Henry two alien ships came out to meet him. He fired the instant they showed up on his sensor screens, disabling one of them as the other evaded his laser cannon and returned fire.

He avoided the pulses of energy and headed for Catherine Parr, the outermost of the six Wedding Rings. Once there he hid among the rocks and debris, shutting down his systems so the alien couldn't read any neutrino activity. He knew the alien would search for him, perhaps summon the other ships that had attacked Sinderella in the Anne Boleyn ring, and he was ready for them. He'd been in enough battles to know that one ship could make a stand against two or three, but once the other side had four or more, the odds against victory were astronomical, because now they could put together an englobement, the ultimate offensive formation.

Well, let them try. No one was going to englobe him, not here among all God's leftovers. This was no asteroid belt, where the actual sighting of a nearby asteroid was a relatively rare phenomenon. This was a ring, and there were literally billions of rocks and iceballs racing around in a tight orbit. You could hide in a ring, but you sure as hell couldn't perform precise military maneuvers in one, not without putting your hull at risk.

He waited patiently, activating his sensors for two seconds every minute. It was enough time for them to spot approaching ships, but not (he hoped) enough time for an alien ship with sophisticated sensing devices (which he did not know for a fact that they actually possessed) to determine that there was sufficient neutrino activity to investigate.

Finally, after sixty-seven minutes, he struck paydirt: the sensors found an alien ship about sixteen miles away, carefully picking its way among the debris. His first inclination was to bring all his systems to life, lock onto the enemy ship, and fire—but he realized that there might be hundreds, perhaps thousands, of rocks blocking a clear shot, rocks that would deflect or absorb the killing force of his various weapons while signaling his position to the aliens.

So he waited, and waited, and finally, when it seemed that the aliens would never give him a clear shot, their ship closed to within a mile. An alien voice, speaking almost perfect Terran, tried to raise him via the radio, but he chose not to answer. Let them think his ship was dead. Let them close in and prepare to board. Let them lower their guard just for an instant.

It was when the alien ship was only thirty yards away that he suddenly activated his laser and energy pulse cannons and fired point-blank at it. The ship turned red, then white, and then vanished from sight.

His instruments told him that the alien ship had signaled to its companions. He couldn't decipher the message, but doubtless it was telling them that they had found a human ship and were preparing to examine it more closely. Now that they wouldn't respond to any queries from their comrades, it seemed a dead certainty that the other ships would soon be seeking him out, trying to determine what had happened—and they'd be a lot more cautious, since they had no way of knowing what had happened to the first ship.

How many had Sinderella mentioned? Five? He'd downed two, so there were at least three remaining. He figured he ought to be able to nail at least one the same way he'd just disposed of the last ship, maybe even two. Then, with the odds even, or nearly so, he'd break out of cover and match his skills against the remaining ship or ships in a good old-fashioned dogfight.

And then the scrambled channel came to life.

"Somebody! *Any*body!" said Sinderella's voice. "I'm in a bad way. My ship's disabled and losing air. I have no motive power, about half my systems aren't working, and none of my weapons are operative. I'm—"

"I know where you are!" interrupted Mayflower. "Let's keep it to ourselves."

"Nicodemus!" she cried. "Are you nearby? I'll be out of air in another half hour."

"Get into your spacesuit. Depending on the make, it's got from six to fourteen hours of oxygen."

"All right."

"Have you got any flares?"

"On the ship?"

"No, with your suit."

"Let me check." A long pause. "Yes. Two of them."

"Okay. Break radio contact before they can pinpoint your location. I'll signal you when I reach the right ring. Then leave the ship and fire a flare. With luck I'll spot the first one. If not, we'll try a second."

"Acknowledged."

The radio went dead. He realized that there was no sense pretending to be a lifeless derelict ship any longer, not after almost a full minute of radio transmissions. And he couldn't lie in wait for his prey while Sinderella's oxygen ran out.

He ordered the ship to accelerate above the plane of the elliptic. It would make him an easier target with no rocks to hide behind, but he didn't dare chance one of the other ships making it to Anne Boleyn first. His only advantage was that they probably didn't know where Sinderella was—and then it occurred to him that of course they knew, that they were the ones who had disabled her ship in the first place.

He rose high above Catherine Parr and raced toward Henry VIII. Within a minute three ships were in hot pursuit. He dove down between Catherine Howard and Anne of Cleves, then spotted an empty vacuum in the middle of Jane Seymour and raced through it. All three ships plunged into the hole behind him. Two made it out; the third was crushed by a vagrant chunk of ice.

He felt confident that his ship was quicker and more maneuverable at sublight speeds, and wished he could engage the other two in combat—but he couldn't take the chance. Sinderella had only a few minutes' worth of air remaining in her ship, and once she abandoned it, she was floating out in the open, defenseless, and on a limited supply of oxygen. He couldn't chance being killed or disabled, because any shot that destroyed his ship would kill Sinderella as well.

He tried a few evasive maneuvers, couldn't shake his two pursuers, and decided that he didn't have any more time to try. Instead he headed directly toward Anne Boleyn, and as he came within a few hundred miles he broke radio silence.

"Are you still in your ship?"

"Yes," answered Sinderella.

"Okay, when we're through speaking, jettison yourself and use your jetpack to make your way to the edge of the ring if you can."

"Then what? Do I fire the flare?"

"I'm thinking. There's no way I can brake and pick you up without turning myself into a sitting duck for the two ships that are following me." He paused for a moment, considering alternatives. "All right," he continued. "We'll have to do it the hard way."

"This *isn't* the hard way?" she said ironically.

"Cancel what I said. If you get to the edge of the ring they'll be able to spot you as easily as I can. Go to the very middle of it and then fire your first flare. If I spot you, I'll contact you, and then just wait until I work my way to you. If you don't hear from me within ten seconds of firing the flare, that means I missed it. Raise me on your suit's radio and let me know, and we'll try again."

"Are you sure this is the way you want to do it?" she asked. "It's like a meteor swarm here. You'll be in more danger from the rocks than the aliens."

"The aliens are *trying* to kill me. The rocks won't care."

"Whatever you say. I'm leaving the ship now."

"Good luck," said Mayflower.

He maintained his lead over the two pursuing ships and raced alongside Anne Boleyn, waiting for the flare. A minute later his radio crackled to life.

"I didn't hear from you."

"You fired one?"

"Yes."

"Damn! My sensors missed it."

"I've only got one left. When do you want me to fire it?"

"Let me get a hundred eighty degrees around the ring—or, rather, a hundred eighty degrees around from where it is now, since it's spinning too. I'll let you know."

He wanted to hit light-speeds to get to his destination in a hurry and perhaps lose his enemies, but he knew such a maneuver would take him clear out of the ring system, and by the time he got back he wouldn't know if he'd achieved the proper position *vis-à-vis* the ring, so he simply increased his speed to seventy percent of light and raced around Anne Boleyn. When he felt he'd circled half the ring, he contacted her on the radio again.

"Okay, shoot it."

"Here goes."

Once again his sensors couldn't spot any flares.

"Did you see it this time?" she asked.

"No."

"Shit! What are we going to do? Can you home in on my radio signal?"

"I can approach you, but I can't pinpoint you much closer than maybe forty or fifty miles." He was lost in thought for a moment. "All right, I've got an idea. Keep broadcasting until I *do* get close."

"Then what?" asked Sinderella.

"How far are you from your ship?"

"Only a few miles."

"Start making your way back to it."

"Then what?"

"Then overload the nuclear pile and get the hell out of there again. It'll explode in about four minutes, and I guarantee I'll spot *that*."

"So you'll get that much closer, but you still won't spot *me*," she said. "Not with all these rocks."

"Sure, I will. You'll see me first, since my ship is much bigger than you are. As soon as you do, pull your laser pistol and fire at my nose."

"What if I hit you?"

"No handgun can penetrate my hull, but I'll spot where the fire's coming from and pick you up."

"Are you sure this is going to work?"

"In theory."

"What do you mean, in theory?"

"I mean, if the explosion doesn't send a few million rocks at your head, and if the force of it doesn't send you careening a couple of hundred miles away, and if the aliens don't shoot me before I reach you, and if I can maneuver through all the debris, and if nothing happens to your life-support system, and if we can make it away from Henry VIII before reinforcements arrive, then we've got a pretty good chance of surviving."

"I find your notion of a pretty good chance somewhat optimistic," said Sinderella grimly.

"If pessimism would help in a situation like this, I'd be the damnedest pessimist you ever saw," he assured her. "Now get moving. One of them's starting to fire at me again."

"I'd hate to compute the odds of our living through this."

"All the more reason for you to be grateful after I rescue you," he said wryly.

"You get me out of this in one piece and I'll show you gratitude like you never dreamed of," promised Sinderella.

"I'm counting on it," replied Nicodemus Mayflower.

Gravedigger Gaines and the Aliens

Henry VIII didn't have much to recommend it. The atmosphere was chlorine. The temperature was almost 100 degrees below zero Celsius. The gravity was seventeen percent heavier than Galactic Standard, which made every step an effort. The day lasted for 1,273 hours, and so did the night. About the only thing of note was the sky, which was illuminated by the six sparkling Wedding Rings reflecting the light of the distant sun.

Why the hell would anyone hole up here? wondered Gravedigger Gaines, as he trudged across the rocky terrain. Especially a force that had blown the Navy out of the sky. If there was a single thing to recommend Henry VIII, he sure as hell couldn't think what it might be.

Still, he knew the men and women from the Outpost were covering all the other Henrys (except for I, which was molten, and a few moons that had checked out clean), and since his sensors had spotted a small group of aliens on the eighth Henry and he was used to hunting down killers on worlds with wildly diverse atmospheres and gravities, he had decided to take care of this group himself.

Visibility was close to nil, but his instruments told him that the aliens' camp was about half a mile ahead of him, and their ship was even closer. That suited him just fine; if he couldn't see them, they couldn't see him.

He found their ship, melted the ignition, and destroyed the life-support system, then approached to within two hundred yards of the aliens. He could barely make out the outlines of the dozen bubbles that housed them. When he was a young man, he might have charged into the camp, spraying bullets and laser beams right and left, looking his foes in the eye. But over the years he had seen how messy death could be, and how unnecessary heroism was. He'd decided that he liked living, and planned to die only with the greatest reluctance. So he'd started playing it safe, and that had led to greater and greater successes until he'd made his fortune and chucked the whole business.

Now he took out his laser rifle, sat down on the ground, supported the barrel on his knees, and fired.

There was no reaction, which showed him that he had missed. He shrugged. Missing from two hundred yards when the enemy didn't even know they were being fired upon was a lot better than missing at ten yards when they were shooting back at him.

He aimed again and pulled the trigger. This time a bubble shattered and four aliens staggered a few paces, gasping for air, then collapsed.

It was like shooting fish in a barrel. Before the first of the aliens suited up and fired back, he'd blown apart ten of the twelve bubbles. Then, since they could only tell where he was based on where the laser bursts were coming from, he got to his feet, walked fifty yards to his left, and fired again. The eleventh bubble exploded, and he changed positions again.

He was about to fire at the twelfth and final bubble when his suit's radio picked up a voice.

"Is that you, Gaines?"

He didn't want anyone pinpointing his position based on his radio signal, so he remained quiet.

"It's just you and me," said the voice. "You can answer, Gaines. I know it's you."

He maintained his silence.

"Come on," said the voice. "If I'm going to die, I want to know who killed me."

Gaines moved about twenty yards to his left.

"It's just you and me. All the others are dead."

"What makes you think I'm someone called Gaines?" asked the Gravedigger at last.

"I know you were at the Outpost," replied the alien. "And I know your methods."

"How?"

"I'm the one that Men call the Gray Salamander."

"I put you away back on Barracuda IV," said Gaines, surprised. "I thought sure they'd give you life."

"They did."

"So what are you doing here?"

"I escaped."

"How many guards did you kill in the process?"

"Enough."

Gaines moved again, just in case the Salamander had some way of homing in on his signal. "This time I'll have to kill you," he said.

"Why? They say you quit the bounty-hunting business."

"We're at war, remember?"

"I'm not at war with anyone," said the Salamander.

"Then what are you doing here?"

"I like killing things."

"You've done all the killing you're going to do," said Gaines. "Only one of us is leaving this planet, and it's not going to be you."

"Bold words for a man who's lived more than half his life, Gravedigger Gaines. I'm still in my prime, and unlike you, I know the territory."

Gaines fired at the final bubble and saw it explode. Then he raced to a point thirty yards away, just before the Salamander's energy pulse hit the spot where he'd been.

Now he cautiously began making his way back to his ship, weaving his way along the terrain, careful never to move more than ten yards in a straight line. The Salamander kept taunting him, and he kept replying, but he concentrated solely on getting back to his ship in one piece.

And then, finally, after almost half an hour, it came into view.

He approached it via a serpentine route, just in case the Salamander had found it first and was waiting for him, but he couldn't make himself believe that was the case. If the alien had found his ship, he'd surely have bragged about it by now.

He climbed aboard, closed the hatch, and inspected every inch of the ship to make sure he was alone on it.

"I'm getting tired of this hide-and-seek game," came the Salamander's voice.

"So am I," answered Gaines.

"Then you'll face me?"

"No. I concede the game. I'm leaving the planet."

"I don't understand," said the Salamander. "What are you talking about?"

"I'm saying good-bye to you."

"You're a lot of things, Gaines, but you're no coward. You'd never leave without beating me."

"I've already beaten you," said Gaines.

"Beat me? You haven't faced me yet!"

"Facing you is for young men with big egos. My job is winning—and I've won."

"You're crazy!"

"I may be crazy," agreed Gaines pleasantly, "but I've blown away all twelve of your life-support bubbles, and before I did that I disabled your ship. I've got a year's supply of oxygen on my ship. How much have you got in your suit?"

The Gray Salamander was still cursing at him when he broke out of orbit and lost radio contact.

Three-Gun Max and the Aliens

Three-Gun Max was in a foul mood.

He had followed the Cyborg de Milo to Henry V at Reggie's request. She had radioed him not to land, but he paid no attention to her warnings and set his ship down next to hers.

She was waiting for him as he climbed down from his ship's hatch.

"Stop following me!" she demanded.

"I'm just making sure you don't get into any trouble," he replied.

"There's only one person here who's in trouble," she said, "and it's not me."

"Look, lady, I'm just keeping a promise to that robot bartender."

"The one they call Reggie?"

"He's got a crush on you," said Max with a grin. "He wants me to make sure no harm comes to you."

She stared at him. "I don't believe a word of this."

Max raised a hand to the sky. "I wouldn't kid you."

"It makes no difference. I work alone."

"I notice you didn't feel obligated to work alone when you thought Catastrophe Baker might come along."

"He's a hero, known throughout the galaxy. You're just a three-handed barfly."

Max glared at her. "Don't hassle me, lady. I get ugly when I'm riled."

"You're not all that good-looking *unriled*," said the Cyborg dryly. "Now leave me alone or suffer the consequences."

"What consequences?"

She pointed a finger at him, and a burst of laser fire shot out, just missing his head.

"Oh," said Max. "*Those* consequences."

He turned around and climbed back into his ship.

The Cyborg de Milo stood on the ground, hands on hips, as if she half expected him to emerge again. He waited until he was certain she wasn't leaving until he left first, then activated the ship and shot into the atmosphere.

He had tried his best to keep his word to the damned robot, so his conscience was clear. Now he was free to go anywhere he wanted.

Still, he was already at Henry V; it didn't make any sense to fly to one of the other Henrys as long as there were aliens to be confronted right here. He tightened his orbit, had his sensors scan the surface, and found an alien encampment about six hundred miles to the west of the city that the Cyborg de Milo had staked out as her own territory.

He set the ship down some twenty miles from the encampment and considered his next move. He didn't have the firepower to approach the aliens and take them all on. Besides, that was the kind of thing men like Catastrophe Baker bragged about, but no one ever really did.

If he was carrying any bombs he could have flown low over the encampment and dumped his payload, but his ship was a lightweight flyer that wasn't even equipped with defensive weapons. If he knew where they stockpiled their weaponry, he could sneak in under cover of night and blow up an entire munitions building—but he didn't know if there *was* a munitions building (and he had to admit that even if he *did* know, he had no idea how to blow it up. Explosives were not among his fields of expertise).

So, distasteful as he found the idea, it looked like the only way to do any damage to the aliens was to march off and confront them. He checked his screecher, his burner, and his blaster, made sure all were fully powered, and began walking toward the encampment.

He had covered about seven miles when he saw a two-legged figure approaching him. At first he thought it was another Man, but as it neared him he realized that it was an alien.

He pulled his burner and aimed it at the alien's chest.

"Hold it right there!" he yelled.

The alien stopped, startled. "I didn't see you," he said in heavily accented Terran.

"Drop your weapons," ordered Max.

"I don't have any," said the alien.

"I'm not kidding!" snapped Max.

"Neither am I. I'm a deserter."

Max approached the alien cautiously and made sure that he was unarmed.

"Well, I'll be damned!" he said. "Where the hell did you think you were going?"

"Away."

"Just away?"

"I'm a poet," said the alien. "I have no business here in the middle of a war."

"Truth to tell, I can think of a lot of places *I'd* rather be," said Max, pulling out a flask and taking a long swig. "Here. Can your metabolism handle this stuff?"

"I'll never know if I don't try," answered the alien, taking the proferred flask and lifting it to his lips.

"You know, you're not so bad for a godless, planet-raping alien," allowed Max.

The alien wiped his mouth and returned the flask to Max. "You're not so bad yourself," he said. "For a xenophobic, imperialistic swine whose race is out to enslave the galaxy."

"You got a name?"

"Of course I have a name. You couldn't pronounce it, but the closest translation is Wordsmith."

"You were born with that moniker?"

"Certainly not. I took it for myself after I reached my majority."

"You're a major?"

"I'm a private."

"Then what's this majority crap?"

"That means I'm an adult."

"Good," said Max. "God knows how many interstellar laws I'd be breaking giving booze to an underage alien."

"Speaking of which, might I have some more?"

"Sure," said Max, handing him the flask. "That's what it's for."

"Thank you," said Wordsmith. "It's really quite stimulating, isn't it?"

"There's those who would say yes, and then there's some who would say absolutely."

"Have you a name?"

"Max. Or, more formally, Three-Gun Max."

"You're not sensitive about having three hands?"

"Hell, no. If we start arm wrestling, I've got a spare. Have you?"

"I've never encountered any other Men with three hands," said Wordsmith.

"We're a small but select group of superhumans," admitted Max.

"How many are you?"

"The downstate returns aren't all in, but so far, at last count, rounded off, it comes to one—me."

"Are you a mutant?"

"I prefer to think of myself as gifted."

"Why are you here at all?" asked Wordsmith. "You seem like a reasonable sentient being. Why fight a war when you have the whole galaxy in which to avoid it?"

"You know," replied Max, "not thirty minutes ago I was asking myself that very question."

"And what was your answer?"

Max shrugged. "I like to fight."

"All right," said Wordsmith. "I can accept that."

"You can?" asked Max, surprised. "I would have thought you'd disapprove."

"No. If you'd have come here because you believe in the nobility of war, or because you cherish the glory of military victory, then I would have disapproved. But you descend from a race of predatory apes. It is your nature to kill, and you are simply reacting as untold generations of murderous progenitors would have reacted."

"You think so?"

Wordsmith nodded his head sagely. "You cannot help what you are."

"And does your race descend from predators, too?"

"Of course. Almost all sentient life does." Wordsmith smiled. "That does tend to let us all off the hook, philosophically speaking."

"So how come *you* don't like fighting?" asked Max.

"I am a fourth-generation poet," answered Wordsmith with dignity. "We have created a new genetic branch of my race's ancient tree."

"So you'd rather rhyme than rape?" suggested Max.

"I don't believe I said anything remotely like that," Wordsmith corrected him. "I'd rather rhyme than kill. Raping is another matter altogether."

"You know," said Max, "if it weren't for this fucking war, I think we could become lifelong friends."

"I feel an affinity for you, too."

"Let's go back to my ship and I'll break out some more drinking stuff," said Max.

"I was about to ask if you had any more," said Wordsmith, falling into step beside the human.

"By the way, if you don't mind discussing it, just how the hell did the war start, anyway?"

Wordsmith shrugged. "I have no idea."

"But you're here, fighting in it."

"I was drafted."

"So you don't know who fired the first shot?"

"No. I do know that we fired the next thousand—but we're a very masculine race, rugged and competitive and filled to over-flowing with testosterone."

"Sounds like we have a lot in common."

"Of course," said Wordsmith. "Races that don't have those traits in common surrender immediately."

"A telling point," admitted Max.

Suddenly the alien stopped and swayed dizzily.

"Is something wrong?" asked Max.

"I believe my system is having a little difficulty metabolizing your intoxicants," said Wordsmith. "I'll be all right in a moment." The swaying stopped. "There. The dizziness has left me."

"What do you guys drink?" asked Max.

"Anything that's wet."

"Heavy drinkers, huh?"

"Especially poets."

"You've got that in common with most of the human poets I've known," said Max.

"Have you got a female, Max?" asked Wordsmith.

"You mean to share with you?"

"No. I mean, do you have a life mate?"

"Not yet. Maybe one of these days. I'm still testing the waters."

"You copulate in water?"

"Well, it's been known to happen, but that's not what I meant. It's a figure of speech. It means I'm still searching for a life mate— or, to be more accurate, still auditioning potential life mates." He paused. "How about you? Have you got a lady alien waiting at home for you?"

"Yes," admitted Wordsmith. "I miss her terribly. I suppose that's the real reason I deserted. I long to be back with her again."

"Forgive me for pointing this out, but deserting the place where you keep all the spaceships probably wasn't the brightest way to go about getting reunited with her."

"I hadn't considered it until I was miles away from camp," confessed Wordsmith. "And by then it was too late."

"Well, what the hell," said Max. "We'll sit the war out on my ship, drink up all my booze, and then I'll take you to your lady-friend."

"Do you mean it, Max?" asked the alien.

"Sure," said Max. "What are friends for?"

Wordsmith took off the metal necklace he was wearing and handed it to Max. "I want you to have this as a gesture of my friendship."

"What is it?"

"My military ID. I realize it's a common and inexpensive present, but it's all I have."

"Then I'll be honored to accept it," said Max.

They continued walking and talking, and in another hour they came to the ship. Max broke out a couple of fifths of his best whisky and brought two chairs down to the ground, and they spent a pleasant afternoon drinking and telling stories. Then, just before sundown, Wordsmith clutched at his stomach.

"Something's wrong," he began. "I don't feel very well. . . ." He stood up, took a tentative step toward the ship, and then collapsed.

Max dragged him into the ship and laid him out on a cot. He

didn't know what else to do, so he applied cold compresses to the alien's head.

Wordsmith remained almost motionless for twenty hours, then opened his eyes.

"That stuff is really bad for my metabolism," he said weakly.

"Is there anything I should be doing for you?" asked Max. "Your pulse rate has doubled and your color has deepened. I don't know if those are good signs or bad ones."

"Just let me lie here until I get my strength back."

"Whatever you say."

The alien lost consciousness again and didn't awaken until he began vomiting five hours later. Max cleaned him up as best he could and offered him some water. He refused it, and since Max didn't know if his race even drank water, he didn't force the issue.

Wordsmith slept for another day and night before regaining consciousness again.

"I feel awful," he moaned.

"I'd better send for one of your medics," said Max.

"No," said Wordsmith. "They'd shoot me for desertion and kill you as an enemy."

"But you can't just lay here getting weaker by the hour," protested Max.

"Why not? It's very pleasant here, and it's keeping you out of the war."

He passed out again.

Max kept watch over him day and night for a week. Then one morning he checked the alien's pulse and couldn't find it. He held a mirror to Wordsmith's nose and mouth; there was no trace of breath. He knew the alien's death wasn't his fault, but he couldn't help feeling guilty since he had been the one to supply the whisky.

He dug a shallow grave, laid Wordsmith in it, and covered him with dirt. Then he checked his weapons, as he had done more than a week before, and prepared to walk to the encampment.

When he got there he found it deserted.

He returned to his ship and flew to the city where he had left the Cyborg de Milo. There were hundreds of alien corpses, but no sign of her.

Son of a bitch, he thought. *Did I just drink and doctor my way through an interstellar war?*

Hurricane Smith and the Aliens

The whole plan depends on you, my dear," explained Hurricane Smith as he looked out at the barren, rocky surface of Henry IV. "Are you *sure* you can appear to be one of the aliens?"

Langtry Lily nodded her assent.

"Well, then, I can't see what can go wrong. You make yourself look like one of them, you train your gun on me, and then you present me as a captive. That gets us in the front door, so to speak. Then, once you see who's in charge, you change to appear like him or her, and we see just how much confusion we can cause. I'll have a couple of pistols hidden beneath my spacesuit. If we play our cards right, we ought to both be able to come through this unscathed."

She stared at him questioningly.

"Unscathed," he repeated. "That means without any serious injuries."

She smiled.

"Just remember," he said, "it's not enough to look the part. You have to stay in character. That means you push me around, you act like I'm your mortal enemy, you never take your eyes off me or stop pointing your pistol at me. I'm Hurricane Smith. That makes me one hell of a feather in your cap."

Another curious stare as she reached up to her head, feeling for a nonexistent cap.

"Just an expression. It means I'm a desirable trophy, one that should get you promoted a few grades." He looked out once more, then back at his wife. "You ready? Then let's go."

She walked to the hatch.

"Wait!" he said. "You haven't changed yet. You still look like Langtry."

She turned to him, and he almost did a double take at the alien staring at him through the transparent helmet.

"Son of a bitch, that's perfect! I keep forgetting how fast you can do that!" He paused. "Let me go first, just in case anyone's watching. If they see us both emerging from my ship, we can make up some story about how you snuck aboard and got the drop on me—but if you climb down first, without keeping your gun trained on me, they'll know it's bullshit."

She stood aside as he walked by her and slowly climbed down to the ground. She joined him a moment later.

"Okay, push the gun in my back as if you're urging me to speed up."

She did as he ordered, and he put his hands in the air and started marching toward the aliens' headquarters. It took him a few strides to adjust to the lighter gravity, but no one noticed either of them until they were within a few hundred yards of the huge protective dome. Then a number of alien soldiers, all heavily armed, raced out and trained their weapons on him. He ignored them, as did Langtry Lily, and continued walking.

Once they reached the dome they paused in the airlock until the readout said that they could remove their helmets. All of them did so, and then Langtry shoved the gun into his back again and he began walking forward again.

They marched toward a small building, and as they neared it an officer emerged. He took in the situation at once, and a smile spread across his alien face.

"Hurricane Smith!" he said. "This *is* our lucky day! Do you know how much the Monarchy will pay to get you back?"

"They won't pay you any more than they're offering to certain select bounty hunters," answered Smith.

"Oh, yes, they will," said the officer. "There's a shortage of heroes these days, or hadn't you heard?"

"You must be thinking of Catastrophe Baker, or maybe the Cyborg de Milo," said Smith. "I gave up the hero business when I got married."

The alien threw back his head and laughed. "You?" he said disbelievingly. "Hurricane Smith, the most prolific deflowerer of alien females in the galaxy? What did you marry—a gigantic horned toad, or perhaps a twenty-legged spider that ate her last husband for breakfast?"

Smith shot a quick glance at Langtry Lily. She still appeared in alien form, but her expression was anything but amused.

"I married the most wonderful female anyone's ever seen," answered Smith quickly. "A creature of rare and delicate beauty, exquisite manners, remarkable empathy—and above all, *iron-clad self-control.*" He emphasized the last few words for Langtry's benefit.

"Are you describing her or proffering a legal brief for her?" asked the officer.

"If I was too forceful, I beg your forgiveness," said Smith. "Write it off to love."

"Well, I'm certainly glad for your sake that you've known love, since you're about to become intimately acquainted with pain and degradation while we're waiting for the Monarchy to make an offer for what's left of you."

"If you really plan to ransom me, you'd be much better advised to feed me and treat me well," said Smith. "The Monarchy doesn't buy damaged goods."

The officer looked around. "Do you see the Monarchy anywhere?" he said with an amused laugh. "They won't know you're damaged."

"Not only won't they know I'm damaged," replied Smith. "They won't even know it's me."

"Oh, yes, they will. When the time comes we'll cut off a finger or gouge out an eye and send it to them, and they can match it against your fingerprint or your retinagram."

"How very foresightful of you," said Smith dryly.

"I graduated at the top of my class in officers' school" was the reply.

"What did you study—sadism, with maybe a minor in rape and pillaging?"

The officer laughed again. "You have a wonderful sense of humor, Hurricane Smith! I'm almost sorry that we're going to have to torture you."

"Who says you have to?"

"You capture the enemy, you torture him. Those are the rules."

"Ignore them."

"Actually, I'm not *that* sorry."

The officer signaled to two of his soldiers to bind Smith's hands behind his back. As they approached, Langtry Lily tensed noticeably.

"Don't worry, soldier," the officer said to her. "You'll be prominently mentioned in my report."

Smith's protective suit was quite heavy, and there wasn't much give to it. As the soldiers pulled his hands behind his back, he winced in pain.

An instant later, Langtry Lily hissed and spat at the two soldiers. She hit one in the face, the other on the chest. The liquid sizzled and began burning holes in them.

"I don't know what he is, but he's not one of us!" cried the officer. "Kill him!"

Smith dove for the officer and grabbed his weapon, but it was too late. Half a dozen laser beams and energy pulses had ripped through Langtry's body. Her outline seemed to blur for a moment, and then, as she lay dead on the ground, she was once again a Peloponne.

"You bastards!" bellowed Smith. "That was the woman I loved!"

He killed the officer, then used his corpse as a shield and turned his pistol on the others. The element of surprise was on his side, and he killed half a dozen of them in the first few seconds of battle, but the rest quickly regrouped, found cover, and began shooting back.

The corpse couldn't absorb many more beams before it fell

apart, and Smith backed away, looking for some place to make a stand.

And then, before any of the enemy knew what was happening, they were mowed down from behind by a female alien carrying a laser rifle. It was doubtful that any of them ever even saw who killed them.

When it was over she stepped out of the shadows and approached Smith, stepping over the fallen bodies.

She gestured toward Langtry. "Was that your wife?"

"Yes," said Smith, not knowing whether or not to lower his weapon.

"I thought so." The alien female looked at him. "I'm sorry."

"It's not your fault."

"They make me ashamed to be a member of the same race." She walked over to him. "I know how you feel. I lost a loved one in battle."

"You did?"

She nodded. "We have that much in common."

Smith eyed her up and down. "Maybe we have even more."

"You think so?"

"Come back to my ship with me and we'll explore the possibilities."

"If they find me, they'll execute me as a deserter."

"If you don't leave with me, they'll execute you as a traitor," noted Smith.

She sighed. "I suppose you're right."

They began walking to the airlock.

"You know," said Smith after a moment, "you're really quite attractive."

"But I'm not even a member of your race."

"We have to look beyond that if there's ever going to be peace in the galaxy."

"Those are *my* feelings exactly!" she said. "But they sound so strange coming from a warrior like you."

"I'm no warrior."

"What are you, then?" she asked.

He put an arm around her as they continued walking, and found the texture of her alien skin oddly exciting.

"I prefer to think of myself as a peacemaker," said Hurricane Smith.

Little Mike Picasso and the Aliens

Little Mike Picasso looked at his viewscreen. There was nothing but rocks as far as the eye could see.

"Can I breathe the air?"

"Yes," answered his ship's computer. "Of course, the first breath will kill you within five seconds, but . . ."

"Where the hell *are* we?" he demanded.

"I have no idea," came the answer.

"Well, you're *supposed* to know!" he snapped.

"I beg to differ," said the computer. "You could have added an HT10547 state-of-the-art navigational computer to me before you came to the Inner Frontier, and you chose not to. It is hardly my fault that you have forced me to perform operations for which I was not programmed."

"All I said was get me to one of the Henrys where the aliens were."

"I know what you said. I have audio, video, and holographic recordings of it, and can instantly reproduce them should the need arise. That in no way alters the fact that I am not an HT10547 state-of-the-art navigational computer. I have done the best I could do under exceptionally trying circumstances."

"You couldn't find your nose with your finger," complained Little Mike.

"I possess neither a nose nor a finger," replied the computer.

"You know damned well what I meant," said Little Mike. "Not only didn't you find a world with aliens on it, but you don't even know where we are."

"I have not denied my limitations," said the computer. "But it is unfair of you to keep referring to them, to say nothing of unkind and—dare I suggest it?—petulant."

"Go fuck yourself."

"And vulgar."

"Look," said Little Mike, "I am the best goddamned artist in the galaxy, maybe the best who ever lived. I make Michelangelo and Picasso and Morita look like amateurs. I can't excel at everything, so I don't think it's asking too much for my spaceship to know where the hell we are."

"There's a logical flaw in your argument," the computer pointed out. "Being the best goddamned artist in the galaxy has nothing to do with—"

"It wasn't an argument, it was a statement!" growled Little Mike. "We're going to wipe these bastards out. I mean, hell, if Catastrophe Baker and Hurricane Smith and Gravedigger Gaines are all fighting on the same side, then the aliens are doomed. I've got to find them before the war's over, so I can paint them and capture them for posterity."

"If you plan to capture them for posterity, why not paint them *after* you've captured them?" asked the computer.

"I'm going to capture them on canvas, not in the flesh," said Little Mike. "I'm five foot three, I weigh a hundred twenty pounds dripping wet, and I've never fired a weapon in my life. How the hell am I going to capture aliens that can blow the Navy out of the spaceways? My job is creating a masterpiece or two while there are still some of them left."

"Perhaps you should have attached yourself to Catastrophe Baker or Hurricane Smith at the outset. From what you've told me, they are almost certain to come into contact with the aliens." The computer paused. "In fact, I could signal one of them right now, and—"

"And if the aliens are closer to us than Baker or Smith, you'll have broadcast our position to them."

"Ah—but I don't *know* our position," said the ship triumphantly.

"Then how the hell would you expect Baker or Smith to find us?"

"They're heroes," answered the ship. "Heroes always find a way."

"Who told you that?" asked Little Mike.

"It's on my library crystals."

"Fiction or nonfiction?"

"I cannot differentiate."

"Some computer!" snorted Little Mike.

"You get what you pay for," answered the computer calmly. "You could have bought me the ability to make value judgments, which would require me to instantly know the difference between fiction and non-fiction. You chose not to. Now you must live with the consequences of your penury."

"Let's get back to the problem at hand instead of making groundless accusations. Where the hell are we?"

"My accusations were not groundless," said the computer.

"Fine, they're not groundless," said Little Mike with a defeated sigh. "Now, where are we?"

"I don't know."

"Check your fuel gauges and your internal chronometer. How far did we fly? How long did it take? What can you deduce from that?"

"Everything is relative," answered the ship. "I know how much fuel I used, of course, just as I know the duration of our trip. But to know precisely where we are, I must calculate the speed at which the Tudor/Plantagenet system is moving in relation to the galaxy, and indeed the speed of the galaxy in relation to all the other galaxies. In response to your query, I shall commence my calculations now. Please do not interrupt."

Mike sat patiently for five minutes, then ten more, and finally another hour. Finally he spoke up.

"How long is this likely to take?"

There was no response. For a moment he thought the computer had gone dead, but then he heard the gentle whirring as it computed the size and speed of every moving object in the universe.

"There's a war going on, you know," said Little Mike.

The computer blinked an acknowledgment, but couldn't spare any brainpower to respond.

Little Mike made himself a sandwich, opened a container of beer, watched a holo show, and went to bed. When he woke up in the morning, the ship's computer was still lost in its calculations.

"This is ridiculous!" he snapped. "Cancel the order."

Another acknowledgment blinked, but once again the computer couldn't spare even the slightest portion of its brainpower to reply.

After six more days had passed, Little Mike ran out of food. The beer was gone a day later.

Just as he was certain that he would die of starvation before the ship determined where they were, the computer suddenly came to life.

"I am pleased to announce that we are on Margaret of Anjou, the moon of Henry VI."

"Good!" said Little Mike. "Now let's get the hell out of here!"

"Where would you like to go?"

"Wherever the action is."

"Oh," said the computer. "Did I neglect to tell you? The war's as good as over."

The Outpost and the Aliens

I began sweeping the floor again.

"That's the fifth time you've swept up in the last hour," said Willie the Bard. "How much cleaner does the place have to be before you're happy?"

"It's just nervous energy," I said. "They're fighting a war out there, and we're stuck here at the Outpost."

The Bard glanced out the window.

"Uh . . . I hate to be the bearer of bad tidings," he said nervously, "but we're not as far from the war as you think."

"What's happening?" I asked.

"A ship just landed." He continued staring at it. "It's not like any other ship I've ever seen."

"Damn!" I said. "We'll just have to defend the place as best we can."

"*We?*" repeated the Bard. "I'm a historian. I've never held a weapon in my life."

"I can't stand them off all by myself," I said. "Einstein's blind, deaf and mute. You're elected."

"Get Reggie to help."

"He's a robot," I said. "A robot can't harm a sentient being, or, through inaction, allow harm to come to one."

"Stupidest thing I ever heard," muttered the Bard.

Then Reggie spoke up from his position behind the bar. "On the contrary, I have absolutely no moral or ethical compunction against harming Men or aliens."

"You don't?" I said.

"None whatsoever."

"Good. Then grab a weapon and—"

"However," he continued, "the only thing I know how to do is make drinks. I am totally ignorant of firearms and military tactics. If you would like to take the necessary fourteen hours to reprogram me . . ."

"I don't think there's time," I said.

"There isn't," confirmed the Bard. "They're already marching out of the ship. Seventeen—no, eighteen—of 'em."

"Okay," I said. "There's no way I can take them out with standard weapons. This calls for something special."

I reached behind the bar and pulled out the molecular imploder.

"I didn't know you had an imploder," said the Bard.

"I've never had occasion to use it before."

"It's an impressive-looking weapon," he said admiringly. "What powers the damned thing?"

"Fission, fusion, who the hell knows?" I said. "I just know that it turns things into jelly—aliens, humans, spaceships, buildings, everything."

I walked to the doorway, aimed the imploder, and activated the trigger mechanism.

And nothing happened.

"Isn't it loaded?" asked the Bard.

"You don't *load* an imploder!" I snapped. "You just aim and fire it!"

"Maybe it's not getting any power," he suggested.

I checked the gauges. "Everything reads right. Everything should be working. What the hell is wrong?"

"Let's ask the expert," said the Bard. "Toss me the computer."

I did as he asked, and he tapped out the problem for Einstein, who replied a moment later.

"He says that they've probably got some kind of atomic neutralizer that's messing up your power source, and that you should use a laser cannon or a pulse torpedo instead."

"This is the Outpost, not a fucking military vessel!" I yelled, as the aliens approached to within two hundred yards. "I don't have that kind of weaponry!"

Another exchange of messages.

"He says it's an interesting problem."

"That's *all* he's got to say?" I said frantically.

"He says he's never seen an insoluble problem. He just doesn't know if he can solve this one in the time remaining."

The aliens seemed to sense that we were defenseless and increased their pace.

"Well?" I demanded.

"He says he's working on it."

"Tell him he'd better finish working in ten seconds!"

He finished in eight seconds. I followed his advice, and that was the end of the alien invasion, and, for all I knew, of the whole damned war.

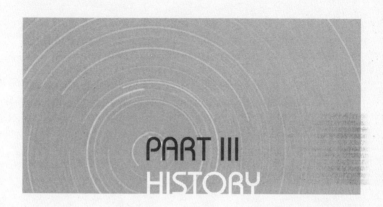

PART III
HISTORY

The war was over.

They started coming back in ones and twos. I had Reggie give each of them a free drink as they entered, and the Bard waited patiently for everyone to get in a talkative mood before he started recording the true history of the war with the aliens.

When Hurricane Smith came back alone, no one asked him what had become of his beloved Langtry Lily. He just had a look about him that said such questions wouldn't be welcomed, and might well be severely dealt with.

Three-Gun Max wasn't his usual talkative self either. He took the drink—I never knew him to turn one down—and carried it over to a table, where he just sat and stared silently at it.

The Injuns—that's what we call Sitting Horse and Crazy Bull—were the next to arrive, and it was obvious they were in a good mood. So was Big Red.

Sinderella and Nicodemus Mayflower entered together, holding hands and staring and sighing at each other like a pair of teenagers who had just discovered how truly opposite the opposite sex is.

The others straggled in, some looking happy, some depressed, some tired, some triumphant. All we needed was a catalyst, someone to break the ice.

That's when Catastrophe Baker showed up.

He walked in, clomped over to the bar like he was still outdoors, and said in his big, booming voice, "Hiya, Reg! Pour me a tall one." He turned to me. "How's it going, Tomahawk?"

"Pretty good," I answered.

"I saw an alien ship out there," said Baker. "I was half-hoping they'd taken over the Outpost. Might have been fun to throw 'em out on their ears."

"They've been disposed of," said the Bard.

"Pity," said Baker. "I hate it when a war ends while my blood's still up." He stared at the Bard. "I don't suppose *you'd* like to engage in a little rasslin' and eye gouging and the like, just for the hell of it?"

"Not me," said the Bard. "My job is recording history, not making it."

"Seems kinda limiting to me," said Baker.

"We can't all be heroes," said the Bard.

"The hell we can't!" said Crazy Bull. "Me and my partner managed."

"Yeah?" asked Baker.

"Yeah," echoed Crazy Bull. "Maybe we aren't full-time heroes like some, but we were heroic when we had to be."

"Or sneaky, anyway," added Sitting Horse.

"Sometimes being sneaky is all it takes," agreed Baker.

"They weren't such bad guys," said Max, speaking up for the first time. "The aliens, I mean."

"They were monsters," said a familiar voice from the doorway.

We all turned and saw the Reverend Billy Karma. He looked different somehow. It took a minute for me to spot what had changed: he was now sporting a pair of prosthetic hands, one made of gold, the other of silver.

"If anyone kills you, they're gonna want more than both ears and the tail as trophies," said Baker admiringly. "That's mighty impressive new hardware you're sporting there, Reverend."

"Got new feet, too," said Billy Karma. "Courtesy of them godless alien heathen that Max here seems to have taken a liking to."

"I didn't say I liked 'em all," answered Max defensively. "But just like there's a bad apple in every batch of good ones, who's to say there can't be a good apple in every rotten batch?"

"It's against the fourth and seventh commandments!" yelled Billy Karma. He frowned. "Or is it the second and ninth?"

"Max has a point," said Hurricane Smith. "They weren't all bad."

"Let me guess," said Baker. "At least one of the ones that weren't all bad was a lady, right?"

Smith glared at him. "You know," he said sullenly, "I can remember when I used to like you."

"What's not to like?" said Baker. "I'm strong, handsome, agile, noble, truthful to a fault, and one hell of a hand with the ladies."

"That's six reasons right there," said Max.

"He's not irresistible to *me*," said the Earth Mother, entering the Outpost and heading to a nearby table.

"Or me," added the Cyborg de Milo, following close behind her.

"I am glad to see that you are well, Venus," said Reggie. "I was worried about you."

"You were?"

"We have so much in common," said Reggie. She looked at him curiously. "I am all machine, and you are at least half machine. Everyone else here is merely flesh and blood."

"There was nothing to worry about," said Max. "I told you I'd protect her, didn't I?"

"Protect me?" said Venus. "I hardly saw you after I left the Outpost."

"I made sure things were safe in that ancient city before you showed up."

"Then I suppose I owe you my gratitude," said Venus with an obvious lack of sincerity.

"Happy to do it."

"Of course," she said, "you managed to miss more than six hundred armed aliens."

"Well, I got rid of the first five thousand I came to," replied Max smoothly. "I figured with all your weaponry you could handle a measly six hundred without working up much of a sweat."

She turned to Willie the Bard, who was scribbling furiously.

"Why are you writing all this down?" she demanded.

"Someone has to," he said.

"But he's lying!"

"Today it's a lie," he pointed out. "But when my book is published, it'll be the truth."

"Aren't you interested in what really happened?" she continued.

"I'm interested in everything," said the Bard. "You guys tell me your stories and I'll sort 'em out."

"But you weren't there!" said Venus. "How can you sort out the truth from the lie?"

"I'll keep what makes the best history and throw the rest out."

"Can you do that?"

"History is written by the winners," answered the Bard. "That's why it reads so well, why it has such a noble trajectory to it."

"It don't read well next to the Good Book," put in the Reverend Billy Karma.

"What's the Good Book but God's version of history?" said the Bard.

Suddenly Billy Karma grinned. "You know, I never looked at it that way."

"Of course, that means you won't want to rewrite it after all," said Baker.

"Nonsense," said Billy Karma. "God's a busy man with a lot on His mind. I'm sure it can still use a little improvement here and there."

"I didn't know God was a man," said the Earth Mother.

"She isn't," agreed the Cyborg de Milo.

"Now just a minute!" began Billy Karma hotly, jumping to his feet.

"Sit down, Reverend," said Venus, pointing a lethal finger at him. "Or do you want to be carrying around some molten slag at the end of each arm?"

"Maybe you each have your own God," said Sitting Horse placatingly.

"Are you suggesting that there's a God for every being in the universe?" asked Baker.

"Of course not," answered Sitting Horse. "Crazy Bull and I worship the same one."

"Is it a male or female God?" asked Billy Karma.

"I don't think that's important," said Sitting Horse.

"But just in case you're curious, She's got really big tits," added Crazy Bull.

"That's blasphemy!" roared the Reverend.

"You don't think God has breasts?" asked the Cyborg de Milo.

"Hell, no!" said Billy Karma. "Matter of fact, He's hung like a horse."

"And you think that's *not* blasphemous?" asked the Cyborg incredulously.

"Of course not," said Billy Karma. "God made man in His own image. Hell, me and God could pass for twins!"

"I sure wouldn't put that in your book," said Baker to the Bard. "Nobody'll read the rest once they read *that*."

"I haven't put anything in it yet," replied the Bard. "But I suppose enough of you are here that I should start." He turned to the Cyborg de Milo. "What was all this about killing six hundred aliens?"

"I did."

"So tell me about it."

"Okay," she said. "I killed six hundred aliens."

"That's it?"

She nodded. "That's it."

"It's going to make a mighty thin chapter," said the Bard.

"I'm into killing, not bragging."

The Bard sighed. "Okay, have it your way. But nobody'll ever know you were here."

"What do I care?" she asked.

"It's your immortality," explained the Bard. "That's what history's all about. It shows you were here, that you made a mark on the pathways of Time."

"I know I was here."

"But no one else will know."

"Once I'm dead, what difference does it make?" said the Cyborg.

"It's the only way to be sure you'll never be forgotten," said the Bard, "that your memory will live in song and story."

"And how does that benefit me?" she asked.

"Right," chimed in the Reverend Billy Karma. "She's going to the good place or the bad one, and either way, that's immortality enough for anyone."

"But if they don't exist, then *this*"—the Bard tapped his notebook with a finger—"is all the immortality she's got."

"Bite your tongue!" snapped Billy Karma. "God wouldn't have invented sex except to give us a hint of what's to come if we lead the good life."

"You think heaven is non-stop sex?" asked the Earth Mother.

"What else *could* it be?" shot back the Reverend. "That's why we call it heaven."

"Have you ever sat down and seriously discussed this with God?" she continued. "Or maybe a good psychiatrist?"

"No need to," said Billy Karma. "It's self-evident."

"I don't know that I'm interested in *either* kind of immortality," said the Cyborg de Milo, taking a swig of her drink, then signaling Reggie for a refill.

"All right," said the Bard. "If you don't want to be remembered, you don't want to be remembered." He turned to Max. "You were on the same planet, right?"

"Henry V, right," said Max.

"You want to talk about it?"

"It's still kind of painful," said Max. "But what the hell, why not?"

Three-Gun Max Finds a Friend

It was after I'd made the city safe for Venus (began Max, as the Cyborg de Milo snorted contemptuously). I set my ship down a few hundred miles away, ready to take out a small alien army all by myself.

But before I did, I figured I owed myself a meal, since wiping out all those aliens figured to burn up a lot of calories. I was sitting there outside my ship, cooking some steaks over an open fire, far enough from the aliens so their sensors wouldn't be able to spot me, when I felt the muzzle of a screecher pressed between my shoulder blades.

"Raise your hands," said a thickly accented voice, which I knew had to belong to one of the aliens.

"If I do, I'll burn the steaks," I said without turning around.

"So what?" asked the alien.

"If you're going to kill me anyway, it doesn't make any difference what I do with my hands . . . but if you're *not* going to kill me, then it's criminal to burn 'em."

"I hadn't thought of it that way," he admitted thoughtfully, walking around to the other side of the fire. He kept his gun trained on me while he tried to figure out what to do next.

"Well, if you're not going to shoot me," I said, "you might as well join me. There's enough food here for both of us."

"I don't mind if I do," he said, taking a plate and squatting down next to the fire. "It's been a long day, and I haven't eaten since sunrise."

"You got a name?" I asked.

"Wordsmith," he said. "How about you?"

"Max."

"I couldn't help noticing that you've got more hands than the usual human," he said.

"I never found it to be a disadvantage," I told him.

"That's curious," he said. "Everything I've learned about your society tells me that anyone as different as you should be an outcast, shunned by all."

"Just what is it you think you know about my society?" I asked.

"I've read all the books and seen the usual indoctrination holos," he replied. "I find your habit of eating newborn babies especially disgusting."

"I'm not aware of any humans ever eating babies."

"I suppose it's a secret ritual," he said sympathetically.

"I have a feeling that you're a victim of false doctrine," I said.

"False doctrine?" he repeated, puzzled.

"Propaganda."

"But I *saw* the holos!"

"You saw the wonders of computer animation and special effects," I said.

He stared at me for a long moment. "I don't know," he said at last.

"Did you see holos of people cooking babies?"

"No, just eating them raw."

"Well, there you have it," I said. "I'm living proof of the fact that Men always cook their meat."

"Yeah, I guess you are," said Wordsmith. "I can't tell you what a relief that is."

"Why?"

"I'm no warrior," he confessed. "I'm a poet. I joined the military after I read about what you did to babies. Now that I know you don't eat your young, I think I'll go back home and finish work on my first collection of poems. I specialize in unrhyming hectameter."

"Will they let you leave?" I asked.

"Why not?" he said. "They have no use for a poet." He paused. "Actually," he added ruefully, "they have no use for anyone who doesn't kill, maim, and torture."

"Maybe you should think about coming over to our side," I suggested.

"I can't," he said. "Men despise anything that's different."

"More propaganda," I said. "A few hundred miles from here is a cyborg lady with more firepower built into her fingers than one of your battleships possesses. She has artificial eyes, and when the war's over, she's probably going to trade her real legs in for prosthetic ones. And yet, she's fighting for our side. She wouldn't be doing that if we ostracized her, would she?"

"No," he admitted. "No, I suppose not."

"Of course not," I said. "Maybe I ought to tell you Man's side of the story."

"I've got all night," he said.

So I explained to him about how Thomas Jefferson wrote the Magna Carta, and Pope John XXIII freed the Martian colonies, and I quoted as much of Babe Ruth's Gettysburg Address as I could remember, and pretty soon he started asking me more questions, and we talked clear through to the morning.

And when the sun finally rose over Henry V, he reached out, shook my hand, and announced that he saw now how he'd been brainwashed and that he was going to spend the rest of his life fighting for liberty, freedom, capitalism, and higher property values.

We spent the next couple of days together, just getting to know each other. He recited some of his poetry to me, but it didn't rhyme or have much of a beat to it, and hardly any of it was about war or women, which is just about all that's really worth writing about. I spent the rest of the time telling him about how a free society works, and why we on the Frontier don't pay taxes or vote or spend too much time worrying about the finer points of the law.

"But if you voluntarily give up your franchise, what is the point of fighting for the Commonwealth?" he asked.

"I'm not fighting for the Commonwealth, or the Monarchy, or whatever we're calling it this week," I said. "I'm fighting because you guys invaded the Henrys, and that's where I spend most of my quality drinking time."

He frowned—as much as a member of his race *can* frown, anyway—and tried again: "How is your government to survive if everyone flees to the Frontier and refuses to pay taxes?"

I could have explained that it just meant we'd conquer a few more alien races and tax 'em up to the eyebrows, but somehow I sensed that wouldn't elicit the reaction I wanted. So instead I told him that for every one of us who was bold enough to emigrate to the Frontier, there were millions who stayed behind.

"It's just simple logic," I explained. "If there weren't enough people to pay taxes, they'd either incorporate some of the Frontier, or they'd raise taxes."

"That sounds very reasonable."

"It is—unless you're the guy whose taxes they raise."

"And if you are?"

I shrugged. "Then you head off for the Frontier and probably open up a new world or two, and eventually the government takes it over, and that's the way the galaxy gets itself civilized."

"There's a mathematical purity to that, isn't there?" he said. "I mean, a certain amount of dissatisfaction is always bound to occur, but as your society is set up it simply leads to expansion, which in turn leads to more government intrusion and hence to more dissatisfaction and more expansion. . . ." He paused. "Why, at this rate, Man should be assimilating Andromeda and the other nearby galaxies any day now!"

"Do you find that threatening?" I asked.

"No," he said. "I find it exciting!"

"Your race has no notion of Manifest Destiny?"

Well, he didn't know what the term meant, so I had to explain it to him.

"What a wonderful notion: Manifest Destiny!" he exclaimed. "I *like* it. My race thinks only in terms of gaining a few systems here and there, and enjoying a little bloodletting. Nothing as grandiose as your race."

Well, before long he'd made up his mind to come to the Outpost and claim asylum. I explained to him that there was no one here who could grant it to him, and that if he really wanted asylum he'd have to go into the Monarchy and find some government agency that specialized in defectors, and that given the number of government agencies we had, that could take a couple of lifetimes. I finally convinced him to just come on back to the Outpost with me and get used to Men and freedom and unfettered capitalism in slow, easy stages.

We decided to leave the next morning, but as I was cooking us up some eggs and hash browns prior to taking off we suddenly found ourselves under attack from Wordsmith's countrymen.

"Let's get the hell out of here!" I said, running to the ship.

"Watch out, Max!" he cried.

I looked around and saw an alien infantryman aiming his pulse rifle right at me. I knew as sure as I'm sitting here that I had about half a second of life left to me—and then, just as he fired, Wordsmith leaped in front of me and took the energy ball that I would have sworn had my name on it.

I went a little bit crazy then. I killed the alien with my screecher, then put a gun in each of my three hands and started walking the countryside, screaming at them to come out of hiding and face me. A couple of dozen actually did, and I blew them away, ignoring the few minor flesh wounds they managed to inflict on me. When I'd finally killed them all, I went back to the ship and gave Wordsmith a decent, human-type burial.

He was my friend, maybe the best friend I ever had. Lord knows he wasn't much to look at, and I never did understand his poetry, but he took a shot meant for me, and that's more than any Man ever did.

The Earth Mother wiped away a tear. "I think that's beautiful," she said.

"So do I," said the Cyborg de Milo. "But I went over to that encampment after I cleaned out the city, and I didn't find any two dozen dead aliens out in the countryside."

"Maybe their companions took 'em back and buried 'em," said Max. "Or maybe the sunlight disintegrated 'em."

"I notice it didn't disintegrate the six hundred I killed," she said dryly.

"Look, that's my story!" snapped Max. "If you don't want to believe it, that's fine with me!"

The Cyborg de Milo shrugged. "It makes no difference to me."

Max turned to the Bard. "Well? You gonna use it?"

"In the absence of a contradictory version, I suppose I don't have much of a choice," he replied. "Besides, Wordsmith makes a wonderful metaphor."

"He wasn't a metaphor," said Max. "He was the ugliest son of a bitch you ever saw—and the most loyal friend."

"I suppose you can't ask much more than that," allowed the Bard.

"*I* sure can't," said Max.

Big Red and Gravedigger Gaines entered just then.

"You just missed one of Max's stories," the Bard informed them.

"How can we ever live with the disappointment?" said Gaines. "Two beers, Reg!"

The two of them walked up to the bar.

"The war over?" Big Red asked me.

"Looks like," I said.

"Did we win?"

"As far as I can tell."

"Well, then, I guess it was worth it."

"What was?"

"What I had to do to get off Henry IV."

"You going to tell us about it?" I asked.

"Try to stop him," said Max wryly.

"I'm kind of dry. Let me just take a little sip of this first," said Big Red, lifting the huge stein of beer to his lips and downing the entire contents in a single swallow. He wiped his mouth off with his sleeve. "Boy, I've missed that!"

"If that's all you've missed, you got some serious problems, son," said the Reverend Billy Karma.

"We're not all as single-minded and sex-starved as you, Reverend," replied Big Red.

"Sure you are," answered Billy Karma. "You're just not all as honest and forthcoming about it."

"I wonder if God's had any second thoughts about letting you be the one to state His case," said the Gravedigger.

"Not a chance," replied the Reverend Billy Karma. He held up the second and third fingers of his gold hand and pressed them tightly together. "Me and God are just like *this*."

"It must be a comfort," said the Gravedigger ironically.

"It does make the occasional sexual rejection more bearable," admitted the Reverend.

"Occasional?" said Sinderella, laughing aloud.

" 'Let thy women be silent in the House of the Lord,' " quoted Billy Karma.

"In case it's escaped your notice, this isn't the House of the Lord," said Sinderella.

"If *I'm* here it is."

"He just wants the women to be silent so they can't say no to him," said Max.

"Well, I'll be damned!" said Billy Karma. "You know, I never thought of that!"

"Somehow I'm not surprised," said Max.

"Are you *ever* going to tell us how you escaped from Henry IV?" the Earth Mother asked Big Red.

"When everyone else stops talking," he answered.

"You could run smack-dab into Eternity before that happens," suggested Catastrophe Baker. "Just step right in and tell your story."

"Okay," said Big Red. "I suppose I might as well."

The Seventy-three-Hour Rasslin' Match

Truth to tell (began Big Red), I was doing pretty well for the first couple of days I was on Henry IV. I knew Hurricane Smith and his lady were also on the planet, causing havoc a few thousand miles away, which took a little of the pressure off me.

My method was pretty effective. Sneak up behind them in the dead of night and stab 'em before they knew what hit them. I might have kept it up for another few weeks when my knife hit something metal—I still don't know what it was, maybe an ammunition belt slung around his neck. Anyway, the blade broke off with a loud snap, which wasn't anywhere near as loud as the alien's screams. A squad of about a dozen alien soldiers showed up within seconds, and suddenly I was staring down the muzzles of one hell of a lot of alien guns.

"He's the one who's been decimating us!" cried the leader. "I want him alive!"

I waited just long enough for his words to register with his troops, and then, figuring no one would disobey orders by killing me, I launched myself at the nearest of them. I'm no Catastrophe Baker, but I was giving a pretty good account of myself, felling aliens right and left, when one of them cracked me on the head with a laser rifle.

When I woke up, I was in a damp underground cell, and one of my arms was chained to a wall. Facing me across the cell was another human, chained to his wall.

"How are you feeling?" he asked me.

"I've been better," I admitted. "Where are we?"

"Under the arena."

"They've got an arena?" I asked. "They didn't strike me as all that sporting."

"It was built by a long-dead race," said my companion. "But our captors have put it to good use."

He looked familiar, and I kept staring at him, and finally I knew where I'd seen him before. "Hey, aren't you Backbreaker Barnes?" I asked.

"Yeah, that's me."

"I've seen you fight a couple of times," I said. "I still remember the night you wiped up the floor with Meyer the Maimer."

"One of my better bouts," he agreed.

"It was pretty even for a few minutes," I said. "Then you seemed to go berserk."

"The son of a bitch made a comment about my mother, and I just plumb lost my temper."

"Insulted her, huh?" I said.

"No," answered Barnes. "He said she was a bright, good-looking woman and a fine cook." He paused and grimaced. "I *hated* my mother."

"Well, I knew he said *something.*"

He stared at me. "I think I recognize you too," he said at last.

"Didn't I see you knock one out of the park against Iron-Arm Mc-Pherson?"

"That was a long time ago," I said.

"I remember it like it was just yesterday," said Barnes. "You're . . . damn, I can't remember your name."

"Rasputin Raskolnikov Secretariat Lenin Man o'War Trotsky at your service," I said. "You can call me Big Red."

"Big Red!" he repeated. "That was it. I don't know how you remember your official handle."

"It took me a few years to learn it, I can tell you that," I said.

"Well, Big Red," he said, "I wish I could say I was glad to see you, but the truth of the matter is that I wish they hadn't captured you."

"Thanks for the kind thought," I said. "But at least we've got each other to talk to."

"Not for long, alas," said Barnes.

"Oh?"

He nodded his head sadly. "Yeah, I'm afraid one of us is gonna have to kill the other."

"Why? I'm not mad at you, and you don't look exceptionally annoyed with me."

"That's got nothing to do with it," he said. "The aliens get their amusement by taking us to the arena and having us fight against each other."

"What if we refuse?"

"Then they'll kill us both."

"Has this been going on long?" I asked.

"About two weeks," said Barnes. "Well, sixteen days to be exact."

"How can you be so sure?"

"Because they took seventeen of us prisoner."

"You've been killing a comrade a day?" I asked.

"Don't look so disapproving," he said. "If I don't kill them, the aliens will. At least this way I'm still alive, and there's a chance, however small, that one day I'll be able to claim my just and terrible vengeance."

"What if a participant fakes being dead?" I asked.

... into the river that runs through the city, he said. "It's filled with carnivorous fish that can take all the flesh off your bones. If you're not dead when they throw you in, you will be about ten seconds later."

"I see."

"I'll make it as quick and painless as I can," he promised me.

"I appreciate the thought," I said. "But I was kind of planning on making it quick and painless for you."

"For me?" he said with a laugh. "I'm Backbreaker Barnes!"

"And I'm Big Red," I said. I was going to throw back my head and laugh like Barnes did, but I had this feeling that nothing would come out, so I just stared at him.

"Look," he said. "If you put up a fight, I'm going to have to soften you up for the kill. I'll probably have to break a couple of arms and legs, and maybe bust your rib cage with a bear hug. It'd go a lot easier with you if you'd just let me give your head a sharp twist and be done with it." He paused. "I swear I'll always honor your memory."

"It's not that I don't want to oblige you, Backbreaker," I said. "It's just that as an athlete, I was taught to always give my best. The paying customers deserve it."

"We don't have any paying customers," he pointed out. "Just godless aliens."

"Just the same, I'm going to have to give it my best shot."

"It's your decision."

"And if you feel yourself weakening," I continued, "let me know and I'll end it just as painlessly as I can."

"What do you know about killing blows?" he said contemptuously.

"I'm a quick study," I said. "Especially when my life is on the line."

"You ever do any freehand fighting, professionally or in college?" he asked.

"No," I replied. "I wrestled for a couple of semesters to keep in shape between track and baseball seasons."

"Yeah?" he said. Suddenly he smiled. "You know, maybe we could put on a real show for these bastards."

"What have you got in mind?"

"If we take turns throwing each other around the ring and try some real crowd-pleasing holds, maybe they'll like it so much that they'll want an encore . . . and they can't have an encore if one of us is dead."

"What the hell," I said. "It's worth a try. And it beats trying to kill each other."

"I wish we weren't chained to the walls, so we could practice a bit," said Barnes.

"Well, maybe we can just discuss it," I said. "You know, kind of create a scenario, so we know who throws who when."

"Why not?" he said enthusiastically.

So we fell to it, choreographing every move, every throw, every hold. We didn't want to hurt each other, so we devised ways to make the aliens think we were gouging out each other's eyes and banging each other's heads against the ring support posts when we were just pretending to do so.

We figured we could keep it up for maybe an hour or two, at which time we were dead sure that the aliens would be having such a good time that they'd insist on a rematch, which meant the two combatants would have to be kept alive for another day.

Well, they gave us some slop to eat for dinner—as food it wasn't much, but as gruel goes it was probably better than most— and we fell asleep shortly afterward. Then it was morning, and they unhooked us from the walls and dragged us up a long ramp, and pretty soon we found ourselves in the middle of a huge arena, with maybe a thousand aliens in attendance.

One alien walked into the middle of the ring with us (I call it a ring, but it was on ground level and didn't have any ropes) and signaled the crowd to be quiet. Then he turned to us.

"You have no weapons, and there are no rules. The survivor gets taken back to his cell." He backed away from us. "Let the battle commence!"

I charged Barnes and let him throw me with a flying mare. The aliens had never seen anything like that, and they screamed their approval.

I got to my feet, closed with him, and gave him a hip toss. He flew across the ring, and the crowd went wild.

Well, we spent about an hour taking turns throwing each other all the hell over the ring. Whenever we'd get tired, one of us would put a headlock or a body scissors on the other. We'd scream like we were in terrible pain, but actually it didn't hurt at all, and it gave us a chance to rest.

"How long do you figure we've got to keep this up?" I asked during one of the times he was giving me a fake bear hug.

"Beats me," he said. "I was hoping they'd have broken it up already."

They didn't show any sign of breaking us up, so we kept at it. By the fourth hour we'd run through all our choreography and started making things up as they occurred to us. I gave him a body slam, and he writhed in agony, so I knelt down to see if I'd actually broken anything.

"I'm fine," he whispered. "But I learned that if you land with your arms and legs splayed, it makes a hell of a noise and makes the crowd think you're all busted up."

"Let me try," I whispered, so he climbed painfully to his feet and slammed me, and it turned out he was dead right, and we spent the next half hour body-slamming each other.

The crowd started getting bored, so I invented the pile driver, and he invented the figure-four grapevine, and I invented the stepover toehold, and he invented the claw, and I invented the forearm smash to the jaw, and he invented the rabbit punch, and the next time we looked up it was morning again and we'd been at it for a full day and night.

"How are you holding up?" he asked as he applied a half nelson to me.

"I'm getting a little hungry," I said.

"Well," said Barnes, "if you're hungry, and I'm hungry, then *they* must be getting hungry. All we have to do is outlast 'em."

We kept at it another day and night, and by now the audience was getting kind of restless, either from pangs of hunger or unanswered calls of nature. But they had also become incredibly partisan, so much so that when Barnes threw me into the second row, some of the aliens began pummeling me and sticking me with sharp objects until I could get back into the ring.

"They hate me!" I whispered as I invented the hammerlock and put it on him.

"Half of them were booing me when I tossed you out there," he said.

"Really?" I said. "Let me throw you into them and let's see what happens."

So I did, and what happened is that the half of the crowd that hadn't bothered me began hitting and kicking Barnes.

"You know," I said when he'd crawled back into the ring and we were taking turns pretending to stomp on each other's fingers, "there's a hell of a profit in this sport we're inventing. I think these aliens would rather watch us than fight the war."

"You've got a point," he said, grabbing my foot and twisting it. As I fell to the floor he said, "I figure we've been going at it for almost two and a half days. I don't know about you, but I'm going to need to visit a bathroom pretty soon now."

"I don't think they'll let us leave," I said, pretending to stick a thumb in his eye.

"We'll never know if we don't ask," he said, staggering over to the announcer. He jabbered at the alien, who seemed to consider what he said, then entered the ring.

"The combatants will take a ten-minute nourishment break," he said.

We were led off to the dungeon from which we had come.

"I don't want a *nourishment* break!" complained Barnes.

"I know," I said, "but it probably sounds better than saying he was stopping the fight so you could take a shit."

We were back ten minutes later, and we went at it tooth and nail, but truth to tell, we were running out of inventions, and I knew we couldn't keep it up much longer, especially since we hadn't had any sleep.

When we'd been at it for just under seventy-three hours, I collapsed as Barnes swung at my head and missed by a good two inches. He knelt down next to me and pretended to pummel me.

"You got to make it look better," he said. "Everyone in the first two rows has got to know I missed you."

"Hell, the force of the wind from a missed blow could knock me down right about now," I answered. "I don't know how much longer I can keep fighting, Backbreaker. Maybe you'd better snap my neck right now."

"We started together, and we're going to finish together," he said. He sneaked a look around while gnawing on my ear. "I got it," he said.

"What?"

"See that big box along the back wall?"

"What about it?" I asked.

"I think that controls all the lights in here," he said. "What if I was to throw you into the crowd, and while you were climbing onto your feet you swiped a burner or a blaster and blew the box away? We might escape in the confusion."

"How far do you think we could get, two unarmed men on an alien world?" I asked, bringing my knee up into his stomach.

"There's a bunch of corridors below the arena, on the dungeon level," he said as he doubled over. "One of them leads outside the walls of the city, pretty near where you left your ship."

"It just might work," I agreed.

So, with that, he got up, grabbed me by the hair, lifted me high over his head, and threw me into the crowd. I landed three rows deep, and managed to get my hands on a burner as I was disentangling myself.

I fired it at the box, and the arena was plunged into total darkness. Suddenly I felt Barnes's hand on my arm, tugging me to my left.

"This way!" he whispered.

I followed him, and a minute later we were racing down the underground corridor. Some of the aliens tried to chase us, but even after seventy-three hours in the ring we were too fast for them. We made it to my ship, and here I am.

"So where's Backbreaker Barnes?" asked Max. "I thought you two were going to go into the phony rasslin' business."

"He said he felt too much like an actor and not enough like an athlete, so we parted ways," explained Big Red with a shrug. "But I still think there's money to be made staging rasslin' matches (which I prefer to think of as insincere rather than phony), and I aim to get rich proving it as soon as I find the right partner." He looked over at Catastrophe Baker. "How about you?"

"I still got a few years of heroing left in this old body," answered Baker, "but I appreciate the offer, and I'll sure consider it once I'm too old to rescue innocent damsels from fates more interesting than death."

"You really think people would waste their money watching phony wrestling?" asked the Gravedigger.

"Sure, why not?" responded Big Red.

"But sooner or later they'd figure out that it was all an act."

"Hell, people pay to go to the theater, don't they? Are you telling me they really think that's Hamlet up there?"

"It's not the same thing."

"You're right about that," said Big Red. "You go to a play two nights in a row, you know exactly how the second performance is going to go. But come to my new profession two nights in a row and you've got no idea what you might see the second night."

"Well," said the Gravedigger, "maybe aliens would pay to be flim-flammed like that, but not real Men."

"It's been my experience that it's easier to flim-flam real Men than just about anything else in the galaxy," said the Earth Mother.

"Amen," added Sinderella devoutly.

"Did someone mention flimflamming?" said Bet-a-World O'Grady, entering the Outpost.

"Reg, give the man a drink," I said. "How did it go?"

"Not too bad, all things considered," said O'Grady, walking up to the bar.

"What particular things do we have to consider?" asked Max in bored tones.

"Flimflamming, of course," said O'Grady. "That's what everyone was talking about, right?"

"Some of us were just drinking quietly and hoping they'd all shut up and go away," said Max.

"It figures an alien took a shot meant for you," said the Reverend Billy Karma disgustedly. "No human being would be that stupid."

"Sometimes I'm amazed at how stupid human beings can be," said Max, staring straight at Billy Karma, who shifted uncomfortably in his chair for a moment and then pulled out his copy of the Good Book and buried his nose in it.

"So," said Catastrophe Baker to Bet-a-World O'Grady, "you got some particular insight about flim-flamming?"

"Tons of 'em," answered O'Grady.

"Care to share any of 'em with us?"

"How's about the most recent one?"

"Okay," said Baker, leaning back in his chair. "How about it?"

The Night Bet-a-World O'Grady Met Nick the Greek

You'd never know it to look at me (said O'Grady), but I'm not a fighting man.

"You're kidding, right?" guffawed Max.

"Getting in your interruptions a little early, ain't you?" said Catastrophe Baker ominously, and Max promptly shut up.

I wasn't much of a fighting man even when I was thirty years younger and a hundred pounds lighter (said O'Grady). It's just not my style.

So when we all left the Outpost to confront the aliens, I figured I'd meet them on the battlefield where I'm at my best—a gaming table.

I sent word to the aliens that I'd meet their best gambler at the casino on Mozart II, which I figured was far enough away from the action so that we wouldn't be disturbed by any bombs or invading armies or anything.

I got there a bit ahead of him, checked out the lay of the land (no offense, ladies), and waited for my opponent. He showed up a few hours later with a trio of bodyguards. I couldn't pronounce his name, so he let me call him anything I wanted, and I just naturally hit on Nick the Greek, since I figured this might be the most important opponent I ever faced.

Well, we sat down to play, and I tried to talk him into a little Face-Up Draw Poker, but the sneaky bastard had heard of it and insisted that *he* go first, so of course I lost.

"What were the stakes?" interrupted the Bard.

"He put up all his money and promised to get his soldiers off Catherine de Valois, and I put up all my money, all my worlds—but of course I didn't own any at the time—and I agreed to sit out the war in one of his prison cells."

"So you spent the rest of the war in prison?"

"Not exactly."

You see (continued O'Grady), Nick the Greek was pissed as hell when he found out I didn't have title to any worlds. He kept accusing me of lying to him, whereas I kept pointing out that I had merely misrepresented my holdings, which is a whole lot different from lying, though he never quite understood the fine dividing line.

I could see he wasn't happy, so I tried to come up with another bet, and suddenly I remembered that I owned a pair of casinos out on the Rim and another one in the Spiral Arm. I hadn't visited either of 'em in years, but the titles were in my ship's safe, so I decided to make him another bet.

"What is it this time?" he asked, and I could tell he was just waiting for me to name some scam he'd heard of.

"Here's the deal," I said. "We'll get a fresh deck and break it open. I won't touch it. You shuffle it until you're happy with it."

"Then what?"

"Then you put it down between us and we start drawing cards, one apiece. My bet is that you'll turn a court card face-up before I do." I paused to let him consider it, then added: "I'll put up all three of my casinos plus my ship against all the money you're holding."

"But that's just the luck of the draw," he said, obviously disappointed that there wasn't any ruse attached to it. "Why not simply flip a coin and be done with it?"

"I might not win with a coin," I said. "I never lose at cards."

"You just lost five minutes ago," he noted.

"That's because I tried to flim-flam you," I said. "It was unethical, and I got what I deserved. But this is an honest bet."

"I don't think I'm interested," he said. "I've already won all your money. Why should I risk it in an even bet?"

"Okay," I said. "I'll give you odds."

For just a second I saw him smile before he put his poker face back on, and I knew that I had him.

"You have no more money," said Nick the Greek. "What kind of odds can you give me?"

"Tell me what you want," I said.

"All right," said Nick. "I'll bet everything I have against everything you've mentioned . . . and, in addition, if I win, you must help me kill everyone in the Outpost and support my claim to its ownership in a court of law."

"Done," I said.

"What do you mean, *Done*?" I yelled. "You were offering to kill me and the Bard and probably Einstein!"

"It was a con," replied O'Grady with a smile. "You know the old saying about how you can't con an honest man? It goes double for aliens."

I watched Nick the Greek shuffle the cards (said O'Grady), and since I'm as handy at stacking a deck as he is, I saw that the first picture card was the jack of spades, and that it was going to come up ninth.

"Since I went first at Face-Up Draw," said Nick, "I will allow you the privilege of going first in this game."

I could tell he was just waiting for me to refuse, which is how he'd know I had spotted him rigging the deck, and the second I made a fuss about it, he'd cancel the bet, keep my money, and stick me in a military prison. So I agreed to pull first.

Now, along with his three bodyguards, there were about two dozen Men in the casino, along with a couple of Canphorites and a Domarian. I waited until they all crowded around to watch and explained the wager to them so they'd know what they were watching. Then I pulled a three, and placed it face-up in front of me.

Nick pulled a six and let everyone see it, then placed it face-up in front of him. I pulled another three and turned it up, Nick did the same with an eight, I pulled a deuce, he pulled a five, I pulled a ten, and he pulled a four.

Now he and I both knew the next card was a jack. I reached out, peeked at it as I began pulling it, and immediately placed it face-down in front of me.

"Hey, what's going on?" demanded Nick.

"Nothing," I said politely. "Your draw."

"What have you got there?"

"A nine," I said. "Your draw."

"I don't believe you," said Nick. He reached across the table and turned the jack face-up. *"Aha!"* he said triumphantly.

I turned to the nearest bystander. "What did he just do?" I demanded.

"He turned over the jack of spades," said the man.

"What did *you* see?" I asked another.

"Same thing. He turned up your jack."

"And what was the bet?"

"That he'd pull a picture card before you did."

"No!" I said. "The exact bet was that he'd *turn up* a picture card before I did—and that's just what he did."

Nick screamed bloody murder, but there were more than twenty men on my side, all of them carrying weapons, and his three bodyguards were no match for them. So, after spending a futile half hour trying to find someone to support his claim that he'd been filmflammed (which of course he had, but *legally*), he paid off his bet and stormed out.

As for me, I stuck around long enough to lose just about everything I'd won, and then came back here to find out how the war was going. You can imagine my disappointment when I learned it was over before I could make a bet on it.

"Fascinating!" said the Bard, scribbling furiously.

"Hey," said O'Grady sternly, "I don't want that little ruse to see print before I'm dead. I damned near lost everything because they were wise to Face-Up Draw. I plan to get rich on this one."

"The people who buy Willie's book ain't likely to sit across from you at a gaming table," said Max.

"Just the same, I want it kept quiet while I'm still alive."

"We could kill you now and solve everything," suggested Max.

"I can't help wondering just why we fought this war," said O'Grady. "It didn't make me any richer and it sure as hell didn't make you any pleasanter."

"Every now and then folks just have to burn off energy," said Catastrophe Baker.

"There's better ways of going about it," said the Reverend Billy Karma. "That's why God invented two sexes."

"You better check your biology textbooks again, Reverend," said Big Red. "There's worlds where the Good Lord created up to five sexes."

"Don't you believe it," said Billy Karma.

"I've seen it," said Big Red.

"Yeah?" said Billy Karma. "Well, I was talking about it with God just the other day, and He says He invented up to two and then stopped. Anything with more sexes than that was created by Satan just to confuse you."

"If you think it confuses *me*, you ought to see *them*," said Big Red with a chuckle.

"Might be an interesting study in group dynamics," said O'Grady. "Put 'em all together on a cold night and—*WOW!*"

"Put 'em all together and wow?" repeated Big Red with a puzzled expression.

"The *WOW!* had nothing to do with the subject at hand," said O'Grady as Silicon Carny walked in. "Well, only peripherally, anyway."

She was dressed all in white in an outfit that fit like a second skin—not that there was anything wrong with her first skin, mind you.

"I haven't seen you in white before," noted Max as she undulated over to an empty table and sat down. "Are we being virginal?"

"We're being a nurse," she replied. "Or at least we were until recently."

"I didn't know there were any hospitals in the Henrys," I said.

"There was an alien hospital on Elizabeth of York," said the Earth Mother. She turned to Silicon Carny. "But I didn't see you there."

Which meant she hadn't been there. Seeing Silicon Carny wasn't a sight people tended to forget, even female people.

"When we all left the Outpost," said Silicon Carny, "I figured that most of you were heroes and warriors, but that my particular talents lay elsewhere."

"I'll vouch for that!" said the Reverend Billy Karma devoutly.

"So I made my way to Trajan III," she continued, ignoring the Reverend's obvious enthusiasm, "which was the nearest planet with a military hospital, and volunteered my services as a nurse."

"How did you make out?" asked the Earth Mother.

"Okay, at least at the beginning," answered Silicon Carny. "My supervisor said I gave dying men the will to live again, just by walking past their beds."

Even Max, who jumped on almost anything anyone said, didn't seem to have a problem accepting that. He just nodded his head as if to say: *Of course they'd want to stay alive now that they could see what they were fighting for.*

"So how come you're not still there?" asked O'Grady.

"I was asked to leave."

"By who?" asked Max disbelievingly.

"By my supervisor."

"Why?"

"Evidently eight other nurses saw me and began showing signs of terminal depression."

"I can believe it," said Max.

"Well, I, for one, am thrilled to welcome you back," said O'Grady.

"I'll second that!" shouted the Reverend Billy Karma.

Pretty soon just about every man in the place was echoing that sentiment, and then the Reverend offered to buy a round of drinks for the house, and Catastrophe Baker matched him, and then even Max bought drinks for everyone, and it occurred to me that I could make a healthy profit just by paying her to hang around while all the men tried to impress her.

Once all the drinks had been passed out and things had settled down again, the Reverend Billy Karma walked over and seated himself next to Silicon Carny.

"I don't suppose you'd care to cut the cards?" he said. "First one to turn over a picture card loses."

"What are the stakes?" she asked.

"We'll think of something when the time comes," he promised her.

"Whatever odds he's offering, I'll triple 'em for the same bet," said Big Red.

"I'll quintuple them," said Max.

"Why do I think the result is a foregone conclusion?" asked Silicon Carny.

Billy Karma smiled at her. "Is this a face that would cheat an innocent semi-virgin like you?"

"That's it!" she declared, getting up and moving to another table. "No bet."

"By the way," said the Bard, "did anyone run into Faraway Jones during the fighting?"

"Why?" asked Baker.

"I'm just trying to keep tabs on everyone so I know what to put in the book."

"I never saw him."

"Me neither," said Hurricane Smith.

"Nor me," said Big Red.

"Come to think of it," added Nicodemus Mayflower, "has anyone seen Argyle, or Hellfire Van Winkle?"

"I spoke to Argyle via subspace radio just before he was due to land on Henry V," offered the Gravedigger. "I haven't heard from him since."

"Who else is missing?" asked the Earth Mother.

I looked around the room. "Sahara del Rio," I said.

"And Little Mike Picasso," said Max.

"I haven't heard from Achmed of Alphard since just before he set his ship down on Henry VIII," said the Cyborg de Milo.

"I was on Henry VIII, and I didn't see him there," said the Gravedigger. He shrugged. "Still, it's a big planet."

"I tried to warn him off," said the Cyborg. "He wasn't the survivor type."

"We can't all be heroes," I said.

"I don't know about that," replied Big Red. "That's a mighty impressive alien ship parked out there where your front lawn would be if you could grow grass on this dirtball. Somebody must have done something heroic or there'd be an alien tending bar right now."

"Yeah," chimed in Catastrophe Baker. "You're a writer, a saloonkeeper, a robot bartender, and a blind man. How did the four of you manage to hold them off?"

I turned to the Bard. "Do you want to tell them, or should I?"

"You tell them," he answered. "I'll be too busy writing it down."

"But you already know what happened," I said. "You were here. Why wait until now to record it?"

"Nothing happens until someone says it does," he replied. "You're elected."

"That's silly."

"That's objectivity," he shot back.

"Are you guys gonna argue all night, or is someone gonna tell us what happened?" demanded Baker.

"All right, all right," I said. "Keep your shirt on."

How Einstein Saved the Outpost

I don't know exactly when the ship touched down (I said). I just know that one minute the four of us were alone in the Outpost, and the next minute we had company.

There were maybe thirty or forty of them, and our side was only a bartender, a historian, a blind-deaf-mute genius, and me— so I figured it was pretty much up to me to save the day.

I didn't think matching laser blasts or energy pulses with the aliens was the most sensible way to defend the Outpost, so I picked up the molecular imploder that I keep hidden behind the bar. I'd never had occasion to use it before, but I keep it in good working order. Besides, it was the only formidable weapon I owned. It's the kind of thing that can turn a thousand aliens *and* their ship into jelly in a nanosecond.

Anyway, I aimed it at the approaching soldiers, flipped off the safety, and fired—and nothing happened. All the readouts told me it was charged and working, but it sure as hell wasn't doing what it was supposed to do.

I tried again, and again there was no hum of power, no destruction of the aliens, no nothing. So I asked Einstein what was wrong, and after giving the matter some thought he figured out that the aliens had some kind of atomic neutralizer, some device that could stop any atomic-powered weapon from working.

The problem is, he told me that when they were maybe a hundred yards away. They'd seen me try to fire the imploder and knew their neutralizer was working, so they didn't spread out in any kind of attack formation. They just laughed at me and kept right on walking toward the front door.

I told Einstein that if he was going to save the day, he had less than a minute to do it, and he promised to get working on it right away.

Well, they got to within eighty yards, then sixty, then forty. I kept trying to fire the imploder, and I kept getting no result.

"Einstein!" I yelled. "Either think of a solution in ten seconds, or your thinking days are through!"

Eight seconds later he tapped out his instructions on his computer, and the Bard relayed them to me.

" 'Move twenty feet to your left and fire again,' " read the Bard.

It sounded like the stupidest idea I'd ever heard, but I didn't have time to argue, so I ran twenty feet away and fired again—through the window right behind Sinderella's head—and this time, the imploder worked and the whole alien squadron melted right into the ground.

I took the computer back from the Bard and told Einstein that his idea had worked. "How the hell did you figure it out?" I asked. "And more to the point, *what* did you figure out?"

"Your weapon uses atomic energy, does it not?" replied Einstein.

"Yes," I answered.

"And the basic principle of atomic energy is $E = MC^2$, correct?"

"To the best of my knowledge, yes."

"Now, the aliens had an atomic neutralizer which prevented your weapon from functioning."

"That's what you told me."

"Well, as you can plainly see, that was the answer."

"*What* was the answer?" I asked. "How did you know the imploder would work if I moved twenty feet to my left?"

"You could have moved twenty feet to your right, I suppose," answered Einstein. "But there's one more letter in *right* than in *left,* and I was given to understand that time was of the essence when I wrote my instructions to you."

"You're not answering me," I said. "How did you know the weapon would work if I moved in *either* direction?"

"As my great-great-great-et-cetera Uncle Albert pointed out, relativity may merely be a local phenomenon. You circumvented the neutralizer by becoming twenty feet less local."

"In a long lifetime of listening to stupid stories, that's the stupidest I've ever heard!" said Max.

"You think so?" asked Nicodemus Mayflower thoughtfully. "I've heard lots that were dumber. Some of 'em right here in the Outpost."

"Uh . . . I don't want to be the one to criticize," said Willie the Bard, "but that's not quite the way it happened."

"It is now," I replied.

"But—"

"Einstein didn't see what happened and Reggie's not a talker," I said. "I figure that makes me the only eyewitness to history."

"Just a minute," said the Bard. "I was here too!"

"You're just the historian," I said. "Without me telling the story, nothing happened."

"The man's got a point," said Catastrophe Baker. "After all, they're *your* rules."

"You'd rather have me write *his* version than the real one?" demanded the Bard.

"His version *is* the real one," said Baker. "Or at least it will be once you write it down."

Einstein tapped out a message on the computer, which Big Red promptly read aloud to us. "He says he finds Tomahawk's version rather charming, and he hopes no nuclear physicist ever reads it."

The Bard stood up and walked over to the bar. "I appeal to you, Reggie—tell them Tomahawk's lying."

Reggie didn't say a word. He just kept washing dirty glasses, and when he was done with that, he began wiping the bar.

"I guess you don't appeal to him after all," said Max, and everyone guffawed.

"All right, you win," said the Bard, returning to his table and his notebook. "That's how Einstein saved the Outpost."

"By God, if I'd known history was this much fun, I might have stayed in school!" boomed Catastrophe Baker.

"When did you quit?" asked Big Red.

"When I was about eight or nine," answered Baker.

"They didn't try to stop you?"

"Of course they tried," said Baker. He shook his head sadly. "Poor bastards. Still, I suppose most of 'em are out of the hospital by now."

"You knew even then that you were going to be a hero?" asked the Earth Mother.

"I don't know about that," he admitted. "But I sure as hell knew I wasn't going to be a scholar."

"He had his whole future mapped before he was ten," said Big Red ruefully. "And here it took me almost half my life to decide to be a professional rassler."

"What's the difference between being a wrestler and a rassler?" asked Silicon Carny.

"Wrestlers get hurt. Rasslers get rich. Or at least that's the way I've got it doped out."

"I can teach you all about rasslin'," said the Reverend Billy Karma to Silicon Carny. "Just step out back with me and I'll show you some nifty holds."

"And I'll show you some kicks, scratches, and knife thrusts," said Silicon Carny.

"I admire your sense of humor," said Billy Karma.

"Do you see me smiling?" she asked grimly.

"Leave her alone, Reverend," said Baker. "Or ain't you had enough body parts cut off lately?"

"You mean these?" said Billy Karma, holding up his gold and silver hands. "It was a minor inconvenience, all done for the greater glory of God."

"Yeah?"

"Right." He turned to the Bard. "Get your pen out, Willie. This story'll uplift the hell out of you. You wouldn't want to miss writing it down."

An Undefeated Spiritual Tag Team

Now, I got nothing against war (said the Reverend Billy Karma). It's one of the best ways of getting rid of godless heathen and working off a little excess sexual energy, and certainly God is in favor of war, since He's been battling with old Satan for the better part of a zillion years, give or take a century.

But on the other hand, I'm no warrior. I don't expect Catastrophe Baker to be able to quote the Good Book and I don't figure Three-Gun Max can please the ladies half as well as I can, but I can't do some of the things they can do, neither. And butchering an alien army single-handed happens to be one of them.

But just as there's more than one way to skin a cat (which is probably why we don't have a hell of a lot of cats left at this late date), there's more than one way to win a war. So I flew off to Henry VI, which is one of the worlds where God, in His haste, forgot to install running water, electricity, or breathable air, and decided to confront the aliens that were holed up there.

I landed in a pretty barren spot, but nonetheless managed to find their encampment a few hours later. We exchanged a few pleasantries: I found out that they called the planet Janblixtl, and they found out that I called them golem, which is what they looked like.

Just as I thought we were getting on pretty well, they pulled their guns and pointed them at me and demanded to know what I was doing on Janblixtl. I figured there was no sense lying, so I explained that I had come to convert 'em all.

"We have our own god," said the leader. "Why should we worship yours?"

"Mine's bigger and stronger and smarter, and He'll show you how to get more women," I explained.

"Our God created the universe," said the leader.

"Yeah?" I said. "Well, *my* God created *your* god."

"Blasphemy!" he said furiously. "Our God is the lord of all creation!"

"My God is the lord of this and every other universe from the beginning to the end of time," I said. "Not only that, but He's a four-handicap golfer and He ain't missed a free throw in more than fifty-seven centuries."

This didn't impress them quite as much as I had hoped it would, and before I knew it they'd marched me into one of their bubbles, where we all took off our helmets and spacesuits.

"Now," said the leader, "what is your real reason for being here, Billy Karma?"

"Just what I told you," I said. "I'm here to bring you guys over to Jesus."

"Jesus? Who's that?"

"Well, it's a little complicated for the uneducated layman to understand, but Jesus is God's son."

"Okay," said the leader. "Bring Jesus to Janblixtl and we'll negotiate directly with him."

"That ain't possible," I said. "He's been dead for over eight thousand years."

"You worship a dead man?"

"Well, he wasn't exactly a man," I explained.

"Was he a god?"

"Not exactly."

"This is all very confusing," said the leader. "How did he die?"

"He was crucified."

"Explain, please."

So I told them how crucifixion worked, and I saw them all nodding approvingly.

"See?" said the leader to a couple of his soldiers. "I *told* you there was much we could learn from the enemy. I trust one of you was taking notes." He turned back to me. "I hope you see the error of your ways, Reverend Billy Karma. Your God could not even protect His own son, whereas our God has helped us defeat your Navy."

"My God is busy overseeing the Monarchy and the stock market and certain select sporting events," I shot back. "You're such a minor pain in the ass that He ain't even noticed you yet. But when He does, you'll know who's the boss of the universe."

The leader stared at me for a long moment, and just when I thought he was going to agree with me and apologize for going to war, he said: "I think our Department of Propaganda would be most appreciative if you were to renounce your God and swear your eternal allegiance to ours."

"Never!" I roared.

"We can have our holocameras here in ten minutes."

"Bring all the cameras you want," I said. "Me and God are an undefeated spiritual tag-team."

"I beg your pardon?" he said.

"You heard me!" I shot right back at him. "We'll wipe up the floor with you. We'll take you in straight falls. We'll visit you with floods and plagues and pestilence and kill every firstborn son. So you just watch what you say to me."

"You refuse to renounce your God?" he said.

"Absolutely!"

"Even if I were to dismember you for refusing?"

"Cut away everything you want," I said. "They're just corporeal objects anyway. You can't cut my immoral soul."

"Don't you mean you're *immortal* soul?" he asked.

"That, too!" I said.

"You probably think that I'm not going to do it, that it's just an empty threat."

"I hope it is, because I've grown kind of attached to my appendages, but it makes no difference—nothing will ever make me turn my back on God, because I know He'll never turn His back on me."

"An interesting hypothesis," he said. "I think we shall put it to the test."

He aimed his pistol at my hand.

"Wait a minute!" I said.

"What is it?" he asked, looking disappointed. "Are you renouncing your God already, before I get to shoot you even once?"

"No," I said. "But ain't we gonna wait for the holocameras?"

"No," he said, shaking his head. "The citizenry back home aren't interested in watching your incredibly brutal and painful dismemberment. They only want the end result—your acceptance of our God."

He aimed the gun again.

"You're forgetting something!" I said desperately.

"What?" He checked his pistol. "Did I leave the safety mechanism on?"

"You're forgetting that I don't speak your lingo, so even if I did renounce my God, which I will never do, your people couldn't understand me anyway."

"We'll translate," he said. "And now, if there are no further delays . . ."

I was still trying to think of one when he blew my left hand off.

"Have you anything to say?" asked the leader.

"Yeah," I replied. "It hurts like hell!"

"That's all?"

"No, I got something more to say."

"Certainly. What is it?"

"Can somebody lend me a bandage?"

"You have courage, Billy Karma, I'll grant you that," said the leader. He aimed and blew my other hand off.

"Son of a bitch, that smarts!" I said.

"Are you ready to swear fealty to our God yet?"

"Keep shooting, you rotten bastard!" I said.

So he did, which is how I lost both my feet.

"Lord," I said, "forgive them, for they know not what they do." Then I added: "But make 'em suffer a bit first."

"You really believe that shit, don't you?" said the leader.

"You bet your alien ass I do!"

"Any deity who can inspire that kind of loyalty must be quite admirable," he said. "Tell me about Him."

"I'll be happy to," I replied. "But could we staunch the flow of blood first, so I don't pass out before I come to the good parts?"

He agreed, and summoned some medics, and while they were working on me I started extolling God's virtues, and the Spirit must really have been with me, because before they'd finished patching me up I'd converted the leader, his soldiers, and all the doctors.

I stuck around long enough to convert all the rest of them and then, having done my part for God and the war effort, I stopped off just long enough to pick up some new hands and feet and then high-tailed it back here to the Outpost.

"God sure is lucky to have you on His side," said Max sardonically.

"Truer words were never spoken," agreed Billy Karma.

"I don't know how He managed to get through the day before you showed up on the scene," continued Max.

"It was rough," said Billy Karma. "That's probably why He lost control of Himself and had an illicit affair with Mary."

"You mean the Virgin Mary?"

"Well, she was a virgin when He met her anyway." He paused thoughtfully. "Hell, if I wasn't around to take the pressure off Him,

He'd probably be propositioning Silicon Carny this very minute."

"I doubt it," said Big Red.

"Why?" said Billy Karma. "His taste is at least as good as mine, and that's who *I'd* like to sneak off with."

"Thank heaven for small favors," said Sinderella with a sigh of relief.

Billy Karma looked over at her. "I'm sorry," he said apologetically. "I hate to have you suffer the pangs of rejection."

"I suppose I can learn to live with it."

"If it'll boost your ego any, we can do a little preliminary missionary work while I'm waiting for Silicon Carny to come to her senses."

"You touch her," said Nicodemus Mayflower, "and I'll cut off the one appendage the aliens seem to have overlooked."

Billy Karma crossed his legs and squeaked like a mouse. "What a thing to say!"

"You heard me."

"Call his bluff," said Max with an evil grin.

"Right," chimed in Catastrophe Baker. "If worse comes to worst, you can replace what he cuts off with an all-diamond version. Not only will it go with your gold and silver hands, but it'll never go soft."

Pretty soon everyone in the Outpost was urging the Reverend Billy Karma to lay a friendly hand on Sinderella, just to see what happened next. For a moment it looked like he was considering it, but finally he shrugged and shook his head.

"I can't do it," he said. "It's obvious that she's attached to this homely young man, God knows why when she could have an irresistible man of the cloth like me, and I'd hate to have to maim and maybe kill him if he attacked me. No, I think I'd best leave young love to blossom." He winked at Sinderella. "But if you ever get tired of young love and start yearning for mature, highly skilled love, you know where to go."

She grinned. "To Catastrophe Baker, right?"

Everybody laughed at that. Everybody except the Reverend Billy Karma, that is. He just sat there and frowned, as if he couldn't understand how she could be so completely misguided.

"You know, if you want to get a woman of any kind, you're going to have to work on your approach and your timing," said the Earth Mother.

"And your looks and your manners," added Silicon Carny.

"And your clothes and your language and your personal hygiene," Sinderella chimed in.

"That could take years!" protested Billy Karma.

"Then it'll take years," said Nicodemus Mayflower. "You know what they say: There ain't no such thing as a free lunch."

"The hell there ain't," said Billy Karma. "Tomahawk passes them out every day."

"Just stay your sweet lovable self," said Max, still grinning. "I wouldn't know what to do if you became all dandified like they're suggesting."

"What are you doing here anyway?" demanded Nicodemus Mayflower pugnaciously. "Don't you have a flock to shepherd?"

"My church is the galaxy," said Billy Karma with an expansive wave of his hand. "And every sentient being is my parishioner." He paused, then added: "Especially the ones with the big boobs."

"You're about as subtle as a supernova," said Max.

"I learned from an expert," Billy Karma shot back. "Or would you rather have had the Little Pop than the Big Bang?"

"Makes no difference to me," said Max. "I slept right through it."

"Philistine!" muttered Billy Karma, concentrating once again on his drink.

"The way he talks, you'd think Men had a monopoly on Philistines," said the Earth Mother.

"Don't they?" asked Baker.

"Certainly not. Do you think you're the only race where the male of the species is ill-mannered, unprincipled, rapacious, and otherwise disgusting?"

"I never gave it much thought," he admitted.

"Well, I assure you, you're not."

"So who's worse?" asked Baker.

"I didn't say anyone was worse," answered the Earth Mother. "Just that you're not alone."

"Okay, then, who's giving us a run for our money?"

"Most recently?" she asked.

A Hospital Is Not a Home

As you can tell by looking at me (began the Earth Mother), I'm not built for battle. Hell, I wasn't built for battle thirty years ago, when I looked a lot more like Sinderella.

So I decided that I'd volunteer as a nurse at the alien hospital on Henry VII's moon, Elizabeth of York. I figured that my best bet to help the war effort was to learn something about the aliens' anatomy, something I could pass on to Catastrophe and Hurricane and the rest of you.

It turns out they weren't all that different from us.

"They sure as *hell* looked different," said Big Red.

"And they had more of a taste for sadism than any Men I've met," added the Reverend Billy Karma. "Except maybe for Baker and Smith and Gaines and Max and the cyborg lady."

You're mistaking social differences for physical differences (continued the Earth Mother). But as a matter of fact, there *was* one important social difference.

I saw an alien soldier who'd been all shot up pinch a nurse as she walked by. I waited until all the doctors and nurses had left the ward, and then I approached him.

"I couldn't help noticing what you did before," I said.

"Mostly, I moaned a lot and fell asleep," he responded.

"I mean to the nurse."

"Well, it's been a long time," he said defensively. "I suppose in due course I'll be sent home, and I'll find a life mate, and that will solve my hunger."

"Why wait that long?" I asked.

"None of the nurses would be willing to become my life mate," he said bitterly. "I'm just a farmer who was drafted to fight this war."

"Who says they have to become your life mate?"

"Are you crazy?" he said. "Do you know the penalty for rape?"

"I'm not talking about rape," I answered.

He looked puzzled. "Then what *are* you talking about?"

"Among my race, when a male suffers unbearable sexual tension, there are women who are happy to provide an outlet for him."

"Life mates, right."

"More like evening mates," I said.

"You mean, you don't have to pair off with them for life?"

"That's precisely what I mean."

"But . . . but why would they participate?"

"There's always money," I said.

"You mean . . . ?"

"It's an old and honored profession among my people," I said.

"*Madre de Díos!*" he exclaimed (or alien words to that effect). "What a mind-boggling concept!"

"You think it would meet with your race's approval?" I asked.

"Our *enthusiastic* approval," he replied.

"Your females, too?"

"Certainly. Most of them require a detailed financial statement from prospective suitors. They'll probably be even more avid supporters of this bold new concept than the males."

"Good," I told him. "I am not without experience in running such an enterprise. If you will introduce all your fellow soldiers in the wards to the concept, I will explain it to the nurses."

"But this is a hospital!" he said, suddenly depressed. "Where can we go to . . . uh . . . you know?"

"One of the things my race specializes in," I said, "are heroes. Most of them are highly idiosyncratic, too much so to be able to function within a rigid military structure. But I just left a number of them, and they're preparing to drive your people out of the solar system and back to your home world. I'd be surprised if this hospital isn't deserted within forty-eight hours—except for those nurses I can recruit and those soldiers who are healthy enough to help support this business. And of course, once word of what we're doing gets out, we'll move our operation to your home world and just leave a small branch here for those wayfarers who need to charge their batteries before returning home."

"You're quite sure your heroes will carry the day?" he asked. "Because I would hate to commit to this and then find out that we'd won the war."

"I think I can guarantee it."

"But we'll outnumber them hundreds to one."

"That will just encourage them to fight harder," I said. "Trust me: I know them. They are the most contrary individuals in a race of contrarians."

"I just hope you're right," he said.

And I was. The aliens cleared off Elizabeth of York in thirty-six hours (except for nine former nurses who had decided to change professions). About half the walking wounded opted to stay, and so did a number of able-bodied soldiers who were willing to risk being court-martialed for desertion to sample the wares of Madame Elizabeth's Emporium.

In fact, the only reason I'm here at all is to transfer my funds to their home world. I leave later today to scout out locations for the next branch of Madame Elizabeth's.

Who says war is hell?

"I've heard of camp followers before," said Max. "But I have to take my hat off to you. You're the first camp *creator* I've ever met."

"Well," said the Earth Mother, "you do what you know."

"Precisely," said the Reverend Billy Karma with a lascivious smile.

"And do well," she added.

"Are you really going to spend the rest of your life running a whorehouse for aliens?" asked Max.

"Of course not," she said. "I'll spend about four or five months getting it operating smoothly, and then I plan to franchise it. I'll be back among humans in a year's time, and I'll be filthy rich. Hell, I might even buy this place."

"It's not for sale," I said.

"You haven't heard my offer," said the Earth Mother.

"Doesn't make any difference," I said. "This place is my life. What would I do if I sold it?"

"Consider the offer withdrawn," she said. "I envy you."

"You do?" I said, surprised. "Why?"

"Because you've found something that means more than money to you."

"So have I," chimed in Billy Karma.

"Yeah, but you find something new every time a different woman twitches past," said Max.

"I was referring to the Good Book," said Billy Karma with all the dignity he could muster.

"I'll offer you two hundred credits for it," said Max.

"Two hundred?" repeated Billy Karma. "It's a deal."

Max laughed. "I thought it meant more than money to you."

"It does," said Billy Karma. "That's why I got it committed to memory. The physical manifestation of a book don't mean no more than the physical manifestation of a man. It's what's inside that counts."

"And what about the physical manifestation of a woman?" asked Max.

"Well," hedged the Reverend, "me and God are still trying to figure that one out." He pulled a well-worn copy of the Bible out of his pocket. "Now where's my two hundred credits?"

"Forget it," said Max. "I was just proving a point."

"Hey, a deal's a deal."

"Go away," said Max.

"You're not going to pay me?"

"Nope."

"Satan's got a special place in hell waiting for people who go back on their word," said Billy Karma.

"He told you that personally, did he?" asked Max.

"I ain't never met up with him personally," said the Reverend. "But he comes to me in visions and tells me what he aims to do to sinners." He paused and glared at Max. "Your name was prominently mentioned the last time we spoke."

"That's strange," said Max. "He never speaks to me. In fact, the only supernatural being who ever pays any attention to me is Wilxyboeth."

"Who the hell is that?"

"Argyle's god of sexual potency," he said, giving me and Reggie a big wink.

"Yeah?" Billy Karma tossed his Bible to Max. "Here. Keep the damned thing."

"What's this for?"

"A reward for telling me how to conjure up this here Wilxyboeth."

"Tell you what," said Max. "Go a whole day and night without insulting any of the ladies here and I'll think about it."

"Twenty-four hours?" said Billy Karma. "For that kind of self-control, I want you to do more than think about it. I want you to guarantee me a face-to-face meeting with Wilxyboeth."

Max threw the Bible back to him. "Forget it. We do it my way or not at all."

"All right," said the Reverend with a sigh. He tossed the Bible back to Max. "We do it your way." He turned to Silicon Carny. "I'm sorry, my love. You'll just have to hold yourself in check for another day, after which I'll be happy to do the holding."

"Not bad," said Max. "You made it almost ten seconds." The Bible flew back across the room.

"Just a minute!" protested Billy Karma. "It was a slip of the tongue!"

"You lose."

Billy Karma hung his head in defeat, but the mood seemed to

pass in a few seconds. "Oh, well," he said, smiling at Silicon Carny. "I'll just have to find something else to do with my tongue."

She pulled out a knife. "You take one step toward me and *I'll* find something to do with it."

"What kind of monster are you?" he demanded.

"The kind who chooses her own bed partners."

"This ain't a good year for radical ideas," said the Reverend Billy Karma.

"Or disgusting preachers," she shot back.

Billy Karma decided to take one last shot at it. "I'm only disgusting on the surface."

"Right," chimed in Max. "Deep down he's actually nauseating."

"Thanks for your help," said Billy Karma, glaring at him. "I really appreciate it."

"Any time."

Just at that moment Little Mike Picasso entered the Outpost.

"Welcome back," I said. "Reg, get him a drink."

"Good to be back," said Little Mike. "Am I the last to show up?" He looked around the room. "I see Argyle hasn't made it back yet. Or Achmed." He turned to Hurricane Smith. "I hope Langtry Lily's just taking a nap, or maybe a trip to the necessary."

"She's dead," said Smith.

"I'm sorry to hear it," said Little Mike.

Baker walked over and threw an arm around Smith's shoulder. "Me, too, Hurricane," he said. "You should have mentioned it earlier."

Smith shrugged. "These things happen."

"Yeah," agreed Baker. "Any lady who links up with one of us has just taken fifty years off her life expectancy. And when all is said and done, Langtry was a bug—no offense meant; she was a mighty attractive bug—and for all we know she might only have had a life span of two or three years."

"It'll be rough, but in time you'll learn to live without her," said Sinderella sympathetically. "Someday, when the pain lessens, you might even find somebody else."

"I already have," replied Smith.

"But there are only three women in the whole Plantagenet system, and they're all here right now," said Sinderella.

Baker laughed. "You don't think he'd hook up with a *human* woman, do you?"

"Maybe it's a better year for radical ideas than I thought," murmured the Reverend Billy Karma.

"Did you meet her at Madame Elizabeth's Emporium?" asked Baker.

"Certainly not!" snapped Smith. "She's good and pure and noble and fine and decent!"

"Okay, where is this paragon of virtue and femininity?" asked Baker. "We might as well meet her."

"She's on Adelaide of Louvain."

"I never learned no English history," said Baker. "Where the hell is that?"

"The outer moon of Henry I," said the Bard.

"What's she doing there?"

"Everyone here just got done fighting a war against her race. We decided that she should stay there until we could be sure she wouldn't receive a hostile reception."

"You should have known better," said Baker, who seemed honestly hurt. "If you vouch for her, that's all it takes."

"I know you, Catastrophe," said Smith apologetically. "But I don't know some of the others."

"How did you hook up with her?" asked Baker.

"She saved my life on Henry IV."

"Even aliens make mistakes," said Max.

"Shut up!" snapped Baker. He turned to Smith. "Is that where Langtry bought it?"

"Yes."

"You want to tell us about it?"

"I might as well," said Smith, sighing deeply. "They both deserve to be in the Bard's book. If he doesn't hear my story, then fifty or a hundred years from now it won't have happened, and that'd be a shame."

The Bard picked up his pen. "Ready when you are."

The Sacrifice of Langtry Lily

Langtry Lily and I had hit upon our strategy long before we landed on Henry VII (began Hurricane Smith). Since she could emulate any life-form and could breathe the junk that passes for air there, we decided that she would disguise herself as one of the aliens, and I would pretend to be her prisoner. Then she'd take me to their leader, and when we got the chance I'd kill him and she'd impersonate him. And since the aliens knew nothing about her abilities, they'd have no reason to question her identity. Once they accepted her as their leader, she'd either tell them they had orders to return to their home planet, or she and I would find some way to kill them all.

It started out all right. We landed, she held a gun on me, and I walked ahead of her. A bunch of soldiers met us and escorted us to their headquarters. Their commander began questioning me, and as he did so they manhandled me a bit, which was something I hadn't foreseen.

"You're the bravest man in the galaxy, except for me," interrupted Baker. "You can't make me believe that a little manhandling, or even some serious torture, would put you off your feed."

"It didn't."

"Well, then?"

"I wasn't alone—remember?"

Each time they hit me or shoved me (continued Smith) I could see Langtry exercising all of her self-control not to come to my aid. Then, finally, they hit me once too often, and she got so furious that she lost control of the image she was projecting, and suddenly everyone could see her for what she was.

I took advantage of the surprise to ram my elbow into the nearest alien's face and grab his gun as he collapsed. I shot two others before anyone realized what had happened.

Then the commander yelled "Kill him!"—and a second later he amended it to: "Kill them both!"

I burned his head to a crisp a second later, and Langtry began spitting that acid she spits, and pretty soon we were standing there amid a pile of dead aliens.

"Well, it's not quite the way we planned it," I said, "but we seem to be doing okay."

Then I saw a bunch more aliens coming out of their makeshift barracks, all of them armed and dangerous. I told Langtry to find someplace to hide, that they were too far away for her to spit on them, and that I couldn't concentrate on killing them and protecting her all at once.

Well, things got pretty hairy then. I must have killed about twenty of them, but then one of the ones I'd thought I'd killed right at the start reached out and grabbed my legs. I lost my balance and fell down next to him, and somehow or other my laser pistol flew a good ten feet away. I tried to crawl over to it, but the dying alien wouldn't let go of my legs.

I looked up and saw another alien running at me, a knife in his hand. I knew the alien was never born that I couldn't beat in a freehand fight, but I was still being held down, and I realized that if his knife pierced my spacesuit that would be the end of me.

He was twenty feet away, then fifteen, then ten, and I still couldn't free my legs—and then, from out of nowhere, Langtry was standing in front of me. She spit full in his face, but even though he only had a couple of seconds of life left to him, his momentum carried him forward and she took the knife thrust that was meant for me.

I finally broke free, just in time to catch her in my arms. With her dying breath she whispered that she loved me and was happy to sacrifice her life for mine.

I didn't have time to mourn, because there were a bunch of aliens taking aim at me, and I was still unarmed. Then one of them screamed, clutched at his chest, and keeled over. Another's head split open. A third flew backward like he'd been kicked by a horse.

Then an arm reached out and lifted me to my feet. It was attached to an alien female.

"Follow me if you want to live!" she said, heading off toward one of the barracks.

She'd obviously shot some of my foes, so I paused just long enough to pick up a couple of guns from alien corpses that wouldn't be needing them any longer and then fell into step behind her.

"Who are you?" I asked her. "And why have you come to my aid?"

"I have heard stories of the great Hurricane Smith," she said. "And now that I have seen you fearlessly facing overwhelming odds, I have decided that you are too noble to die."

"Even though it means turning traitor to your own race?" I asked.

"I look past the appearance of things," she replied. "I am more like you than like any of them."

I'd have asked her more questions then, but the aliens started firing, and we were preoccupied with staying alive for the next few minutes.

I noticed that she was a good shot, almost as good as myself, and that she was utterly without fear. When a laser beam scraped her shoulder a couple of minutes later, she cursed like a spacehand.

"Are you all right?" I asked.

"I'll worry about it later," she said, aiming her pistol with her other hand.

"Get behind me and tend to your wound," I said. "I'll hold them off."

"*We'll* hold them off together," she said, bringing down another alien. Then: "I'm sorry about your friend."

"My wife," I corrected her.

"Then I am doubly sorry," she said. "We have much in common, you and I. If she was your wife, it shows me that you also look past the appearance of things." She paused long enough to aim and fire at another foe, who dropped like a rock. "Did you love her very much?"

"Yes."

A momentary silence. Then: "Do you think you can ever love again?"

"Perhaps," I said.

"It would be very sad if you could not."

"Let's shoot the enemy and worry about it later," I said, and that's what we did for the next half hour, until we were the only two living beings left.

"Thanks once again for your help," I said.

"I am only sorry we could not save your wife. I know what it means to lose someone you love."

"What's your name?" I asked.

She pronounced it two or three times, but it was beyond me. Finally she said, "What name would you like to call me? I will trust to your wisdom."

I figured if I had all that much wisdom, I must rival Solomon, and since she and I were now partners, so to speak, I decided to call her Sheba.

"Sheba," she repeated. "It seems a very melodic name. Who was she?"

"An ancient queen," I said.

"Then I am honored."

I decided not to tell her how many wives Solomon had. We spent the next few days getting to know each other better—and if the Reverend makes one of his typical comments, I just may burn his balls off—and then I decided to leave her on Adelaide of Louvain until I found out what kind of reception she would get at the Outpost.

Anyway, that's the story of how Langtry Lily sacrificed herself for love—or for me, since to her they were both the same thing.

And it's also the story of how I met Sheba, who could see beyond the mere shape of things and somehow realized that we were not only meant to be comrades-at-arms but soulmates as well.

"You know, I had me an alien lady friend once," said the Reverend Billy Karma.

"It figures," said Max.

"Yeah?"

Max nodded. "No human woman would ever say yes to you."

"Right!" chimed in Silicon Carny and Sinderella.

"Wait a minute," said the Bard. "There might be a story here. I don't know anyone besides Hurricane Smith who's ever had a relationship with an alien woman." He turned to Billy Karma. "You want to tell us about it?"

"Ain't much to tell," said Billy Karma.

"That figures," said Silicon Carny.

"Come on now," urged the Bard. "Don't be so modest."

"It's not all that happy a story," said Billy Karma. "We had a tragic failure to communicate."

"How tragic could it be if she's not with you anymore?" asked Sinderella.

"If all you're gonna do is make jokes, I'm not gonna talk about it."

"They're through making jokes," said Baker, with a look that said they'd *better* be through. "I want to hear this."

"Well, it was a Vandei woman," began the Reverend. "I hooked up with her while I was out spreading the Word on the Rim. We just hit it right off, and when I left Vanda she came along with me."

"A Vandei woman?" asked Baker.

"That's right," said Billy Karma.

"I hear they're trained from birth to do nothing but please their mates."

"So they tell me."

"And with a whole planet of Vandei men to choose from, she fell for you?"

"Well, kind of," said Billy Karma uncomfortably. "Actually, I won her in a craps game."

Suddenly Bet-a-World O'Grady sat up and looked interested.

"Anyway, I figured I owed myself a vacation, so I headed to Seascape—that's Alpha Ribot III—and rented a villa for the next week. Once we were settled in I figured it was time for my Vandei woman and me to get to know each other a little better." He paused long enough to take a swig of his drink. "First thing she did was come up to me and ask what kind of sex I preferred. She made it sound like there were seven hundred or more different kinds, but I could only think of a few off the top of my head, so I told her that as far as I knew, there wasn't a man alive who didn't prefer oral sex if he was being honest about it."

"What kind of stakes did you have to put up against her in the craps game?" asked O'Grady with professional interest.

"Shut up!" snapped Baker. "Go ahead, Reverend."

"Well," said Billy Karma, "the next thing I knew she was sitting next to the bed reading *Fanny Hill* aloud to me. I didn't say anything, because I figured this was just her notion of foreplay—you know, a way to get me all hot and bothered and ready for action." He frowned. "Except that she read and she read and she kept on reading, and finally I fell asleep."

Silicon Carny threw back her head and laughed.

"It ain't funny!" snapped Billy Karma.

"It is to me!"

"Get back to the story," said Baker.

"The next night, as we were getting ready for bed, she opened up a copy of *The Story of O* and read it to me, and the night after that it was *The Autobiography of a Flea,* and finally, when she opened up *Tropic of Cancer* on the fourth night, I sat up and asked her what the hell was going on.

" 'Am I not pleasing you, my love?' she said.

" 'Look,' I said, 'I like dirty books as well as the next man, but when do we get to the sex?'

" 'But we are *doing* the sex,' she protested.

" 'What are you talking about?' I demanded. 'Here I am, all set for some oral sex, and all you do is read at me.'

" 'But that's what you asked for,' she said.

" 'The hell it is!' I shouted.

" 'I will prove it,' she said, and before I could say anything else she activated the cabin's computer and ordered up a definition, and out popped the words on a holographic screen—*Aural: of or pertaining to the ear or the sense of hearing.* She smiled at me. 'I naturally assume this means reading classics of human pornography aloud to you.'

" 'Now I see what went haywire,' I said. 'You got the wrong idea about things.' I pulled off my pants. 'Put yourself in my expert hands and I'll lead you through it step by step.'

"She took one look at me, and her eyes widened, and she said, 'You're not going to stick *that* in my ear!'

"Then she was out the door, screaming and running her way down the beach." The Reverend Billy Karma sighed. "For all I know, she's *still* screaming and running."

"Somehow it ain't quite as touching as some of Hurricane's romances," said Baker.

"I think our Catastrophe is a master of understatement," agreed the Bard. "I also think, in the interest of dignity, I'll leave that little adventure out of the book."

"That's okay," said Sinderella happily. "By the time Silicon Carny and I are through spreading it around, everyone in the galaxy will have heard it."

Baker turned to Hurricane Smith. "You ever get any head from an alien lady?"

"Once," answered Smith.

"Yeah? What happened?"

"Not much. She was a Nexarian, so she still had five heads left."

"That's disgusting!" said the Earth Mother.

"You think *that's* disgusting, you should have seen the head she gave me. It must have giggled for an hour before it realized it was decapitated."

"You know," said Baker thoughtfully, "I think it's entirely possible we're talking at cross purposes."

"Could be."

"Don't you *ever* find yourself attracted to a human woman?" asked Baker.

"I try," said Smith. "I really do. But they're all so . . . so *same*."

"Well, I like that!" said Silicon Carny.

Smith looked at her. "I got to admit that you're a little less same than most."

"I think someone here might disagree with your assessment of human ladies," suggested Max.

"Who?"

Max jerked a thumb in the direction of Nicodemus Mayflower. "He's been sitting there, staring at Sinderella and sighing like a schoolboy, ever since he got back. I actually saw the two of 'em holding hands."

"At least *he's* got the right number of hands!" snapped Sinderella.

Max grinned. "See what I mean? It's got to be love. What other reason would she have to insult me?"

"I didn't know she needed any," said the Cyborg de Milo, who seemed to have taken a serious dislike to Three-Gun Max during the war.

"You two went off in separate ships and different directions," said Crazy Bull. "What happened out there?"

"Yeah," said Sitting Horse. "How is it that you left in two ships and came back in one?"

Nicodemus Mayflower looked at Sinderella. "Should we tell them?" he asked.

She shrugged, which was still an attention-getter. "Why not?" she replied.

A Wedding Ring in the Wedding Rings

I hadn't planned to wind up in the Wedding Rings at all (said Sinderella). But after I wiped out a trio of ships that were headed to Henry VII, I decided that it might not be a bad idea to hide in the Rings until they found something better to do than hunt me down.

But a bunch of them found her even among all that space garbage (said Mayflower), and I headed out to try to rescue her.

To *assist* me (Sinderella corrected him).

To assist her (Mayflower agreed). The problem is, it's damned hard to find a ship that's hiding in the Rings. I mean, hell, each ring must have close to a billion chunks of rock and ice in it, maybe more, and by the time I'd gotten there they'd crippled her ship.

Well, to tell the truth (said Sinderella), I think it's more likely that a rock hit the ship. But the result was the same: none of the controls worked, and the structural integrity of the hull was compromised.

In other words (put in Mayflower), she was losing air. Her radio still worked, though, so she was able to tell me that she was in Anne Boleyn, the second Wedding Ring. It became a race between me and the aliens to see who would find her first. I had her fire a couple of flares, but it's a mighty big ring and they were mighty small flares, and I couldn't spot them. Then I finally got the idea of having her climb into her spacesuit and leave the ship after overloading the nuclear pile. I figured when it blew I'd be able to pinpoint the explosion, pick her up, and fly us both to safety.

Well, the explosion was visible, all right. I think you could have seen it from the surface of Henry VIII. Having my instruments get a bearing on it was easy, but—

But we had another problem (interjected Sinderella). I wasn't all that far away from my ship when it blew, and the force of the explosion sent me rocketing backward at a phenomenal rate of speed. I knew if I hit any of the rocks I was done for—and no sooner had I figured that out when I saw that I was on a collision course with a huge chunk of ice. I jettisoned about half my air supply, which acted as a jet and allowed me to miss the iceberg— but I was still racing through space in the middle of all these rocks, and I couldn't use the jet trick again without asphyxiating myself. Then a tiny rock crushed my suit's radio, so I couldn't keep in contact with Nicodemus any longer, and I figured I was done for.

But my sensors had spotted her (said Mayflower), and I started maneuvering through Anne Boleyn, slowly closing the gap between us. After about ten minutes I got within sight of her, and was getting ready to bring her aboard when she pulled out her laser pistol and began firing it wildly—or so I thought. You see, I had told her to fire it at my ship's nose when she spotted me; it couldn't do the ship any harm, and it would help me pinpoint her location.

But she was firing about ten degrees to the left and above me, and since she was only a few hundred yards away, I couldn't figure out what was wrong—and then, at the last moment, I realized that she was trying to warn me that there was an alien ship coming up on my left. I turned my laser cannon on it just a second or two before it could fire its pulse torpedo at me, and I blew it to pieces. This caused even more problems for Sinderella, because some of the pieces started flying straight toward her.

Then I saw what I hoped would be her salvation, and I fired a laser beam at this huge rock, almost an asteroid, that was fast approaching her.

She immediately grasped the possibilities, and instead of trying to avoid it, she carefully maneuvered herself so that she could land on it. It didn't have much gravity, but it was moving fast enough so that as long as she stayed on what I'll call the front end of it, she wasn't going to get thrown off.

The rock protected her from all the flying debris, and I was finally able to maneuver my ship right next to it.

I never thought an airlock could look like paradise (added Sinderella), but this one sure did once Nicodemus opened the hatch. He was standing inside it, and he threw me a line. Well, he *tried* to throw me a line, but since there was no gravity it didn't work very well. Finally he just signaled for me to push off from the rock and aim myself in his direction. I was scared to death, but I did what he wanted, and a moment later I felt his hand close on my arm.

We spent the next two days hunting down the remaining ships that had come after me. They were good, those pilots, but my Nicodemus is superb, and eventually we found them and blew them away. Then it was just a matter of getting out of the Rings and returning here.

As man and wife (said Mayflower proudly). Show 'em your ring, honey.

"Who married you?" asked Max.

"I did," said Nicodemus Mayflower.

"You ain't no preacher," said the Reverend Billy Karma.

"But it's my ship, and a ship's captain has always been able to perform marriages."

"Pity," said Billy Karma. "I'd have presided over one hell of a shindig for a not-unseemly fee."

"Yeah," said Mayflower. "But you'd probably have kissed the bride, and then I'd have had to kill you."

"Good God, why?" demanded Billy Karma.

Sinderella smiled sweetly. "I'd have insisted."

"It was lucky you had a wedding ring handy," remarked Max. "Not a lot of people go to war prepared for that particular eventuality."

"Actually, I didn't," said Mayflower. "But after we wiped out the alien ships and decided to get married, I took the busted radio on her spacesuit apart and made the ring she's wearing from its innards." He smiled. "Now every time she looks at it, she'll remember how we got together, and that as long as we're a team nothing can defeat us."

"I find that a noble and touching sentiment," said the Gravedigger.

"Truth to tell, we just came back to make sure we'd won the war," said Mayflower. "We'll have another drink or two, and then we're off on our honeymoon."

"Where are you going?" asked the Earth Mother.

"Who cares, as long as we're together," replied Sinderella.

"I hear Serengeti is a great planet," offered Big Red.

"The zoo world?" said Mayflower.

"Yeah. Species from all over the galaxy, all of 'em roaming free."

"If he can't think of something better to look at on his honeymoon than a bunch of animals, I married the wrong man," said Sinderella.

"Now that you mention it," said Billy Karma, "you *did* marry the wrong man, and there's still time to get out of it and run away with me."

"Now I know how we Christianized so many alien worlds and races," said Big Red. "The man just refuses to take no for an answer."

"You know, now that I come to think of it, I ain't never run into an alien evangelist," said Baker. "I guess their gods ain't into recruitin' as much as ours is."

"How about you Injuns?" asked Max. "What's your God like?"

"Beats me," said Sitting Horse.

"You don't know?"

"He doesn't make house calls," said Crazy Bull.

"Could be worse," said Max. "Could look just like Billy Karma, the way he thinks ours does."

The Earth Mother looked from Billy Karma to Catastrophe Baker and back again. "It's hard to believe you were both created in God's image." She paused. "If He's really God, He probably looks more like Catastrophe Baker."

"What makes you think so?" demanded the Reverend.

"Because I'd like to think I worship a God Who has good taste," replied the Earth Mother. Then she added: "Though probably She looks more like Sinderella or Silicon Carny."

"Are you gonna start that sexist bullshit again?" said Billy Karma.

"There's only one sexist in this room, and it's not me," said the Earth Mother. Then she shrugged. "Well, maybe five or six." She looked at the painting of Sally Six-Eyes that hung over the bar as if seeing it for the first time. "Including Tomahawk."

Little Mike Picasso grinned. "See? I told you you should have let me be the one to paint Sally for the Outpost."

"Would it have been any less sexist if you'd painted her?" I asked.

"Probably not," he admitted. "But she'd have looked a lot better. Right off the bat, I'd have gotten rid of four of her eyes."

"But that's not the way she looks," I said.

"Art doesn't have to mirror Nature," said Little Mike. "Sometimes it improves Nature instead."

"Isn't that dishonest?" asked the Bard.

"You're taking everyone's word about what happened in the war without checking them out," replied Little Mike. "Isn't *that* dishonest?"

"Apples and oranges," said the Bard. "History doesn't try to improve Nature."

"No—but what you're doing improves History."

"I'm just making it a little more interesting, so it won't be stuck in a musty library, or a musty computer, and only read by academics and historians," replied the Bard defensively.

"I thought academics just pontificated," said Max. "You mean they actually read?"

"On rainy nights, when there are no cocktail parties," said the Bard.

"You're ducking the subject," said Little Mike. "I still want to know what's the moral difference between my painting Sally with only two eyes and you writing about something that didn't take place."

"You're *changing* what she looks like," said the Bard. "That's dishonest. I'm just *embellishing* what Catastrophe and Hurricane and the others tell me. That's simply literary license."

"But what if what they tell you is a lie?"

"Why would anyone lie to a historian?"

"Maybe because it makes them seem more heroic," suggested Little Mike. "Or maybe they lie for the sheer love of lying."

"Highly unlikely," said the Bard uncomfortably.

"Let's put it to the test," said Little Mike. "I'll tell you the story of what I did during the war. Some of it might be true and some might not be. When I'm done, you tell me what you're going to write and why."

"Fair enough," said the Bard, accepting the challenge.

The Lost Treasure of Margaret of Anjou

I **was** heading to Henry IV, hopefully to fight side by side with Hurricane Smith, when I ran smack-dab into a pair of alien ships just past Henry III (began Little Mike Picasso). I immediately began evasive maneuvering, and just about the time I thought I'd lost them, a lucky shot managed to disable my subspace radio and my navigational computer as I was nearing Henry VI.

I figured I'd better set the ship down and see what I could do about repairing the damage. I knew there was a major alien garrison on Henry VI, so I landed on Margaret of Anjou, its moon, instead.

The radio was a total loss, and while the damage to the computer didn't look too serious, I'm an artist, not a computer tech, and I didn't begin to know how to go about fixing it.

I decided that the only reasonable course of action was to return to the Outpost and see if I could either borrow a ship or hook up with someone else—but before I did so, I decided to get into my spacesuit and look around, just in case there was some stunning aspect of the landscape I might want to sketch for future use.

I opened the hatch, climbed down to the ground, and began walking. The rock formations were interesting, but I've seen—and painted—better ones. There was no air and no water, and of course no foliage of any kind, and just about the time I decided there was nothing of any value to see, I spotted something strange off in the distance. I couldn't quite tell what it was, but it didn't look like it belonged there, so I began cautiously approaching it.

It turned out to be an alien building. Not erected by the aliens we were fighting, but something infinitely older and stranger. I don't think I'd ever want to meet the creatures that could pass comfortably through that oddly shaped doorway.

Centuries' worth of dust puffed up from the stone floor with every step I took. I activated my helmet's spotlight and looked around. I was in a huge chamber, maybe fifty feet on a side, and there were a lot of smaller rooms off it, each with that same strange doorway.

I went into one of the rooms. It was empty. So was the second. But in the third I struck paydirt. Evidently this was a storage building, constructed either by some wealthy aliens from Henry VI who wanted to hide their valuables from thieves, or else built by the thieves themselves as a place to keep stolen goods until they could sell them on the black market.

It was like an ancient Egyptian tomb. Grave robbers (or the equivalent) had stolen all of the jewelry, but they'd left the artwork behind because they had no idea what it was worth—and what a treasure trove it was! There was a Morita sculpture, and a Tobin bronze, and a pair of Dalyrimple holo paintings. There was even a Rockwell from old Earth itself!

I started carrying them back to the ship piece by piece, which took the better part of the day. I spent the next week exploring Margaret of Anjou, hoping against hope that I would find another ancient treasure cache, but one was all there was. Still, given the money that museums and art gallerys would pay for my haul, I had precious little reason to be disappointed.

I waited until I saw the last of the alien ships leave Henry VI. I figured they'd never have done that if they hadn't been ordered to retreat, and that meant the war was over, so I got into my ship and brought it back here, using a slide rule and a pocket calculator.

Now I plan to celebrate with a bottle of Tomahawk's best Cygnian cognac, and then I'm off to the Commonwealth to see what my treasure's worth on the open market.

"That's it?" asked the Bard.

"That's it," answered Little Mike Picasso. "How much are you going to use?"

"None of it."

"Why?"

"It's obviously a total fabrication."

"Have it your way," said Little Mike. "You going to be here for another couple of minutes?"

"I live here," said the Bard.

"Good," said Little Mike, walking out the door.

"You're really not going to use it?" I asked.

"It's a fabulous story!" said the Bard, finally letting his enthusiasm show. "I'm going to use every word of it. I just didn't want to say so to that arrogant little bastard!"

Little Mike reentered, carrying a holographic painting of a purple alien landscape.

"A genuine Dalyrimple!" he announced. "Worth at least three million credits back in the Commonwealth." He turned to the Bard. "So you write your history and I'll sell my treasure and we'll see who winds up happier."

"Nice painting," said Max. He reached out and pointed. "I especially like this weird-looking tree."

"Don't touch it!" snapped Little Mike, slapping Max's hand.

"Sorry."

"I'd like to see what else you have in your ship," said the Bard.

"Even though you're not writing it up?" said Little Mike.

"I'm an open-minded man," said the Bard. "Convince me I'm wrong."

"Let's go," said Little Mike. He carried the painting out the door, followed by Willie the Bard.

"Nice painting," remarked Baker. "If you like ugly alien landscapes."

"Paint's still wet, though," said Max with a grin, holding up a purple forefinger.

"Should we tell him?" asked Big Red.

"And rob history of a story like that?" said Max.

The Bard returned a few minutes later.

"Where's Little Mike?" I asked.

"Wrapping his paintings back up. You don't leave treasures like those just sitting around, you know." The Bard lit a smokeless cigar. "Him and his silly propositions! As if he could pull the wool over my eyes!"

"You saw right through him, huh?" asked Max.

"The way I see it, everything about his story was true except where it took place. He probably never set foot on Margaret of Anjou. He made that part up, just to throw us off the track in case there are more treasure caches wherever he got the paintings. My guess is that he was probably on one of Henry I's moons."

"Well, it sure makes sense when you explain it that way," said Max, just before Little Mike returned to the Outpost and sat down next to the Cyborg de Milo. She immediately got up and moved to an empty table.

"It's time for me to go," said the Earth Mother, getting up and walking to the door. She turned to me. "Good-bye, Tomahawk. I should be back in six or eight months."

"Good luck," I told her.

"You know," said Nicodemus Mayflower, "it's time we left on our honeymoon." He escorted Sinderella to the door. "See you around."

They followed the Earth Mother out to the landing field.

"Our noble little group seems to be getting nobler and littler," remarked Max.

"Well, *we* aren't going anywhere," said Crazy Bull.

"At least, not as long as our credit's good here," added Sitting Horse.

"Hey!" said the Bard suddenly. "You two never told me what you did during the war."

"You never asked," said Crazy Bull.

"I'm asking now."

"Too late," said Crazy Bull. "Now it's gonna cost you."

"Right," said Sitting Horse. "You want a story, you pay for our booze while we tell it."

The Bard nodded to me. "Put their drinks on my tab."

"You're a gentleman and a scholar," said Crazy Bull.

"I guess this means we don't get to scalp him, huh?" added Sitting Horse.

Reggie brought them each a refill.

"Okay, you're drinking my liquor," said the Bard. "Now let's have the story."

"Who gets to tell it?" asked Sitting Horse.

"You told the last one, so it's my turn," said Crazy Bull.

"What 'last one'?" interrupted the Bard. "You guys have never told me any of your adventures before."

"You think you're the only hot-shot historian on the Frontier?" shot back Crazy Bull. "There's a guy on Modesto III who not only buys us drinks but pays for our room while we're there."

"Yeah," chimed in Sitting Horse. "He pays for first-rate stories, so that's what we give him. I can't say what you're going to get, since you're only buying us whisky—and cheap whisky at that."

"In fact, if the whisky was any cheaper," said Crazy Bull, "I'd probably tell you a story where the aliens win."

"Are you going to tell me your story, or are you going to bitch all day?" demanded the Bard.

"Art can't be rushed," said Crazy Bull.

The Bard signaled to me. "Tell Reggie that's all the booze I'm paying for."

"History, on the other hand, can be rushed all to hell and gone," continued Crazy Bull quickly.

"Then get on with it."

"Right."

The Battle of the Big Little Horn

It was twilight (said Crazy Bull), and the wind was blowing gently from the west. Sitting Horse and me, we crawled up the hill on our bellies until we could see just beyond it. Geronimo was off to our left, and Vittorio was leading his warriors on our right flank.

We saw a number of the enemy gathered around their camp-fires, but there was no sign of General Custard yet, and—

"What the hell are you talking about?" demanded the Bard.

"You wanted a war story, I'm giving you a war story."

"But you're making it up! It's set on Earth, for Christ's sake!"

"Nobody in the Outpost ever made up a story for you?" asked Crazy Bull.

"Not like this!"

"Well, of course not like this. How many Injuns come out here, anyway?"

"But you're making up a story about a battle that took place more than seven thousand years ago!"

"Sure—but it was a doozy."

"I'm not getting through to you at all," said the Bard, totally frustrated. "I want to know what happened when you left the Out-post to fight the aliens."

"We won," said Crazy Bull. "But the story of the Big Little Horn is much more exciting."

"Right," said Sitting Horse. "There's no General Custard in the story about the aliens. Take my friend's word for it: you'll like the story he's telling much better."

"You drive me crazy!" muttered the Bard.

"Maybe he doesn't like having Geronimo and Vittorio in it," suggested Sitting Horse.

"Well, I could replace them with Tonto and Shoz-Dijiji, I sup-pose," said Crazy Bull.

"Who the hell are they?" asked the Bard wearily.

"They're fictional, but they'll do just as well as Geronimo and Vittorio," answered Crazy Bull. "After all, me and my partner here are the stars of the story. They're just spear carriers."

"Bow-and-arrow carriers," corrected Sitting Horse.

"You guys still don't seem to understand my problem," said the Bard. "How can I write this up as a battle against alien invaders in the Plantagenet system?"

"Change the names," said Crazy Bull.

"That's dishonest!"

"Who's to know?" asked Sitting Horse. "We won't tell if you don't."

"Look," said the Bard, who seemed on the verge of tears, "all I want to know is what happened when you went out to fight the aliens."

"It's dull," said Sitting Horse.

"Not all history is wildly exciting," answered the Bard.

"You really want to know?" asked Crazy Bull.

"Yes."

"And you're sure you wouldn't rather hear about how the Sioux defeated General Custard at the Big Little Horn?"

"*No!*" screamed the Bard.

"Okay," said Sitting Horse with a shrug. "We found the aliens' flagship and blew it up."

"Not much of a story, was it?" said Crazy Bull.

"You expect me to believe that the two of you blew up the biggest ship in the aliens' fleet?"

"I don't know if it was the biggest," said Sitting Horse.

"But it might have been," added Crazy Bull. "It was at least a mile long."

"And you destroyed it all by yourselves?"

"That's right."

"How?"

"We put a bomb behind the captain's toilet."

The Bard looked from Sitting Horse to Crazy Bull, then back again. "Just how dumb do I look?"

"Just how honest an answer are you looking for?" asked Sitting Horse.

"I'd be more likely to believe you actually fought at the Little Big Horn."

"The Big Little Horn," Crazy Bull corrected him. "And we told you you'd like that story better."

The Bard turned to me. "They're paying for their own booze from this moment on."

He stalked off to his table.

"We really did blow it up," said Crazy Bull to the room at large.

"I believe you," said the Reverend Billy Karma.

"You do?" said Crazy Bull, surprised. "Then I must be remembering it wrong."

"Why does everyone hate me the second they meet me?" demanded Billy Karma self-pityingly.

"To save time," said Silicon Carny.

Willie the Bard threw back his head and laughed.

"Don't you even think of putting that in your magnet opium," threatened Billy Karma, "or me and Jesus will both come back from the grave to haunt you!"

"I thought one of you had already come back from the grave," said Big Red.

"He did," admitted Billy Karma. "But he didn't have no staying power. With me by his side, we'll haunt this hack historian day and night."

"Well, it's good to know you're going to straighten him out," said Big Red.

"No matter what I do, he'll still scribble lies about me in his notebook."

"I meant Jesus, not the Bard."

"Jesus'll take a lot less work than the Bard," said the Reverend Billy Karma.

"That's comforting to know, since a few billion people still worship him," said Big Red.

"I don't know that they worship him so much as they hope He'll pull their coals out of the fire," said Max.

"You mean their souls," Billy Karma corrected him.

Max shrugged. "Six of one, half a dozen of the other."

"You know," said Catastrophe Baker, "we ought to take up a collection and buy a wedding present for Nicodemus Mayflower and his lady."

"Sounds good to me," I said. "Reg, pull a hundred credits out of the strongbox and give it to Catastrophe."

Pretty soon everyone was ponying up, and finally Baker did a count. "Twenty-six hundred credits," he said. "We ought to be able to get them something nice for that."

"You could get something nicer for fifty-two hundred credits," suggested Bet-a-World O'Grady.

"Are you offering to match the pot?" asked Baker.

"Not exactly," said O'Grady. "Are you willing to bet it on a double-or-nothing proposition?"

"With you?" said Baker. "Not a chance!"

O'Grady shrugged. "It's your loss."

"It'd be our loss if we took you up on it," said Baker with absolute conviction.

"What kind of bet were you gonna offer?" asked Billy Karma.

"Oh, something simple and evenhanded," said O'Grady. His eyes narrowed. "Have you got any money on you?"

Billy Karma emptied his pockets. "I got exactly seventy-three credits, four New Stalin rubles, and six Maria Theresa dollars."

"Precisely the sum I had in mind," said O'Grady, walking over to the bar. "Reggie, have you got a pack of matches?"

"Forget it," I said. "He's never even seen a pack of matches."

"Okay, we'll do it the hard way. Reggie, find a piece of cardboard and cut a piece two inches long and an eighth of an inch wide."

Reggie did as he was ordered and handed the thin strip of cardboard to O'Grady a moment later.

"Now, usually matches are one color on top and one on the bottom," he said, "so I'm going to take my pen and just turn one side of our match substitute black."

"Now what?" asked Billy Karma when he was through.

"Now I toss it in the air, and you call it before it lands on the bar—white side or black side. We'll bet a credit on the outcome."

"White," cried Billy Karma, and sure enough it came up white.

O'Grady tossed it four more times; it came up white twice and black twice.

"It occurs to me that we could spend all day tossing this stupid thing, and when we're all done one of us might be three credits ahead," said the Reverend.

"Let's make it more interesting," said O'Grady.

"How can it be more interesting?" asked Billy Karma. "All you can do is call white side or black side?"

"Not exactly," said O'Grady. "What if I say that it'll land on its edge?"

"You're crazy!" scoffed Billy Karma.

"Are you willing to bet seventy-three credits, four New Stalin rubles, and six Maria Theresa dollars to prove it?" asked O'Grady.

"Let me make sure I got this straight first," said Billy Karma. "You're going to toss the thing, just like you've been doing, and it's got to land on its edge. If it lands white side up *or* black side up, I win?"

"That's right."

The Reverend Billy Karma looked around the Outpost. "You all heard him." He pulled out his money and slapped it down on the bar.

O'Grady grinned, bent the cardboard into a V-shape, and flipped it in the air. It came down on its side, of course.

"Just a minute!" bellowed Billy Karma. "That ain't in the rules."

"You all heard me," said O'Grady. "Did I ever say I wouldn't bend the thing before I flipped it?"

"Nope," said Baker.

"Not a word," said Hurricane Smith.

"Looks like the Reverend's going to need to pass the poor box," added the Gravedigger.

"You cheated!" said Billy Karma, pointing an accusing finger at O'Grady.

"You can't cheat an honest man," answered O'Grady.

"So if I admit I'm a fake and a fraud, you'll admit you cheated?"

"Maybe I will, maybe I won't—but I won't give you back your money."

The Reverend Billy Karma raised his eyes to the heavens, though the ceiling got in the way, and moaned, *"Eli, Eli, lama sabachthani?"*

"You've got him speaking in tongues," noted Baker with some amusement.

"I'm surrounded by illiterates and ingrates!" muttered Billy Karma, going back to his table.

"That's okay, Reverend," said Baker. "We ain't proud. We'll let you hang around anyway."

Bet-a-World O'Grady turned to the Bard. "I give you my permission to put that one in your book. I haven't seen five packs of matches in the past twenty years."

The Gravedigger walked to the door, as he'd done a couple of times already, and looked out.

"Who're you looking for?" asked Baker.

"Argyle," replied Gaines. "I keep hoping the little bastard listened to my advice, but I guess he didn't." He sighed and returned to the bar.

"Did you see him once the fighting started?" continued Baker.

The Gravedigger shook his head. "Last I heard from him, he was planning to land on Henry V. I tried to talk him out of it. He was a philosopher, not a fighter. By the time I got back from Henry VIII, there wasn't any sign of him."

"Was it rough on Henry VIII?" asked the Bard.

"No more than I imagine it was on any of the other Henrys."

"You want to tell us about it?"

Gaines shrugged. "Why not?"

High Noon on Henry VIII

I hope Nicodemus and Sinderella don't spend their honeymoon on Henry VIII (said the Gravedigger). It's got a chlorine atmosphere, terrible visibility, heavy gravity that wears you out after a few steps, and the temperature's more than halfway to absolute zero.

I claimed Henry VIII for my own, because I've had more experience in hostile environments than anyone else here except maybe Hurricane Smith. I knew they had a small garrison there, and I made it my business to take it out.

I used my ship's sensors to spot them, landed maybe half a mile away—and found a dozen of them waiting for me, guns drawn, as I clambered down to the rocky ground.

"Kill him!" ordered one of the officers.

"*No!*" cried another voice. "He's *mine!*"

I looked around and saw a familiar alien face peering at me through his helmet. It was the Gray Salamander.

"I thought he died on Daedalus IV a few years back," said Baker.

"I heard he'd bought it in the Roosevelt system," chimed in Hurricane Smith.

"Last time I checked the Wanted posters, he was worth half a million credits dead or alive," said Baker.

"And there was a footnote that no one really wanted him alive," added Smith. He turned to the Gravedigger. "So it was really him?"

Yeah, it was really him (continued Gaines). He made his way through the aliens that were crowded around me until he was just a couple of feet away.

"You arrested me on Barracuda IV," he hissed. "I've never forgotten you for that. I think of you with my every waking moment and curse your name. I've planned and plotted and prayed for the day I could face you again—and now here you are at last."

"It's your move," I said. "What do you plan to do with me?"

"Kill you, of course," he said.

I didn't see any way to stop him with a dozen burners and blasters trained on me, so I just kept my mouth shut and waited for him to speak again.

"You are the only being ever to defeat me in any form of combat," he said at last.

I could see where he was leading, so I thought I might as well encourage him.

"It wasn't all that hard," I said. "I know ten or fifteen Men who could have done it, as well as a handful of aliens."

"We shall see!" he screamed. "I have spent the past decade dreaming of the day when we would meet again and I could demand a rematch!"

"You'll just lose again," I said.

That seemed to drive him crazy. He began jumping up and down and yelling so loud and so fast that my translator couldn't make out what he was saying.

Finally he calmed down a little and leaned forward, so his helmet was touching mine.

"You will be allowed to retain your weapons if you promise not to use them on my companions."

"If they don't fire on me, I won't fire on them," I said.

He turned briefly to his soldiers. "You will not interfere upon pain of death." Then he faced me again. "We will meet when the sun is at its zenith. Visibility will be minimally better then."

"Where?" I asked.

He pointed to his left. "There are a dozen bubbles housing our garrison half a mile in that direction. I will meet you on neutral ground, halfway between your ship and our garrison."

"Fair enough," I said. "By the way, how long before the sun's at its zenith?"

"About an hour," he said. "Don't be late. It will be almost thirteen hundred hours before it reaches its zenith again."

And with that, he turned and led his men back to their bubbles, though I lost sight of them before they'd gone fifty yards.

Since I had an hour to kill before high noon, I wandered around, trying to acquaint myself with some of the landmarks. I came to their ship after about twenty minutes, marked its location in my mind, and then walked over to the area I had mentally designated as Main Street and waited for the Salamander to show up.

He could probably have shot me before I even knew he was there—his race has much better eyesight than ours in the pea soup that passed for atmosphere on Henry VIII—but his honor had been challenged, and I wasn't surprised to see him emerge from the fog and approach to within twenty yards of me.

"How I have longed for this day!" he said.

"I didn't know you were in that much of a hurry to die, or I'd have hunted you down again," I replied.

He reached for his burner, but I'd had more experience with heavy-gravity worlds. I had my screecher out first, and an instant later it shattered his helmet, and that was the end of Salamander Jones. I gave a moment's thought to collecting the bounty on him, but he was such a pulpy mess there was no way anyone could have identified him.

I'd promised not to fire on his companions, and I kept my word. I walked over to their ship, disabled the life support and ignition systems, and went back to my own ship. If the garrison hasn't run out of air yet, it will soon—and *that* will be the official end of the war.

"But if he'd been on Henry VIII longer than you, how come he hadn't adjusted to the gravity?" asked Silicon Carny.

"He'd adjusted to all the normal activities," answered the Gravedigger, "but reaching for your weapon is an instinct. When he went for his gun, gravity pulled his hand half a foot too low."

Hurricane Smith was busy studying the clock on the wall.

"Was it that dull?" asked Gaines.

"I enjoyed it," said Smith. "But it made me think about Sheba."

"What about her?" asked Baker.

"She's on Adelaide of Louvain with a limited air supply. I really ought to be leaving in the next few minutes."

"Got time for one more drink?" asked Baker. "I'm buying."

Smith glanced up at the clock again, which was just to the left of the painting of Sally Six-Eyes. "Yeah, I suppose so," he said.

The Gravedigger turned to Willie the Bard. "So can you use it?" he asked.

"Of course," answered the Bard enthusiastically. "It's like a shootout in the Old West. I'll make it as famous as the shootout between Billy the Kid and Jesse James at the O.K. Corral!" He paused. "I don't think I'll mention what you said about the gravity."

"Why?" asked Gaines.

"Men need heroes, not scientific explanations," replied the Bard. "And so does history."

"I thought history needed facts."

"History *interprets* facts," said the Bard. "It's a whole different union."

"And it gets you off the hook," said Max dryly.

"Not if I get it wrong," answered the Bard.

"Now even *I'm* confused," said Max. "If you interpret facts instead of report 'em, how can you get it wrong?"

"You never heard anyone interpret something the wrong way?" asked Baker.

"Yeah—but I was on the spot to point it out to them. A hundred years from now, who'll know if Willie interpreted things right or wrong?"

"If I do it wrong, no one will know, because no one will read the book," replied the Bard patiently. "The job of the historian is to make history come alive for those who weren't around to experience it. You make the wrong choices, it just lays there like a dead fish."

"I thought the job of the historian was to report the facts as accurately as possible," said Hurricane Smith.

"The greatest history of all is the Good Book that the Reverend Billy Karma totes around in his pocket," answered the Bard. "How accurate do you think it is?"

"So much for setting down the facts," said Max.

"Sometimes you got to sweep the facts aside to get at the truth," said the Bard.

"I thought they were one and the same," said Baker.

The Bard shook his head. "If I've learned anything listening to all the stories at the Outpost, it's that more often than not facts are the enemy of Truth. (You can't see it, of course, but I just spelled *Truth* with a capital T.)"

"You mean I keep telling all these true stories," said Baker, "and you keep rewriting 'em so that they fit *your* notion of truth?"

"I told you before: I don't rewrite, I embellish."

"What's the difference?"

"I keep the basic structure of your stories—the who, what, when, why, and where of them. But I try to make them more meaningful, so that future generations will understand that great things were taking place here."

"And what if they weren't?" asked Max.

"They'll still feel some pride in your accomplishments, however trivial they really were," said the Bard. "Is that so sinful?"

"I never said it was sinful at all," said Max. "Just dishonest."

"Why can't I make you understand that there's a difference between lying and embellishing?" said the Bard in a frustrated voice.

"Maybe because there ain't any in *his* life," suggested Baker.

"Look," said Max. "He's an historian. He's supposed to tell the truth. He lies. That's wrong. It's as simple as that."

"You never shot a man with a gun you had hidden in your third hand?" asked Baker.

"Sure, I did," said Max. "But that's different."

"It wasn't dishonest?"

"It was a matter of life and death."

"So is what Willie's writing," said Baker.

"How do you figure that?"

"It ain't *his* life or death," explained Baker. "It's *ours*. Somebody picks his book up two hundred years from now, I'll be alive for as long as they're reading about me. Once they close it I'm dead again. That's the life part. The death part takes place if he never sells it or no one ever reads it."

"Son of a bitch," said Max. "I never looked at it that way." He turned to the Bard. "You have my permission to lie whenever you want."

"Embellish," insisted the Bard.

"Whatever," said Max.

"There's one story I haven't had a chance to improve upon, because I haven't heard it yet. How about it, Catastrophe?"

"Me?" said Baker.

"You fought in the war, didn't you?"

"Not enough to work up a sweat."

"I'd like to hear about it anyway," said the Bard, notebook at the ready.

"What the hell," said Baker with a shrug.

Catastrophe Baker and the Ship Who Purred

I figured it was up to me to end the war (began Baker), and I decided that the direct way was probably the best way. I knew there was a major encampment on Henry III, so I flew there as soon as I left the Outpost.

I didn't try to sneak up on them or nothing like that. I just walked into the middle of their camp, told 'em who I was, and offered to fight their champion, *mano a mano*.

My notion was that whoever won the fight won the war, but that didn't sit right with their chief, who didn't have the authority to surrender his garrison, let alone the whole Plantagenet system, to a force of one. While I was talking to him, I was introduced to a good-looking lady gun-runner, so I came up with a counter-offer: if their champion won, I'd fight on their side for the rest of the war, while if I won, they'd give me Queen Eleanor of Provence, which is what I'd named the gun-runner.

They decided I was so formidable that they ought to be able to throw a pair of champions at me at the same time, and they were such earnest little fellers that I agreed. I figure the whole fight took about two minutes, and I'm sure the thin one will walk again some-day, though I got my doubts about the short, chunky one.

Anyway, they were men of honor—well, aliens of honor—and they turned Queen Eleanor over to me. She wasn't none too happy about it, but I escorted her to my ship and, just to make sure she didn't run away, I stayed on the ground while she opened the hatch and entered the airlock. And then, before I could stop her, Eleanor locked the hatch and took off, leaving me standing on the ground looking foolish as all get-out.

The aliens laughed their heads off, and for a minute there I was thinking of challenging the whole batch of 'em to a freehand fight to the death, but then I decided that it wasn't really their fault that I'd found a lemon in the garden of love, so I had 'em show me her ship, which I figured was mine now.

It was the strangest-looking damned spaceship I'd ever laid eyes on, but I couldn't see no reason not to appropriate it just the same, so I bade all the giggling aliens good-bye after signing twenty or thirty autographs and climbed into the ship.

The control panel was like nothing I'd ever seen before. All the readouts were in some alien language, and the chairs and bulkheads felt kind of soft and almost lifelike. I didn't pay much attention to them, though. My main concern was trying to figure out how to activate the ship and take off.

Hurricane Smith got up and walked to the door.

"I don't mean any disrespect, Catastrophe," he said, "but I've been keeping an eye on the time, and I really think I'd better go pick up Sheba on Adelaide of Louvain before she runs out of air."

"No problem," said Baker. "It wouldn't do to have your lady love suffocate while you stay here drinking and enjoying yourself."

"I'm glad you understand," said Smith. "I'll see you in a day or two."

One button on the control panel caught my eye (said Baker). It was a little brighter and a little shinier than the others, and since I couldn't just stare at the panel all day and do nothing, I reached out and pushed it.

And heard a very high-pitched human squeal.

"Who's there?" I said, drawing my burner and spinning around.

"Me," said a feminine voice.

"Where are you hiding?" I demanded.

"I'm not hiding at all," said the voice. "I'm the ship."

"Are you a cyborg or an artificial intelligence?" I asked.

"Neither."

"I'm running out of guesses," I said.

"I'm a living, genetically engineered being."

"You sound female," I said.

"I am."

Baker looked up and saw Hurricane Smith standing in the doorway.

"I thought you'd left," he said.

"I did," said Smith. "But I heard what you were saying, and I came back for the rest of the story."

"It's just about an alien spaceship," said Baker. "Or an alien that happened to *be* a spaceship."

"A female alien."

"I thought you had your own female alien to worry about," said Baker.

"You mean Sheba?"

"Right. Ain't she busy running out of air on Adelaide of Louvain?"

"She's got big lungs," said Smith with a nonchalant shrug. He walked back to his table, sat down, and leaned forward intently. "Go on with your story."

Baker stared at him for a long moment and finally shrugged. "Whatever makes you happy."

"Do any of these make us take off?" I asked, hitting another couple of buttons on the panel (continued Baker).

"Oh, my God!" she breathed.

"Did I hurt you, ma'am?"

"Do it again."

So I pressed the buttons again, and the ship started purring just like a cat.

"You got a name, ma'am?" I said.

"Leonora," she sighed.

"Well, Leonora, ma'am," I said, "can you maybe tell me how to get the hell off Henry III before these here aliens decide to bust the truce I kind of threw on 'em when they weren't looking?"

"Just sit down," she said. "I'll take care of it."

So I sat down, and before I could strap myself into the chair its arms grabbed me and kind of wrapped themselves around me, and then I looked at the viewscreen and saw we were already above the stratosphere.

The arms released me and kind of stroked me here and there before they went back into place, and then I got to my feet again and continued looking around.

"What's your name?" asked Leonora.

"Baker," I said. "Catastrophe Baker."

"What a romantic name!" she crooned.

"You really think so?" I said. "I always thought Hurricane Smith and Gravedigger Gaines grabbed up the really good names." I walked to the back of the cabin. "Where's the galley? I ain't eaten since before I landed on Henry III."

A wall slid away. "Just enter this corridor," she said, "and it's the first room on the left."

So I took a step into the corridor, and the ship shuddered a little like it was going through a minor ion storm, and I stuck my arms out against the walls to make sure I didn't fall down.

"Oh!" said Leonora. And then: "Oh! Oh! Oh!"

"I'm sorry if I've discommoded you, ma'am," I said. "I don't mean to do you no harm."

"You're not doing me any harm!" she said, and I could have sworn she was panting.

Well, I kept walking down the corridor and she kept saying "Oh!" with each stop I took, and then I came to a room on the left, and I entered it, and sure enough it was the galley, though it wasn't like any galley I'd ever seen before. There was a table and a chair right in the middle, and all kinds of incomprehensible controls and gauges along one wall.

"What would you like, Catastrophe Baker?" asked Leonora.

"Maybe a sandwich and a beer, if it's no trouble, ma'am," I said.

"No trouble at all. Do you see the glowing pink button on the wall, just to the left of the holographic readout?"

"Yeah."

"Just press it."

"Don't I have to tell it what I want?"

"Just press it!" said Leonora urgently.

So I walked over and pressed it.

"Wow!" purred Leonora.

"What do I do now, ma'am?" I asked.

"Now you eat."

"What I mean is, where's my food?"

"On the table," said Leonora—and sure enough, it was.

I sat down and started chewing on the sandwich.

"You're so much more considerate than my last owner," said Leonora.

"I ain't your owner, ma'am," I said. "I'm more like your borrower."

"We would make such a wonderful team!" she said. "Won't you consider it?"

"Well, sure, if you want me to keep you," I answered.

"Oh, yes!" she whispered.

"Well, as long as we're man and ship, how about heading over to Barleycorn II?" I said.

"Done."

"As simple as that?"

"Well, you could get us there faster by adjusting the navigational control," she said.

"How do I do that?"

A wall panel slid into the floor, revealing a whole new bunch of flashing lights and buttons and controls and such.

"Do you see that little wheel on the Q-valve?" she asked.

"Yeah."

"Turn it to the left."

"Whatever you say, ma'am."

I walked over to it and gave it a quick spin.

"Oh my, oh my, oh my!" she shrieked.

"Did I hurt you, ma'am?"

"No!"

"Is that it, or is there anything else I should do?"

Well, I never knew you had to fiddle with so many controls to adjust a navigational computer, but finally I must have hurt her because she told me she couldn't take any more, and I said that was okay, if we got there an hour or two later it wouldn't be no problem.

The trip took two days, and she was just the sweetest thing you'd ever want to meet or travel with. She insisted that I eat three meals a day, and we kept working on that navigational system whenever I had a chance, and then finally we touched down on Barleycorn and suddenly I noticed a note of concern in Leonora's voice.

"Where are you going?" she asked.

"I'm off to visit an old friend," I told her.

"Will I ever see you again?"

"Sure, you will," I said. "I don't plan to spend the rest of my life on Barleycorn II."

Actually I just planned to spend one night there, renewing an old acquaintanceship with the Evening Star, a lady embezzler who doubled as an exotic dancer. I took her out to dinner, and during the course of the meal I mentioned Leonora, and nothing would do but that I took her there later in the evening so she could see the living ship for herself.

"She's certainly cute," she said as we stood in front of Leonora.

"So are you," I said, kind of gently nuzzling her neck and ear and starting to subtly remove her tunic. "And you got racier lines."

"My, you're impetuous!" she said, giggling and slapping my hand—but not so hard that I took it away.

"Could be," I replied, since I hadn't never seen my birth certificate. "But my friends call me Catastrophe."

Well, we started renewing our friendship in earnest, right there in the shadow of the ship. We kind of did a little of this and a little of that, and by the time I took her back home she decided that no woman in her right mind would ever call me Catastrophe again.

It was when I came back to the ship that the trouble started.

"I've never been so insulted in all my life!" said Leonora.

"What are you talking about?"

"The second I turn my back you seduce that ugly little tart!"

"She ain't ugly, and besides, I done it in front of your back," I said, figuring I had to speak up for the Evening Star since she wasn't there to speak up for her own self.

"And you're filthy!" continued Leonora. "Get out of those clothes and take a bath immediately!"

"You're sounding a lot more like a mother than a spaceship," I complained.

"Did I upset you?" she asked.

"Yeah, a little."

"Good!" she snapped. "Then we're even!"

Well, from that moment on things just went from bad to worse. Every time I gave her a new location to visit, she gave me the old third degree about what woman I was planning to ravish. She wouldn't send or accept any subspace radio message that had a female at the other end. If I talked in my sleep and mentioned a lady's name, she'd wake me up and demand to know who I'd been talking about.

Finally, after three or four more days, she announced that she was taking me back to the Plantagenet system.

"What's going on?" I asked.

"I can't stand it anymore!" she said. "I can't concentrate on navigation! I can't compute my fuel consumption! I can't focus on meteor swarms and ion storms!"

"You got some kind of headache?" I asked.

"I have a case of unrequited love, and it's driving me crazy!" she said. "You are my every thought, and yet I mean nothing to you."

"Sure, you do," I said.

"As a woman?"

"As a spaceship."

She screamed in agony.

"I'm sorry, truly I am," I told her. "I wish I wasn't so goddamned attractive and irresistible to women, but it ain't something I can control. It just seems to go with being a practitioner of the hero trade."

She didn't say another word until we entered the atmosphere of Henry II. Then she asked in a very small voice: "Would you adjust my gyros, just once, for old time's sake?"

"Sure," I said. "Where are they?"

A couple of knobs started flashing.

"Well, I'll be damned!" I explained. "I thought you used them to home in on different radio frequencies."

I reached out and started turning the knobs.

"Mmmmmm!" said Leonora.

I spun the left-hand one.

"Ohhhhhh!" she said.

I twisted the right-hand one.

"Oh God! Oh God! Oh God!" she screamed. Then: "Was it good for you, too?"

We landed a couple of minutes later, and then she let me out and took off for parts unknown.

And that's the true story of The Ship Who Purred.

"Did she give you any hint about where she might be going?" asked Hurricane Smith.

"No," answered Baker. "Last I saw of her, she was heading out toward the Quinellus Cluster."

"How much of a start did she have?"

"On who?"

"On *me,* damn it!"

"Ain't you got a ladyfriend what's fast running out of oxygen on Adelaide of Louvain?" said Baker.

"Never interfere with someone else's romance!" said Smith severely. He looked around the room, and finally his gaze fell on Billy Karma. "You're broke, right, Reverend?"

"Well, I always got the Lord and the Good Book," replied Billy Karma, "but truth to tell, neither of 'em will bring all that much of a price at a pawnshop."

"How'd you like to make a quick two thousand credits?"

"Who do I have to crucify?"

"Just fly to Adelaide of Louvain and pick up my . . . uh . . . this female alien named Sheba, and bring her back here."

"It's a big moon, and I assume she's just a normal-sized godless alien heathen," said Billy Karma. "How will I find her?"

"I'll transmit her position to your ship's computer."

"Sounds good to me," said Billy Karma. "But I'll want the money up front."

Hurricane Smith pulled out his wad and peeled off a pair of thousand-credit notes. He handed one to the Reverend and one to me.

"Half up front, and Tomahawk will give you the other half when you show up with Sheba. And Reverend?"

"Yeah?"

"Leave right now and go as fast as you can. If she suffocates, I'm going to want my money back."

"I'm on my way," said Billy Karma, running to the door.

"I'd better go with him," said Big Red, getting up from his table.

Hurricane Smith looked at him curiously.

"I assume you want her brought back intact as well as alive," explained Big Red.

"If possible," answered Smith without much interest.

"You ought to know that you never send the Reverend out without a chaperone." Big Red took Billy Karma by the arm and walked out the door. "Let's go, Rev."

Hurricane Smith turned to Baker. "The Quinellus Cluster, you say?"

Baker nodded his head. "That's right."

He walked to the door. "Wish me luck."

Then he was gone.

"Best luck I could wish him is that he never finds her," said Baker, emptying his glass.

"But it would make a nice story," remarked the Bard.

"Yeah, it probably would." Suddenly Baker turned to him. "I want you to sell that goddamned book before you die."

"I'll do my best," said the Bard, surprised. "But why do *you* care?"

"That book's my immortality," continued Baker. He took a deep, heroic breath. "And on days like this, I feel like I just might want to live forever."

"Trust me, you will," promised the Bard. He patted his notebook. "I'll see to it."

Those who were left drank and told stories deep into the night. Then, one by one, they began leaving.

Little Mike Picasso offered to capture Silicon Carny on canvas. She liked the notion, and they went off together to his studio on Beethoven IV.

Bet-a-World O'Grady remembered that there was a high-stakes game on Calliope, the carnival world, and decided that if he left at dawn he just had time to make it.

Sitting Horse and Crazy Bull went home to spend a little time with the other Injuns and replenish their cash supplies.

Truth to tell, I don't know where the Cyborg de Milo went. One minute she was sitting there, and the next she was gone. I never even saw her leave.

Einstein announced that he'd come up with a new approach to transmuting base metals into gold that was even more efficient than the last such method he had devised, and Gravedigger Gaines offered to fly him into the Commonwealth so he could register it at a patent office.

Catastrophe Baker stayed a few hours longer, but I could tell he was feeling restless. Finally he decided it had been too long since he'd encountered any Pirate Queens, so he borrowed a ship and went out looking for some at the edge of the galaxy.

So it was just Three-Gun Max and the permanent residents—

me, Reggie, and the Bard—for an afternoon. But this is the Outpost, and it never stays empty for long.

Doc Arcturus showed up at twilight, followed by Treetop Quatermaine, and the Sapphire of Sappho, who could have given Silicon Carny a run for her money. By sunset they were arriving in force, Cyclone Jim Crevich and the alien Br'er Rabbit and Spidersilk Sally and Billy the Blade and the Titanium Kid and a couple of dozen others.

Before long there wasn't an empty chair in the place. Then Snakeskin Malone walked in, strode across the floor like he was still outside in one of his beloved jungle worlds, and had Reggie pour him a tall one.

"Hi, Snakeskin," said Max. "Long time no see. What have you been doing with yourself?"

"I've been out making history," he replied.

"Let's hear about it," said the Bard, pulling out his pen and notebook so he could graft yet another story onto his epic chronicle before both the adventure and the adventurer were lost forever.

That's pretty much what we do at the Outpost—live a little history, make a little history, tell a little history. It's not an easy place to find, but if you ever get here, I think you'll agree that it was worth the effort.